GHOSTS

GHOSTS

MARSHA PARKER

E. P. DUTTON, INC.   NEW YORK

Published in the United States by
E. P. Dutton, Inc., 2 Park Avenue, New York, N.Y. 10016

Library of Congress Cataloging in Publication Data
Parker, Marsha.
Ghosts.
I. Title.
PS3566.A682G5 1982   813'.54   81-19497
AACR2

ISBN: 0-525-24109-4

Published simultaneously in Canada by
Clarke, Irwin & Company Limited, Toronto and Vancouver

Designed by Nancy Etheredge

10 9 8 7 6 5 4 3 2 1
First Edition

For William

GHOSTS

1

---

*But man dieth, and wasteth away: yea, man
giveth up the ghost, and where is he?*

—JOB 14:10

WHEN you are young and the
moon is full and your experience is small, what seems like nothing
to some old onlooker can still be a terrible milestone in your little
life. And sometimes when you get older and you can look back
without wincing, you see that it really was a milestone, or something
like that: a glimpse into yourself; a quick snitch at the future, memorable only because of what happened later to remind you that even
though you were young and frail and blind, God, or someone,
always had His eyes open.

The ghosts are everywhere. In a breeze, in a whisper, in a scrap
of scribbled paper lying at the bottom of an old box. They are in old
barns, in new cellars, in classrooms, in towers, attics, closets, in the
very air around us. Ghosts can walk the bare winter fields; they can
walk through walls and they can step across the centuries as easily
as we step over thresholds. They are the ghosts of our memories, the
assemblage of parts nonexistent, forgotten and then remembered;
blushes, omnipresent and then magically, suddenly gone, the ghosts
of ourselves, of our friends, our families. We are only the living souls
of today, the ghosts of tomorrow.

Ghosts are more likely to occur in places with tumultuous histories, perhaps because people are ready to see them there; but that does not mean that they cannot appear as well in a modern suburban backyard. People will more than likely remember the unfamiliar ghost. For instance, if you were to see a strange woman in your backyard wearing twentieth-century clothing, you might suspect she was just a new neighbor; but if the woman was carrying a pomander, and wearing a farthingale and a ruffly white collar that framed her face like a jack-in-the-box, you might be more suspicious. It really seems to depend on where you look, and it depends on how you look.

I have heard of people who are gifted with a sixth sense that feels beyond touching: a sense that combines sight and touch and "sees" what is invisible to most people. I have heard stories of such people walking into suspect houses and saying: "There is a ghost in this house. I cannot see him, but I sense that he is standing on the landing with a box of chocolates in his left hand," when the others present won't feel a thing. Then the owner of the house will reveal his secret poltergeist stories, of plates flying in the dead of night, spectral hands shaking the children awake, furniture levitating, chocolates disappearing.

I have always wanted to see the ghosts, just as so many people have a morbid desire to see things that are better left unseen, and at the same time I have wanted not to see them. If it is possible to love and hate the same person, it is equally possible to accept and deny something at the same time. I can deny that ghosts exist in any material form, quite convincingly, I think. Yet funny things continue to happen to me, as if these inexplicable, immaterial spirits have singled me out for a concentrated physical assault because I was a soft spot in the front lines; yet not soft enough to preach the gospel of what I *thought* I saw, or felt, on several occasions. That is one of the great beauties of ghosts: that they are so evanescent as to defy description and conviction, and that no one would believe you anyway. A level-headed person should always remain open to the possibility that she could be mistaken. Those who stoutly claim that they have encountered ghosts are probably dreamers. A ghost can be no more than a misconception, a puff of smoke, a whiff of perfume, love at first sight, a nonsense word that cannot be defined, a muzzy concept dreamed so clearly in a dream that you can never remember it the morning after, no matter how hard you try.

[2]

Dreams are not composed of real men. Yet when an incongruous presence, if you will, a ghost, or an energy force (depending upon your pet theory) confronts you head-on, do you tell yourself that it doesn't exist? That it isn't happening, and just turn and walk away? When you know, or at least strongly suspect, that you are wide awake and perfectly sane and there is a shrieking banshee, a quavering white sheet, or a stark naked man with a bald spot in the center of his skull standing in front of you, do you faint? Scream? Dash? Pray? Stand transfixed and stare eternity right in the eyes? And afterward, the saddest part is when you realize that memory does not provide tangible proof. Memory is not positive evidence of anything. Memories are dreams, only existing in the present tense, before or behind our eyes.

I have done a great deal of thinking about ghosts; of what they might be, if they are at all. They might be real people masquerading in period costumes, using special effects to seem to disappear, or to appear indistinct or whitish, but I have decided that that is not very likely. They might be products of a fertile, or a drugged, imagination. And then, of course, they might be nothing at all, blown up into something by an overactive mind eager for adventure or anxious to find easy answers. But a ghost is not an answer, I have come to realize; if anything, it is the first word in a question. If it is none of these things then maybe it really *is* a ghost. A soul that has not yet found peace. A soul that resisted the sedative influence of God in life and is frittering away eternity in its continuously elusive search for something. Something that will close the circle. Something that will soothe the unseen wounds. An answer. A balm. A peek beneath the surface that will modify, alter, explain, and absolve. A gospel, or a reason.

Children adore gospels: gospels in the form of pat statements, unequivocally true, too simple and straightforward ever to consider contradicting, because it is oftentimes fun to believe blindly. Gospels make life very easy sometimes. Before the age of reason, before I had developed the skills of asking questions and doubting, my gospel was my best friend, Carole, who, once a year, would venture up north with my mother and me and stay with us for a week at our summer cabin in the north woods of Wisconsin. Carole made my life very simple: she was the prime mover and I was a little moon, just following her gravitational pull. I believed implicitly in what Carole told me, and for that one week every summer I was her slave, her pupil, glad to be doing whatever she suggested in her infinite wisdom.

Our last summer together, a hair before adolescence and different schools separated us forever, we were eleven years old and anxious for a different sort of excitement from the frog catching and fishing of years past. Carole wanted to sleep out in the woods one night, armed with a gold ring, to watch for ghosts.

She led me out that night like a starved and foolish puppy. Carole said that it was possible to see ghosts if you looked through the gold ring after midnight when the moon was full. My mother reluctantly let us drag our cots and wool blankets out into a dry, wooded spot on the edge of the thicket surrounding the swamp; too far from the cabin for my feeble comfort but close enough to see pinpricks of light from the windows. We set our flashlight on the dry leaves between the cots.

It was past ten but we were too excited to sleep. A wind in the tall birch trees shushed the mosquitoes away. Every so often a heavy-shelled beetle or a moth would smack into the plastic case of the flashlight. There were rustlings in the underbrush, and sometimes a brief but frantic splashing somewhere in the pitch-black moistness of the swamp. But mostly it was Carole, waiting for midnight with the flashlight, the full moon, and the shiny gold ring that she held up to the greenish moonlight between her index finger and her thumb, turning it slowly between her fingers.

"Can't we try it now?" I pleaded. Time does not exist the same way for youth as it does for old age, and I did not like the idea of waiting so long for the excitement to begin.

"You won't see anything now," Carole advised. I envisioned an army of moldering bodies wearing only the rotting shreds of their mortality. Precocious child. Maybe I didn't really want to see them. Imagination was always better, or at least more lurid, than reality. Better to look now, see nothing, and pretend that it was all just a hoax, I feebly reasoned. If I denied the ghosts perhaps they would deny me their presence. Perhaps.

"Let me try anyway."

Carole weakened. "It's not even eleven yet. And besides, only people born between midnight and six in the morning can see ghosts through a gold ring. When were you born?"

"I don't know. In the morning, I think."

"Well, you can try, but you probably won't see anything."

[4]

She was right, to a point. I could see only her face lit up like the round center of a clean china plate in the flashlight, the rest of her body stretched out dreamily on the cot, faintly visible and relaxed in the moonlight. I admired her composure. In fact I admired everything about Carole: her dark, short, curly hair beside my long, lank, albino-white hair, her mother's exotic Australian accent, her smell of Ivory soap and clean clothes, even her buckteeth which I tried to emulate in the dark. She passed the magic ring over to me ceremoniously. "Watch it. It's my mom's," she warned.

I held the ring in the palm of my hand and wondered why it wasn't hot, or sending off sparks, or at least glowing. It seemed like any old gold ring, not that I had seen many real gold rings in my eleven years. I felt funny when I touched it. Not funny like I had touched a live wire or a vibrating washing machine, but simply queer.

"What do I look at?"

"Look at the moon first," Carole said, "but you won't see anything 'cause it's too early."

It was August and I felt a slight chill, but it was only slight because the magic of the ring was working on me and I was warming to it. Autumn began in late July in northern Wisconsin, winter lasted until June, but that night the temperature was not very important. The woods were washed with greeny-white light from the moon. It was a wonder to me that moons could get that full and bright and not be called suns.

I held the gold ring to my eye, squinted, and framed the moon in the center. I half expected to see witches on brooms, or perhaps one or two gossamer-winged fairies riding fireflies. All I saw was the moon, big and cheesy and brilliant, framed by a misty golden cloud as round as an orange, reflected in the bay by the swamp.

"Nothing," I said, still searching.

"Told you so."

"There's just this shiny circle around the moon."

Carole snatched the ring back from me and held it up to the moon. It behaved as any normal ring would behave: the light bounced off the surface as she rotated it in front of her eye. I noticed that there was no ring around the moon now. Everything seemed quite normal again, but I was conscious of something different in the woods—a sound that I could not immediately identify, or maybe it was just the evening chill moving up from the swamp, making my ears pop and the white hairs on my bare arms stand up on end.

"I don't see any circle around the moon," Carole said, challenging. "Everyone knows that the fairies dance when there's a ring around the moon. You making it up?" Carole moved to the edge of her cot and became noticeably less relaxed.

Carole knew me better than that, I thought. I had little imagination, and even less skill when it came to telling lies. I virtually worshiped her, and I would never dream of lying or pulling a prank on her. I didn't want to see strange circles around the moon that she didn't see, or hear unidentifiable sounds in the night if she didn't. I wanted her to see and hear these things, and then tell me about them once we were back in the warm, bright safety of my mother's cabin kitchen.

"Maybe I didn't see it then," I lied. Carole seemed momentarily satisfied, and she passed the ring back across to me. "But do you hear something funny?" I foolishly added.

Carole made a violent motion with her hands meant to silence me. She bent over and did the unspeakable: she switched off the flashlight. We sat on the edges of our cots facing each other in the dark woods. It was terribly hard work, holding our breaths back, concentrating on the sounds in the night. I saw my mother's reading light go out, felt my skin start to bristle up and down my spine, and pledged all of my future allowances to the Lutheran Sunday school if only I could be back inside the cabin, safe with the comfortable and familiar sounds of the refrigerator and the eight-day clock. Before long it was obvious what the funny new sound was: it was no sound at all. The wind had stopped, the water of the bay was no longer washing the dock. Even the peepers in the bog had shut up, probably perched immobile on the edges of their lily pads, staring into each other's slimy, impenetrable yellow eyes, wondering why the earth had suddenly gone quiet on them.

"Something's awfully wrong," I moaned. "I read that the animals only go quiet like this when an enemy is approaching, like a bear, or a wolf!" (Or an army, I thought—an army of skeletons.) I listened for the sound of distant marching, of bones clattering. I regretted having seen *Jason and the Argonauts* that spring.

"Shut up, will you? Then why would the wind stop, too?"

The bristling feeling traveling along my spine was almost unbearable. My shoulders felt as if they might sprout wings. Now I understood how ghosts could claim victims: they died of fright. If dying of fright meant that every part of your body wanted to fly off in a different direction, then I was on my deathbed that moment. But it seemed infinitely worse to race all that distance off to the cabin alone (it must have been a full city block of woods in between with untold pairs of clammy hands concealed behind each thick tree trunk and a monstrous creature ready to spring out of every bush), and so I remained rooted to the cot.

"What are you waiting for?" I whispered. I felt sand in my throat, burdock barbs in my eyes. My voice did not want to work, I wanted to wet my pants, I wanted to run, knees to my chin, but I couldn't possibly run all alone into the anxious arms of a phantom. It was so confusing, and at the same time I wanted to commit myself to the supreme torture. I wanted to look through that wretched gold ring again. I wanted to scream, but I wasn't quite sure of the most effective scream to make to keep the terrors at bay—a scream that would make me hoarse for days, or a scream that would just be enough to send me flying home.

"Look through the ring again!" Carole barked. I was horrified by her command, but I obeyed. First I looked at the moon, and I saw the circle surrounding it, shimmering like the pupil of a cat's eye. I desperately wanted to throw myself back onto the cot, to get rid of the awful feeling in my spine, but then Carole barked out another order. "Check all around us now!"

I looked dutifully at Carole first: she was pale and frowning and as rigid and as serious as I had ever seen her. I wanted to believe that this was all just a joke that she had contrived—the moon's ring, the silence in the woods, the deathly seriousness so unlike her—but she wouldn't relax and reassure me. I had no choice but to keep on playing her game as much as it frightened me. I had a fleeting notion that perhaps Carole herself was a ghost. I held the ring to my eye and framed her face in the center. Nothing extraordinary.

"Don't look at *me!*" she hissed. "Look *around* us!" I didn't want to move. Her eyes were inscrutable wet slits in the dark, her face as pasty as spilled flour. I turned away slowly, the ring pressed to my eye, looking toward the swamp and the bay first. It was very hard work because I did not *want* to see anything. I imagined the worst: skeletons of hunters and Indians lost in the bogs and quicksand (although my mother insisted that there was no quicksand in that swamp), will-o'-the-wisps, swamp gas turning into phantom shapes as it rose toward the moon, bearded and bleeding hermits stumbling out of the heavy grasses and lunging for us, their animal-bone knives sharpened to lethal points. Expecting the worst, I saw nothing. Only the edge of the moon's mysterious halo stretching into the tall swamp grasses and lighting them up like rows of silver tinsel in Christmas candlelight.

"Nothing in the swamp," I whispered, hoping. I didn't want to turn toward the dark forest behind me for fear that I would come face to face with a terror hovering immediately over me. Best to remain ignorant. It was less frightening that way. I decided to check with Carole first before I ventured a look to my rear.

"See anything behind me?"

"No. You look."

Her curtness gave me some peculiar courage. I swung around and glared at the terror through the ring. A dark wood looked back, manifestly uninteresting, yet infinitely secretive.

"Nothing there."

"There's *got* to be something!" Carole insisted, and she ordered me to look all around the cabin. I took the ring away from my eye and looked at her instead. The bristly feeling was going away.

"There won't be anything up there," I said. "My mother's in the cabin."

"You'd better check everywhere," Carole admonished. "This is really weird. Can you look around the cabin?" Her voice broke. She was more frightened than I was. This was awfully disconcerting to me; after all, she was my idol. Her tension was terribly contagious. Shaking anew, I was about to focus the ring on the cabin when the wind quickly blew back, as perfectly timed as if God were operating the bellows backstage. The birch leaves above started rustling, the swamp grass whistled, and the bay lapped at the dock. I hesitated for just a second, and then looked through the ring.

The cabin looked small and artificial in the strong moonlight. Only two sides of it were visible from that angle: the steeply sloping side facing us, and the porch. The wind continued to blow even harder and the treetops made a constant roar, drowning out the sound of the water. It felt like a storm coming, I thought, and storms always excited me. But then I saw something move from around the corner of the porch. I watched, paralyzed, as the figure of a man became more and more clear, standing there, facing me. He was looking directly at me, just standing there and staring, a precise but colorless figure in the dark wearing some kind of a robe with a metal

[8]

plate on it, like a shield, that flashed dully in the moonlight. He sat down stiffly on the ground beside the edge of the cabin, pointed his finger at me for one long tremulous second, and then just lay down there, on the forest floor, fifteen feet from my mother's bed, and turned his head toward me. I saw tears in his old eyes as he vanished. He just vanished.

All the bristles swept back up my spine, all the horror of bloody hermits and spewing entrails flooded back. I threw the gold ring up into the wind and I screamed as hard, as loud, as satisfyingly as I could. I tried to scream loud enough to shake the phantoms and visions and tears from my soul. I tore through the woods, my arms moving like the rotors of a helicopter warding off the clammy hands and colorless men.

I ran all the way to the cabin on Olympian feet that had never ever run so fast, and around the back of the cabin, avoiding the tainted porch where he no longer lay, too breathless and crazy to think about it rationally. I knew he was still around there somewhere: a man with gray hair, who was following me. A poor, insane man in rags with a kind of shield on his chest, with letters, or maybe they were snakes, engraved on it, making a small imprecise gesture toward me, a lure, as if I would ever be so mad as to go to him! I slammed the kitchen door thunderously behind me, waking my mother and the dog. I pounded up the stairs to her bedside where I rubbed my aching and spiny back against the comforting hardness of the wall, her wall, and waited for my breath, my senses, my voice to catch up, whining and slobbering beyond control about some goon chasing me.

My mother fumbled for her glasses. The ions of civilization flooded over me. I loved electricity just then, but the look I saw on my mother's face sobered me up fast.

"Carole!" I managed to croak. "Did he get Carole?"

"Did who get Carole?" my mother muttered, always cold and Norwegian and very practical, slowly waking up and trying to make some sense of me sitting there on the floor beside her bed, covered with leaves, cobwebs, and scratches.

"Did who get me?" I heard Carole's sickened tremolo downstairs. I suddenly began to see what a fool I had been to believe my eyes, and how angry my mother would be with me if I tried to explain it to her. Nonsense, she would call it. She might even slap me, and scold me for scaring Carole. In front of Carole, that kind of embarrassment could be life-threatening. I had to think fast. I stood up, knees weak and arms still aching from the incredible dash through the woods, and I lied to my mother. I told her that I had seen a wolf's green eyes in the dark only a few feet from our cots.

"You goofball!" she growled as she fluffed her pillows and rolled over. "It was probably just Fred Schmidt's Labrador. Now turn out the lights and go to sleep."

It was probably just Fred Schmidt's Labrador. Of course. What else could it have been? What did it matter that Fred Schmidt never let his Lab out at night because it ravaged all the trash barrels on that side of the lake? And what did it matter that what I saw was a man, not a wolf or a dog? I turned out my mother's light for her and went downstairs.

Clouds were blowing over the moon. There would certainly be a storm. The gods were angry. With the fortitude of a fool I peeked out the stairwell window that gave me a perfect view of the corner where the man had stood and where he had disappeared, but I couldn't see a thing there now. Not a shadow, not a footprint in the sand. Men are real; dreams are not. It had to be a dream, then. Carole was whimpering on the davenport. I felt utterly crushed by the enormity of what I had seen, or thought I had seen, and of what I had done. I had abandoned my best friend to a ghoul. I had reduced my strongest, my cleverest friend to Jell-O, and if I told her the truth she would probably just call me the liar that perhaps I was and insist on going back on the next Greyhound bus from Eagle River.

"What was it? What was it? I didn't see nothing!" she blubbered, her round clean face framed in knotted black curls. She was still clutching her woolen blanket from the cot, and I noticed a nasty scratch on her cheek. She looked like she wanted to cry. I really didn't want to make matters worse. It was like watching your own mother cry. I felt numb and helpless.

"I thought it was a wolf, but Mom said it was just Fred Schmidt's Labrador."

"A wolf?" Carole stopped whimpering and her eyes widened. A wolf was more reassuring, real, explicable, than a ghost. But I still had the impression that she didn't believe me.

"No. Fred Schmidt's Lab."

Carole didn't say anything else, but at least she stopped trying to cry. She didn't believe me. I knew it.

I locked the kitchen door, then put some salve on her scratch and told her that we would have to hunt for her mother's gold ring in the morning. It was late, well past eleven, and I'd be damned before I'd set foot outside again that night.

"Don't worry about it," Carole said before she fell asleep. "It wasn't really my mother's ring. I got it out of a bubble-gum machine last week."

Carole never again came up north with me, nor did our tender preadolescent friendship survive that experience. Yet the incident did not die there with our friendship. Year after year I never felt the same about the woods. The forests of northern Wisconsin were pretty enough: safe, lovely, peaceful, fragrant, and gentle havens for city folk from as far afield as Indiana and Illinois who came up in droves in the summertime. But at night in my bed in the cabin I would hear noises coming from the woods and the swamp that defied description: terrible slopping noises, thrashing in the underbrush, guttural cries so deliberately modulated that I swore they must be human. No one else seemed to hear the noises, though, so I had to stop talking about them; but then no one else was quite aware of the utter endless blackness that I felt in the woods at night without the comforting blink of city streetlights through the shades. The dark there covered me like a gauzy shroud all alone in my trundle bed like a grave. In certain desolate moments of panic I would have to turn on the light, to reassure myself that I was still living in the present tense, and not cloaked in iron, a soulless shadowless thing without feet, floating away beyond the control of my senses into the timeless blackness.

I could not forget the way he stood there dimly lit in the full moonlight, but as hard as I tried I could not remember whether or not he cast a shadow. I had scarcely seen his face. I could not recall any sensation or expression that belied a personality behind the breastplate, a heart that beat, a soul that wept, nor did I care. What mattered was that he stood there in the moonlight and he scared me. He existed for a moment. Or maybe he didn't. It *could* have been Fred Schmidt's Labrador. It could have been Fred, for that matter; he liked to drink, and perhaps he had had a whim that night to dress up in ragged cowl and breastplate and scare the pants off a couple of whiny eleven-year-old girls. Yet that really didn't make good sense to me because even at eleven I knew that adults had better things to do than to go to such lengths to amuse children, particularly if they weren't their own children. Fred came from the south side of Milwaukee and he told dirty jokes and my mother told me to stay away from him. He was not the sort of man who would play pranks like that. Fred had probably never seen a cowl or a breastplate in his life.

It still bothers me, that old gospel: ghosts do not cast shadows. Nor are they reflected in mirrors, nor do they leave footprints. I regret not checking for prints the next day. Still, the ghost, the man (my opinion wavers) had probably not existed at all, except in that rare combination of childish imagination and moonlight. So sayeth the adult.

I still wish to God I could remember a shadow.

2

"THIS kitchen's a mess. I told you that we should have scheduled our classes on the same days. I go out for four hours and you turn the place into a rubber factory!" I harped at poor Robert, who sat, oblivious, on the steel-bentwood-and-vinyl kitchen chair tapping his fingers over crumpled sheets of Big Chief paper and eraser filings.

"It's not *that* bad," he said, still up to his cheeks in quantum. I wasn't sure which I objected to more: the mess or his ability to tune me out in favor of calculus.

"You never even try to sweep this crap up," I snorted, pushing a pile of sticky pink rubbery stuff in the direction of the floor. It hardly moved. By then I knew that you had to wait for it to dry out, then gently coax it off into a dustpan.

"It's not that bad."

"Is that all you can say?" I almost screamed. There was some-

---

*If anyone looks at me
Please tell me
I am too flighty
As I well know

thing awful digging into my soul those last few months of college, and just then I blamed Robert. The noise I made forced him to look up from his work at the source of the annoyance. The face was never annoyed, but instead blank and all-comprehending, as if the answer to the problem he was working on, the source of my anguish, the answers to the questions of the universe, were emblazoned on my T-shirt. "Can't you say anything else?" I added, unnecessarily loud. I was perfectly aware that I was being bitchy. I knew it, I liked it, and I planned to keep on doing it. It made the digging sensation subside for a while.

"Sure I can. What's for supper?"

I slammed my books down flat on the kitchen floor. They made a wonderfully loud bang when they hit just right, and the people downstairs could shove it up their noses for all I cared. Bugger them, bugger him, I thought, and bugger me too. I was a lost soul with erasers and quantum and supper to contend with. It seemed so much easier to succumb to the fury than to try to reason it away. What had poor Robert ever done to harm me, except to get in my way for the past six months?

It had all started almost four years before in the Commons on our first day of college. I remember being alone, not having followed my high school classmates to any of the more conventional eastern schools. At the other end of the dining table sat Robert. At that time he seemed to me to be very much like all the rest of the boys with his too-long blond hair, a saggy, tattered T-shirt with a ripped pocket, old corduroy jeans with food caught in the cracks of the fabric, and peach fuzz.

Except that Robert didn't talk like the other boys did. He just sat there grinning a big, shapeless, Swedish grin. I finished my dinner, cleaned my plate (unlike the others who, even if they were starving, would not eat the food in order to maintain a state of grace with their peers, since it was fashionable to criticize college Commons cuisine), and stood up to leave when Robert finally said something.

"The applesauce isn't that bad."

Everyone at the table was silent. What could they possibly say to counter that? How could even the college Commons destroy commercially bottled applesauce? The inanity of Robert's simple statement silenced them all. I decided that I liked him. I picked up my tray and moved discreetly toward the kitchen with it when a girl sitting beside Robert, a dark, unsmiling, butchy sort of girl with hairy black armpits and a man's sleeveless T-shirt, took her dish of applesauce and dumped it over his head.

I left as quickly as I could without stumbling. I couldn't bear to watch the expression on Robert's doughy face. The din of the Commons drowned out the noise from the table, and I ran back to Gilbert Hall, the first coeducational dormitory on campus, to find my roommate there, unpacking.

First days in new places are always memorable even if more exciting things happen later. My roommate had driven there from New York with her boyfriend, a tough sort of fellow, much older (at least twenty-two), who was training to be a pilot at a technical college in Missouri. The dormitory maid had already made the beds and my parents had helped me to unpack all of my things, so I sat there rather uselessly at my own very scratched metal desk watching Tina and her boyfriend, Alan, unpack. She didn't even flinch when he piled her underwear into one drawer of her tin bureau. I thought that was a bad sign.

Tina was cheerful enough, pretty enough. She had a peculiarly long eastern accent, she was taller and much darker than me, and she ignored me. That was about all I knew of her after two hours in the same room, except that she had a dog named Timmy and liked to play tennis. She was paying more attention to Alan than to me, and within that two-hour period it became manifestly obvious that I was unwelcome there. I began to doubt the sense behind the concept of open, coed dormitories. Tina stopped talking to me altogether after a while, and then she stopped looking in my direction. It was getting dark outside and I wasn't sure of where to go, but I knew that I had to go somewhere. I tried to wander unobtrusively out the door of room 107, which Tina rapidly shut behind me without so much as a polite "So long," and down the hall into the lounge. I sat on a plastic-covered couch, pretending to read *Siddhartha* for at least another two hours, until I started to stick to the upholstery.

It was past eleven when I ventured back to the room. The plastic upholstery had given me a rash. My name and Tina's were stuck on the door, written in black Magic Marker pen on two sticky-backed HELLO! MY NAME IS cards. The door was locked. I heard voices inside, whispers, then nothing. No one came to open the door when I knocked.

The first floor of Gilbert Hall was pretty active that night. I know, because I could see it all from the lounge where I slept. I turned out the lights and tried to relax on the plastic couch, but it stung the backs of my legs. I was afraid that I might stick permanently. About one in the morning some knocking woke me out of a half-sleep. There was Robert, the applesauce washed out of his hair, rapping at a door directly across from the lounge. The door opened, and the dark, butchy girl in the T-shirt appeared. Robert went into her room with her and she locked the door behind them. I heard it click.

When Tina's boyfriend wasn't there I had a bed to sleep in, although Tina did her best to keep me awake most nights. We were an ill-matched pair. Tina, from a liberal Italian family in New York, was very lively and sociable, smoking cigarettes and dope, drinking coffee and beer and chatting cross-legged on the floor until the most ungodly hours with all the "darlings," as she called her friends, up and down the hall. I worried quietly about cancer, criminal arrest, coronary disease, hemorrhoids. All I wanted to do was to go to sleep or to crawl off with my knitting or my latest historical novel. I honestly tried to contribute to these sessions once or twice, but my contributions were feeble, few, far between, and substantially ignored. It wasn't until December that I actually broke down under the pressure and made a supreme effort to conform.

I never saw Robert with the butchy girl in public. I never saw much of either of them, in fact, and she dropped out in mid-November of that first term, a victim of one of Tina's darlings, who accused her of leaving a pile of feces in one of the showers. I could sometimes hear Robert playing the piano in the ground floor lounge after supper: meaningless chords, jumbled notes that poured out of his mathematician's brain in mathematically precise chaos. I never talked to him. We just looked at each other over the ivory keys from distant ends of the first floor hall.

Gilbert Hall had not been built with the notion that two sexes would cohabit there. Each floor was conveniently divided in half by a lounge; but this arrangement was unfortunately complicated by the fact that there were three bathrooms on each floor, and three does not divide evenly. On our end it was unanimously the ladies' room, on their end it was the men's room, but no ultimate decision was ever reached about the bathroom in the middle, the only one with bathtubs, beside the central lounge. Most of the ladies were too shy to use it when there was the danger of a gentleman in underwear wandering in on them, yet it was never officially designated a men's room because of the tubs. And so it became coed.

Round about early December, when the pressure of exams seemed to bear heavily upon everyone's nerves but mine, someone discovered that by closing the windows and by turning on all of the hot taps in the sinks, bathtubs, and showers, they could create a very effective steambath in the coed bathroom. The men were the first ones to take advantage of this newest amenity in old Gilbert Hall, but soon enough the darlings were joining them. Tina would return to our room in the evening after supper, clad only in a towel, flushed to the gills and dark and lovely from the heat, praising its soothing effects on a nervous, study-worn body. I never studied very hard so I wasn't too concerned about relaxing, but before long there were only four of us who didn't participate in the nightly steambaths: two fat girls from Nebraska who roomed together, and wore crucifixes and identical T-shirts; one thin Oriental boy who had pimples and wore thick glasses and always looked confused; and me. For fear of ending up blackballed like the poor, butchy girl who threw applesauce and fouled the shower, I broke down.

And so one tense evening the night before the Christmas break began, after my last exam, I put on my bathing suit, wrapped a very large beach towel around my body, and walked resolutely down the hall into the steambath. I darted right into one of the toilet stalls at first and gingerly removed the towel. The steam was too thick to see more than twelve inches in any direction, so I bravely swam out of the stall toward the source of the most heat—the corner where the bathtubs were.

Everyone over there was stark naked. Like lost souls in hell, which is how it looked to me after eighteen years of never seeing a naked parent or hearing a sex education lecture: breasts and penises and pubic hair swimming at me out of the coiling steam, a pornographic inundation. I never even noticed their faces: lost souls have no identity. I kept colliding with the genitals, and the genitals would stare at me in my bathing suit as if I were Dante in my civilian robes being led through their damned mist like a freak, and suddenly I knew that I *was* a freak. The steamy, hellish atmosphere was having a peculiarly immoral effect on me. I realized, with a piggish frisson of excitement, that I *wanted* to be as naked as they were, damned and all. Because I felt almost cloaked in the heavy steam anyway, I gleefully removed my bathing suit, and for the first time since the age of two I walked naked before other people. Since everyone else was equally naked it did not seem odd. In fact, after a few minutes it felt positively normal, and all my thoughts of hell vanished like vapor.

I had never seen a naked man before, and I was intrigued by what looked like a ridiculous rubber hose dangling. The boys puffed valiantly to hold back erections, the girls were as cool and settled as the December snowdrifts outdoors. And thus I came face to face, so to speak, with Robert, still quiet, still grinning his huge, shapeless, Swedish grin, unknowingly the only one standing in there with an erection as large as a fence post, unashamedly ogling all the naked girls. He tossed a glass of cold water on my back when I wasn't looking. I turned around and did the same to him. He seemed to like it. He grinned even harder, and his erection didn't flinch.

We went our separate ways the next day, Robert back to Iowa and me just eighty miles north, home. Robert kissed me on the forehead as I stood in the lobby of Gilbert Hall with my suitcase, waiting for my father to pick me up.

He telephoned me long distance from Iowa that Christmas break and I was entranced. No one had ever telephoned me long distance before, and my parents were impressed because he was Scandinavian, a Youngson.

Robert and I met again in Gilbert Hall in January for the spring term, and as fate would have it, or perhaps a lack of imagination, we stayed together until that last semester. Amid the eraser filings, off campus in the squalid two-room flat, I began to hate his monotone.

On a frigid January night with the campus as still as an Antarctic dewdrop and Tina and Alan away for the weekend, Robert coaxed me into my bed. With a few rapid, efficient strokes, he undid eighteen-and-a-half years of fierce Norwegian chastity, retained not on any lofty principles but simply because no one had asked for it. I remember a rubbery object with an unpleasant smell, a lot of wet kissing and then a mysteriously pleasant sensation downstairs all of a sudden. Robert fell alseep on top of me and I almost died of suffocation and claustrophobia before I managed to wake him and wriggle free.

I spent the next two weeks suffering from an acute case of what the college physician so indelicately referred to as "honeymoon cystitis." Rather than see the doctor as soon as the painful symptoms appeared, I suffered with it for two weeks, deriving a certain masochistic pleasure from the agony. It was only when Tina started complaining about my frequent trips to the toilet throughout the night, and when Robert got fed up with my agonized cries whenever he pressed his lustful attentions upon me that I was driven to the infirmary.

But four years later I was starting to become aware of insidious changes, new pressures, forces operating against us, unseen, barely felt. Life had to change. School looked suddenly meaningless beside the specters of career and self-support. I never liked changes, and have often been guilty of ignoring them; yet as it was with Carole's gold ring, as much as I hated to look, I *had* to look. The future was suddenly mine, and I had to face that Robert was simply boring me, keeping me on square two when I was ready for square one.

Before the echo of the slamming books had faded into the greasy acoustical ceiling tiles, Robert was back into his problem, his straight blond hair, cut bluntly across like a little Dutch boy's, hanging over his cheeks. I couldn't stand to look at him. The mail was on the countertop. There was a letter for me on top of the pile. It looked like another rejection. I had exhausted all of the universities within a fifty-mile radius of M.I.T., where Robert was bound. I took the half-bottle of wine from the refrigerator and went into the bathroom with it. There was nowhere else to escape, the apartment was so small; I could hear his fingers drumming through the walls, and I hated him.

"What's for supper?" he called over, maddeningly cheerful.

"Nothing." I sucked at my bottle like the self-pitying wretch I felt, a notebook balanced on my knees, squatting beside the toilet, hoping for the words of an English assignment to pour forth.

"Sounds good!" he hollered back, the sound of his tapping fading with the sound of buzzing in my ears from the wine.

And that June, into our last summer term after graduation, almost four years after it had all begun, I started to make life very miserable for poor Robert. He spent more nights sleeping in eraser filings than I care to remember; I drank more bottles of Valpolicella than I can remember. And the saddest part of all was that perhaps it could so easily have been avoided if I had done something more sensible that last semester than take a course in Middle English poetry and literature.

Since childhood I had been obsessed with things medieval. I was the first one in my fourth grade class, for instance, to understand that there was a difference between medieval and Renaissance, although I never quite grasped the fine distinctions until years later. By age eleven I had read Dante's *Inferno* and had done a book report on it, noting in grisly detail the scenes that a macabre, slightly introverted child of normal intelligence might well note: creatures wielding iron gaff hooks at the souls floating helplessly in pits of boiling oil; and condemned gnawing the napes of other condemned in icy eternal entombment.

It wasn't until I was older, perhaps thirteen, after the Beatles had washed over the Midwest, that my general fascination with things medieval—Dante's Hell and Milton's Paradise, ladies wearing pointed hats that resembled the loathsome cones in my first geometry book, instruments of torture on display at the public museum—began to shape itself into an almost ravenous interest in things distinctively English and medieval. The process might be attributed to my father, whose sole cultural activity then was a penchant for listening to medieval music which, he insisted, was soothing and unobtrusive, and reminded him of the music he had heard as a boy in the small village back in Norway where he was born.

My father did not have a keenly honed taste for medieval music: he could not distinguish a harp from a sackbut; he simply enjoyed listening to it after a Sunday dinner, fat and dozy after a big meal, buried beneath newspapers on the couch. I listened to it at first because I had no alternative, but it appealed to me nonetheless in a careless sort of way until I eventually found myself humming snippets of "Worldes bliss" rather than any of the popular rock tunes. I wasn't yet sure what I wanted, but I sensed that it had something to do with that music, with Dante, with England, with castles. It made me shiver. I dreamed softly of dampness and dark green hillsides while my classmates dreamed of orchids on chiffon dresses. God had a plan, but plots took time to develop, and I wasn't rushing anything.

In college the fascination survived and I snapped up every course even vaguely related to the time and place: Shakespeare first of all, then all of the histories from Roman on up to Georgian, trying to find a place that felt comfortable; then Latin, French, English Renaissance prose, and a history of science. At last, by my senior year, frustrated by Matthew Arnold, disgusted with Milton, and still searching, I turned for my final credits to Middle English literature.

The professor was a tiny, jumpy young fellow whom we all at

first suspected of being homosexual, particularly when he started bringing all of his friends in to class. The friends themselves stayed around for only a day or two at a time. They appeared to be perfectly normal young men with rucksacks and blue jeans, only distinguishable from the rest of us by their shorter, tidier haircuts and the English accents in their polite whispers. As it turned out, the professor—who asked that we call him David—had gotten his degree at Oxford and he was playing host to his more adventuresome classmates, all hitchhiking through America after term ended. By late June we were almost thoroughly convinced that David was not a pantywaist because he read Layamon's *Brut* in such a hirsute fashion that one could almost watch his silky little beard thicken.

One day one of his friends was sitting in the corner front desk beside my usual seat. He was rather nice looking. I personally forgave David for his persnickety grammatical corrections to my last paper on the *Morte d'Arthur,* for his tiny butt that disappeared into buttless, baggy trousers, for his clear-bottomed glasses and nasty greenish teeth. Feeling up to my eyebrows in eraser filings, I boldly sat down next to this one and introduced myself.

He had wonderful eyes, I saw that right away. My father had warned me never to be taken in by men who told me that *I* had beautiful eyes, yet I rather felt like telling just that to this fellow; but the words simply would not come. Four years with the same boy, the only boy, had made me behave like him in many ways: awkward, shy, quiet, clumsy. I needed to fall in love for once, voluntarily, with someone smooth. I stared at my notebook. I realized that that is exactly what Robert would have done in a similar situation. I turned to face him, and I stuttered a greeting.

And I looked him over closely. He wasn't terribly tall like Robert—a gigantic, white-haired Swede—but he was tall enough. I needed that change. He was very dark ("Looks like a Jew boy," my very Norwegian-looking father said later), and he seemed very well mannered. He was wearing his Oxford University necktie with a sports jacket, well rumpled, and blue jeans. After four years of seeing blond men in scruffy corduroys and tattered T-shirts covered in cookie crumbs, I was impressed.

"Have you read the assignment?" I asked, palms sweating, trying to keep from staring at the notebook again, trying to keep my hands from shaking too noticeably as I rooted in my purse for a pen. I had never flirted before. It was unprecedented. It was exhilarating.

It was shocking. I hardly recognized myself. I would turn over a new leaf. Robert didn't know it, but he had just been pushed overboard.

"What was I supposed to have read?" he asked, with deep brown eyes so beautiful that I could not possibly keep my pen from dropping and making a splot of ink on the green linoleum floor. I bent over to pick it up, conscious that my breath probably reeked of coffee and that I probably had sleep stuck in the corners of my eyes. The sun was full in my face. He would be able to see every spot in all its glory.

"The Auntirs of Arthure at the Terne Wathelyn," I said, with the utmost lack of cleverness.

"As a matter of fact, I have read it," he said and he smiled. A smile that came out of his eyes, his ears, up my nose and into my brain before I could manage to exhale.

"I haven't," I said. "Can you tell me about it in thirty seconds or less? David is always on time and this class is too small to avoid being questioned." I had in fact read it, but I had suddenly, conveniently, forgotten it.

And he actually remembered, and he told me all about it: about the horrible battlelike hunt so unusually gory, but characteristic of northern writing, about Guinevere's petulant reaction to the ghost, about the horrid creature with a toad on its head that was her mother, and about speculation that it might be two stories loosely connected rather than just one. "Are you an English major?" I asked him stupidly.

"Literature?" He pronounced it beautifully, without the *e.* "No. I read Geography."

We went to the student union afterward where I neurotically drank another cup of coffee to keep me alert enough to talk to him, and he had a chocolate milk. His name was Michael Jones. I skipped the rest of my classes that day and we walked around the campus together talking, Michael rather effortlessly it seemed, me nervously with my *a*'s and *r*'s softening until by five we were holding hands and no one could have guessed that I had been born and bred in Milwaukee. We had dinner together at the Burger King, a fascinating experience for Michael, raised on home cooking and fish and chips. We walked back up the hill to the campus to watch the long day unobtrusively slide into a short night from the top of an Indian mound.

After almost twelve hours, my jaw was sore from talking and my chest ached from love and tension. It was hard to relax because the only other man I had ever so much as held hands with was Robert, who never talked much. It was all so different. Even in the beginning it had never been so exciting with Robert. I revised my master plan. I did not need or want a lifetime of towheads and cold Scandinavian blood in the *Snus* belt. I needed Michael Jones. I would have done anything that night to secure the dream firmly to my bosom; and it was frightening and wonderful to feel that way.

We stopped talking when the last of the blue sky disappeared, and we started kissing then. By ten-thirty I had been unfaithful to Robert twice on top of an Indian mound in the center of the campus. By eleven we had made love four times and I was afraid that if it went on much longer we might get too relaxed and be discovered, even though it was Tuesday and most students were home studying for mid-terms. We were on the shadowy side of the mound, but I still didn't want to relax too much. Since Michael was staying on David's living room floor I could not very well follow him home for more and so we had to part, me miserable, sore, sticky, Michael I don't know. He did say that he wanted to meet me again the next day in the union, which was enough to keep me awake most of the night in a near-matrimonial frenzy.

I walked back to the apartment in midsummer moonlight all sweaty and enraptured. The town was as quiet and backlit as a vacant movie set, the air smelling unreally of dewy cut grass and fresh roses. I could not think of what to tell Robert, who would not ask but would expect an explanation. I was too inexperienced to know any better. If I had, it might not have felt so exquisitely painful to be in love. My womb danced at the thought of Michael Jones, so clever, so English, so strange, such a gentleman, such a cad, such fun, so hard, so dark and different. My heart thumped a dull thump and dropped into my liver at the thought of Robert, who loomed before me suddenly through the kitchen window. He sat at the table, tapping his fingers in piles of eraser filings, clacking a slide rule, eating a banana, those blue soupy eyes staring up into the ceiling searching for the correct number, only to erase it seconds later in favor of a more correct number. The floor was littered with Twinkie wrappers and orange juice spills. For some reason Robert ate only yellow food, the junkier the better.

I dropped my purse and books on the floor beside his stereo and his collection of electronic music and Frank Zappa records. As soon as I breathed the air of the apartment I felt oppressed, squashed, suffocated. Bananas, rubber, and sperm. How could I ever have thought that I loved him? How could I have slept with him and have been moved by him all those years, those wasted young years? Robert, six foot one, with yellow hair and yellow skin and yellow T-shirts and yellow pencils and even a yellow penis. His watery eyes sloshed around to greet me dispassionately. Robert was always dispassionate except when he came, or when he was asked to eat something nonyellow.

"It's late." His eyes lapped at the hands of the plastic kitchen clock in the shape of a coffee grinder.

"Yes," I said, and volunteered nothing else. I couldn't talk to him after what I had just done. I had nothing to say to him after saying everything to Michael. It was like dropping from heaven to earth in fifteen minutes. It hurt everywhere. I could only talk to Robert as I would talk to a pet cat or dog. I knew nothing about math, he knew nothing about British constitutional history. But Michael knew everything. Robert looked like me, too: for that I might as well look in a mirror. I needed the contrast of Michael. My parents were both blond and watery-eyed. So were all of my relatives, and it was damn boring.

I went into the bathroom and stared at myself in the mirror, hoping to see something beautiful there that would be worthy of Michael Jones; but all I saw was that I needed some color in my cheeks, some body in my baby-thin white hair. I noticed that there was grass all over the back of my white shirt and blue jeans, and I tried to brush it onto the floor, but it stuck tenaciously. I wondered if Robert would notice. Probably not. He did not usually notice very much. I could hear his fingers tapping wildly. He was already deeply, darkly back into his calculus. I decided not to tell him anything, to wisely wait and see if Michael Jones would remain interested the next day, and possibly the next, in spite of having had all of me after only a twelve-hour acquaintance. I took a bath, reluctantly washing away all traces of him, and tried to sleep that night on the couch in case Robert came to bed. But he didn't. He tapped until two in the morning, and then fell asleep on top of the kitchen table, a guiltless sleep induced by the innocence of quadratics.

I waited for Michael Jones in the student union that second day. He had arranged to have breakfast beforehand with David and another faculty member with an Oxford background. I had planned to skip all of my classes again if things progressed favorably. I was early, as usual, and had finished off two unnecessary cups of coffee when he walked in, late, wearing the same shirt, necktie, jeans, and jacket he had worn the day before. I was still impressed, and noticed with a stab of pleasure that he had grass stains on his knees. He nodded. I remembered the way he felt on top of me and I blushed back. It had been too dark and quiet on the Indian mound the night before to feel any embarrassment, but in the brash light of the union's fluorescent tubes and the fierce June sunlight it reared up red and hard, like a hive. I wondered why on earth I was there at all and not hiding under a damp leaf in someone's back garden.

"Good morning, Miss Mortenson."

Mr. Jones? I couldn't bring myself to say it. No matter what I said to this man, this brilliant Oxford M.A., this dark-haired foreign mystery, I would sound doltish. If Robert hadn't just that moment come loping into the union all yellow and distracted, I might have made up an excuse to Michael and left.

"Had a good day so far?" I strained. Michael pulled out the chair next to mine with a flourish and sat down, behaving Englishly, I thought. Robert was ordering something to eat at the counter. It would be either a custard ice cream or egg salad. He hadn't noticed us yet.

"Oh, reasonably. David is a tiresome talker, but one can't complain when the accommodation is free."

Suddenly I couldn't think of anything else to say. My lungs billowed up into my throat, choking me, and my hands went numb gripping the arms of the chair. It had all been said and done the night before, I realized in a panic. I wondered how I had ever managed to think of things to say to Robert for four years, but then it wasn't much of a challenge to keep him amused. My bladder was tightening up, and I wanted to leave. I rooted for words the way I had rooted for a pen in class twenty-four hours before.

"I don't think that you told me where you were from in England." Of course he had told me.

"It doesn't really matter because my family moved so often. I was actually born near London, but I've probably lived a year or two in most of the large cities in the country, since my father worked for British Rail."

"Funny, I've lived in the same place all my life. But my parents have moved now that Dad's retired." I heard myself talking and I was amazed at how boring I sounded.

"Oh, really? Where have they moved to?" So polite. He couldn't possibly be interested, but still I was impressed. Love tolerates, love forgives, love tries to obliterate and smother.

"A farm. Near the city. Not too far from here."

Robert paid for his ice cream. He turned around and spotted us immediately. I could see that he was surprised. Normally he would have pushed his face right into the ice cream and finished it standing still beside the counter, but instead he just stood there with it melting down his big hands, staring at us. I hoped he would come over and learn for himself, see how exalted Michael Jones was beside him, to save me the trouble of telling him later. I also hoped that he would just go away and forget what he had seen to save me the effort of explaining. He loped over to the table and stared at me like a sheep. He didn't have to say anything. His face had no expression, which was expression enough to me. Robert was never very proficient in the social graces. The extent of his hospitality and sense of humor was handing out green string beans on Halloween. He saved the yellow ones for himself.

"Robert, this is Michael Jones. He's visiting from England."

Michael actually stood up and extended his hand, but Robert's was runny with custard and all he could do was look at it dripping on the Astroturf carpeting of the union floor. "Hi, sport," Robert finally said. I think he was trying to be casual, clever. It never worked with Robert. My chest collapsed, my heart strings sprang. He wiped his hand on his dirty, baggy corduroys and sat down in a heap in the other chair at our table.

"Are you studying history as well?" Michael asked him.

Robert's eyes were bigger and doughier and sheepier than usual, taking in Michael and me sitting side by side, strained and guilty grins spread obviously on our faces. He stared at Michael, he stared at me, he stared at his custard and started to glom it down with the vehemence of a starving mongrel. With a sticky sneer of custard spread up both his cheeks he emerged long enough to say, "No, math."

"Oh dear," Michael said, "I can't say that I have ever had much to do with mathematics, although I certainly admire those people who can manage it."

"I can't stand it either," I added, tactlessly, but Robert wasn't

[26]

listening anyway. "But then he can't bear to look at a history book."

Robert reached the cone, ignoring us, and he made a lot of noise chewing it, on purpose, I suspected. His eyes had moved from contemplation of us to the acoustical tiles on the ceiling, looking for answers.

"Where are you headed now, Robert?" I asked, not really wanting to know but desperate to fill in the silence and get him on his way.

Robert just looked at me like a sick sheep with those blue eyes of his and belched. A nice, rich, long, custardy, moist belch. He grabbed his quantum text and stood up. "Ta ta," he said, and he loped, baggy and yellow and unfunny, right out of the union.

"You have some unusual friends," Michael said.

"He's a math major."

"Yes. I expect he is."

There was in those first days an intoxicating and novel quality to the relationship with Michael that even I was suspiciously aware of. Michael was everything that Robert and I were not: he was foreign, he was dark-haired, well spoken, gracious, and gregarious. He spoke of having more friends than I had classmates at college. I especially liked his looks. He was not handsome in the conventional sense. Handsome men like that were usually very boring or neurotic or arrogant. But Michael was certainly good-looking: a bit long in the nose perhaps, slightly weak in the chin, but deliciously un-Norwegian, pale-skinned and English, with strange, deep-set, smily brown eyes with a wicked, sarcastic, genius life of their own. His hands were the hands of a peasant, short fingers with bluntly trimmed wide nails, but white and soft. And he was strong. God only knew how he got those powerful muscles in his arms and his legs because he never seemed to do much physical work or exercise, or any sport that I knew of; but he was certainly very strong, and very impressive in the nude, rather like my very own toy Adonis with a funny accent. He was too polite to show his scars in the beginning, and I never probed for them. In fact, he was too polite even later to show them, or perhaps too proud. I seldom exhibited the same self-control.

I left Robert a week to the day after meeting Michael in class. He extended his visit to two weeks, because of me. I stopped doing my homework and spent my few hours alone just thinking of him and of what happened on the Indian mound, on Robert's bed that night while Robert monitored the telescope at the college observatory, the third night very late and quietly on David's dusty living room floor, the fourth and fifth days periodically in my Volkswagen parked in a cornfield, the sixth day again quietly and repeatedly at David's while he was at class, and the seventh on the couch where I took up residence in my friend Cynthia's living room. If there had been any guilt with Robert in the beginning, there was perhaps less with Michael because I was acting deliberately and I loved him more than I could ever remember having loved Robert. I felt a different sort of sexual guilt with Michael than with Robert: a good guilt, if that was possible. It was bad enough having disported myself for almost four years with Robert and then having abandoned him practically at the altar like some Gothic rake; but now coupled with Michael whose mere Englishness, age, neckties, and Oxford degree made him seem more respectable, at least superficially, the burden of the tawdry sexual liaison with Robert was a little hard to bear without trying to smear some of it off onto my partner.

However, it was 1974. And, according to the media, who ought to know, people in 1974 had sex everywhere all the time, and I shouldn't feel bad about Robert. I suspected that such feelings as mine were peculiarly out of date. I tried not to discuss them too much with Michael because, based upon some of his early, brief confessions, his morals were very much up to date. Yet my small guilt persisted. I clung to him like a spring peeper desperate in June, and did very little to combat it. Silently, I felt guilty for both of us, and that made me feel good. It just seemed right. It made me feel cleaner, this token guilt. In the thirteenth century my sexual habits might have been cause for local banishment, or even death. It didn't seem entirely right to me that fornication could suddenly be so easy, so acceptable now.

I learned that Michael's childhood home had been just about everywhere. His parents had moved at least nine times before he was eighteen when, through his own cleverness, he finally escaped the gypsy caravan of their life to study at Oxford. His father, at one time some kind of a food manager for British Rail, had retired a few years earlier to an ancient, rotting, two-acre farm in Gloucestershire, but, according to Michael, he was already feeling restless there. I worried that this same nomadic blood ran in Michael's veins since his first priority after finishing at Oxford was to tour America by thumb. I felt that my fears were even more justified when the two weeks were over and Michael said that he had to go. After all, that was why he had come in the first place, he said: to see America, and not just to spend his precious two months in the green, liberated cloister of a small, private, midwestern college.

He was right, of course. Still on my best behavior, gnashing back the jealousy, I agreed that it probably was time he continued his travels, wondering at once why I had given up the sheep-in-hand in favor of a transient Englishman who was, without a doubt, the supreme catch, very horny and attracted to me, but also manifestly unwed, well educated, footloose. The two weeks had been a dream of junk food banquets and bicycle rides and orgasms and Middle English mythology. I had stopped studying altogether and not even the prospect of a marginally lower grade point average could coax me back to my books while he was there. I had all the credits I needed. The only thing I thought I lacked was Michael Jones. I thought about him before I fell asleep, as soon as I woke up, while I brushed my teeth, peed, spread peanut butter on toast. I ate, laughed, drank, walked, breathed, blinked, and heard Michael Jones.

"Where do you go from here?" I asked him that last night with the strength of a lamb, not really wanting to hear an answer from him at all, preferring the bliss of ignorance to the stab of truth. We were on the campus, leaning back against the old oak trees that swaddled the Indian mounds beneath them. I kept thinking of the words to a lyric I had read earlier that day: *"Go hert with adversitee and let my lady thy woundis see."* I was a good girl with Michael and I hid my wounds, speaking of Robert and of guilt as little as possible. He followed suit. He never discussed Other Women.

"I should ask you the same question," he said.

"Why?"

"Well, you will be graduating and leaving next month. What then?"

"I hadn't thought."

"That surprises me. You seem to do everything so deliberately. You don't have trouble making big decisions."

"I don't really want to think about graduation just yet. It's a whole month away. I asked you first anyway. You have this bus ticket —so where are you going with it?"

"Oh, I'd like to see the West."

"The West?" Men were so annoyingly vague. I had visions of

silly foreigners in ten-gallon hats and spurs combing the vast tracts west of the Mississippi in search of red Injuns and cowboys. I didn't want Michael to be a silly foreigner. The relationship was young enough to be very tolerant, but in time I knew I might hate him for this kind of naïveté.

"Vancouver, Washington, you know."

"No. Never been there."

"I can't very well invite you, although I'd like to."

"I'm not asking to be invited."

"I know."

We were sharing a bottle of wine rather poorly concealed in a brown paper sack. The sky was not spinning yet, but I was close to being embarrassingly frank.

"Do you think you'll be coming back this way?"

"Yes."

Exactly what I wanted to hear, and no more. It pleased me so much that I didn't say anything for a few minutes, just enjoying the yes, and Michael leaned back on the tree trunk smiling with English lips and something else to say.

"What do you think about it here?" I finally asked when the silence grew too large.

"Where?"

"Here. America."

"That's not a fair question. I've only been here for three weeks."

"But you've seen enough to venture a generalization."

"Perhaps. I think I like capitalism, then. I like the notion that you can still become a millionaire here if you're clever enough. You can be awfully clever in Britain and still be a pauper. At least a person has a chance here. I like that."

"Well, why don't you just move here and become a capitalist?"

"I wish it were that easy, little girl."

"What's so difficult about it?"

"Red tape. Visas. Work permits. Besides, I may not be all that ambitious. It would be a matter of trading one set of values for another, and I'm not sure that I'm quite prepared to make such a decision."

"If it's so difficult then why are there so many foreigners over here? Isn't that what this country was predicated upon?"

"They're patient, I suppose, or businesses sponsor them. Maybe they marry Americans."

The silence was delicious. I took another pull at the bottle, and let the sky jiggle and bob into sunset.

"When might you be back this way?"

"I'll be here for your graduation, if I'm invited."

I left my fan and a garlic press behind in my haste to move to Cynthia's. A week after I saw Michael off on a Greyhound bus westward I went back to Robert's apartment to pick them up. I still had my key and I had hoped that he would be gone, rubbing and tapping away on some tabletop out of sight in the calculus lab. But he was there at the kitchen table where he had practically worn perfect rump-shaped indentations in the vinyl chair and bony elbow marks on the Formica tabletop. He seemed abnormally yellow, or perhaps it was just my absence of two weeks, looking at pinker men, that made him appear so. The sink was full of glasses with a gummy residue in them—orange juice or lemonade, most likely—and the waste can was overflowing with squash and carrot skins and egg bread wrappers. A jar of peanut butter with a dark, hardened crust on top was open on the counter. It looked as if rigor mortis had set in everywhere.

"Forget your hunting horn, or have you caught your fox already? Tut-tut-tut," said Robert, tapping all the while he spoke with more malice than I had ever heard him muster. His humor was always pathetic, belabored. I had never known him to be vindictive or bitter about anything; not even when his lab partner cold-bloodedly broke his new slide rule when Robert exceeded his score on an exam. He had always been simply Robert, easygoing, odd, quiet. For some reason he seemed to have shrunk. I felt like a germ.

"Do you mind if I take the fan?" I was careful with my choice of words. We had gone fifty-fifty on that fan, but the math building was air-conditioned and none of the history buildings were. I knew he wouldn't miss the garlic press, since he didn't know how to use it (and anyway garlic was white), yet I still felt like apologizing.

"Why not? You've taken almost everything else." He stopped tapping and stared at me. He had been crying. There were pinkish half-moons on yellow. I had never seen him cry before. When I thought about it later, I recalled never having seen him so upset either.

"I'm sorry, Robert. Do you want me to leave the fan?"

"You don't have to."

"I'd rather not then."

"I'm boring, right?"

"No. Not exactly."

"Take your fan. I'd like the lemon squeezer back."

He started drumming like two rock bands out of sync, each hand pounding a separate beat across the flaky surface of the kitchen table, rubbery puffs of eraser filings flying off the edge onto the floor, tapping with all ten fingertips until I thought that they would have cracked off. Drumming almost cacophonically, crazily, like his piano playing, with his head down instead of his eyes up toward the ceiling. I couldn't bear to see Robert—gentle, nondescript, innocuous Robert—behave that way. I hated changes. I didn't want to be responsible for that.

"Stop it, Robert. You're driving me nuts."

He kept right on pounding. He was crying again. I took the garlic press from a kitchen drawer and I left him the fan.

I graduated. It was neither a time of woe nor exultation; it was merely a tedious process to be got through on a hot day when I would rather have been sitting underneath a torrent of silty, cool water at Shopiere Falls, with Michael Jones. He had come back the night before, as silently as a toad on soft, moist earth, coming up to Cynthia's front door and knocking softly, salty and tanned, the same man only six thousand miles larger. He had called twice during his travels, once from Vancouver, once from Chattanooga, but something inside of me more than half assumed that it had all been a dream, that Robert was my only hope in life. But still I clung to the dream as a bullfrog clings fiercely to a stick in misguided amplexus. When he did appear there underneath the yellow bug light on the rotted front porch with gnats about his head zitting on the light and that same smile, I invited him in and felt the exquisite, lush, massaging fingers of love requited touch every pore of my skin.

It was late. Cynthia was in bed upstairs. Michael set his pack down on the floor and collapsed onto the couch. I felt as if we, or I, should celebrate. Celebrate his homecoming, my graduation, our love. All I had on hand were two cans of Pabst. I had given up wine when I gave up Robert. I handed one of the cans to Michael. At least it was cold.

"Cheers," he said, and he drank like a sponge while I sipped, watching him.

We didn't say much that night. There was too much to do. We drank the beer, pulled out the sofa bed and made love. He was sweaty and he dirtied my sheets but even that was exciting and forgivable. Afterward I wanted to say something but I couldn't because he had fallen asleep. The night outdoors was full of fireflies and the syrupy lush peace caused by high late summer humidity. I heard every car pass by in the street that night. I heard windows opening, windows banging shut, air conditioners and fans humming and buzzing all liquefied and cushioned by the moisture and ozone thick in the air. Michael snored a little bit, but I didn't mind because it didn't keep me awake. I wanted to talk, and that was what kept me awake.

My parents were due to arrive the next day at ten, in time to photograph me in embarrassing black gown and mortar board on the college lawns. They knew about Michael, inasmuch as they knew that my telephone number had changed and I was no longer living with Robert. When they stopped at the apartment they hardly seemed surprised to see Michael there. I suspected that all the surprise had been knocked out of them two years before when they walked in on Robert and me in my bedroom at home undulating shamelessly together like two naked beached whales, and again when I announced that we were going to live together off campus. They stopped asking questions then, and just winced instead whenever I came home for the weekend, anticipating the worst.

Fortunately Robert was off near the end of the alphabet, in the Y's, and I was in the middle, so we were spared any more than the most fleeting glances at the commencement ceremony. When I would rather have cycled down to the A&W with Michael afterward, my parents insisted on taking me out to dinner in the poshest restaurant that small town could summon forth, complete with paper napkins and ketchup bottles. Michael came along and I was amazed at his agility in talking with my parents. He did it as effortlessly as he did it with me, and they were impressed. When they were ready to leave, my father stood aside with me on the front porch and told me that I had "a good one there. At least he eats meat, like a man." Math did not a man make. Meat did. Michael won.

It was tense at first after such a long time apart. There was little enough ground to stand on. I had thought of so much to say to him in those four weeks that I could not recall a single thing, and besides the situations never seemed quite right. I knew that I wanted to marry Michael, to keep him there, but at the same time I tried to fight down that snatching, smothering urge. Four years of parasitism with Robert (I wasn't sure who was the parasite and who was the host, but it certainly was not a healthy symbiosis) had set me in a bad way. I tried not to glower when he mentioned other women acquaintances. I tried not to pry into where he had spent all those nights away (did he make a habit of settling onto college campuses and looking for dissatisfied blond coeds?). Of course he had had sex before me, and hadn't I as well? But he was just too smooth, too good to have had only one other partner in all his twenty-five years. I tried to swallow the maddening doubts. I tried to love the dream and forget the man. Dreams are faithful; men are not.

We were in the kitchen. There was no fan. I was trying to make shepherd's pie from a recipe in Cynthia's *Betty Crocker's Cookbook.* This meat stuff was new to me. I had to concentrate harder than when I read Langland. Michael was wearing his swimming trunks and yellow rubber flip-flops, drinking a can of beer at the table. I could hear Cynthia singing to herself upstairs as she packed to go home to St. Louis. The lease expired in a week. I didn't want to think about that.

"This is just meat loaf with mashies on top," I announced finally, after deciphering Betty's hieroglyphs. "It's disgusting!"

"Oh, no! It's wonderful!" Michael insisted. "You just make it sound disgusting."

"Does your mother really make this stuff?" I brandished a wooden spoon covered with globules of reddish hamburger meat, strung together weakly with spermlike bands of egg yolk, all dangling grotesquely over the mixing bowl.

"Definitely. I was raised on it," he said proudly.

"I've heard that pizza was invented in New York and you can't even find it in Italy. Are you sure your mother makes shepherd's pie?"

"Would I lie to you?"

He touched a nerve. "Yes," I said, banging down the lid on a pot full of boiling potatoes. I knew that I was about to behave very badly, for the first time in front of him, and that it was irrational, but still I let myself succumb. It was just a game for him, I thought. I was as exotic to him as he was to me, only he saw it as simply a temporary arrangement, a fling. I grabbed my can of beer from the stove top and thundered into the living room with it. The sofa bed had not been made up yet. I threw myself across it in an abandoned heap. I prayed he'd follow. He did. Flip-flops on linoleum, on wood parquet, on shag carpeting. I felt his weight depress a corner of the bed.

"Are you all right, Gay?"

"Sure. Just hot." Every hair on my body was wrong. Every corpuscle rankled.

"I think it's more than that," he said. I hadn't expected quite that much sensitivity from him; not that it took much, but Robert had all he could do to tell a frown from a smile. I wasn't sure that I wanted him to know exactly what was bothering me. I was afraid that by telling him my dream, by spilling my wishes out loud, he would go away forever.

"How do you know?"

"You've been tense for days. Ever since I got here, really."

"So have you," I groped.

"Have I?"

"Of course you have."

"What's your reason? 'Fess up now."

"Robert called me," I lied again. I justified the lie to myself by not specifying the time or the day that he called. Robert *had* called me, but only once in the past month and that was to squeal about all of his pencils that I had inadvertently moved out. He seemed to have recovered.

"Oh?" Michael seemed to recoil, like a big beetle that has run into a large obstacle that it cannot, or does not want to, comprehend. "What did he want?"

"We were going to get married in a month, you know."

"I know. But you called it off." He had been well versed by me. I hoped that by hammering in my separation from Robert, my distaste for marriage and commitments like that, he might ignore the other side of me that wanted like life to clasp him to my matrimonial bosom with hooks of steel.

"He still wants to get married." I wasn't at all sure if this was the truth or not (I strongly suspected it wasn't), but it sounded good and dramatic. Robert and I had never discussed it. It had all been assumed, and forgotten. We floated apart like clouds on a windy spring day. Neither of us ever asked the other why.

"What about you?" He fiddled with his flip-flop.

"I don't know. I've known Robert a long time, but that doesn't mean that I still love him."

"I see."

He wasn't rising to the bait.

"I have to be out of here in a week."

"Yes. You're going back home?"

"I suppose. For lack of a better offer. For the time being."

"And Robert? Where's he going?"

"M.I.T."

"I presume you don't mean the Milwaukee Institute of Technology?"

"No."

"I see."

We were getting nowhere. I gave up. "How does your mother spice up the meat loaf ?"

"Don't use that dreadful name for it. It's minced beef, and she doesn't spice it at all."

He stayed on that whole week, watching me pack, each minute a mystery, each second melting as fragile as ice. I felt as if we could have done anything together and it would have been exciting; he appeared to feel the same way. He talked about his old cars, I talked about my history advisor who wrote pornography for bread and butter. He talked about going back to England to finish his training as a chartered surveyor with a firm of estate agents, I talked about a volunteer job I had had at the county zoo one summer, keeping the llamas from eating children's clothing in the petting zoo. We took walks around the block and I listened to him so hard, watching the way his lips moved, memorizing the outline of his front teeth, that once I tripped over the clumps of crabgrass that grew boldly up through the cracks in the sidewalk.

He talked about England and told me things that I would never believe until I saw them for myself. Things that my collections of books and brochures had said, too, but things that seemed too good, too fanciful to be true. Castles that were more than eight hundred years old. Green like green was meant to be, in ivy, in leaf, in meadow, in hedge, in January and in June. Cottages with roofs like woolly hats covered in roses. Inglenook fireplaces with worn hearths and niches for sitting and drinking something warm on a chilly night. Nice people. People with burst blood vessels in their rosy cheeks who actually said things like "ta" and "cheers" and "I say" and "bloody hell."

What Michael told me all sounded vaguely familiar, but I had rejected it years ago as so much monstrous romance that could never be as good as all that. Real thatched cottages? The same one or two were probably photographed to death for those ads. Ancient ruins? I had seen the site of an Indian village on the shores of Lake Aztalan near home that archaeologists said was five hundred years old. But that's all it was. A site. Some pimples on the earth, a few swells and a pouf here and there that I might, stretching the limits of credibility, attribute to an errant glacier. But a five-hundred-year-old Indian village? It was like calling an urn full of dust "John Smith."

But the difference between Aztalan and John Smith's dust and what Michael told me about England was that Michael told me, and so I believed. I remembered how it felt as a child to want to go there so badly that I could sit for an hour wadded into an impossible posture of arms, legs, and fingers crossed, wishing to open my eyes and find myself on top of Mount Snowdon wrapped in fox fur and tweeds, or at least to find an airline ticket on the floor in front of me. But all that gave me was a cramp and many frustrating moments when all I saw before me was the tacky blue-plastered bedroom walls. Yet I believed in Michael like I had never believed in crossed fingers and wishes on stars and seeding dandelions and the first words uttered on the first day of the month. He had said that he would come back, and he did come back. I wanted more promises than he could make come true. I floated along all week, waiting for another dream to turn into reality, not wanting to think at all that men do not make dreams, but dreams make men.

"What's it like in Cotswold country?" I asked. The words meant almost as little to me as "Moebius strip." Never having traveled, I did not have the traveler's scope of imagination. Cotswold was a funny word that I mispronounced.

"That's like asking me what it's like on the moon. Do I get twenty-five words or less?"

"Don't make fun of me."

"Honestly, Gay, I can't do justice to a question like that. Can't you be more specific?"

"Not really. All I know is that there are some special sheep there, but is there more than one thatched cottage too?"

"Hell, yes! Hundreds of them. Thousands, maybe." We were walking in the ten o'clock darkness and I could not see his face. As far as I knew he didn't lie, but he liked to be sarcastic at my expense sometimes. I brought out the worst in him, too. My midwestern honk, my parents' Oldsmobile, my addiction to root beer floats, my faith in *Time* magazine, my total ignorance of the *Financial Times,* my liberal stance on things like drugs and women's rights and racial prejudice.

"Seriously, Michael, they all look alike in the pictures."

"That's right. They all look alike. Like the wogs in Africa."

"Like what?"

"No, sunshine. There are thousands of them and they all look different. Each thatcher has a distinctive way of thatching, so the roofs vary from place to place. Some are older than others, and list to one side, or ripple like your Wisconsin cornsilk in the wind. Some are half-timber crucks, some are post and span with close or widely spaced timbering. Some are plastered over, some are filled in with brick, or with wattle and daub, and, most important of all, some are covered with pink roses, some are covered with white roses, and some are even covered with red roses."

We walked on in our circumnavigation of the block, almost swimming through air thick with corn pollen, the must of jungly wet August overgrowth, sticky petunia and cats. There was part of a yellow moon just stalking up over the trees. Michael's flip-flops slapped the pavement. I was barefoot, padding swiftly beside him, three of my steps to one of his.

"I don't believe you."

"Suit yourself."

"I want to believe you."

"Then come and see for yourself."

"When?"

"In June the red rose blooms."

"That's a long time to wait."

"I can't make roses bloom in September. Not even for you, sunshine." He took my hand and squeezed it. I believed him. "But have you ever heard of the Christmas rose?"

"It can't really be true. Can it?"

"Why can't it?"

"You're just homesick. You remember it as much nicer than it really is. What about ugly, cracked pavements and bad industrial smells?"

"I just stay away from them."

"That's too easy, Michael. All I ever read or hear about are thatched cottages and sheep and roses. England must have sewage treatment plants and buses that stink and loonies."

"Oh, plenty of them. But why would you ever want to hear about all that?"

"Because it's real."

"But who is interested in reality anyway?"

I believed him. We stopped at the A&W for a black cow because the name amused him, and then we walked back to the apartment, to bed.

I had to pack, feeling sick the whole time. I didn't want to go home. I toyed with the idea of graduate school. The University of Wisconsin had to accept me, even on such short notice, because I was a tax-paying resident with a reasonable grade point average; and in fact they did, which was better than some dreary secretarial job, which was probably the best I could have done with a B.A. in history. Michael helped me pack, and he came along on the first two journeys home. I had managed to accumulate three carloads full of junk in my four years. I fastidiously avoided asking questions about the future as long as he did, but I couldn't stand it anymore by the time the last night in the empty apartment rolled around, with even Cynthia and her singing long gone and the whole college town now a barren shell for me.

"What do you think of my parents?" I asked him. We were sitting on the porch in the eerie brilliance of the bug light and the moonlight. Every few minutes a bug would hit and it would make a *bzit* noise, signaling the end of yet another short life on earth.

"Nice. Typical American folk. Friendly, overweight, a big car, and they like Englishmen. Something about the accent inspires trust, I think."

"Until they get to know you." It was a bitchy thing to say, but I was so unsure of myself that I felt I was obliged to say it.

"Don't you trust me?" For once he rose to the bait.

"Why should I?"

"I love you. That's why."

"Since when has that been a good reason for trust? Me and countless others, right?"

"There's no one else, Gay."

"Why can't I believe you, then? Why doesn't your accent inspire trust in *me*?"

"Don't make fun of me."

"I can afford to. I love you. And you're the one with the Oxford M.A. who's leaving me tomorrow."

We sat in the stark glow of dim lights. Cynthia had absconded with the lawn chairs, so we were perched on the edge of the porch rail. It gave off smells of mortality. Damp rot. Fungus in dark, deep, hidden places, under the floorboards. Something had to be said now.

"You haven't told me what you plan to do tomorrow. I'm going home. You can't come along and sleep with me in my parents' house. Where are you going?"

"I have two weeks left before I have to fly back."

"I know that."

"I'm flying from Kennedy."

"I know."

"I thought I'd go east. I'd like to visit Pennsylvania and New York."

"Oh." I felt sick. The wretch had a mind of his own. "Will I ever see you again?"

"You really don't trust me, do you?"

"Why should I?"

"I told you why."

"I guess I don't believe you, then."

"You should try to get over that. Not just with me. With everything. You're too suspicious."

"You count more than anything else."

"Right now, perhaps. Give yourself a chance."

I wanted to fight him with my fists, but all I had were words. "I am. I left Robert, didn't I?"

"For the wrong reasons, perhaps, but it was still a good thing, I'm sure."

"Do you want me to visit you in England?"

"Let's not discuss that now. It's too soon."

"Too soon for what? I love you, you say you love me, and tomorrow we're going off in separate directions. In two weeks we'll be four thousand miles apart."

"Don't forget, love, I have your telephone number."

"Well, I don't have yours."

"Ladies should never call gentlemen anyway."

It ended inconclusively and I couldn't sleep all night, although Michael snored like a bulldozer. I miserably turned the apartment keys over to the landlord the next morning and left Michael carrying his dirty, Union Jack-emblazoned pack on the entrance ramp to the Chicago expressway just outside of town. Once he was dumped I felt curiously unbereaved, lightened. Nothing to study for, no one to wash my hair for, nothing to do but go home to my parents' farm and let my mother cook big meals for me again. I drove like a bird, light on the pedals. It was so strange to be utterly free.

"Telephone, Gay."

It was my mother calling. I had been home for ten days and no one had called me. None of my high school friends knew that I was back home, and anyway they couldn't have found me since my parents had moved from the city. There was no one who would telephone, other than Michael, who conspicuously didn't. I had almost stopped hoping except for dull pain alone at night. Registration at Madison was the next day and pain was temporarily superseded by anxiety. I dropped the newspaper I had been reading and plodded into the kitchen where my mother was washing cabbages from the garden for some reeking Norwegian lamb stew. The receiver was lying in a puddle on the blue tile counter. "I think it's long distance," she said. My heart stopped.

"Hello?"

"Hello?"

"Hello?"

"Hello. Have I got the Maharaja's Palace in Jaipur?"

"Michael!"

"Who else? I love you."

"Where are you?"

"Does it matter?"

"No. I suppose not."

"I'm at JFK Airport. Soon to be airborne, ahead of schedule. Where will you be a week Tuesday?"

"Here."

"Just as I thought. Can you meet me at O'Hare at four-thirty?"

"Of course! But why?"

"I should think that would be obvious. I'm coming back to claim you. At least I expect to be coming back, contingent upon the lady's desires."

"What desires?"

"You tell me: yes or no?"

"Of course! I'd love to see you again!"

"You'll do more than see me this time, dear girl. You'll marry me."

My heart fell from my neck to my knees. There was a Santa Claus after all. The cabbages, the kitchen, Daddy rustling my discarded newspaper, everything blurred into one huge pink rosy bubble. A dream come true, yet too good to be true. Thatched cottages with roses.

"Of course I will."

"Is that all you can say? Can't you say 'Yes' or 'I'll think on it'?"

"I don't have to think on it. Yes. Yes. When?"

"I'll leave that up to you and your mother. We can discuss the details next week. Ta, ducks. I love you."

"I love you!" I screamed, oblivious of my mother chopping cabbage just five feet away. My elbows and knees were jelled as I set the receiver back into its cradle. I wanted to tell, but I wanted to savor my secret a while longer, too. They would be pleased, I knew. All things were possible. I wobbled back into the living room propelled by a smile and whumped down into an easy chair, seeing and smelling roses.

"Who called?" my father asked, distracted, from behind the classifieds. The whole conversation had taken place within earshot, but he never listened.

"Michael."

"Nice boy. Eats meat."

"He asked me to marry him." I couldn't wait.

"He did?" The newspaper came down. A momentous occasion. "Ing, did you hear?" he called toward the kitchen. The sound of chopping cabbage ceased and my mother's red face ringed in drooping orange curls appeared at the door. "Gay's still going to get married!"

"How nice, dear," she said, and, after wiping her hands on her apron she came over and gave me a hot little kiss on the cheek. "To who?"

3

Shall we all die
We shall die all
All die shall we
Die all we shall

—GRAVESTONE IN
GUNWALLOE, CORNWALL

AT one time Robert and I had
tentatively decided upon September the fifteenth as a good day, a
month after graduation, enough time to locate an apartment and a
little bit of furniture, enough time to make the simplest of arrangements. All of those reasons were still valid, but on September the
fifteenth I married Michael Jones instead of Robert Youngson, and
we moved into a little farmhouse on an extremity of my parents' 150
acres.

It was a tedious wedding. I kept thinking of how much better
it could have been if it had not been in Milwaukee and if I had not
been born, baptized, and confirmed a Lutheran. We kept it mercifully small and were able to escape with just a cursory ceremony at
St. John's, the ancestral family church dating from 1953, and a small
reception on the farm, in the fresh hay-and-mignonette-scented garden under an alternately brilliant and ominous Indian summer sky
with roasted pig and watermelon and strawberries and fresh cider
and cardamom bread that I was too excited to eat. After one forgetta-
ble night in a grand downtown hotel we moved into the smaller of
the two houses on the property, across the long buckwheat field from

their slightly newer house, separated by a wall of white flowers and the nearly mechanical buzz of a million busily pollinating bees.

Downtown Milwaukee was not anyone's idea of the perfect honeymoon situation; nor was it ours. But I had to be in class at ten in Madison on Monday morning; we had no money to speak of; my parents felt some remote obligation to give us a good time even though Michael and I had agreed beforehand that honeymoons were a lot of old Victorian nonsense anyway—a poor excuse for a vacation. That was easy enough for him to swallow, I thought, having just spent three months on holiday; it was not difficult for me either, never having been on a real holiday, not knowing what I was missing. I still vaguely correlated the idea of a vacation with going up north, and had nasty recollections of uncomfortably woodsy scenes, ticks, blackness, spooks, mosquitoes, spiders, and swamps. As the reception wound down and after Auntie Inez left with all of the leftover pork and watermelon, there wasn't much point in hanging around. I gathered up a small case full of deodorant and toothpaste, feeling guilty at seeing my mother's kitchen a solid block of dirty plates, hoisted my long skirt up into the Volkswagen and we purred off downtown.

They smirked at us in the hotel lobby. We went to a suite of rooms full of marble-topped tables, a four-poster tester bed with a white lace canopy, velvety thick blood-red carpeting (so stains wouldn't show? the color of love? I wondered, with a shred of guilt), pink upholstered velvet chairs so grossly overstuffed that they looked more like fat cartoonish pigs, and even a fireplace with a wrought-iron grille drawn over it, decorated with hearts and flowers. We laughed at the oversized bathtub and promptly fell asleep. The next morning they woke us up with champagne and roses. A terrible combination. There was no time to do what we were supposed to do, and I was anxious to get back to our house to clean it, to put the new shades on the windows, to read the chapters in Stenton that I had to have finished by ten on Monday.

We finally got around to consummating the union late Sunday night, my head reeling with the oaths of frankpledge, heriot, and scutage that I'd been studying, Michael wasted and reeking of damp after a day spent clearing a corner of the cellar for a small workshop area. He drove me to Madison on Monday with half a notion to locate a car of his own there, somewhere, while I pursued my education. He left me outside the union, fortresslike and red, glowering over the fishy shores of Lake Mendota, and drove off in search of transport.

I sat in Feudalism that morning looking at my left hand. Fingernails brownish and soft from scrubbing woodwork covered with grime of the ages. Skin crisscrossed and hatched with tiny lines. Was it really the same hand that I had had attached to my body for twenty-two years? Somehow I felt it should have aged more since Saturday. It was a married hand now. With an eighteen-carat gold ring on it. Married hands grew old and wizened and unappealing overnight. I was going to become asexual. Amoeboid. Time to fasten the top three buttons on my blouses, let out the seams in my jeans. Soon enough the smooth skin on my chest would turn to chicken flesh like my mother's. I wrote "Jones" all over my notebook. It was easier to write than "Mortenson." The air smelled of drying hay, sweat, rubber, and Indian corn. "Scutage" and "heriot" were very ugly words. I was married.

I had lived a curiously nonexistent childhood at home with my parents. It was odd to be back near them, and unsettling. I could only remember the most obstreperous highlights: a birthday party at age eight that turned into a fart-lighting tournament until my mother walked in: seeing a ghost at age eleven: my first taste of hard liquor and the ensuing drunken brawl with my girlfriend Wendy at age fifteen. But there was nothing really memorable in between. I suppose that meant my parents had done their job well, since bad things are usually more memorable than good. Living at home now seemed a bit like living at college: temporary, a stage of life to be endured, but minus the scent of erasers and the sound of electronic music in the background.

They had left the rough painted plaster walls of their farmhouse like the plain walls in our old house in the city because Daddy hated wallpaper. He said that people only used it to conceal cracks, and then insects bred underneath it. They had transformed the farmhouse into a facsimile of the city house, with a gold living room, gold painted walls, gold painted ceiling, gold painted mantel, gold shag carpets, gold upholstered chairs, gold throw rugs, a gold couch, gold drapes, gold Tiffany lamps. The oddly dry and cushiony cellar became my father's office when he retired. The toothmarks remained in their mahogany bedposts where I had sacrilegiously teethed as a child. Funnily enough, even the waxy tile floors of the bathrooms were the same as in the old house, the rolling noise the sliding shower doors made, the hard mattress and the same green striped sheets on my bed, now our bed, moved across the field to the other little farmhouse. They still had their color television that made everyone purple-faced and ready to pop with aneurysm, and the place still smelled of bayberry, pork chops, apples, dust. The wind even made the same sound as it drove through the stormdoors, like a baby goat crying.

It was too familiar, too close, too uncomfortably comfortable. Although it was a different house from the one I had been raised in, all the components were the same. They had carried their smells, their colors, their atmosphere along with them, unconsciously. I suspected from the start that it would not last forever for me because these things were only eternal in their place; I was young and too kinetic to bear them any longer than it took for Michael and me to decide to go.

Michael was not very keen on living in the little farmhouse, yet as far as I could determine the only really bad thing about it was its proximity to a cancerous subdivision. Most of the farmers had sold out to developers by the late sixties and their rubber-stamped handiwork was everywhere. My father had had dreams of subinfeudating the farm, but he found out too late that most of the soil was not suited for septic systems, and it would either have to remain a farm and wait for city sewers, or perhaps be donated to the city posthumously as Mortenson Park. In the greener months of the year a long row of thick, scrubby, unkempt lilac bushes shielded the subdivision from our view, but in the winter that was all you could see: a billowing sea of ranch houses—split-level colonials with asymmetric windows, nondescript aluminum siding, and black eagles mounted over front doors. There were houses trying to be trendy modern but really only small variations on a model home theme. The subdivision next to the farm was forgettably named Towering Oaks, a name both incomprehensible and pretentious, for the only oaks around were on my father's land which enclosed the entire ghastly development in a paternal L-shape.

In a way I could perfectly understand Michael's displeasure. The farmhouse needed so much work done to it in the wake of unsympathetic tenants that we could not justify doing it on a short-term basis. It was frustrating even to think about it: the leaking, moldy basement which he had tried, and given up, working on; the porous, rusted gutters; the crabby overgrown lawns; the moldering barn; the chipped and ancient asbestos siding; broken and rotted window sashes; cracked walls—and architecturally it was boring, although not nearly so bad as the things that continued to sprout like so many mysterious warts and mushrooms in Towering Oaks. At least the little old farmhouse could claim some legitimate age, boast real hardwood floors, and it had a pitch to the roof.

Michael also could have been afraid of what he had once light-heartedly accused me of emulating: a *normal* housewife with a beaver wagon, three kids, a dishwasher, a microwave oven, and a cheating husband. A marriage without obvious blemish. Smiling children with minibikes and clean clothes. A life without cockroaches and red roses. Michael looked out the bedroom window and saw the Buicks parked in the asphalt driveways across the property line. He saw the perfectly new shingled roofs, the rider mowers manicuring perfect lawns, the flagpoles and rock gardens, the spoiled children riding ten-speeds, the dumpy wives with short, shapeless, blown-dry hair dressed in baggy trousers to hide stretchmarks like war wounds, hanging out rows of white shirts and sheets and brassieres (for they all had Dydee Wash for the little guys), and he saw me wanting the same things because we had not known each other long enough for him to think otherwise.

He saw me contriving that scene for him through the bedroom window like some big billboard: "Look! You are not going to be able to live up to my American dreams! Buy me a flat ranch house with asymmetric windows and a patio with a Weber grill on it and a huge garage, and make me everlastingly happy! Bugger your silly roses and thatched cottages!" That is what he believed I wanted, and that is what he started to hate above all. But so did I. I think. Only it was very difficult trying to get him to believe that. Somehow our dreams existed on separate, parallel planes, the same dreams separated by so much air, and it appeared to me that it might be hard to get them to intersect.

Michael, with his customary ingenuity, found work through my father's contacts as a real estate salesman the week after we were married, and by the end of the month he was working as an appraiser, charging fees rather than earning commissions. By the time he got his green alien card he had already been working for almost two months and had saved enough money for two plane tickets to England, one way. At least that was the way he phrased it to me. We were still feeling our way with each other, learning which side of the bed the other one preferred, still on our best behavior most of the time, too shy to sigh in bed, not familiar enough to use the bathroom with the door open, still two strangers reluctant to expose our dreams for fear that then they would never come true.

In mid-October there was a great burst of wet, blustery weather across the state. My father received a long-distance call from Fred Schmidt up north in the woods who said that a tall, heavy birch tree had blown over onto the roof of the cabin there. The storm hadn't reached us in the southeastern part of the state, but it had been unusually severe up north. My parents left on a Wednesday morning to survey the damage, and called when they arrived there early that evening.

"Is it as bad as Fred said?" I asked my father.

"The hole's big enough," Daddy answered. I was still the baby as far as he was concerned and one did not disturb babies with adult problems like holes in roofs.

"Well, what can you do about it?"

"I'll use your mother to plug it," he joked. I heard her mutter to herself in the background along with the song of pots and plates ringing in a soapy sink.

"You won't try anything silly like pulling it down yourself, will you?" I had seen him do things impulsively like that many times before. He gave himself a hernia and many pulled muscles by heaving boulders, logs, trailers, concrete blocks, automobiles, and iron stoves out of his path rather than wait for someone else to come along and do it. I had inherited some of that impatience and impetuosity and I knew how hard it was to suppress. It was all right if you were twenty-two and healthy, but not if you were sixty-two and had heart trouble.

"Nah. I got a guy coming in from Eagle River tomorrow to pull it down and chop it up for me. We'll be home late Friday with lots of firewood."

He made a few more benignly deprecating remarks about my mother's size, using her to plug the hole in the roof, or making her chop the wood. He still saw her as a size eighteen even though she had shrunk to a fourteen after two years with Weight Watchers. I heard some silverware crashing loudly somewhere across the state, and then we hung up. Michael came in about nine and we ate a cold supper.

He drove me to Madison the next morning: an oddly benevolent gesture since we did have two cars at that point, one of them my mother's. But it was raining, he had an appraisal to do near Madison, and he must have felt slightly sorry for me, daily victim of bus rescheduling and delays. I appreciated the ride. I had gotten used to taking the Badger Express bus from Goerke's Corners, to leave him use of the car since he had not found one to buy and had stopped looking in disgust. The bus also gave me more time to read my tedious assignments for Documentation, which I was finding increasingly hard to tolerate. The seeds of the idea of living in England that he had sown were not at all bad ones, and if we left in January it meant that I could avoid Documentation II.

It was dark when Michael met me outside the union at five: a cloudy sky, thick and bulbous and bluish-gray. The car was parked down the street, in front of one of the big fraternity houses. Michael had a funny look on his face. He grabbed my hand, held it tight. Honeymooners, I thought. Cute. It felt good. He wasn't ever affectionate in public, like a good Englishman, and I was enjoying this rare moment of feeling wanted in front of the world.

"How was your day?" he asked me as we walked toward the car.

"The Bishop of Durham wears a full suit of armor over his vestments."

"Nothing new though? Nothing interesting?"

"I thought that was interesting. How was your day?"

"The usual toil."

"How's the car behaving?"

"Better than your mother's hog would, I daresay."

"Needless to say."

And then he stopped on the sidewalk and he hugged me. Very odd, I thought. I wondered what this was leading up to. "Do you love me?" he asked.

"Of course! I've been telling you that for months. What a silly thing to ask me right here."

I looked up into his eyes on the ill-lit sidewalk in front of the old, prisonlike union. We were standing underneath a streetlight that was trying hard to come on. There was an awfully funny expression on his dark face. Michael had never talked to or looked at me quite that way. As little as I perhaps knew him after only four months' acquaintance, I suspected then that he had something important to say. A flitting image of two one-way airline tickets passed through my mind. Was this a prelude to the announcement of our ultimate move?

"Yes, I love you," I said.

We stepped out of the well of flickering light and on down Langdon Street toward the car. A spotlight on the flagpole in front of the State Historical Society across the street revealed a flag at half-staff. I thought that was most unusual. Half-staff for what? Had I missed something in the news that day? Not likely. Important news spread like dust across campus. A strong gust of wind wheeled my skirt up and around and I leaned over to grab it.

"Your father was killed today," he said, and I stopped to let the wind blow past, the voices of spirits whispering, the voice of my father in the air.

Honor thy father and thy mother. I thought all the drive home: What had I done but to ignore them both? A squawling, selfish child, a scowling, sour adolescent, an abrasive, unappreciative teenager, a disobedient, fornicating college student, and now an unemployed adult, a professional student. Daddy is dead, Daddy has died, and it was all my fault for disappointing him, I thought, for the sins of the daughters are visited upon the fathers. Daddy is gone, with the fleeting memory of a hateful, ungrateful daughter seared onto his soul's memory for eternity; a daughter too anxious to abandon him, "hot to trot" he had called me once when he first saw me kissing Robert. What had I ever given my father but grief and the expense of an embarrassingly unexpected wedding?

Death lurks behind the dark corners like a thief. It was too late to give him more love, to make up for twenty-two years of spiteful-ness and aggravation. It was too late to honor him, and God knows he deserved it. He who never did me any harm. He who gave me life, food, clothing, shelter, love, education, conscience. He who tried to shelter me from harm and wickedness and unhappiness and hurt. I ground his Old World values up in my fist and sprinkled them spitefully, like so much worthless dust, over his graying head. I laughed at his discomfort, ignored his pains.

At noon when Michael said he died I was selfishly enjoying a cheeseburger in the union. I was oblivious when his heart finally stopped. I was tabulating meaningless data on the number of wheat sheaves produced in a defunct English hamlet in the year 1237 while he lay dead hundreds of miles away on the forest floor. He and I were one flesh, and yet I never knew until Michael said so that part of my flesh was gone. Daddy was gone. So suddenly, so unfairly it seemed, but death is always that way. It cheats. God accept him, I prayed to myself over the Dane and Jefferson county lines: he wasn't even given his three score and ten. Only sixty-two. I ended up praying for myself, because he was in a better bargaining position than I was then.

Was he riding a silver cloud, I wondered, looking across the seas with the wide empty eyes of eternity, looking through the roof at me, my face to the filthy farmhouse carpet, my shoulders sagging, my breath coming in self-pitying gasps? The pain was fierce and physical. Was he wrapped in some white sheet, knotted at head and at foot, waiting for the hyenas to powder his face, redden his lips, wire his jaws shut: to say "Oh, my, he looks good, doesn't he?" like some Thanksgiving turkey. Horrible thoughts passed through my mind that night. Daddy was not a corpse. Daddy was a bodiless angel, building a castle for us all in heaven. Daddy was gone. But gone where? Such awful expressions they were. Could Daddy see Michael take me up off the floor, lead me to the couch and make love to me then and there? Could Daddy see me humping wildly in my sorrow, despite the thought of him dead and cold and so very distant? God forbid that anyone should have seen or known. The flesh is despicable.

Between long, wet pauses in the conversation, our voices echoing off the wires and clouds and creosoted poles across the state, my mother said that Daddy was going to be cremated the next day. He had tried to remove the birch tree from the roof himself with a little handsaw. His heart just stopped, she said, and he rolled off the roof, dying instantly on the ground. She was all right, she cried. All right, she cried. I miss you, I cried. We cried for ourselves, orphaned and widowed, and not as much for Daddy. We had never been that close. There was something very cold and crystalline about the Norwegian soul that prevented too much close affection. The icicle had fallen, and shattered. Daddy was gone.

In the *Mabinogion,* a collection of early Celtic folk tales from Wales that borrow from the Arthurian legends of Geoffrey of Monmouth, there is a story about the plague of the screaming hearth.

Once a year on May Eve the people of Britain were plagued by a terrible scream that emanated from somewhere over the hearth. The terrible scream caused pregnant women to miscarry, other women to become barren; it halted the growth of crops, animals, trees. Children were rendered senseless. The King of France, one Llevelys, and his brother the King of Britain, Lludd, solved the problem. It was revealed to them that a foreign dragon was fighting a local Welsh dragon, and on May Eve the local dragon would scream horribly in battle. King Lludd had to locate the geographical center of the kingdom, dig a pit there, fill it with good mead, and then cover it up with a silk sheet. On May Eve the dragons fought up in the air, grew weary after a while, sank down into the pit, drank the mead, and when they were drunk and sleeping King Lludd tied up the silk sheet, locked it in a stone chest, and buried it.

Stories similar to the tale of the screaming hearth have always possessed human imagination. A popular version of the mysterious scream-announcing-doom is the banshee, who will appear to a person, or to a member of a family, when someone close to them is about to die. Or the people will see a spectral monk, cowl down over his eyes, passing through the garden on some inexplicable errand. Some tell of having seen monks enter gardens and start digging, as if they were opening graves, or they may hear choirs of ghostly monks chanting.

It might be nonsense. It must be. If we tried to interpret all of the omens that seem to pop up every day, all of the black cats, the spilled salt, the broken pyramids, we would probably spend the rest of our days living with knots in our stomachs and lumps in our throats. But there was that flag at half-staff. It was entirely a coincidence that we walked down Langdon Street that night, that I noticed it at all and even remembered, and a coincidence again a few weeks later when again I saw it spotlit at half-staff. We had our first terrible quarrel then. I spent the night alone on the couch, crying, shivering there under the dusty, moth-eaten Afghan in my cotton nightdress. Something else had died, but I wasn't quite sure what it was.

I had cried for Daddy, but not a lot. I wished I could have. The nastiest thing that God ever did to us was to saddle us with memory and conscience. At four in the morning, waking up from a deep, forgotten dream to smell Michael's hair, to feel and hear his long, low, unconscious breath, I would remember, and the sweet darkness and warmth of bed vanished, rematerialized as grayness and cold.

[52]

Was the world really so different? Even as ashes, Daddy's atoms were still there. I kissed my husband and tried to forget.

"I've done it. I've made the reservations," he announced from the bathroom. The toilet seat clanked down, he flushed, he came into the kitchen where I was peeling carrots and reading from *The English Church Under Henry I.* "I've made the reservations," he repeated, coming up behind me and coddling my elbows in his palms. "You'll get peel on your book."

"Might make it more interesting."

"And less valuable. Have you no respect for books?"

"So you finally decided. Absolutely?"

"Just so long as you have no violent objections. You don't find the idea repugnant, do you?"

"No. But I haven't really thought about it seriously. I suppose it's just a nuisance to move again, but it would be an even greater nuisance in a year's time." In a way it didn't surprise me. I had hoped he would make this decision now. When someone died, it left a great hole in your life: through the hole, all you could see was a flux, like oily patterns on moving water. Somehow, without Daddy there to order the universe, I needed Michael more than ever. It hadn't been his father; he could still be rational and detached. I didn't want to be sloppy and dependent, but death was unsettling. Talk of a move refocused my attention. I knew that my mother wouldn't keep the farm. It had been Daddy's idea, Daddy's hobby. We would have to move eventually anyway. "What about Mom?"

"I wouldn't think of leaving until she was settled. You told me she seems to be in good shape, didn't break down on the telephone or anything."

"No. My aunt's been with her, though. We really ought to wait and see how she is after she gets home and is left all alone." I felt a heavy, solid mass of guilt nudging aside the relief I had first felt when Michael told me of his decision. It was somehow callous, almost sacrilegious, even to consider abandoning my mother two days after her bereavement. It was perhaps a good idea for us, but I had yet to test it on her before I could be unabashedly eager to leave.

"Are the reservations really made?"

"Early part of January."

"Can't we just buy the tickets and leave the exact departure date open? I can't hit Mom with this just yet."

"I can always exchange them."

"Do you understand, Michael?"

"Of course."

"What happened to all of this nonsense about capitalism too?"

He shrugged his shoulders. "Still there. Somewhere. Some people have to climb the mountain to satisfy themselves, others can be content to approach it in their hiking gear and leave just knowing that they *could* have climbed it, if they had wanted to."

"What about work?"

"I'm not exactly unemployable."

"You said that salaries were abysmally low there."

"Does it really matter, if the quality of life is better?"

It was my turn to shrug. I didn't know. I couldn't think. Queen Matilda had just granted some gold to Llanthony Priory, and my father had just died. "Quality's relative. I can't honestly say that we're spoiling ourselves here. No Cadillacs, color televisions or steaks on the table every night."

"Is that what you really want?" he asked.

"I doubt it. Do you?"

"Maybe I do. I don't know, but it's not worth climbing a mountain and risking a life to get it."

"What made you decide?"

"Your father, I expect. Seems a good time to go, like you said, after we've made sure that your mother is secure."

I marked my place in the book with a peeled carrot and went over to where he stood, hands in tweedy pockets in Oxford posture, looking out the window over the unkempt orchard, the sun setting behind unpruned trees with suckers upraised like a brace of pikes and lances, the drooping snow fence, the Armageddon of autumn, the crinkling, vacant sound of dried corn audible even through the window glass, and I put my arms around him. "When do you want to leave?"

"Early part of January."

"Roll on January."

She came down in a bus four days later and left his car up north where he had been cremated. I met her at the bus depot downtown, after school. We hugged, almost embarrassed, she said "Oh, Gigi" about five times in her sweetest maternal voice reserved for happy or momentous meetings, and we drove back to the empty house in my old Volkswagen. There was nothing I could say. She could never understand, and neither could I.

"Where is Michael?" she asked, her eyes wandering around the familiar living room of the big farmhouse, wanting instead to talk about Daddy whose very nonpresence was like a giant piece of furniture missing, with a certain stillness in the air that was not at all right.

"He thought it would be best if we were alone," I said, and, after a pause, "He's upset. He liked Daddy a lot, you know."

She cried then, but the wound was five days old and the edges were just beginning to heal over.

"We had such a good marriage," she said between sniffs. "I'm much too young to be a widow. We had so much to do, so much to look forward to once he had retired."

"I know," I said, not knowing. "But God has a reason for everything He does. We can't hope to understand, and we can't try to argue with Him."

"Daddy was just so full of *life.* . . ."

"And we have no alternative but to learn to cope. . . ."

"You know, I'm really going to miss just talking to someone my own age. And it's a terrible feeling to have to eat out all alone like I had to do during the bus ride. What can you do between sips of coffee? Stare at the tabletop. That's all." She started to cry again and I tried to imagine what it would be like to eat out alone. I couldn't imagine. Robert and I could never afford to eat out; Michael and I hadn't been together long enough to have gone out much, and I would hardly consider doing it alone as long as I had access to a grocery store. The chasm widened; the bridge swayed. I looked ahead to my own widowhood. It was a terrible thing to be all alone when you didn't want to be. For those nights, weeks when Michael was gone the summer before, I could remember how terrible it was, the feeling that he might not come back, the rejection, the feeling of not being good enough to be asked to go along. Widows had no choice. It was worse when someone left you deliberately, I thought.

It wasn't as if Daddy had died on purpose just to get away from her once and for all.

"It is terrible to have to be alone, Mom. You just have to keep yourself busy, I guess."

"Oh, I'll have enough estate work to keep me busy, all right," she sniffed, finally, and then she seemed to dry up—or else it was the Norwegian in her freezing up. "That's how I've managed to come this far."

"That's good. I love you, Mom, and don't forget that I'm right across the field if you need me." Affectionate words between us were rare enough to be meaningful. Physical affection was equally rare and usually embarrassing. Still, she hugged me there on the gold couch in the gold room and I smelled her strong, flowery perfume, her clean blouse, her face powder. This was familiar, I thought, and this was nice. I really did love her. She had always been good to me in her own distracted sort of way. Daddy had had such a strong personality that she had never really had a chance to develop on her own, to give me as much attention as he demanded from her, living always for and through him.

"You know that Michael has been talking about going back to England?" It might have been the wrong time to bring it up, but I was very bad at keeping secrets. She seemed very lucid to me, and I thought she might take it well.

"Why ever would he want to leave Milwaukee?" She seemed genuinely puzzled. I felt like covering tracks, but it was too late.

"I guess he's homesick."

"Oh. I never thought of that."

"We'd visit, of course, and you could come over any time to visit us, too."

"Where?"

"In England. We're moving."

"Moving? Why?"

"I don't know why. Because Michael wants to, I guess. Because I do, too. It won't be for a while, though. I would never leave you at a time like this."

"Hum," she said. And, like me, she forgot. She denied. She stood up, wavered like the fragile petal of a fading poppy in July, then lunged toward the kitchen. "Would you like some coffee, honey?"

I felt suddenly angry. She treated me like a baby. It was as if she didn't believe me. Just as it had always been—if they didn't like what I said they just ignored it and it went away. Silence intimidated me. Lack of response was usually enough to shut me up and turn me from my errant ways. But it wouldn't work now, I thought; I was big, I had an airplane ticket, I was leaving with my husband. It occurred to me, with awful clarity, that I oftentimes behaved just like my mother did: blindly, unthinkingly, denying. Who had died anyway?

"We're leaving in January." I pursued it cruelly. She had disappeared around the corner and I could hear her banging cupboard doors and knocking pots together to drown out what she did not want to hear.

"All I have here is Sanka. Daddy couldn't have caffeine."

"Do you mind if I send Grandma's tablecloth over?"

"How about some tea instead?"

"I can always send it back. It's not heavy."

She thrust her head around the corner, eyes red and swollen, telling me to hush, and I remembered a hundred things past now: how she had thrust her head around that same corner and smiled in August after Daddy told her I was getting married; Robert's eyes when I took the garlic press; those terrible, hollow, silent sobs I made on nights when Michael was gone I didn't know where; when the future seemed more unsure and precarious and lonely than it ever had before. "I can't hear you, dear. Is tea all right?"

"Yes," I whispered, brought low like a baby. "Yes. Give me tea."

By late October I knew all of the landmarks by heart between Madison and home. The white church on the right was one-third of the way. Johnson Creek was halfway. The Jefferson County line was two-thirds of the way. The landscape had turned that desperate deep green that happens just before the first frost. Within a week it would give way to shocks of yellow, of pinky maple on its way to red, flecks of autumn up the leafy roadside eskers: a presentiment of mortality. A brilliant flame before the candle goes out. A bang and then the finish.

It was one of those days when Michael spared me the bus, when he had another appraisal to do near Madison. It was a long ride alone: we appreciated each other's company. Daddy had been dead for almost two weeks and was preoccupying my thoughts less and less. Michael and I had just passed the white church on the right, and I was railing on about feudalism. Not that I had listened much in class that day; it was still my best course. The huge old professor was hard to ignore with his peg leg and booming theatrical voice that went on ceaselessly fascinating. He made frankpledge sound sexy. My mind rarely wandered during his lectures. The other courses, the Historic Documentation I, the Intro to Medieval Thought, were a bit pedestrian beside this professor's theatricality. I learned a lot from him, and I tried to impress that upon Michael.

"It's not much different now than it was in the twelfth century," I ranted to Michael, secretly mimicking my professor, using some of his pet phrases that might sound erudite. Michael did not seem terribly responsive that afternoon. I was half serious, half still trying to impress him. He probably sensed that. "I mean, don't we pledge ourselves to our employers? Don't we sign contracts that stipulate 'in return for so many hours on duty for My Lord, this vassal will receive x amount of compensation'? You know, some lords made their vassals work most of the week for them, then the rest of the time the poor clods had to sandwich in their own lives. And what did they get in exchange? Protection. Like Blue Cross coverage. A big intangible."

"Surely they got more than that," Michael said to the steering wheel.

"Oh, sure. A small strip of land, permission to let their pig root for acorns in the precious forest maybe once a year, use of the communal plow team, if the lord was a generous one. It's really only a translation of that today."

"How do you mean?"

"We might get paid more, but only because a few vassals were lucky enough to get on top, to step on a few necks. Our bosses only give us as much as they have to, by law. Whenever workers get some extraordinary bonus from their boss, it hits the papers: a thirty-two-hour week, or a fifteen percent raise, whatever. It's news. It's unnatural. Normally we plod along working our forty-hour weeks, then race home to be human beings for the remaining eight waking hours."

"Some of us enjoy working," he said.

"Some of us don't. Not that I've ever tried, but to take an oath in exchange for a livelihood seems so *feudal,* so archaic. To render yourself servile to some lord, some company, in exchange for money just doesn't seem civilized."

"What makes you think that they weren't civilized in a feudal society?"

"Well, look what happened in the fourteenth century."

"What happened in the fourteenth century?"

"They revolted, didn't they? Personal service was largely replaced by a rental payment. Peasants were in a good bargaining position then. They were being picked off like flies by the plague. Labor was scarce, and they were a precious commodity. They could afford to revolt with yawning chasms on either side: servitude or plague. Look at us now: too much labor, not enough jobs. It's no wonder the lords have an upper hand again."

"With so much labor about you'd think that the majority would rule. Look at the trade unions in England."

We were rapidly getting out of my depth. The day's lecture had not gone that far. I stayed away from history after the Industrial Revolution anyway.

"Speaking of unions, are you still looking for a car?"

"No. It doesn't matter. We'll be leaving soon enough anyway."

We rode on in silence. The sun was at an impossible angle to the earth and shot sharp gold beams of setting light at the woody hillsides rippling alongside the expressway. Lately, ever since he had decided to leave, there was an odd blank, something unsaid between us. It might have been English reticence and tact versus Norwegian frigidity, but still we did not even try to discuss it. It had something to do with the moving, with whys and hows, but I couldn't pinpoint the exact question, and so I asked none.

"What happened today?"

"Nothing. Americans are fat."

"What kind of an answer is that?"

"Cars are expensive. And I'm not sure that I like this lifestyle, this kind of work."

"Consider yourself normal. After what we've just been talking about, how could you say you liked any job anyway?"

"Because I'm a serf at heart. My ancestors painted themselves blue."

"Bull."

"They did. And I *like* to work. I wasn't raised by rich, fat, liberal parents. I never even had an allowance. I got through university on government grants. It's just *this* job I don't like. *This* job in *this* country."

"You're starting to sound like my father when he talked about the golden age of the nickel hamburger, during the Depression, when he had to walk everywhere he went and he loved it."

"I used a push-bike."

It had never occurred to me that there was that much of a cultural difference between us. We spoke the same language, we shared a lot of the same attitudes and ideas, we even had simultaneous orgasms on occasion. I never realized that it would take the utilization of a push-bike to make me think differently. I used my fancy French ten-speed for vain, body-building exercise, cruises to the A&W, for time-wasting, verdant rides through the cornfield countryside; he had used his rusty, single-speed for serious transportation. "You're not being serious."

"I'm bloody well serious. My parents gave me money for the bus, but I saved it and walked the three miles to school instead. Can't you understand that?"

"Not really. Seems silly."

"We ate tripe at home. Did you ever eat tripe?"

"No. I don't even know what it is."

"It's the lining of a sheep's bloody stomach! It looks and tastes as dreadful as it sounds."

"I thought that England was all thatched cottages and roses."

"It is. But you have a push-bike balanced outside the front door and tripe frying on the stove inside."

I wasn't sure that I liked what I was hearing, so I didn't pursue it. He was evidently not in a good mood, unimpressionable, and perhaps a bit homesick and confused all at once. I feigned understanding. Rather than aggravate him, I just quietly turned to my Stenton and read the rest of the way home.

4

All flesh is grass . . .

—ISAIAH 40:6

PICTURE a ghost town in the cold autumn rain. An abandoned farm is like that, only much worse. At least the derelict buildings of a ghost town have each other to keep them company in their decrepitude; an old farm has only the rats, the weatherbeaten boards, the ragweedy meadows, the broken yokes and dull plow blades to accompany it on the last lap of its journey back to the earth. *Nos habebat humus.* We return to earth. All of us, everything.

One soul's energy and sporadic enthusiasm cannot breathe life back into a dying barn once the roof starts to go. It requires the combined talents of masons, carpenters, roofers, landscapers, exterminators, and money. As much as it hurt me to see the old bank barn that my father had partially saved sinking back into the heavy midwestern clay from whence it sprang more than a century before, there was little I could do alone to save it, and Daddy had had little inclination to sink the thousands into it that would ensure its standing for another hundred years. To him it meant little more than a picturesque backyard shed, about as valuable as the cast-iron bathtub rusting in the orchard that was once kept full of summer flowers. I made sure that the doors stayed locked from vandals after he was gone. I poked the soggy, worm-eaten beams of the stable to check the slow but certain advance of the decay. I shifted loads of junk around inside to make certain areas more esthetically pleasing, and I swept up the pigeon feathers and droppings that accumulated geometrically once a month; but these feeble efforts could not even be termed stopgap. When the light inevitably began to show through the cedar shingles, then the old barn's mortality was clearly visible even to my own dimmed, loving eyes that could, at one time, block out even the ugliest decay.

I had seen the barn through four sets of seasons before, since my parents moved to the farm. Yet once winter nudged aside the wetness and foreboding of autumn I was always fascinated how the old barn would go into a sort of ageless hibernation—the damp beams freezing deceptively solid, the birds in the rafters quiet and shivering, the abandoned odors of cat urine, mildew, rotting wood and hay, and dust suspended in a frozen dream. Under the blanket of snow and ice the old barn held its feeble, dying breath, only letting out the barest of groans when wintry storms blasted snow through the imperfect slats of the haymow story, or faint sighs when the early March winds lifted yet another precious shingle, to be deposited in the cornfield and run underground at spring plowing. Hovering motionless and eternal, I could forget the old barn's ailments for a while and content myself indoors before my parents' fireplace, selfish and warm and oblivious of the barn's time passing.

Springtime was too busy a season for anyone to be concerned about the old barn. Between mowing, tilling, planting, and spraying there was no time to bother about the quiet old wreck of a rampart that stood damply long-suffering across the fields. The swallows nesting, noisy and lively in the topmost beams, the fresh breezes blowing clover through the broken windows, made it easy to ignore the old barn's real plight.

And when summer came, vacations at home, when I first knew the barn intimately, day after day, the magic of sun, rain, and earth sent up green vines, overgrowing scrubby trees and tall quack to cover it. It hid from the summer heat behind a mask of dense foliage, harboring its private birds, its old broken-down tools, its rotting timbers. There was weeding to do in the summer, periodic harvests to make, canning and preserving, sunbathing, grass mowing. There was little time to be concerned with the great, faded, reddish barn now cowering beneath summer's obnoxious glory. When the heavy purple thunderheads glowered overhead like floating mountains and the sirens far off warned of tornadoes, then I would look anxiously toward the old barn and wonder if she could last through yet another violent storm. She always did. But if London Bridge could fall, then so could she. One day. But not now.

One late summer night before the wedding, my last summer home, sandwiched between singleness and wedded bliss, I threw every window open in my parents' farmhouse, as wide as they would go, to smell the quiet summer farm smells floating in like faraway music. The marigolds were the trumpets, with a harsh pitch, the flowering tobacco plants were violins all buttery and smooth, the petunias were the percussion. I kneeled, chin to my bedroom windowsill, thinking of Michael still in England. All the lights in the house were out behind me, and I watched the big hunter's moon move like a yellow cat up over the lilac bushes so bright that I could see everything in the backyard as if it were day. Each little wooden pin on the clothesline showed up, and I saw the big stump where a giant oak tree had been felled. My mother's little, triangular-shaped flower bed in the center of the lawn was surrounded by shadowy, ominous chicken wire, there to keep the neighbor's dog from mauling her dahlias. I could see a lot of movement in the too-long grass: the crickets, the glint of moisture on toads' backs as they arched through dewy grass in search of dinner, and even the barn, standing across the meadow.

I padded barefoot outside to see it all, the light, moisture, smells, all of it around me like an exquisitely wrought quilt. The barn stood out against the blacker fields in silhouette, its jagged edges perfectly delineated, every stone a perfect circle set in its mortar bed. I loved that barn with a hopeless, dying love that could not do it any good. To me, it symbolized freedom, creativity, antiquity, cheerful hard labor—things either unknown to or reviled by the good folk of Towering Oaks and a million other developments just like it who would probably cheer and applaud when the nasty old barn was finally gone. One subdivision down the road had leaned hard enough on the owner of another old barn so that it was razed. The remaining pathetic stone foundation was their monument to progress.

The moon made the old barn almost glow, almost come alive. I remembered a poem from David's class:

The mone mandeth hire light
So doth the semly sonne bright,
When briddes singeth breme.
Deawes donketh the dounes;
Deores with here derne rounes,
Domes for to deme . . .

And all those Garth Williams illustrations of my childhood—of the beautiful green-skinned girl preserved forever in the magical pond holding a fresh nosegay of flowers, her hair floating around her head like rays of sunlight and all the trolls peering down into the water at her. I remembered pictures of full moons and red-cheeked little boys who received large sacks of resplendent marbles from fairies, playing mystical marble games in the moonlight with the round gems glowing like fireballs. I thought of the barn resurrected, sprouting legs or wings, and dancing a jig to the tune of the fiddle played by the cow who jumped over the moon. It seemed my life was a succession of fantasies all come true that night, although I was in danger (I didn't realize then) of never being able to see through them. I remembered that night later, in October, when the neighbors across the road told me a funny story about the barn.

The Morgans knew everything about everyone who lived within a one-mile radius of their property. Mr. Morgan had been born in the old, dilapidated farmhouse on top of the hill across the road, Mrs. Morgan in a then-extinct farmhouse on Hergest Road just around the corner; but they had since settled into a little ranch-style cottage on one acre just across the road from us. The old farmhouse hovered over the young upstart like a doddering old dowager, now at the mercy of tenants who hardly cared that the porch was falling off and the roof blowing away. Mr. Morgan kept his new ranch house in immaculate repair as if in defiance, the lawn always perfectly mowed, clipped, trimmed, and raked, the paint never allowed to peel, the gutters never permitted to rust or to accumulate sludge, the windows always kept rainbow clean. He even shoveled his roof in the winter.

The Morgans were not nosy people by any means because they kept mostly to themselves; yet they *knew.* They seemed to know everything about everyone and only God knew how since Mrs. Morgan only left the house three times a week: to go grocery shopping on Thursdays, to go to the beauty parlor on Saturdays, and to go out to dinner at the local supper club on Sundays. She must have watched the world go by through her kitchen window, and had even asked me once why I frequently got up at night around three and turned on the kitchen lights. I told her that I had a weak bladder. She cared.

The Morgans told me that on the night of the big windstorm a year before—a year to the day before my father died—they had never seen such a mess, short of a few brief tornadoes, in all of their fifty-odd years there. The wind blew all across the state, they said, collapsing trees, television towers, aerials, whipping shingles everywhere, even blowing over automobiles. I tried to remember the details of that storm and I couldn't. I was still away at college, oblivious of weather, probably ensconced with Robert in our kitchen arguing over messes. All I could recall was that it was indeed very windy one night the autumn before, and that then there was a storm. A terrible storm.

The wind was still raging late that night when Mr. Morgan went outside to check his property for damage from the flying branches. He said that he thought he saw something out by our barn. The Morgans knew every person, every car, every thing that belonged on our land across the street. He called Mrs. Morgan outside to take a look, to ask her what she thought it might be. She was stumped.

"Honest to God," he told Michael and me that October, after we had gotten to know them in the exchange of eggs and local gossip, "it looked like some kinda UFO or something!"

"It was glowing like a star," Mrs. Morgan added, "but it wasn't round or saucer-shaped or nothing. It was shaped more like a giant clothespin, wasn't it, Tom? It was like a person, honest to God."

"I suppose it coulda been some kinda weird lightning," Mr. Morgan ventured.

"No, Tom. There wasn't no lightning till later that night, and besides it hung there for too long. Musta been a good three minutes before it upped and disappeared."

"*Hung* there?" we queried.

"Yeah. Right over the roof of your old barn. Just sorta hung, or floated like, up there," he said, wiggling a long, bony forefinger roughly in the direction of Sirius. I believed what the Morgans had told me, after a fashion, but because I could make no sense of it I just ignored it and it was never discussed again.

On a night like that one back in early September, with barely a breeze and autumn and death and burning so distant, the barn was just a benevolent old prop out there on top of its low, littered bank. The grass was dewy moist. I could almost feel the worms wriggling between my toes. The tree frogs and cicadas were peeping. In some far-off puddle there were bull toads belching and honking. And crickets everywhere. Even Towering Oaks was silent for a change, awed into submission by summer's peace and the moon's overpowering glow. No odors of nasty-burning charcoal briquettes. No car wheels squealing. No minibikes buzzing. No crying babies with heat rash. I remembered Michael then. I missed him until it hurt. I padded back into the dark house with the windows open to write him another letter. Why was peace so ephemeral?

That autumn of 1974 when the Canadian blasts brought late, crazy color to the trees, the grass turned brown and flat, and the corn dried up and crackled in the wind, the old barn reemerged like a problem once forgotten but never really gone. The new cracks in its foundation were distressingly visible. The rain came in through the new holes in the roof and saturated the haymow floor. Against the gray, low, slow-moving skies of autumn, beside bonfires and brilliantly painted trees, and soon enough leafless trees, the old barn spoke of abandonment, desolation, hopelessness. What Farmer Kern —old Uncle Mooshie—had raised in 1849 in anticipation of a new, prosperous life in America after emigrating from Hesse-Darmstadt was now returning to the same earth in which Mooshie lay, a few miles to the south in the local graveyard. A new roof, a bit of concrete to patch the crevices in the rock walls, a beam or a joist replaced here and there, would only postpone the inevitable for a short time. The suburbs were moving in on all sides. Time was passing. The old barn was already gone; yet I could not passively watch its picturesque decline. I checked the locks, I swept the floors, I poked the spongy beams, and I worried. If dreams could resurrect, the old barn would have been new again that autumn. But, alas, dead men do not rise like flowers in the spring.

Shortly after the Morgans told us about the UFO, something happened in the barn that I could not explain, although Michael seemed content that whatever it was could be made sense of. It was late that same October, after Daddy died, when he asked if I would please fetch a yardstick he had seen hanging from the rafter in the stable. I tried to avoid going into the barn unless driven there by either guilt or dire necessity. The spiders bothered me; large and weightless things, all body and legs and no eyes or other obvious organs of sense or intelligence, suspended from invisible filaments, invisible until you ran into them and they stuck. On cold days when the spiders were hibernating it wasn't as bad. I could enjoy it then: its roughly adzed beams, notched and pegged together, the cathedral-like majesty of the soaring haymow with pigeons winging through like angels. I went in to fetch the yardstick shortly after arriving home on the bus that evening. My mother had our flashlight in her car, so I carried an oil lamp with a hurricane shade over the lawn. We had found it in the barn, almost brand new. I lit it just before opening the door, and going into the barn.

Very little light was coming through the windows on three of the walls, the fourth wall having been built into an earthen bank. Most of the windows were broken and had been hastily covered with chicken wire to keep varmints and vandals out. I adjusted the flame on the lamp and cautiously stepped over a compendium of rotting bushel baskets, feed sacks, sawhorses, paint cans, flat tires, troughs, lumber scraps, baling wire, and wagon wheels, over to the corner where some forgotten farmer had once had a little workbench. It was now a sad hodgepodge of dull and rusted tools, still hanging tidily from nails on a slab of wood somehow secured to the rock wall. I held my light up to the row of tools. Michael said that the yardstick was hanging around there, but I couldn't see it. The feed chute opened up just to the right of the tool bench. It was as still as Christmas midnight. I thought I saw something feather out of the chute, and I turned the light to the right. A spider perhaps, shocked awake by the light, but no. It was only a few bits of straw, probably disturbed by some birds or rodents or a wild cat upstairs in the haymow.

I thought I'd just take one quick walk around the whole lower stable, checking the walls and rafters for the elusive yardstick, when I heard the most awful clatter from directly above. I could only stand there and listen. The stable was too dangerously cluttered to move anywhere very fast, and within seconds my lamp was out. I was alone in the dark with terrible loud noises happening not only above me now but in front of me and at my feet: metallic noises; sounds like heavy, hard objects dropping; shatteringly loud noises, louder yet in darkness. And yet, there was not the slightest insinuation of a breeze that might have been responsible for snuffing out my lamp (and only a hurricane could really blow it out with all that oil in it and the shade on) and for sending something upstairs tumbling.

[67]

I didn't stop to relight my lamp. I left it on the worktable and hurried out, scraping my leg savagely on an outstretched roll of chicken wire. I ran back across the lawn feeling like a fool. A fool chased by phantoms. Phantoms in cowls. I felt like an eleven-year-old.

Michael was reading the paper, drinking a can of beer, unflappable. "Find it?"

"God, no. Something came after me out there." I wadded up a moist paper towel in the kitchen and held it to my bleeding leg.

"A dog? Was it that wretched Alsatian from down the road? He didn't bite you, did he?"

"I don't know what it was. It blew out my lamp and it made a terrible racket. I did this on that fucking chicken wire."

"You're not making much sense tonight. What happened?"

"I'm not going back out there tonight for a million bucks!"

"You don't have to. Did you find the yardstick?"

"Hell, no. Go get it yourself."

"Tomorrow, perhaps. It's not that urgent. You'd best put some Bactine on that scratch. Looks nasty."

We talked about it again in the bathroom before bed, but his mouth was full of toothpaste and all he ventured before he fell asleep was that some animal had probably knocked something over upstairs in the haymow and the light went out because either the wick had burned up or the oil was gone. I didn't like his explanations, resented them in fact—the way he treated the issue as if it were somehow distasteful, beneath contempt. He had made a simple request, I had simply failed: that was the absolute and final truth of the matter. I didn't like seeing it that way. It was not hysteria or feminine weakness that failed to retrieve the yardstick. My experience deserved more concern.

I watched him roll his pillow into a ball that night, set his righteous cheek upon it, and fall asleep within three minutes. I wondered if men had souls. Souls that could turn on and off at will. Robert had been like that, too. Everything was explicable, and at bedtime he flipped the yellow switch and went into his sleep mode, tuning me out: a statement to the world that God was nothing more than a gigantic computer that would, in good time, be fathomed, and would be contained within the walls of the Great American Math Text. Michael was yellowish all of a sudden. There *was* no simple explanation. I found my comfort in believing that. I found solace in the inexplicable. I could not cope with his good sense, his calm, his

[68]

doubting me. I wanted him to acknowledge the nonsense that would lift my burden of guilt, make my life easier. Say it's a ghost, Michael, and I'll sleep. Call me an inept coward, and I won't. And I didn't.

I made him go back into the barn with me in the early morning before driving me to meet the seven o'clock Badger Express, and we found the lamp on the table where I had left it, only it had tipped over and the oil had run out onto the floor. "That's why it went out," he trumpeted, finally.

"It didn't tip, Michael. It went out while I was holding it."

He looked at me like a teacher who has to listen to a bad excuse for tardiness and then he looked down on the floor beneath the feed chute. "Here it is." He bent over, shuffled some other objects around, and picked up the yardstick. It was lying there along with all the other tools from the bench. It appeared as if someone had removed them all and dropped them down the feed chute, God knows why. It seemed an awfully strange thing to do.

"I think we have ourselves a vandal," he said, "or else a very clever skunk." We went upstairs, but only the pigeons flapped back at us, and the lock on the door had not been touched. Michael didn't suggest anything else. I didn't ask anyway; we locked up the stable behind us, and he drove me to the bus stop. It was all too nonsensical to discuss again until the next morning, Saturday, when I couldn't hold it back anymore.

He was eating semiturgid waffles, rubbery bathmat-like slabs that I had tried to thaw out in the toaster, to little avail. I was looking into the artificially beige depths of a cup of bitterly strong instant coffee, hoping for a caffeine high to send me lunging into studying for finals. "Those tools were all on the bench when I first went in the other night. I have no idea how they got down the feed chute."

"Vandals, I expect," he said with a full mouth, over the newspaper.

"But the locks hadn't been forced. You saw that." I stirred the coffee, for no reason except perhaps to alleviate an uncomfortable silence.

"Did you know that rats don't have spines, and they can slip underneath doors?"

"What does that have to do with this?"

"Well, when we were living in the country outside York, our neighbors said that they were troubled by noises and objects moving in one of their barns. Mind you, English barns are a little bit different from your Dutch barn out there. It was a stone barn, long and low with a gabled roof and no windows. It had little slits for ventilation, like you might see in castle towers where the soldiers shot their crossbows. This barn was maybe three hundred years old, and since all the troughs were made of stone, and the roof was covered with slates, it wasn't very likely that any part of it could have rotted away to the extent that someone could force entry. The neighbors kept just one milk cow in there, and a little smithy, and almost every morning, only in the month of December mind, the feed bowls would be moved from the top of one of the workbenches in the smithy to below it, all heaped to one side. They were sure it was an evil spirit, and Mr. Church claimed he heard odd noises in the loft during evening milking."

I noticed that he had, rather eagerly, abandoned his waffle.

"So?"

"So one Boxing Day I was up there with my father visiting and Mr. Church started telling us about these sounds, and the bowls moving, and before long we were out there having a look around. The barn was sealed as tight as a drum and as dark as a tomb inside. Mr. Church said that he had sprinkled some lime powder on the threshold to capture footprints, but had never seen any, so my father and I volunteered to sit out there with our torches that night and watch over the bowls."

"Whatever it was, Michael, it happened four thousand miles away, and I don't see what connection it could possibly have with this . . ."

"Patience, little girl. You want to jump to the most complicated, illogical conclusions and then pretend that nothing else matters. We went out there after milking and sat down on some bales of hay with the torches out and we waited and we listened. It was so dark that even after half an hour in there we still couldn't see a thing, but we could hear the noises all right: kind of a scampering and scraping. My father switched the light on when we heard the noises within a few feet of us, and sure enough we caught six bloody great rats veritably oozing under that door and two more on the bench. Church had never thought to tell us that he ate his lunch in the same place he filled the cow's feed bucket."

"Why only in December?"

"Who knows? Maybe the rats like to be indoors when the days are so short. Maybe Church altered his cow's diet and fed her things more palatable to rats in December. In any case, we just set out some rat poison and by the next December his poltergeist had vanished."

"You're saying we've got rats in the barn then?"

"Well, all this activity *did* occur at the feed chute, and even though there haven't been cows or fresh feed in there for years, there must still be some edible crumbs about."

"That doesn't explain the lamp going out, or the incredible noise."

"I can't explain everything, little girl. No one can offer you everything. Am I forgiven?"

"No. It's not that easy. I don't like your implication that I'm hysterical and I jump to conclusions. A 'little girl.' I don't particularly relish the idea of ghosts or poltergeists in my barn either, but I'm not going to disallow the possibility!"

"I'm afraid you're making rather a ridiculous contention then. Life is simply not like that."

"Life *is* like that!" I was angry. As much as I needed his anchor, I hated his obstinacy. I adored his good sense, but I needed my nonsense at the same time. It was *fun* to believe in ghosts; it didn't hurt to believe.

"Can we change the subject, please?"

"Maybe." I wanted to change the subject, too. I didn't believe the rat theory anyway. I had never seen a rat out there. And I didn't want to keep locking horns with him. It was pointless aggravation. "What would you do with an old barn like that? Rotting and, theoretically, full of rats?"

"I expect I'd move back to England and forget about it. It really is hopeless."

"But as long as it's standing, there *should* be some hope for it! There's so little history left around here with all the subdivisions and shopping centers that even a century-old barn full of rot and rats has a right, a duty, to survive."

"Fat chance you'd have of trying to convince a city council of that, let alone your mother. They'd rather see a split-level colonial on that site. If you really are concerned, though, I'd keep quiet about the rats."

A week later, wanting to bury myself in mindless work in order to forget exams, packing, leaving my mother behind, I decided to try to pitch all of the old, moldering hay into one corner of the haymow floor of the barn. It was presently scattered six to twelve inches deep everywhere, providing a nesting ground for the rats that I had come to believe in. It wouldn't be a pleasant job, but at least it would enable me to see the overall condition of the haymow floorboards. It would probably make me feel even worse that I was leaving, but it would allow the floor to dry out a little bit before springtime and rain, because my mother would certainly never touch it.

The air smelled of rain, of clouds low and thick, of leaves, and crisp burning wood. The same combination of elements would have smelled differently in any other month, but it was distinctly the smell of November. It was Saturday and Michael had gone off to work. Michael worked an awful lot: until eight or nine most week nights, and usually all weekend. I wondered why anyone would really want to work that much, but then I remembered how determined he was to squirrel away enough money to return home in triumph. Still, pitching filthy hay and dead mice was hardly to be considered play. If Michael chose to labor away at a desk, that was his problem; but I chose to work in the barn. Although I still must have had some obscure hopes that his disgust with work and America would temper with time, I was beginning to doubt it.

It was a little scary to think of moving so far away. He did not see the move as a lowering of his new standard of living; he had discovered and rejected some important things about America that I had always taken for granted—money and waste. Never having lived without efficient transportation, red meat, and central heating, I could not appreciate the culture shock that he kept so well hidden. I just thought that he was being contrary when he spoke of those things. I didn't actually object to moving, but at the same time I could not really imagine living permanently in a foreign land. Englishmen were curious and mute. We seldom spoke of the move once the decision was made. He simply changed the subject. He could not explain a way of life that was so close to him, just as I probably could not have comprehended his explanation anyway. I just accepted the decision and waited for the airline tickets to arrive in the mail to prove that we were really going to leave. I was a little bit fed up with people who were cold and uncommunicative. I had lived around Norwegians all my life. It was somewhat distressing to learn that Englishmen, beyond the courtship, were rather similar.

I tried to enjoy November at its face value. It smelled good and the air felt crystalline, pure, purged. It was my favorite sort of day, too: overcast, cool, an occasional breeze that sent eddies of dry, fallen leaves pirouetting into the air. It was the sort of day when a person could pitch foul hay, pull up dried weeds, read a bad novel, appraise real estate, and not feel guilty over the passage of time. The Italians say that one does not grow old at table; I say that one does not grow old on a gray, crisp November day. Time stands still. Past, present, and future.

"What did you do today?" The newspaper flapped, rustled, he turned to the next page. It could have been any night of a hundred. The coffin clock that my father had built ticking on the mantel made the only sound except for an occasional wet *shush* of a car passing by on a slick road.

"Pitched dirty hay." I didn't think that that would interest him particularly. Things farmlike seldom did; and he had his own work to get on with. "And you?"

"Toiled away bravely, as usual." He always said the same thing. He did toil away bravely, judging by the money he brought home; but I wanted to know more than that yet hated to pry if he wouldn't volunteer anything more, as if by eking out the details of his hard labor it would somehow make the labors seem less hard. He always used those annoying Victorian words and phrases, too, as if they were so clever that no more need be said. "Toiling bravely," "girding up my loins," and "I daresay."

"I found an old iron baling hook in the barn," I said, half excited yet expecting the cold, wet blanket of apathy to descend any second. He didn't do it intentionally: an old decaying farm that belonged to an unresponsive mother-in-law was not a very interesting topic of conversation for an entrepreneurial Oxford graduate. I accepted that, but I still wished that he could at least feign some interest, for my sake. Sometimes his affected boredom seemed so contrived that I often wondered how much of my own interest in the farm was provoked by his lack of it.

The pages of the newspaper fluttered. I had a passing fancy to put my foot through the front page, but realized that would not have solved anything. He would make me feel like an emotional fool then, muttering to himself, retreating into the cellar to potter with the sump pump or something ridiculous. Either he really didn't hear me, or else he was just pretending that he didn't hear me. More than likely the latter. He was only twenty-five and, as far as I knew, not deaf yet.

"I found an iron hay baler in the barn," I repeated.

"Um," he said. The infamous British "um." It meant anything the speaker wished it to mean. It could mean "yes." It could mean "no." It could mean "how utterly boring." It could mean "go away and leave me alone." It could mean "point acknowledged so pray do not continue in this same tiresome vein." I hated it, no matter what it meant. It was so insensitive, so *nasty*.

"What does 'um' mean tonight?" I asked.

Silence.

"What does 'um' mean?"

"What are you talking about?" He snapped the newspaper down. Another British tactic I had come to recognize: answer a question with another question. The total absence of communication that night was embodied in that one unintelligible sound: *um*. If I had bothered to think about it, I might have let it pass by as a cultural difference. But I had been cosseted and sheltered from any culture other than that of my parents, and was not well trained in tolerance. I saw a boor behind that newspaper: not a man who had worn knee pants till he was twelve; who had never eaten out at a restaurant, other than a fish and chip shop, until he was seventeen; who only owned one suit; and who had never owned an automobile.

"Nothing." The pages fluttered back up again.

"Did you say that supper was almost ready?"

"Almost."

"Good. I'm starving. What is it?"

"You'll like it."

He bent over and switched on the television. He tuned into a football game.

"I saw a man in armor in the barn today."

Silence.

A pan bubbled over on the stove and the lid clacked up and down. The inane banter of the sportscasters drowned out the softer sounds of the clock, the cars, the wind.

"Did you hear me, Michael?"

"No. What did you say?"

"Nothing."

"There's a pot overflowing in the kitchen. See to it."

I would not belabor the point. I had tested him one time too many already, and the last thing I needed then, on the verge of leaving all that was familiar behind, was to lose my credibility. Besides, I was certain this time there would be no logical explanation.

I felt such sorrow for the barn. In a way it had become an inanimate translation of my father. Shortly after he died, I had been walking past it, to cross the field on my way to my mother's house, and I saw that the recent frost had flattened the vegetation in one corner that had been hidden all summer long. There were some odd marks on the stones there. I went closer, to check, saw the initials "W.K." and the date "31 Aug 1913" carved faintly into one of the rocks in the wall. Daddy had been born in 1913. Daddy became the barn.

My concern for the barn was somehow related to the postmortem respect for Daddy that I felt. *He* would have liked to have restored the barn. He had said as much to me, although he never did much about it. I stacked the hay that day with him in mind, pleasing a dead man: a lightning-like clothespin watching over me in my futile pitchforking. It was not pleasant, as I had expected, all dusty and sneezing, but it was satisfying work. I preferred it to studying, or to trying to think of things that I would not be able to find in England that I should pack and send. At least here I was surrounded by history, a simple sort of history perhaps, but touchable nevertheless, and I could see some progress being made. There were clumps of cat and bird droppings hardened into the hay, lots of spiders, centipedes, cobwebs, sowbugs, skeletons of baby birds, eggshells, old fallen nests. If a rat had emerged impaled on the tine of my fork I might well have given up the job in utter civilized disgust and left the barn to the bulldozers, but I could tolerate the droppings and the insects. I worked myself into a lather, and it felt good. The threshing floor was big. Before long I could not reach the top of the first haystack near the door. I started another stack beside it.

There were two small rooms for grain storage in the barn. Neither one had a window and the slats there were fitted very snugly together. The little rooms were perfectly dark, watertight, built specifically to keep the wet and the rodents out of the feed. I had peered into these small, tidy rooms once before with a flashlight, but they were quite empty except for the old grain scoops lying discarded in the corners. I had my back to the grain rooms as I pitched and I would not have thought of them at all that day if I hadn't all of a sudden heard something unusual.

It was not a simple sort of sound, like a raindrop on still water, or glass breaking in the distance: it was more like the *feeling* of a sound, or even a breeze. It was a feeling so strong that I thought I could hear it: a sense of someone watching me through a wall, holding his breath, aware of me while I was unaware of him.

I let go my grip on the fork and it almost flew out of my hands, clattering across the bare wooden floor. I did not go to retrieve it. Instead I listened carefully. I tried to feel again whatever it was I had felt at first. It felt like the woods did that night with Carole. It felt like a net was coming down over me. My spine bristled, my back wanted to sprout wings, my rump tingled: but a few more years of maturity and marriage to a firm-lipped Englishman had taught me to doubt. I hollered deliberately, a "Who's there?" and a "Come on out," and I pounded the floor with my feet, not out of any real fear but to scare off any wild animal (a *wolf?*) that might be lurking there. But the consciousness of some other animate object previously unseen, unfelt, but now manifest, persisted even after my noise died away into the rafters far above my head.

"Is anyone in here?" I tried to sound as matter-of-fact as I could, but I felt ridiculous talking to air, wondering if it was perhaps just the farmer who leased the land moving quietly about downstairs in search of old, reusable equipment. I had to admit that I was frightened. Genuinely. I hadn't felt quite that way for years, but then I hadn't really had the opportunity, first surrounded by Robert, and then having the aegis of Michael beside me in bed every night. I seldom worked alone like this. It was a desolate sound. A sound of November. Of mortality. Of hopes turned back into earth. My insides went hollow. I felt it, I heard it, and then I saw.

He came out of the dark grain rooms as silently as a cat. If I hadn't been facing him I never would have known that there was another soul there. He was not distinct in the overcast afternoon light that sifted weakly through the wooden slats of the barn, but he stood as a solid, absolute mass before me. I felt no need to scream, now that I could see him. There was no one around to hear me anyway. He did not threaten, this stranger. He had simply taken me by surprise.

"What is it?" I asked him. It was a stupid thing to say, I knew, but I would not be frightened away without asking this time.

Silence.

Oddly enough I felt less frightened than I had a minute before I saw him. I could cope with reality; I could not cope with my imagination. He stepped out of the shadows of the grain rooms and I could see him well enough now. A man in armor.

A man in armor. Standing in an old, rotting barn in the American Midwest. It was all dreadfully wrong, almost silly. He did not belong there, but then neither did I, all of a sudden: I would not be there for long either, laboring for causes long lost. Still I was not frightened or put off, only surprised.

"Gay," he said to me and he raised his arm as if to put his hand out for me to grasp, in a handshake. The gesture reminded me uncomfortably of something I had seen once before, but preferred to forget. It was a long time ago.

"What is it?" That was all I could say, like some mindless talking doll. Nothing logical or interesting came to mind, like "Who are you?" or "What do you want?" or "Trick or treat?" It didn't make sense, and neither did I. I wondered if it might be some belated Halloween prank. Would Michael have gone that far? No. That was too easy, and this man was only slightly familiar, too unreal to be real. He was wearing an iron breastplate with skin-tight leggings and cordovan leather boots of rough construction laced up almost to his knees. Chain mail covered his neck and his head, but not his face. He was short, about my height, and still only vaguely visible in the dusty shadow of the grain rooms.

"Please come on out here," I said to him. "What do you want?" I talked in a soft voice, in contrast to how I had shouted just seconds before, deliberately enunciating my words carefully, sensing that he was having trouble understanding me. I moved toward him like a marionette on wooden limbs. I wanted to touch him, to reassure him, to feel that he was bone and blood, to affirm to myself that I was really there watching him. I felt like I knew him. I wanted to make sure. It was silly.

"Gaie."

"What are you saying?"

Gay.

He lifted his arm to me again in that same familiar gesture and he held his hand out to me. I could see his face then as he moved into a shaft of light, pale, sallow, handsome. His dark hair was cut short underneath the mail, and he was tonsured. He didn't look that old after all. His eyes were large, hollow, exquisitely sorrowful. I *knew* him from somewhere, I was sure, but from where? He was beautiful, delicate, sad, and I wanted to know him better, have him close to me. I wanted to know why he was following me, who he was, what was wrong with him. I wanted him, and then I remembered Michael. I was married, and he was forbidden.

"What are you . . . " I started to say again like a broken record when he put his hand over his eyes and bent his head down, away from the light. For a moment I wondered if I should run for the open door while I still could. But he seemed so gentle and kind and sad that I felt it would be cruel to move. There was surely nothing to fear from him. His costume did not make much sense to me, but I hardly cared about that then. He evidently had a good reason for seeking me out, and I wanted to know what it was.

After a few seconds he took his hand away from his eyes and looked back up at me. I remembered then where I had seen him before, a long time ago. There were tears in his eyes. I felt such incredible sorrow for him. It was an intense, mothering longing to comfort him, to hold him, to touch him, to lie down in the hay with him, to command all the miseries of the ages to be gone. I wanted to smear away all the guilt and all the pain of death and sadness between now and then and him and me. I had to move toward him again, to reach him, to touch him, to stop him from crying. I couldn't stand it. A tear rolled down his cheek.

"Gaie, non," he said to me, but as I came within an arm's length of him he relinquished and held out his hand to me again. Then I touched him for just an instant. It felt at first as if I had touched a warm, live person, but then suddenly there was no hard material object underneath my fingertips—instead just a painful nothing that blinded me for a second. The next thing I remembered was the sun coming through a place where a large board had rotted out, hazy with the dust and dirt I had raised in pitching the hay about. There was nothing else there. Nothing at all. Not a scent, not a footprint in the dust, not a sound—only the roiling dust filtering down again to cover the barn boards and leftover clumps of hay with a shroud-like layer of humus. *Nos habebat humus.* We travel on toward earth,

over earth like so many small particles of dust. Whoever he was, he was gone.

I kicked my fork aside and walked back to the house. My spine wasn't even tingling. I was thinking of nothing at all but the nonsense and the beauty of what had just happened. Or what I imagined happened. In my barn. In my benign, moldering, century-old barn. *A man in armor.* God, what nonsense. I was going mad.

The wind had picked up in the three hours since I had left the house. I had time for a cup of tea, and then I went back out to secure the barn doors, lest the wind tear them off. I heaved the sliding doors shut as best I could in the rising wind, pinning them with long iron bars, and turned to rush back to the bright, cold, innocuous safety of the house; but as I shoved the last bar into place and adjusted the padlock I thought I smelled something funny. Some odd, spicy aroma not indigenous to the barn. Something like cloves, or maybe it was scented candlewax. I shivered.

Rain was coming. The wind felt wet. I had to get Michael's supper on.

Lightning struck the old barn that night in a violent, unseasonable thunderstorm that swept the southeastern part of the state. By morning all that was left were the crumbling fieldstone walls of the foundation. No one felt bereaved, except for me.

But it *wasn't* all nonsense. I wasn't that kind of a person. I thought that all loonies deserved to be penned up forever, and I never paid any attention to spectacular predictions of the future made by soothsayers and mediums. My first reaction to anything marginally extraordinary was to deny that it had happened. I was very normal in that respect, I suppose: it is only human to deny, reject.

The early bus to Madison was never as crowded as the one at nine. Even though it got me to campus two hours before my first class, I preferred taking it to the later one. Time to be lulled to sleep by the whine and whistle of the bus engine on the freeway, fewer people to cough and jar me awake. I must have had a severe jolt to the subconscious, though—a delayed reaction—because as soon as I sat down that morning, three days afterward, I knew that something had to be resolved.

I had, feebly, tried to discuss it with Michael again. Should have known better than to try. One does not broach the subject of nonsense with a supremely logical husband like that. I had to sift out the fantastic elements—the armor, his explosive departure—and isolate the man himself. The cordovan boots. The grayish surcoat. The tonsure, and mail over his head, neck, and shoulders. I had to take him out of the barn and put him into a more suitable place. A book? No. Books had captions explaining illustrations like that. More isolation and distance needed. A picture. Sketched onto sheepskin. A Jones family heirloom. No one knew its origin, but my Feudalism professor, Dr. Peters, might be able to furnish some clues. I hoped madly that I could keep from sounding like an idiot.

I didn't have an appointment that morning, but I was lucky. His secretary asked him if I could interrupt, and big and jolly and enthusiastic as he always was, he let me come in. I had tried to make some drawings of the man's clothing on the bus, but they were jerky, rudimentary, from lack of skill as well as potholes in the road. Dr. Peters beamed over the desk at me, diddling a pen between two fingers. I thought, fleetingly, of Robert, yellow pencils, and then of what a potential maniac I was.

"Mrs. Jones, what can we do for you today?" I liked that. Mrs. Jones. That's how he addressed all his students: never by their first names, or *Ms.* Only his colleagues had first names. I allowed him to make me feel important.

"It's not a question about class, but I thought you might be able to help me out with something else I've found."

He made a large and gracious nod, urging me to continue with the waggling pen. Professors didn't have to talk to say things.

"My husband is English, and we have this picture. We got it as a wedding gift from his family, and it's very old, extremely old I think, but just how old we're not sure, and I thought maybe you could give me some idea."

"I'm not a connoisseur of antiques or an art expert, Mrs. Jones, but ask me about English constitutional history and I'm sure I'd be of more help to you."

"It's not the actual age of the picture I'd like to know—it's more like the *period* of the person depicted in the picture. It's a portrait of an ancestor, you see, and no one seems to know which ancestor."

"Well, I'd be honored to have a look at it. Why don't you bring it in next week?"

Lies. One just led right into another. I squirmed a little, hoped he didn't notice. "Oh, I can't bring it in. It's still in England! I've only seen a picture of it. Or, rather, only a description of a picture of it. It's a great family mystery, you see."

"I'm still not sure I can be of much help to you on the strength of a description, but try me." He pushed himself up from behind his massive mahogany desk and moved toward the bookshelves to the right of the door. "Just give me some rough idea of what age we're talking about and let's see if we can't look him up in one of these books on historic costume."

"He's wearing armor."

Peters laughed. "Armor! You've narrowed it down to about ten thousand years right there!"

"And chain mail over his head and shoulders."

"That's better. What kind of armor?"

"Not really armor, I guess; not like a knight wears, at least."

"Knights wore all different kinds of armor."

"Sorry. I meant not a full suit. Just a breastplate. It was a flat sort of thing, over the mail."

"Okay, that puts us before 1400. Was his face covered?"

"No, and he was wearing thick leggings. Not as thick as trousers, but not as snug as leotards either. And he had boots on. Reddish leather boots, that laced all the way up to his knees, with cuffs on top."

Peters pulled a book from the shelf and started to snap through the pages. I wanted to ask him what he thought, but I felt it was best just then not to interrupt. I had an uncomfortable feeling that I was asking this professor to find some anachronism in one of his sourcebooks: to identify bits and pieces spanning six centuries: a conglomerate knight whose costume was contrived by some subdivision cretin who wanted to scare me. I hoped to God not. He seemed to settle at last onto four pages. He kept flipping back and forth between them. "I think we've found your man." He rotated the book around and set it on the desk in front of me. "It's still a wide span of time —two hundred years or so—but I think he's right here somewhere." A large fat finger pointed to one of the pages.

It was a man in armor all right, only the breastplate was wrong. His had not been so stylized: it was much simpler. It had not come to a pert ridge at the front like that. His was flat, rusty, with sort of rough scrollwork tooled into the iron. I turned back a page. I found him. Boots and all. "This one. It says Plate 36. Where's the caption?"

Peters sat back down at the desk across from me and took the book. He found the list of plates at the back. "He's an Englishman, it appears. From the eleventh or twelfth century. That's a mighty old ancestor you've got, if he is indeed contemporary with this kind of a costume."

"But he can't be English. He spoke French."

Peters raised his eyebrows. I thought about what I had just said. "They didn't make talkies in the twelfth century."

I blushed. Idiot. Maniac. "I meant there's some script on the picture, and I think it's in French. I couldn't read it. Or, rather, no one in the family's been able to decipher it."

"What happened in England in 1066, Mrs. Jones?"

"Oh. That. Yes, I suppose he could be English then."

"The Normans changed the whole language. You've read *Beowulf*, haven't you? Even Chaucer's English is vastly different from that, so you can appreciate how widespread and all-pervasive the invasion was. The Normans replaced most of the Saxons in positions of power with their own men: government officials, even scribes. They couldn't speak the Saxons' language, so they used their own. But the two mingled. I think you have yourself a Norman knight there."

"May I make a xerox of this picture?"

"Of course. You can return it in class later. And if you ever get that picture, Mrs. Jones, I'd like to see it."

I grinned with my teeth, nonchalantly trying to wipe sweat from my upper lip. "Yes!"

I took the xerox. I had his picture now. Proof. He was real. He was there on paper. He could not be denied. I could not have dreamed up a Norman soldier, if I had never seen one before. He was *real*.

It wasn't until near Christmas that my mother asked me if I would like to visit my father's grave with her. She had been paying weekly pilgrimages out to Arlington Cemetery where Daddy's urn had been nestled into the earth beside the graves of her parents. With eleven children, Grandpa Jorgenson had had the foresight in the twenties to buy out a sizable corner of the Norwegian sector of Arlington when it first opened, just before the Crash. Grandpa was the first one to make use of the investment: a victim of failing business, felled by a stroke which was complicated and finished by pneumonia. He was only fifty-two. Baby Jorgenson was next, the first child of an uncle and an aunt who survived only one day. Then a young cousin joined them in the late fifties, of premature heart attack, followed by old Grandma Jorgenson of cirrhosis at age eighty-six. The rest of the plots were still attending, although not multiplying like the next generation of Jorgensons was. Although most of Daddy's relatives still lived up north, around Rosholt, in the midst of the boring, beige midlands, my mother could not bear to part with him. So she bought an extra one of the Jorgenson plots from her brother, right next to the one that had been reserved for her, and Daddy became the sole Mortenson in that territory.

My mother made sure that in that first winter the grave was covered with pine boughs, and was kept clear of snow. On Christmas she took Daddy a wreath on a wicker stand.

I had declined her first invitation to visit the grave. It would have been too emotional for both of us, and she did have high blood pressure. I remembered him in the kitchen the morning he left for up north in October, dressed in his favorite blue parka, the nondescript, baggy, cuffed trousers he always wore, and the carefully polished but worn black tie shoes. He had his usual apprehensive, sustained grin on his still summer-tanned face under a wild swatch of stick-straight white hair, the toothpick perpetually perched in the corner of his mouth ever since he quit smoking.

Instead I went alone one wintry Saturday in late December, after exams, without Michael. I wasn't quite sure why I was going at all, since I did not have a maudlin streak in me. Daddy would never know, or care, whether or not I had been there. I would only upset myself all over again. I knew all of this, but I went anyway, partly because I felt guilty for not seeing him one last time, and partly, the biggest part, because I loved him.

I knew exactly where the Jorgenson plot was because my mother used to drag me out there to work over the graves of her parents in the summertime, planting begonia bulbs and alyssum. My job was to fetch water from the tap beside the road. I was always suspicious of that water. I never let a drop of it touch my skin. After all, water came from underground, and there were a lot of awfully dead people down there. Even if they were related to me. One did not have to be loyal to decay. I parked the Volkswagen and hiked through the knee-deep snow. I could see from the road that there was a new stone there. My heart felt like it was dropping. The effect of actually seeing the truth was worse than bare imagination. I stopped short, caught my breath, and suddenly felt quite embarrassingly theatrical. I looked around. No one in sight. I walked over to the grave.

Although there was only one small urn beneath that huge granite stone, the pine boughs covered a six-foot-long rectangle as if there were a real coffin underneath. I bent over to brush some new snow from the boughs. Daddy was always fond of the smells of pine boughs and tomato plants. I thought that perhaps I could remind my mother to plant some tomatoes on the grave come summer. But ashes cannot smell, I thought, and dead men do not rise like flowers in the spring. How awful that was.

I tried to imagine Grandpa and Grandma there beside him, Grandpa now just a box of bones after forty-six years, Grandma maybe not after only fourteen . . . but such thoughts were really too ugly to keep in mind for long. I succumbed to a morbid, masochistic urge and knelt down on Daddy's grave, right on top of all the boughs. I read the words on the stone then. Hard to miss them. Big bold Roman letters carved deeply into the red granite: ALBERT HANS AND INGE GERTRUDE MORTENSON—WHAT WE ARE IS GOD'S GIFT TO US: WHAT WE BECOME IS OUR GIFT TO GOD. Someone had glued a weatherbeaten toothpick into the T of his first name. I was stricken.

I cried then like a storm, like a downpour, more than I had cried when I first heard the news less than three months before. I cried over that toothpick until my stomach hurt, until my face was chapped and stinging with frozen December tears. I cried for me, fatherless; for my mother, widowed; for Grandpa and Grandma and Baby Jorgenson and cousin Greta who had no pine boughs over their graves. I cried for all of the unburied Jorgensons, for the old barn, for the nameless sad soul in armor pleading to a stranger for something unknown from centuries past.

I had seen a film once of people who claimed that you could tape record the voices of spirits. They said that graveyards were full of spiritual voices. I could almost hear them in the wind, an eerie comfort, like reluctant souls blowing past from one dimension into the next, trying to touch me in their passage. Although these voices could not normally be heard by human ears, the tape could pick them up. The film showed these people setting up their tape recorder on top of a gravestone at night. An owl hooted effectively in a tree overshadowing the moving reels. It was dead quiet. When they replayed the tape, sure enough, there was a voice recorded on it. Just remembering what it said made my spine crawl. I wished I hadn't remembered it. The voice on the reel—it was a man's—said just one thing: *I'm scared.* And who isn't?

There *are* ghosts; I am sure of it. But I am not yet sure of what they are supposed to be. They come in so many different forms. I didn't want to leave my grief behind at Daddy's graveside; it felt too good. There was an awful relief in sobbing out loud, in wailing, in suffering chapped cheeks, in watching tear after tear fall and melt the snow around my bended knees. I wailed like a baby until I was too exhausted to utter another cry. I blew my nose on my woolen scarf, and, rather disgusted with myself, I dried up, froze like a fjord in January, and marched back through the snow to the Volkswagen. My eyes were still swollen on Sunday morning, but I was all frozen inside. Every time I thought of that visit I felt a little sick, but I didn't cry again. Perhaps it was my new immersion in history at the university that changed the way I felt, but death was no longer something that carried with it a physical hurt. Death was living; it had to be lived with, and written about.

My mother asked me if I had been out to the cemetery. She had seen the snow brushed aside and the footprints. I said yes. I thought how awful it must be for her to see her own name on a gravestone, the birth date already there, the other date just aching to be filled in: the unfinished time line in the frontispiece of her biography.

5

In wele be ware ore thou be woo;
Thenke wens thou come, wheder to goo.

—BODLEIAN MS DOUCE 302,
JOHN AUDELAY,
FIFTEENTH CENTURY

THE decision was irretrievably made by early December, seven weeks after Daddy died, and three weeks after the barn burned. A week before, the city announced that sewers were coming through the farm, and two days after that my mother agreed to sell the farm to a developer who arranged to have it surveyed and set up for subdividing. The vultures had started circling the day he died; they swooped in the day of the funeral. Their offers were too tempting. The farm had been my father's idea and my mother had just gone along for the ride. Presented with offers from subdividers to purchase the farm for a price five times as much as she and Daddy had paid for it less than five years before, she was dazzled. By Christmas my mother had secured herself a spacious modern apartment back in the Milwaukee suburb where she was born, raised, wed, where she had bred and raised me, and where her heart had always remained.

Within a week the surveyors employed by the real estate company produced a disgusting grid of one-acre "minifarms," which of course necessitated razing all of the existing farm buildings; and, simultaneously, the Planning Commission pronounced the new subdivision site fit for one-acre lot development. Daddy might have been inclined to leave well enough alone, leaving a Mortenson Park to posterity; without him, my mother was just as inclined to leave her mark on the future in the guise of a Mortenson Acres Subdivision. I could already see the road names: Albert Lane, Inge Court, Gay Street. Or maybe she would call it Little Norway and the streets would be named Oslo Drive, Risor Run, Bergen Alley, Lutefisk Lane. The best thing that came out of it was her state of mind: she was too busy transforming herself from a bereaved housewife into a land baroness to grieve. "Daddy would have wanted it this way," she kept telling herself, and me. I hated her death clichés, but she was still too tender to argue with. "We'll never have to worry about money again." The arguments demanded no response from me. I did not look to my father for money or security anymore.

"But we never had to worry anyway," I argued, uselessly. He had made enough money in farming and real estate to keep six widows rolling in pearls and color televisions for the next fifty years. But she had been raised during the Depression and had never been able to purge herself of the fear of being in need, of having to live on cornflakes, bread, and Spam again. There would never be enough to cure her of that disease. Even with enough money in hand to live extravagantly until she was over a hundred, she would still use the same bedsheets until they were unmendable. Thrift and saving were as basic to her as eating. She would never become one of those diamond-bedecked women who carried alligator bags and ate long lunches in Marshall Fields' tea room before the afternoon matinee at the symphony. She would still only buy summer clothes when they went on sale in August, and winter things in June.

Even Michael had tried to reason with her, and failed. "The longer you keep it, the more it will be worth," he argued. "They're not making any more of this stuff, Mrs. Mortenson. If you don't need the money, don't sell. It will still be in demand in five years." But she wouldn't listen. She was scared. She wanted to move back to her old hometown. Albert was gone and she had to fend for herself. She was desperately trying to keep her hands on the reins.

The British Airways tickets arrived in early December. We had given her six weeks, and she seemed fine, so Michael made the final reservations. There wasn't much preparation to make for our move; it was more thinking than acting. I shipped off seven or eight twenty-pound boxes just before Christmas, full of clothes mostly, with a smattering of cookbooks, colanders, and saucepans. Michael said that he had already acquired most of the basic homely requirements. He wrote his father and asked if he could please try to find a cottage for us to rent near Oxford. He wrote back within a week that a former colleague of his owned a house in Warborough with a tiny eighteenth-century cottage out back that was just that day being vacated by students. Understanding the difficulty of finding housing near Oxford, Michael immediately wired the man forty pounds for a deposit and it was pronounced ours by return post. We were due to leave in mid-January. By that time Michael hoped to have ratted away enough money for a downpayment on our own cottage. It would be a poor cottage, he warned: no central heating, and very likely no indoor toilet either. I nodded eagerly. Our own place. I had never lived in a place without central heating or an indoor toilet. I had no idea of what he was talking about.

He had given me ample warning, yet the reality of moving myself and everything I owned overseas had shockingly little physical or mental effect on me. It didn't interfere with my studying, and I never felt the depressing compulsion of having to make wet and panicked final goodbyes to a lot of people. I had been taught to accept most decisions that way. Maybe it was the unflappable, crusty Norwegian character, or else an inability to face the truth: all things were mutable. Somehow the idea, the act of moving to England did not in itself seem to me to be terribly momentous. It just seemed *right,* as if everything I had ever done was leading up to that. I suppose I had a gullible, trusting tendency to approach most of my life that way. To muddle through the minuscule essentials without a grand view to the end. To see odd elements of a thing without being able to interpret the whole thing. To believe in the fantasy and deny the actual.

The move became real to me when I went to the library in Madison after classes one day, and withdrew three touristy books on England: one a compendium of every haunted church, house, hall, castle, outhouse, and well in the kingdom; one a 1974 Michelin guide; one a selection of folk legends from the south, disappointingly written, as it turned out, in some hieroglyphic attempt at duplicating the Zomerzet dialect which Michael found hilarious. The book of haunts turned out to be my best bet of the three, even though I had to hide it from Michael. When he eventually found it he snatched it up from its hiding place in a drawer, gave a superior, cursory, utterly deprecating sniff over the title page, slapped it back down into the shirts and socks and asked me why I wasted my time looking at "such rubbish." I had no defense other than morbid curiosity. Why does anyone read trashy literature? It's better than listening to your heart beat all alone in an empty room on a dark, cold evening.

I read of some of the places that Michael had mentioned, and even in its terse, definitive style the wretched book caught me up helplessly, painfully. The road to Burford, it claimed, was haunted by a black cloud that engulfed and terrorized its victims, both human and animal. And the priory in that same town was reportedly full of ghastly, inexplicable screams, chantings, levitations. There was some horrid pleasure I derived in scaring myself, just as there was pleasure in experiencing some other kinds of pain. Crying, for instance, felt awfully good sometimes, to howl and wail away the hurt. Fright was a comfort in the same kind of way: afterward it was reassuring to think that there might be things in this world that did not, could not make sense:

> *The remains of a Young Lady whose artless beauty, innocence of Mind and gentle manner once obtained her the love and esteem of all who knew her. But when nerves were too delicately spun to bear the rude Shakes and Jostlings which we meet with in this transitory world, she sunk and died, a Martyr to Excessive Sensibility.*

I had come across the epitaph in a chapter devoted to spooks of Oxford. Sensitive Sarah Fletcher had been buried in Dorchester Abbey Church. Gay to the end of my days. And the man who saw poor Sarah, according to the book, in black silk cloak, with purple ribbons in her hair, "was so struck by the anguish in her eyes that he was overwhelmed with the desire to comfort and cherish her." I empathized. It had happened to me once, out in the barn.

Michael seemed determined those last days to wring every last drop he possibly could out of America. We ate out a lot, at McDonald's, at Arby's. He had developed a rabid fascination for large discount department stores and when he wasn't in his office or out inspecting buildings I could be certain that he would be wandering the caramel-corn and plastic-scented aisles of some local Treasure Island, K-Mart or Target store, forever returning with a gem or two: flashlights that floated, smiling face coasters, plastic cookie jars shaped like tomatoes or giant frogs, Johnny Cash or Glenn Miller records, pieces of decorative Japanese-made rubber fruit. He thought it was all "dreadfully amusing": I thought it was a disease and the resulting clutter faintly annoyed me because I didn't know whether to pack it and mail it or leave it behind.

It was late on a Sunday morning and I had wrested Michael from his newspaper. The night before he had brought home a pair of denim overalls large enough to fit an adult hippo. "They don't have people this large in Britain," he cackled, carefully setting the overalls in the last special pile we were gathering together to ship. I removed them later that evening, after he was asleep.

He had seen Target's usual Sunday morning color spread in the paper and was anxious to sample the sales there on barbecue lighter fluid and tube sox, but I diverted him onto the skis. A sporty aunt and uncle had bought us two pairs of cross-country skis in the August sales as a wedding gift, but we were able to use them only three times before we had to think of selling them. It didn't snow enough in Oxford to justify the shipping expense, Michael said. And we had never had the opportunity to master the wax tricks anyway. Our first two sallies out into the disemboweled and newly powdered fields were terrible, unfunny jokes. After ten minutes of floundering like legless mammals on distant Arctic beaches, we removed the skis and walked back. But the third time, that Sunday early afternoon, we must have, quite by chance, hit upon the correct wax for those specific outdoor conditions.

There was more snow, which helped considerably: no tripping over outstanding muddy furrows in the fields. It was colder; it was gray and still coming down in huge, sporadic, shapeless flakes that would attach to your clothing and not melt until you breathed on them. It was, at best, a mediocre idea until we got out onto the long field between the houses and discovered, with a few glad thumps and spinouts, that for once the skis were actually moving forward without out a great deal of effort: in fact were moving us along effortlessly, with white tracks spreading out behind us like endless vermicelli. The tractor ruts and footprints of surveyors were covered by the previous night's snow, and if one looked only straight ahead or to the right, into the neighboring field, it was possible to forget that Towering Oaks was there at all, ready and anxious to reproduce itself a hundred times over on the virgin land beneath our boots.

We skied like professionals, or at least it seemed that way for lack of a professional skier in our midst. We reached the end of the long field, the field that had nurtured buckwheat and a billion bumblebees just three months before, and carried on over toward the next field's corn stubble, between the rows, toward the woods. The crop residue on the back fields slowed us down. It had not been plowed there: the ousted farmer evidently had seen no point since he would not be back to plant the next spring. We split into single file there and followed the same track. The temperature barely approached fifteen degrees. As long as the snow fell the wind was calm, and we were warm enough by that time to ski in just our sweaters; but there was no place to dump our jackets. The snow would have covered them in no time. We would have to stop for a while soon, to cool off.

"Why is it fun all of a sudden?" I said.

"That's the way it always works," Michael answered. "Once you've made up your mind to do something, this sort of thing always happens to weaken your resolve."

"I hope your resolve isn't too weakened. Remember that in a year's time this won't exist. And besides, I'd rather forget that Methods of Historic Documentation II existed too."

"I wouldn't put you through that, don't worry." He had a healthy, thriving scorn for American education. When I told him that Madison had a department of Women's Studies he almost choked on his supper, laughing. "Are women so thickheaded here that they require their own special departments?" he said. "I thought they were all out for equality! Do they have a special department of Men's Studies as well?" Even before he entertained serious notions of returning home, he maintained that if we ever should breed, the resulting stock would be educated in Britain. American schools were all geared for the mediocre-to-cretin level; in Britain, the paths diverged at age eleven.

We skied on in the falling snow that absorbed all sound except for the numbing *zuzz* of a snowblower from the murky, aluminum depths of Towering Oaks. But even that was almost tolerably weak and distant. We stopped to admire a doe nibbling at a remnant of the farm's last crop of field corn. Its last crop of anything, I sourly mused, except maybe crabgrass, dandelions, and Big Wheels. In a year that doe would be the target of dozens of little boys' BB guns.

If it was lucky. If it was unlucky some slimy sod would set up a salt lick and illegally pick it off that winter. We had noticed a cache of empty cartridges in a thicket beside the field. Evidence of civilization. Only the raccoons and the rabbits would remain. They thrived on civilization, like rats and roaches. Trash cans for the coons, gardens full of lettuce, beans, and peas for the rabbits. They never bothered us on the farm: trash cans and gardens were more plentiful and closer together in Towering Oaks.

It was like a modern-day plague of toads, I thought as we coasted along, too far apart to casually chat. The trouble was that the good suburban folk had got their signals crossed in their haste to tame the wilderness and live the Good Life. While the cute little bunnies and raccoons grew fat on their victory gardens and sumptuous garbage, the poor toads were relentlessly blown away by unappreciative, misguided, stomping housewives, lawnmowers, rototillers, and little boys with mayonnaise jars. No matter that the toad was worth ten times its weight in No-Pest strips; it was easy to catch and it screamed. No one would think of putting a firecracker inside of a cute little ravenous bunny's mouth. And so the gardens in Towering Oaks always looked tacky, marginally productive, frayed about the edges, well chewed by coons and rabbits and squirrels, attacked by insects left uneaten by scores of exploded toads, while my mother's garden, boiling with toads, thrived, lush and tall and productive. The corn stubble was already crisscrossed by the nasty little handprints of raccoons, foraging, stealing from the deer, growing fat and ready to heave their disgusting bodies upon a thousand unsuspecting trash cans next spring. Horrible, semirabid things, I thought. No better than the mixed-up people they plagued. I tried to catch up to Michael.

"Did you plan to go in to the office today?" I called across the falling snow to him, blue and oversized in my father's old down parka.

"I'm not sure yet." He danced forward on his skis. A daring trick. I tried to copy the maneuver and succeeded only in plowing one ski tip under a drift. I fell on my side. Michael was again too far ahead to hear me fall. I called out to him to wait. "You ought to take a few lessons!" he called back, his voice sounding as if it were filtered through a blanket. He skied back and deliberately fell down beside me. "Good excuse to rest and cool off."

"Your butt will get soaked."

"Not in this temperature. Besides, I'm hot. Nothing but extremes in this bloody country." Michael did not like thermostats and central heating and the extreme cold that settled over Wisconsin in winter. He was always complaining about it being too hot inside, even when I thought it was too cold. I wondered if it might have been a manifestation of masculine pride: to withstand cold was a sign of strength. I turned down the thermostat to humor him, but sat closer to the fire in the evening, not anxious to admit that I was not quite as stoic as he was. I had been raised at seventy-two degrees, and he had not.

"What do you have to do at the office today?" I wished that he wouldn't go in, but I knew that I couldn't stop him if his mind was made up. We were leaving in ten days. He seemed demonically determined to stow away one final thousand before quitting.

"Odds and sods. Nothing too urgent. It *is* starting to wear me down a bit now."

"I never thought I'd hear you say that. I believed for years that the only person who could work that much and never complain was my father. And look what happened to him."

"He said that business was his vocation as well as his only hobby. That's how you get rich, sunshine."

"Is it worth it?"

"Apparently not. But I'm bound to see it through to the bitter end. It's all well and good for that lot of yahoos—" he waved a woolen mitten to the east where Towering Oaks rumbled like a volcano about to explode over the farm—"but I'm an Englishman, thank God, and I have principles. This is all good for a laugh, but I couldn't take a steady diet of it. You realize, my dear, that the main reason why I have been so successful and have made nearly twice as much money as the other appraisers in the office is that I have this marvelously salable accent. The education is irrelevant. The experience means nothing. What matters is that I can talk with this incredibly convincing, trust-inspiring accent. People buy the accent, not the appraisal. They pay good money to hear me talk, and what I say is Truth."

"Never trust a man with a foreign accent in an oversized parka."

"Or a woman with a feeble-minded mother. They grow up in their image."

"Michael!"

"She's the only person I have failed to convince of my sincerity and good judgment. And she is probably the only person I have given one hundred percent heartfelt, sensible, sound advice to. She personifies American gullibility. She ignores the voice of reason and good sense. Where have I gone wrong?"

"You married her baby. By mere physical contact you've taken on characteristics of the baby. She doesn't hear an English accent any more than I do now. She hears the voice of Gay's *boyfriend*."

"Is that so meaningless that she would throw away all of this land rather than listen to good sense and reason?"

"It isn't reasonable to her. Land means nothing to her, but money does. There's more of everything here, Michael. More land, more money. It isn't precious. She feels no moral obligation to hinder suburban encroachment like this. In fact, she rather likes the idea."

"I don't understand. I mean, I do understand, in a broad detached sense, but I can't possibly subscribe to that philosophy. It's immoral. I work with these developer idiots all of the time. Do you know that there is one in Creekdale erecting monstrous ten-foot-high statues of knights in armor to place at the entrance gates to his Canterbury Manors? I saw the plans for the statues and they're dressed like conquistadores. Sancho Panzas. Fat ones. Christ."

"I think I'm sick."

"Oh, it gets even better! He has building regulations whereby only Chewders can be built in there, thirty-five hundred square feet or more."

"Chewders?"

"I dare not profane the name 'Tudor.' There's Jeffrey Avenue, misspelled of course and not really an avenue, Wife of Bath Court, the Miller's Lane. And each manor is a full half-acre with sewer. I won't believe that any of this has really happened once I'm back home. It's too horrible to be true. The waste here is appalling."

"You remember you once told me how much the freedom of capitalism appealed to you? Infinite opportunities here to fiddle? Surprising how a little familiarity can sour you."

"It's still there, though. Spread out before me like some Roman bacchanal. But I guess I've just lost my appetite for it. I don't see much point in eating to the point of vomiting, then eating some more. It's the way I've been raised. Your mother may thrive on it, but I can't stomach the waste."

There was something unreal about the snow that afternoon, with us sitting in it like two dark tree stumps. I had a niggling impression that it was going to be the last time. Momentous. An ache rose in my throat. It was more than that, but I wasn't sure why, or what. So quiet, fresh, the snow hissed and hummed and sighed as it fell. Resigned. The last time. As if the snow would never again fall white. It would just turn black and all creation would forever after be spoiled. It was moving, forward, inside. I wanted to share it.

"I don't want to leave."

"Tickets can't be refunded."

"I don't mean that. I mean this. Sitting here. In the snow. I don't believe how quiet and white it is. I can't imagine anything more perfect and peaceful."

"You're right. It's not even cold, is it? As one would imagine fairyland or sitting on top of a cloud."

"It's not like you to be so lyrical."

"There's a lot you don't know about me yet, my dear," he said in a mock-villainous voice. "Did I ever tell you about my brace of custom meat cleavers?"

"Don't spoil this. It's nice to know that you have the capacity to be—or feel—poetical. You're usually so serious. Sometimes it's fun to dream, imagining you're in another dimension. I used to play Mary-in-the-Mirror when I was a little kid. For lack of a brother or a sister to play with, I resorted to the mirror."

"I used to lie back and watch the clouds and pretend I was up there moving right along with them. I watched the shapes always changing and imagined they were really buffaloes or elephants or Rolls-Royces . . . "

"Did anything really unusual ever happen to you, Michael? I mean like a dream come true, or a dream sort of run on into reality, so that you couldn't tell the difference between them? Once I'm sure that I actually *did* walk through the bathroom mirror. I clearly recall the feeling of the glass giving way like butter, and then walking upside down on the ceiling on the other side of the mirror, as if it were the floor. And then I flew."

"You *flew?*"

"Yes. I remember it distinctly. I flew from the toilet seat to the countertop. Didn't you ever do anything like that?"

"Not exactly. I never flew, that is. God was not generous in His allotment of aerodynamic skills for humans."

"Don't go all serious on me now, Michael. You must have had something like that happen to you at least once in your lifetime."

"I had a dream once." He said it softly, like he might have been embarrassed by it. He picked up a handful of snow in one mitten, letting it run out. He was looking at his hands, the snowflakes melting on his palms.

"You mean to say you've only had one dream in your whole life?"

"Silly. Of course not. I just had one dream of the variety you described. So real that I couldn't quite shake the feel of it for days afterward. It still bothers me when I think of it."

"Tell me."

"It happened my first year at Oxford, when I was living in rooms at college. I was alone for the whole weekend. My roommate went home for some family affair. There was no provocation for the dream, at least none that I can remember. It wasn't as if I had been studying to distraction or felt otherwise exhausted or distraught in any way. I hadn't spoken with anyone about anything that might have been even subconsciously disturbing. It just came over me like a fever, uncontrollable. I couldn't even wake myself up. It wasn't a bad dream: nothing like a nightmare. It was just endless, and so terribly vivid, and sort of awe-inspiring."

"A glimpse into the black hole? The secrets of the universe?"

"I suppose, if you must be melodramatic. Something like that, but not quite so ominous. It just seemed staggeringly big, incomprehensible."

"Did you actually see anything, or was it just this awe-inspiring bigness you felt?"

"Oh, I saw quite a lot. Indeed, it was very colorful, and very familiar, too—as if I were experiencing some primordial form of my own being, like a reincarnation I suppose. Sounds like sci-fi trash, doesn't it?"

"No. Not at all. Please go on."

"Well, I was lying down, and I couldn't see myself—my face, that is—but I could feel that I was lying down on the ground. It was damp, cool beneath me, and I was watching clouds. Those heavy dark rain-soaked clouds that race across England from the sea. And then the clouds above me split and there was this incredible rainbow that almost exploded across the valley I was in. I could see these smooth, undulating green mountains all around me, like the ones I saw in the Santa Lucia Range in California last summer. Yet these mountains were somehow bleaker, anonymous, dream-mountains. I couldn't see beyond them but I felt I could soar *over* them if only I could concentrate hard enough. I remember this vivid, sharp rainbow slicing through the wet air over me. I was feeling the earth—stones, grass, soil—underneath me, and at the same time I was soaring up with this rainbow, over the valley. It was an extremely unsettling sensation. And one other thing."

"What?"

"Nonsense, really. There always has to be something to spoil it, make it sound silly. Something that's not quite right. Something that reminds us that we should get control of ourselves and look at this objectively. I remember looking down from the sky, for just a split second, and seeing my body stretched out on the ground in front of me."

"What's so strange about that? Were you blue or something?"

"Of course not. But I had this terrible weight on my chest. Pressure, like I was being stepped on, held down, or pressed between two sheets of metal, but I couldn't see it, or anything that could have caused it. Maybe it was a premature heart attack."

We sat there and felt the snowflakes touching us—or rather heard them: an indistinct susurration over our heads, over the fields, over the woods. I did not ask him any more about the dream. I had a rough idea of how he might have felt when I confessed my own ghost stories. Uncomfortable in the realm of the inexplicable. Eager to change the subject. It was obviously too big a thing to make light of with him. I had to respect his sense, his reluctance to admit even this much to me. I had to tread carefully. I liked it that he had told me. It was hard work for him to do that. I had felt him doing battle with all the words, all the way: the admission, then the denial. I loved him all the more for it. He had let me peer inside his soul where it was sensitive, private, solitary. He had let me see inside the most intimate corner, and it had not been easy for him. I found it awesome. And I loved him more. For the briefest second, a mutual awe of the inexplicable had allowed some of his soul's precious elixir to overflow onto mine, into mine. I wished that it could always be that way, at the same time knowing full well that one could not build a foundation of life on the basis of a dream.

We were not far from the winter solstice, and by three the sky was already turning from gray to evening orange, the color of winter sky after a day of unending snow. We got up and skied on to the woods, over the deer paths, up and down the low glacial hills, past majestic clumps of old black walnut trees as straight as rods, and ancient red oaks. The branches over our heads were black and bleak and powdered with snow, piteous with snow, all the more beautiful for the fact that they were doomed, would be gone in six months. The rolling path beneath our skis would be bulldozed flat, the thickets laid waste, the glades leveled and exhumed for poured concrete cellars. We swept like zephyrs around in a westerly circle through the forest, slickly moving forms dwarfed by the trees, by the dignity of the land, humble and joyful that we could take this last taste of Uncle Mooshie's empire with us to the ends of our lives.

We skied back over the fields like gentle hands stroking a beloved head, like unobtrusive elements that belonged to the frozen landscape, leaving finally, our skinny tracks covered over with fat snowflakes before they were beyond our sight: ventifacts, in gentle blue camouflage: ghosts before our time.

We flew out of Chicago on a 707 that, it seemed to me, was held together with hairpins and Elmer's Glue. Never having flown before, I couldn't quite understand how something so large could defy gravity, and I didn't like it one bit. It didn't seem to bother Michael. I had planned to take a Quaalude before takeoff with another one saved for landing, illicit relics of my youth that I had saved from college the summer before. But the fear of being thrown into prison for possession or, worse yet, possibly dying of it (for all I knew I was allergic to it) made me flush it down a toilet in the airport lounge. I took three licit Valiums instead. Unfortunately mind triumphed over drug and by the time we boarded the deathtrap forty-five minutes later I was still as coherent as I had been that morning, when my hand had kept moving in the direction of the telephone with a mind of its own, ready to cancel the reservations.

The plane was very cramped, very long, and very narrow, rather like a giant, foil-wrapped, airborne suppository. I insisted on an aisle seat, much to the delight of the other passengers who, God forbid, *wanted* to look out the windows. I buckled my seat belt, took the gold cross around my neck into sweaty palms, and started to pray to a nonspecific God. Whoever was listening. Michael nonchalantly leafed through a copy of *Fortune* magazine that he had extracted from his briefcase. The plane began to make odd noises, to back up, to go forward, to turn slowly. I really did not want to look out the window but I did anyway, masochistically, craning my neck around Michael's relaxed body, watching the blue lights on the runway appear and disappear. Finally the plane started to pick up speed, and moved swiftly toward the specified runway. It made louder noises, awful noises, and then it started to move faster, faster, too fast, but not fast enough to fly, I thought, until with a great grunt we were suddenly in a vertical position, my cross still sandwiched between my palms, praying, wondering why in heaven's name I had let myself be talked into this.

Hovering between two worlds, breathless, without a foothold, blackness and mist rolling past the windows, this was like being *dead* already, I thought. The engines were at first loud and then annoyingly soft and then unnervingly silent, drifting, falling, up and down, then loud again. Michael casually leafed through the magazine as if everything was normal and he was just sitting on the living room sofa, as if the engines weren't really about to die, the cargo door about to blow off and suck everyone out into the winter darkness, Atropos about to explode a can of deodorant in the baggage compartment, a flock of geese about to be sucked into the engines, God only knew.

I wanted to get off. I didn't want to be in a skinny tin tube rushing through the albuminous clouds where only birds and raindrops belonged, when I should have been snugly ensconced in my bed on the earth darning socks or reading Stenton, or usefully wasting my time in housewifely endeavors. Up there I was too nervous to read: I could see the words and repeat them, but they were meaningless. I couldn't write: my hands shook and sweated. I couldn't sew: I had sent on my darning kit. I couldn't concentrate. I couldn't look out the window. I couldn't wash dishes. I could hardly breathe. Fear made you an animal. It was a waste. A terrible, terrible waste. My father had often told me that time was the one thing that you could never find again once you had lost it. Here was eight hours written out of my life.

It finally occurred to me that although I was incapable of doing anything constructive I could still drink. At last the stewardess climbed up the aisle of the plane, which was still pointing up (a reassuring sign) and she handed me a bottle of wine. I finished it with a few quick tosses, then took another Valium for good measure. It was probably enough to have sedated a horse. I was ready to order more wine when, quite unexpectedly, the plane began to spin.

This was it. I knew. Into Thy hands, Lord, I commend my spirit. What's left of it. I tried to clutch at my cross again but my hands wouldn't work. I heard funny noises, roars, booms, buzzes, thunder, dragons fighting in midair. And then I died.

I rose from the dead on our descent to Heathrow. Michael shook me until I could open one dry eye. "Look!" he said, pointing out a very bright window. The sun was shining; that was all I could see. I thought that hell was supposed to be dark. I shut my eye again. It hurt. The flames of hell. It was all a dream. A nasty, cruel dream, like Tantalus's. I had to go through Purgatory on my way down to hell. At least Michael was condemned along with me. Small comfort. To be strapped faces together on a spit, rotating eternally over the infernal coals.

My mouth tasted like garbage in hot sun. He continued to shake me, and point out the window. A crackling voice announced over the intercom that it was time to fasten seatbelts for landing. The plane made an unsettling dip that almost pushed my eyeballs out onto my lap. "You missed it," Michael said. I had caught the bit about the seatbelts: but mine had been buckled for the last eight hours. I was slowly reviving, gathering up cornea, iris, retina. I knew then how Lazarus must have felt. What a letdown. I could have used a dog to lick my wounds just then. It might have helped me to wake up. I felt awful. Like ten thousand brain cells had just died violent, untimely deaths.

"What did I miss?" I finally croaked.

"We flew right over Windsor Castle."

So what. Big deal, I thought. I had seen pictures of Windsor Castle before. It was big and gray and surrounded by a curtain wall. It had been there since 1167 and would more than likely be there in 2067. What was important was supervising the landing. I clutched my cross with both hands and renewed faith and started the countdown.

His father met us and drove us to the cottage in Warborough which was dark and smelled of wet stones. After the ordeal of the flight, I was not in much of a mood to be sociable. Michael had not seen his father for five months and there was no need for me to do anything more than just sit, looking green and rumpled, in the back seat of his unheated Land-Rover, rendering cursory yeses, noes, and giggles whenever a politely British nonquestion was tossed in my direction. The journey was tortuously long, since Mr. Jones, Sr., avoided motorways and A roads like the plague; along twisting, treacherous, narrow B roads whenever possible. It was gray outdoors, slate, flat gray, by the time we landed at Heathrow, and positively bucketing by the time we reached Oxford.

I had had few real expectations: it was all so foreign beforehand. I had been in Canada once, with a school group, and even that seemed foreign to me although I couldn't remember why. Michael had not told me much. He had shown me some pictures: a snap of his parents in their vegetable garden looking stout, anonymously middle-aged, foreign; a snap of his college quadrangle at Oxford looking stony and sunlit and rather boring, although I didn't tell him that; a snap of one of his childhood homes—the bungalow near York —next door to Mr. Church's ratty barn. The pictures did not tell me much either. All I had to go on were my own impressions, from books, from Michael's speech and behavior. It was perhaps a bit bleaker, poorer than I had imagined, peering out the windows at the back of the Land-Rover; and it struck me then that foreign lands are only foreign when contemplated from great distances. Faced with massive green ivy-clad beech trees, hedgerows swaddling narrow roads, enclosed fields, and oddly consistent architecture, Wisconsin was suddenly the foreign place, and I was home here.

I already knew that I didn't like opening my mouth in front of English people. What I heard was an idiot Midwestern honk, invisible in Wisconsin, but outstanding, mortifying here. I let Michael do all the talking at customs, and tried to fade into the stripes of his shirt, English by association. I didn't like being foreign. I *wanted* to be home.

Our cottage in Warborough, near Oxford, had not been inhabited for over a month, and even before then it had been full of students, the vilest of tenants, who left it looking as if Australopithecus had descended from the dingy mists of Jericho and spent a term or two there. Mrs. Jones had, according to her husband, descended as well with her buckets and brooms and the place had a faint unhomely scent of public loo disinfectant about it. Michael's things had been moved in already. There was a stack of five boxes, three yet in transit I presumed, piled near the front door, all well pulverized by the post office. Like a good wife I floated, still recovering optic nerve and regenerating brain cells, into what I assumed was the kitchen, and struggled to put together a tea. The landlord had been kind enough to furnish us with a pint of milk, and Mrs. Jones had left a box of PG Tips tea and some biscuits.

Michael and his father were struggling to light a fire with wet wood when I brought the hot tea in on an old, warped, Babycham tray. Apparently the roof was leaking right over the woodbox. I set the tray down in the dark and foolishly began clawing at the walls for a thermostat. It seemed so much simpler than lighting a fire, until Michael asked me what in heaven's name I was doing. It suddenly occurred to me that there would be no thermostat there. I had been forewarned, I had forgotten. The fireplace was our only source of heat. It was January, it was raining, it was three in the afternoon and as dark as well-advanced dusk outside. It was, with a bit of luck, forty degrees inside, and very damp. I lied, said that I was looking for a light switch.

The fire turned out to be more smoke than flame, and they were forced to plug in the electric fire. There were no lamps in the room. We drank our tea and crunched our Nice biscuits by the ineffective cold orange glow of the fire's single operative bar. I refueled the pot once. At least the tea was warm, for a while. I hadn't taken off my wool coat since we deplaned, although Michael and his father had, just on principle I think, removed theirs when they got indoors.

Mr. Jones left around five. It was already completely dark outside, and still drizzling a chronic drizzle. Mrs. Jones expected him for supper at eight, he said, and their farm was a good seventy miles away. Thank you for collecting us, I said, accepting his apprehensive, cool handshake, knowing that I would never even recognize him on the street after that one meeting. I had only seen the back of his head on the drive to Oxford, and it was too dark inside the cottage to see more than an indistinct elderly blur moving about alongside Michael's more youthful, trim blur. There was a certain similarity in the way they moved, I noted: an inherited hunch to the shoulders, a Jonesian stride. Michael went as far as the village store with his father and walked back in the rain with a plastic carrier bag full of groceries. It was Friday, he explained, and the shops were open late. Until six.

I rescued some bedsheets, surprisingly unscathed, from one of the battered boxes and took them up a frightfully steep and narrow staircase. There was one large room upstairs with two small windows, both on the same wall, overlooking the garden. There was a bed, a bureau, but no light. The floor sloped dangerously to the west. The ceilings were low. I waited until my eyes had adjusted to the dark, then groped about the bed in an attempt to make it up. I heard Michael come in and carefully maneuvered myself back downstairs. He was researching the kitchen.

"There's coal in the stove," he announced. There was an overhead light in the kitchen with a forty-watt bulb in it—the brightest in the house—but no electrical outlets. Evidently man had not yet invented electric mixers, blenders, and toasters when that kitchen was designed.

"I thought it was a gas stove."

"It is. I can't imagine why there's coal in it."

I opened the oven door. By the Stygian glimmer of the overhead light I could see a blackish pile at the bottom of it. "Perhaps they had difficulty lighting it."

"I doubt that. I had better ask the landlord." Michael lobbed the food alternately into the cupboard and the tiny refrigerator. I extracted a nasty-looking and-smelling plastic packet from his shopping bag.

"What's this?" I held it up to the light and could make no sense of it. Cylindrical things with pointy ends, glistening ominously.

"Kippers." Suddenly the cupboard loomed before me full of foreign names. Oxo. HP Sauce. Carr's Table Water Biscuits. McVities Jamaica Ginger Cake.

"What in God's name are *kippers?*" I was getting tired of wearing the heavy wool coat. My mouth still tasted of wine and Valium and garbage. I wanted a Big Mac. Or maybe a Dunkin' Donut.

"Lovely things, really. You fry them up for breakfast with tomato and bread." A loaf of bread appeared on the shelf. Mother's Pride. Idiotic name, I thought. But then Wonder wasn't so clever either.

"Oh. You mean sausages." I put the plastic things into the refrigerator. Michael was busy rooting in the cupboard for an ice tray. "We need some light upstairs. Are there any candles around?" I already knew better than to ask for electric lights. Michael handed me a box marked "Bougies."

"Your wish is my command. Imported ones, even. You'll need a bottle or two to use as candlesticks."

The doorbell rang. It was the landlord, Mr. Phibbs. All smiling, trousers pulled up to mid-chest, shiny cheeks, well polished but antiquated black tie shoes, hair slicked back; not a face that one would ever dream of complaining to, nor a face that would ever acknowledge fault. After politely meaningless introductions, Michael asked him about the coal in the stove.

"Oh, that." Phibbs chuckled, waving a fat, freckled hand at the oven. "Chappie used to live here thought it would light faster in the fireplace if he warmed it in the oven beforehand. Sorry." We arranged for two pints of milk to be delivered every morning. Michael paid him for a month in advance, and asked if he had any old bottles to spare. Phibbs directed us to a shed in the garden and told us that we could take two. I crept out over the slick garden flagstones after he left and pawed around in the dark. The shed was filled to the roof beams with empty glass bottles. The man was a maniac hoarder.

I took three, and later wished I hadn't. The bedroom proved to be much nicer unlit. What we didn't know wouldn't hurt us. I left the bougie burning all night to keep a careful watch on the progress a large spider was making across the low ceiling over the bed. Michael would not let me squash it. "If you want to live and thrive, let the spider run alive," he had said, repeatedly.

When we were in bed he hugged me. We were both very tired from jet lag, but he didn't want to let go, trying, I think, to create a coziness there, in bed, that he knew didn't yet exist in the cottage —the first home he had provided for me. The sheets smelled of diesel and damp. "Well, how do you like it?" he finally asked, in a tone that defied any negativism on my part. I chose my word carefully. I had not taken off my wool coat until seconds before leaping into bed. I shivered. Should have left it on.

"Extraordinary."

"Yes, isn't it though? Compared with some of the places I lived in around here as a student. Needs some work done on it. Like that moss over there on the wall. Must go. I think that's where we get our leak over the woodbox." I had not noticed the moss on the wall. Now I was torn between watching that *and* the spider. "I have all next week to help you put the place in order," he said. He started work with a private firm of estate agents a week from Monday. Harper Crawley Appleyard & Titts. One of the partners, a junior Harper, had been at college with him. I still could not think of the firm's name without laughing. I snorted rudely, and the bed convulsed. "What's so funny?" he asked.

"Harper Crawley Appleyard & Titts. Can't help it." The bed lurched again. It was all so horrid that it was funny: the coal in the stove, the twisty roads, the cold, the spider, the dark, the moss.

"Poor Mr. Titts," he clucked. "Imagine living with a flag like that waving over your head."

"I feel more sorry for Mrs. Titts. I hope they have more than two children."

"Two little Titts? Actually old Crawley has really got the best name of all."

"What's so funny about George Crawley?"

"His middle name's Crapper."

"Oh, God. Whatever possesses parents?"

"Lord knows. I'm just thankful that I don't have to skip up to folks and say, 'Hi—I'm Gay!' " I gouged at him under the blankets and we laughed. The bed swayed dangerously and the floor groaned; the noise and the sudden movement upset the spider. It trickled along a few paces and took the fun out of everything. It was directly above my head. Michael put his hand on my knee and started to hoist up my flannel nightdress. I put my hand over his, and he stopped.

"We must initiate our new bed," he explained, but I didn't say anything. I was trying to imagine what it would feel like if that spider dropped underneath the bedclothes. My skin crawled on eight legs. I shivered again. "Are you cold?" He wrapped himself around me like a hot octopus.

"Michael, please let go. I can't breathe. I can't move." I pushed his arms away. I could tell that I had hurt his feelings. "It's nothing personal, really. I'm just not in the mood."

Silence.

"I couldn't concentrate anyway with that spider up there. What if it should fall?" The room was full of breath: drafts of musty air, cold breezes from the staircase, the wind sighing like a faraway banshee over Warborough Green. "It must be the jet lag. Maybe tomorrow night. All right?"

I turned over to look at him, to soothe the unseen wound with balm from loving eyes, but he was sound asleep.

6

Homo luge,
Fuge, fuge mortalia
cur amas labilia
sunt sompnia omnia.
Brumans est mors. *

—ANONYMOUS,
THIRTEENTH CENTURY

T HERE is a lot about Oxford that
has been exactly the same for hundreds of years. At home, the oldest
thing around had been the barn. In Oxford, one gets the impression
that even the soil is antique, having passed through more hands,
having clung to more roots, than the nearly virgin soil of our buckwheat field. Trees and shrubs grow deliberately there, to massive old
age. Even the houses seem organic, immovable, permanent. The
whole country, or what little I had seen of it, seemed so rigid, rooted,
solid. No clapboard barns to blow away there: they were built of stone
in England, and seemed as eternal as miniature mountain ranges.

I was very much made to feel like an outsider there, with barely a
fingertip inside the privileged door. Michael had been a student at
Oxford for four years, but he was not a man to share the collegiate

---

Lament, man,
Flee, flee mortality
Why do you love fleeting things?
All are dreams
Death is menacing.

secrets with anyone outside of the unbreakable druidic circle of classmates from his college. There was something humorously sinister about it all. The graduates would certainly have sniffed and called it sacred, tradition, but I thought it was just silliness. Michael could spend hours watching a football match on the television, scrawling his name and his exalted titles over and over again until the page was almost one complete inkspot: Michael A. Jones, M.A. (Oxon), A.R.I.C.S.

When Michael was with an old college friend, it reminded me of cartoons of the Loyal Order of Moose. At any moment I expected them to commence elaborate handshakes, hands over feet, feet over knees, ears over eyes, elbows over ankles, and then to don great horned headdresses and perform ritual dances around the brussels sprouts in the garden. To these peculiar, proud Oxford men, the fact that I had received a degree from an American college seemed hardly worth acknowledging. When they asked me where I had studied, I told them.

"That's in America?"

"Yes, in Wisconsin."

I might as well have said New Guinea. They would sniff then. Not nice, long, loud sniffs redolent of outright disapproval like my mother's, but barely audible, brief little sniffs which were far, far worse than words can describe. To me, college, like adolescence, was an embarrassment, a means to an end, best over and done with and then safely forgotten. One grew, one developed away from that, one changed, life got bigger. Memories just hurt, good ones and bad ones alike, because they reminded one that time passed and could never be recovered again. To them, Oxford was all-pervasive: past, present, and future. It was so deeply fixed into their dispositions that it was like a different culture altogether. It was almost *genetic.* It was a culture that could, by dint of its manifestly great intelligence, merge successfully with any other, yet soundly refused to do so for unspoken reasons that an outsider could only idly guess at. I wondered if they were overly educated to the point of acute narcissism, or if it was just fashionable bigotry? The worst speculation of all, that Americans really *were* brash and piggish beyond civilized comprehension, was too awful to contemplate, but always at the back of my mind. The ones who had never left Oxford were the worst, although even those who had broken away and lived as far as Newcastle, or the Oman, still retained traces of that untouchably esoteric scent.

I usually left Michael and his friends alone in the parlor and returned to the kitchen or to the bedroom where I belonged, or where they evidently felt I belonged. I felt the animosity that an invading army feels from an invaded people. I inhibited their spontaniety, threatened their traditions, their prestige, their values, their superiority, their *way*. The fact that I had graduated from an American college and I could still speak in complete sentences was, to them, at first a curiosity, but later a threat. I tried to keep my mouth shut as often as possible, as much to hide my accent as to stave off any inadvertently spilled vapidities. It was not polite to threaten or to offend your guests.

My feelings of being subhuman, theirs of being intellectual supermen, were not ameliorated by the position in which I found myself after less than a month. Michael had been in touch with another man in his same year at Pembroke whose father was a history don. I had fiddled with the notion of doing another B.A. in history there (they would never have me for a postgraduate degree, Michael said: American certifications were worthless), but it was well into Hilary term and I would have to wait until Michaelmas anyway. Michael suggested that I get a job, and when he learned from his friend Joseph that his father, Dr. Barnes, needed a secretary, I was sent packing on the first bus from Dorchester.

Of course old Barnes had to hire me. I had an old Olivetti and a vast, untidy wooden desk in front of me before I knew what had gone wrong. The pay was abysmal—£1,250 per annum and no benefits worthy of mention—but it kept me inside, out of the rain, and gave me access to Barnes's private library and most of the university's collections and libraries. It was a stroke of luck that Barnes's specialty was medieval history. Medieval English history. And even early English/Welsh history. Infrequently I had letters, lectures, notes, examinations, memoranda, or fragments of one of his manuscripts to type. Frequently I had great oases of time in which to read. In fact, I felt rather guilty collecting even the paltry paycheck once every fortnight.

But it was nice to have the money. After nothing, even twenty-five pounds seemed like a lot. I had not yet been able to make an adequate transition from American to English ways, especially in the kitchen, especially after a near-fatal disaster that first morning when what I assumed were sausages turned out to be smelly, loathsome fish with terrible glutinous eyes bulging out of the frying pan at me as if accusing me of some unutterable cultural atrocity. *Kippers.* I never forgot the name. The cottage, and the frying pan, reeked of the word for weeks. My inability to adapt quickly was expensive at first, and the twenty-odd pounds I earned each week was usually all spent on food.

I could not purge myself of the belief that kidneys belonged *inside* the body, or else in the cat's dish, and *not* in a pie with steak. Puddings were supposed to be sweet, creamy desserts made with sugar and milk and chocolate or butterscotch. The English made puddings out of bread or, worse yet, *blood.* The thought of a blood pudding was almost as repulsive to my Midwestern sensibilities as the sticky, pickled, traditional Christmas pudding. Michael's mother saved Christmas puddings for years. She claimed they improved with age. The trick was to inoculate them regularly with large doses of rum, rather like embalming a corpse. She had saved two antique Christmas puddings for us that first year. Mr. Jones left them with us the first night, but I never knew what the blocky dark piles swathed in mummylike cheesecloth were until Michael told me, several days later. I tried steaming one of them in its cheesecloth shroud for Michael soon after that, as per his mother's instructions, but when we cut it open it was teeming with rum-proof maggots. Steamed rum-proof maggots. And there were always inexplicable dark objects swimming through the watery, bland, English restaurant food on those few occasions we ate out. The portions were always minuscule. The ice cream in England tasted like library paste. The hamburger, or minced beef, tasted like dead cows stuffed with oatmeal. The chickens tasted of fish. The oatmeal tasted like newsprint. Chips, disappointingly, were nothing more than soggy strips of uncooked, fat-saturated potato. I stuck to my healthy American ways and as a result spent a great deal of time and money scouring the shop shelves in Oxford for oddities such as creamed corn, kidney beans, cranberries, wild rice, and Betty Crocker cake mixes.

But when in Rome one should at least try to behave like the Romans, even though it is much harder in some places than in others. For example, if you have an American accent when everyone else has an English one, and as soon as you open your mouth people hear "Gee, Elmer, this is kinda neat but we have one back home that's bigger and newer and better . . ." no matter what you've said; and I *was* guilty, in my criticism of the food. Eventually I did try buying more English products, trying English recipes, but I could never disguise my accent. I refused to try, knowing that a failed attempt, a hammered *r* out of place, would do me more harm than good, and so I tried to disguise other ethnic propensities of mine, within reason and good taste.

Bryngessy Priory lies in a crack between two peaks of the Black Mountains known as the Honddu Valley. It is perhaps one of fifteen hundred such monastic ruins that speckle the British Isles, noteworthy only in that its situation is more picturesque than most. The guidebooks mention the temperamental late eighteenth-century Romantic poet who once lived there. Some may delve a bit deeper and reveal its roiling Augustinian past; a few will retreat to its darkest origins in the sixth century, as a hermitage. All that really matters, for the sake of modern tourism, is that the ruins of the thirteenth-century priory buildings are still there, and if you like you can buy a pint of Penrhos porter at the Abbey Pub, wrongly named, for it was once, technically, a priory. You can sit in, or on, the ruins, watching the early sunset over the mountains, listening to the sheep up the slopes bleating out their mute souls.

We had been in England for just two weeks when I saw Bryngessy for the first time. En route to Michael's friend's castle, we were caught in a rainstorm, lost on the primitive B roads of our inadequate map. We weathered the ferocity of the winter rain in his old Volkswagen bug on a beech-lined gravel drive. When it subsided we got out of the car to take a closer look at the sodden pile of stones before us, at the base of a great green mountain. It was too early in the season for most sane tourists to be walking about on the mountain paths, so we were alone in what was once Bryngessy's cloister, now a perfectly manicured Department of the Environment lawn. I could not have guessed how Michael would behave there. Normally he paced through places like that with an intensity bordering on the insane, guidebook firmly in hand, eyes alternately glued to the pages and riveted to some architectural attraction. I was new to the business. It was such a novelty to me that I didn't need the guidebooks: looking, incredulously, at such great age was enough to keep me happy.

He had been quiet as soon as we turned off the main road, trying to find a shortcut across the mountains. I thought at first that he was just upset at being lost. He hated that: wasting time and petrol, battling frustration at each wrong turn. I didn't say anything. I thought that would only have made matters worse. He sat silently in the car, just glowering out the windshield, as I read the guidebook out loud. I suggested we get out of the car when the rain started to let up. I had to say it twice. "Oh. Yes. Of course," he finally said, distracted by something.

As we walked up the drive to the ruins I asked him if he would like me to read more from the guidebook. There was only one more paragraph, giving a brief history of the priory since the dissolution. But Michael waved me off. I had to run to catch up with him. It wasn't at all like him to sulk, to be so distant. He was usually very attentive, especially when it came to showing me historic sites. I wondered what sin I had unconsciously committed, or what might possibly have happened to him since we left the A road.

"Are you feeling all right, Michael?"

"Um."

"What does that mean?"

He suddenly wrenched forward again, heading toward a tiny parish church beside the ruins of the priory. St. David's Chapel of Ease, the sign read. Services every other week. I thought there would hardly be enough people in the mountains around there to justify even a small church like that. Michael stopped short at the south door. "There's a church here."

"I see that. We didn't need the guidebook after all."

"I was here before, but I don't remember the church."

"Prefab Norman construction, right?"

He didn't even listen to me. I sensed that humor was not appropriate. He charged into the church. I ran after him, to soothe, and to compensate for whatever graceless, unsympathizing effect my comment had had on him.

"I've been here. It's so changed."

"I thought listed buildings couldn't be altered without a lot of red tape?"

"I don't mean it that way. You'll think I'm mad if I tell you."

"I won't think you're mad, Michael. Tell me."

"I've been here before."

"That's the third time you've told me, and it doesn't surprise me at all. Your parents live less than fifty miles away from here, don't they?"

He didn't say anything. It was not in his character to fly around like a cat shitting glass and then to suddenly announce that he was experiencing some manifestation of déjà vu. I didn't like it one bit either. I wanted him to be serious again. I needed my anchor.

Formulas for projecting future cost data. Market predictions. Interest rates and comparables. Nonsense was not beoming to him: that was my province. But it seemed neither the time nor the place to question him about it. He was obviously uncomfortable having to admit that much. I stood at the rear of the church while he charged around it, trying to leap up and peer out of the windows which were built up high into the walls, as a defensive measure in the Middle Ages perhaps. I felt a chill. January. Goose pimples. Someone walking over my grave. At last he gave up, announced that he was going back outside, to have a quick look around. I could see him trying to keep a straight face, hands in his pockets. I zipped the guidebook into my purse. Wouldn't need it.

We crossed over to the nave, the original fine columns now flattened and buried, once decorated by the good graces of Henry I's devout Queen Maud, according to what I had read in the book: newer columns from a later church brought low to mere stoops here and there for the benefit of beer-swilling pub-goers. The roof was now God's heaven, the walls and floor were His earth.

As we stood there facing north, one lone corner of the north transept standing out against the mountainside, a slice of sun split through the clouds. From one end of the valley to the other there was an instantaneous rainbow, pure color vaulting over the ruins and turning the dull colors of all things around us into surreal shades of rich iron red, spring green, aquamarines, and emeralds. It seemed to be going through Michael like a sharp sword. He stood there watching like he was in pain, his arms crossed tightly over his chest, silent. Within seconds the sky had clouded over again, the fast-moving ocean clouds pushed the magical sideshow along, and we were left there as it was, the rain starting up again softly, drizzling down the mossy walls, collecting in small, desolate pools on the weathered hollows of fallen stones, drenching us.

We ran for the car, and without another word drove on, within half an hour reaching the better roads again, leaving Bryngessy, its ghosts, its rainbows, its buried treasure, safely behind. Michael's silent humor persisted.

That next day—Sunday—we went back on our way home to Oxford, at Michael's insistence, partly, I suspected, to undo the odd behavior of the day before, to regain his composure. He hadn't slept well at the castle the night before.

The pub and the small hotel in the tower at Bryngessy were closed because it was January and sensible tourists did not venture thereabouts until the weather settled in May. It was still morning, and a hiker passing down off Offa's Dyke path told us that the pub would probably be open at noon. Coal smoke rose in a thin, blue line from one of the attached farmhouse's chimneys, and there were footprints in the fresh snow outside the old cellar doors. I looked at the reconstructed tower, the top sprinkled with snow blazing in that rare winter sunshine, the windows locked up tight till spring. I wondered then, as many people like to wonder when they walk through old ruins, how many eyes had seen that same tower, whose eyes had seen it, thought what I was thinking, felt what I felt, stood where I was standing. Even then I was sure that we were not alone, but the sun was shining like gold and there were only the souls of Michael and me visible and exposed in the cloister that morning.

"I've remembered now," he blurted. I hadn't expected him to say anything, he'd been so quiet overnight at the castle, and all the drive back there that morning.

"Remembered what?"

"Remembered this place."

"You mean you really remember being here before?"

Even though the sun was shining and the sky was the blue of Wisconsin winter—a sharp change from a solid two weeks of drizzle —it still felt chill and crawly in the valley with a wind blowing through the bare beeches that you could hear, but could not feel on the earth. Souls blowing past.

"I told you yesterday I'd been here before. That's what has been bothering me. I couldn't remember *when* or *why.* The name wasn't even familiar to me. But I remember it now."

"Long time ago?"

"Yes. Very. I don't remember the roads at all, of course, and that's what threw me yesterday; but then I wasn't driving the first time I came. You know how it is when you're not behind the wheel yourself. You don't pay proper attention."

"What jogged your memory?"

"I don't really know. Perhaps that rainbow yesterday. I was only a child, but you remember things like that—rainbows, storms. They're almost like turning points in one's life."

"That's true enough." I remembered the great windstorm the year before Daddy died, when the UFO appeared over the barn; and the electrical storm the night the barn burned. A prelude to our departure. Points of reference in life.

"Did you come with a school group?"

"No. This was too far for a school group to come. I was nine, I think. I was here on a week's outing in South Wales, with my mother. And with someone else."

"Your father?"

"No. He was in South Africa at the time."

He turned away from me then, and strode over to the door of the pub. You could see through the glass doors: stone steps led down into the cellar, but the doors were locked, and it did not look as if it would be open that day at all. We looked, but we couldn't find a sign anywhere with its opening hours.

"How about if we drive around, then come back at opening time and ask them about the hotel?" Michael suggested, nervously, eager to move on yet still morbidly attracted to the place, so different in glaring damp winter sunshine from the gloom and rainbows of the day before. We got back into the car, and drove north, along Gospel Pass, up the road with a view down the cleavage of the valley like so many hills of putty covered in mist on either side. The hills were green, dotted with lousy-looking sheep walking on impossible slopes, into Hay-on-Wye, through Bronllys, the Forest, Crickhowell, then Monmouth and home, the January evening creeping up so suddenly that I almost felt cheated out of a day of my life. I did not mention going back to ask about the Abbey Hotel. Either he had conveniently forgotten, or hoped that I had. My husband was behaving peculiarly. He had a secret. And I didn't like it.

We spent our first weekend and many subsequent weekends in England together at Cadfor Castle. Michael's old college friend, Richard Crawford, the owner, was trying to restore it from a mass of dung-encrusted rubble to some semblance of its former twelfth-century glory by slowly, laboriously, cheaply, excavating the dry moat, by ripping out rotten floorboards and beams, or knocking down walls and plaster that he felt should not be there. Cadfor was one of a string of Welsh border castles. Part of it was built in the twelfth century, complete with a crenellated Norman keep, doves in the courtyard, cobwebs in every corner, and an absence of most typical modern conveniences. There was a toilet in the sixteenth-century wing, the newest portion of the castle. The toilet flushed all right, making life there tolerable, but it was usually cordoned off by thick webs of huge spiders. I was often badly constipated after a weekend at Cadfor. All it lacked was a ghost, or so I thought at the beginning.

Richard was a sometime film technician, a backstage prima donna, who could drop names like Ponti and Fellini as easily as a housewife can drop names of soap products. It took me a while to learn that it was not all empty puffery either. Richard really *did* work with such people, if fitfully. He had furnished his castle with the tacky remains of old movie sets, so that walking from room to room was like moving from a twelfth-century romance to the World War I battlefields at Passchendaele and Ypres. He was a brilliant fellow, but very contrary and jealous of his genius. Richard could not tolerate any competition, in anything, and he made it clear that he had a distinct monopoly on both genius and novel dwelling places. Any talk of our quaint eighteenth-century cottage with the mossy walls was abruptly stopped by talk of ramparts and great halls.

Richard seemed to be permanently between jobs, trying to obtain grants from the Welsh Office for restoring the castle when he wasn't relieving derelict churches of their pews or windows, or freebooting on nearby forest land for fallen wood to fill his fifteen fireplaces. Some of the fireplaces were concealed behind more modern walls, but he still counted them, because he expected them to emerge eventually if he had his way.

Cadfor Castle, luckily purchased in 1972, a hair before property prices started to skyrocket in the United Kingdom, was still mortgaged to the dovecotes even though Richard had made a hefty profit on the sale of a previous residence in Wimbledon. He had a fantastically macabre streak in him that made him paint the rooms purple, red, dark green, justifying it by claiming that "*they* used a lot of color," and cluttering the place with bizarre objects, juxtaposed incongruously and casually before such eclecticism became fashionable—old Portuguese plates decorated with three-dimensional ceramic insects and snakes hung on the dining room walls; an eighteenth-century funeral invitation framed and hung over the bathroom basin where one would expect to find a mirror; a NO STOPPING OR WAITING traffic sign in the W.C.; a naked, bald shop manikin standing around a blind corner up the staircase that I never succeeded in getting used to; a plaster head with a concrete grin wearing chain mail and perched on a bedside table; a collection of teapots shaped like cabbages, water faucets, Sherman tanks, elephants, airplanes and ducks, roosting on windowsills and prie-dieux and tabletops everywhere.

The first time I met Richard he barely acknowledged my existence before launching into a discussion of dry rot in the gallery joists with Michael. He was only partly serious about resurrecting the castle sympathetically, although I could never quite put a percentage on that part. It was not being done to impress a purist: hence his wariness of foreign intelligence. It was more a monument to himself, I guessed, and an attempt to impress—or perhaps to fool—those less knowledgeable. Richard fancied having eighteenth-century statues and a Civil War cannon out in front of the Norman tower. A humble woodshed, perhaps built as a chicken coop in the farthest reaches of the nineteenth century, was to be transformed into a "summer kitchen" full of reproductions of medieval culinary tools. He even had plans to build a chapel in the bailey that had never been there, "But could have been," he insisted. I disapproved of the sham, but I was American and had no right to do so. Richard had served his sentence in Hollywood and he felt he knew all there was to know about Americans. Including me.

That first evening together at supper, back in January, Richard condescended to speak to me at last over the chicken and brussels sprouts that I had cooked. He had spent the day with Michael excavating a fireplace in the old keep, while I was silently relegated to the library in the newer wing, only called upon to periodically deliver the odd cup of tea or biscuit.

"Why are turds pointed on the end?" he suddenly barked across to me, taking me by surprise. I hardly had time to consider the inappropriateness of the question or the subject matter.

"I don't know. Why?" I rose like a Mississippi bullhead to the bait.

"So your ass doesn't shut with a bang!" He pronounced "ass" like a true Midwesterner. Thanks to Michael's influence, I had stopped pronouncing it that way months ago. I then committed the cardinal sin that locked me into the eternally American mold in Richard's mind: I laughed. I realized afterward that I should have pursed my lips and asked him to please pass the vinaigrette.

Another unpleasant habit Richard had absorbed in California was to refer to clichés by obscure initials, then expect you to understand him. Describing how a titled local businessman had succeeded in paying off the county council for permission to raze a medieval barn on his property to make way for an asphalt driveway, Richard called it "the old RRO." Royal Rip Off. When I once asked him if the tremendous expenses necessary to restore the whole castle were at all daunting, and were tempting him to sell, he muttered something about the solicitors S G & R arranging it all for him. Michael later deciphered for me: Sue Grabbit and Run. Americans were either M's, E's, or YD's: Marshas, Elmers, or Yankee Doodles. OD's were female English pensioners—Old Dears. He referred to one of his cars, a 1964 Austin-Healey 3000, a scion of the original lemon, persnickety and blue, temperamental and tinny, as HRH.

In spite of his mildly acidic personality, Richard was phenomenally good-looking: large and blond and Aryan; but his blanket scorn for Americans grievously offended me. There were seldom any other women about the castle—he suspected all women of trying to get themselves pregnant by him in order to trap him, Michael said —and the odd one who did share his bed on a weekend was usually as specious as he was: beautiful, but somehow *wrong,* lacking sympathetic human attributes. I enjoyed the castle and Richard's excellent library enough to tolerate his discourteousness. And Michael seemed not to notice. Perhaps he was willing to make concessions for the dubious prestige of being able to tell the other men at work that he was spending the weekend "at the castle." No matter that he slept on a scratchy straw tick and inevitably showed up on Monday morning with blisters, cuts, plaster dust in his hair, paint specks freckling his nose, and bruises on his arms.

In Wales the mist never seems to rise from October until May. Later that same January, the Saturday we came out of the Black Mountains from Bryngessy Priory, for the first time, it seemed a perfect night for seeing ghosts. The mist was low and heavy as Michael and I arrived at Cadfor about eight, the Volkswagen's headlamps making feeble pinpoints of light in the soupy air. But ghosts seldom materialize when they ought to. It was only Richard who cranked down the drawbridge for us and opened up the gatehouse. We parked the car in the cobbled courtyard, slick with dove droppings, and entered the castle through the keep, into the kitchen.

It was never much warmer inside Cadfor than outside, and only marginally lighter. The kitchen was a chaos of discarded archaeological tools, crumbling plaster, rising damp, strips of curled flypaper complete with legions of dead flies, moldy vegetables, empty brown cider bottles, several broken electric cookers that Richard was meaning to fix, old tea bags, paper bags, spider webs, and half-eaten loaves of weeks-old bread. It was a nightmarish kitchen to a tidy American housewife. Its only excuse was that it was eight hundred years old in places. Richard took a hot chicken brick from the coal-fired Rayburn stove as Michael and I sat down to what would become our usual drafty weekend dinner in the adjacent Great Hall. The sound of knives, forks, and china echoed off the flagstone floor and stone walls into the full, warm fireplace. There was hot spiced wine on the hearth for dessert. The subject turned to food, as it so often does during meals.

"There really aren't any good restaurants out here," Richard noted. He had been spoiled, he admitted, by five years of living in London. Not only that, but he had just become *persona non grata* at the local pub when he left without paying. He had claimed that the food wasn't worth paying for, and he was probably right, but the pub's owner had failed to agree. "I have heard that the food is decent at the Abbey Hotel in Bryngessy. But it's only open for lunches on weekends this time of the year and it's full of sweating, inveterate hikers." Richard directed his conversation at Michael. I didn't mind especially since I was hungry and preferred eating to talking just then. Richard sent a quick flash of disapproval in my direction when I picked my chicken leg up with my fingers.

"This is good manners in America," I said, with a mouth full and greasy fingers, but his eyeball had relocated and I was ignored once again. My words fell on empty air; I was faintly uncomfortable and embarrassed by the ensuing silence which meant that it was *not* good manners at Cadfor.

"Actually, we drove right by there this morning," Michael said, still a slight trace of nerves and sulkiness in his voice. "The pub was closed, but there was evidence of life."

"Yes. It has quite the reputation. Some Hell's Angels-type disturbance there last summer, and a local priest has been trying to have it shut down for years now. Claims it's a sacrilege to serve spirits on consecrated ground, but I say if the monks of old did it then why can't the present occupants?"

"They were canons," I squeezed in, my mouth full of potato.

"What were cannons?" Richard stared at me. I gulped down the potato like a hungry pelican. It stuck in my throat, and my voice came out unnaturally high.

"At the abbey. It was actually a priory, and they were called canons. Not monks."

Richard gave me a penetrating and daggerlike stare. "In any case," he continued, to Michael, "the whole business rather snowballed and with the publicity they got more business than ever."

"How extraordinarily lucky," Michael said.

"Not so entirely. All of the press attracted the attention of the local authorities, and they began to press the owners on the fire regulations. Seems the thirteenth-century tower needs a fire escape if it's to be used for guests, but they're not about to tack one on and destroy the character of the place."

"Good for them," said Michael.

"Yes. It really is all rather ridiculous, isn't it? Too much government, I say. If they keep that sort of thing up it'll soon look like America, won't it? 'Europe's Theme Park: England.' Antiseptic. So safe you could puke and it would come out white and sweet-smelling. Man needs a little danger in his life, right? Like going and staying at the Abbey Hotel in the top room of the tower. Thumb your nose at the old GR, right? Twaddle."

I assumed he referred to the Grim Reaper, but I didn't want to ask. He gave me a defiant look. I had a brussels sprout leaf stuck to my chin. Canons, indeed. "And you, Mizz Jones—" he mimicked an American accent, as he usually did when he addressed me, or when he was imitating a moronic comment someone else had made— "what do you think of English cuisine? Warm beer, pablum, and mush? Miss your burgers and fries?"

"I can't complain."

"Well, well. You *have* got an odd one there, haven't you, Mr. Jones?"

With that Richard retreated into the kitchen and returned with his heart's delight: an apple crumble. We ate it in front of the fire, with the *Hippocras*, playing a few rounds of Happy Families. Richard always won. Michael started to nod off in his chair: a hungry, red, velveteen object direct from some late medieval stage set. It made me nervous to be alone with Richard, so I nudged him awake. Richard poured water over the fire to save the coals for another night. The flames turned blue, simmered down. I remembered a childhood gospel: when the flames turn blue, a ghost is present. They were still flickering bluish when I shut the dining room door, the last one upstairs to bed, carrying Sinistra, Richard's fat black patriarchal cat, in my arms.

There were spooks in the house.

Richard maintained that Cadfor was not a haunted castle, except perhaps in perverted American imaginations, but I retained my doubts. A building that has stood for over eight hundred years, harbored births, love affairs, deaths, plots, good men and bad men, cannot be entirely free from its ghosts, whether they are manifested as bits of jewelry and pottery unearthed by accident while digging in the garden, words scrawled on plaster and exposed after centuries hidden, or those funny things in white sheets that appear from around dark corners. There *are* ghosts at Cadfor, and I believe that I have heard them.

It was the first weekend of February. I had just started working in Oxford. That Saturday I was sent off to the library again like a naughty child while Richard and Michael worked on another fireplace in the Norman keep beside the fifteenth-century Great Hall, hacking away Victorian plaster to expose the original stone lintel some five hundred years old. While Michael wheeled the debris about, Richard chipped away furiously for several hours before he noticed some peculiar recurring patterns on the wall. He held the lamp closer and saw that he had destroyed most of what appeared to be a poem, scratched in an archaic hand into an earlier layer of plaster. He abandoned his work, a little sick over what he had done, and asked Michael if he could read what the remainder of the words said. He could not. They resorted to me. I walked over, up the steps, took their lantern and held it close to the wall.

It said *Forget mee not.* How could I ever?

An unseasonably gelid wind rattled the iron windowpanes. The chandelier swayed high up on the ceiling, the ancient oak beams over our heads complained bitterly of woodworm in their great old age. The deathwatch beetles ticked in the icy, empty, vast hall. We returned to the fire in the blue sitting room and changed the subject over tea.

Later that night in, of all places, the W.C. (Richard had painted the small closet vivid flamingo pink, with an old World War I gas mask hung on the door, and a set of false teeth perched incongruously on the windowsill beside two naked Kewpie dolls), scanning an old issue of the *Sunday Times* magazine, I heard something that made me catch my breath and hold it, to hear better. I wondered for a moment if I was really alone upstairs, if there wasn't someone in the hall with an ear glued to the door. I was momentarily embarrassed, when I realized that it was the sound of someone hurt, someone nearby, in the castle, directly upstairs, or in the empty bedroom next to the W.C. Someone was moaning. I had left the others downstairs before the fire, on the other side of the building, and there were only the three of us there that weekend anyway. I was the only woman around, yet it was definitely a woman's voice I heard. A gentle sighing at first, which I almost mistook for wind, then moaning, then nothing, then suddenly a louder, higher, more agonized cry, incredibly sad, so that the air was hushed, heavily burdened with spectral sorrow.

Forget mee not.

I dropped the magazine on the floor beside the toilet and I jumped up. I listened closely once again, my jeans down around my ankles. Someone was crying. Man or beast? It was now hard to tell, drowned out by the wind picking up on top of the crag, whirling around the ramparts. But it was human. Only an intelligent creature could radiate such titanic sorrow. I hurried back downstairs, my spine just starting to prickle.

No. They had not left the room. They were still discussing the new roof for the keep. Their glasses were an ounce lighter and the fire was as merry as ever. Richard refused to believe my story. "The wind," he pooh-poohed. To his knowledge, no one had ever died in or near that toilet. "I'm sure it was your own backside, dear."

Richard had a fixed attitude about ghosts. I think his reasoning was that no one would visit him in his castle if word got around that it was haunted. At the time he was considering letting two rooms for bed and breakfast. He admitted to only one ghostly encounter in his whole life, and that took place when he was very young. His uncle had been filming Richard and his brother playing in the small back garden of their urban Brighton home. Nothing extraordinary happened during the filming, but when the reel was developed they saw a woman in early Victorian dress with a parasol strolling back and forth across the back of the garden just beyond where the boys were playing. As far as Richard, his brother, and the uncle knew, they had been alone in the garden that afternoon. So who was she? Richard refused to speculate.

It was about a fortnight later, in mid-February, that a similar incident took place at Cadfor, and this time Richard could not deny it because he was right there. Again before the fire, this time in the dining room, below the Great Hall, four of us were playing Snakes and Ladders after the usual supper of chicken, potatoes, and apple crumble. The fourth was a vapid, whey-faced but gorgeous coalpit girl whom Richard had collected on the train from Bristol. It was very dark and quiet except for·the odd gust of wind down the chimney at the other end of the room that sent tiny ash fairies scurrying around the grate.

Richard left the room for a minute. While he was out the coalpit girl started to complain to us that he was a lousy lay. She asked if we could drive her home early the next morning. As Richard came back in the room a minute later, we heard it together: the sound of a recorder, a tambourine, a shawm. It was simple and sweet, unrehearsed and unmistakably medieval. The room became noticeably chillier.

"What's going on?" I asked, stupidly. We stopped the game and all listened to the faint music, barely audible over the hissing, snapping fire that had ceased to produce heat. I was shivering for no apparent reason.

"Did you leave the wireless on in the attic?" the coalpit girl suggested. We had been up there earlier in the day, checking the old electric wiring for dangerous frays. Richard appeared distracted. He waved his arm for her to be quiet, trying to locate the source of the drafts and the music. The music was gay and infectious. It seemed to be drifting down the far chimney from someplace upstairs in the Great Hall. The pipes made amateurish "peeps" as if the musicians were self-taught, and not very well practiced. Another strong wind blasted through the chimney. The ashes in the grate rose and fell, and the music and the chill were gone as fast as they had come.

We went back to our game and Richard said that it had just been the noise of the cars on the M4 motorway behind the hill. He said that his brother had heard something like it once before, and had developed the car noise theory, which seemed to explain it well enough for a skeptic.

It wasn't music at all, then. Rather it was tires on the tarmac. Those specific atmospheric conditions made imperfect medieval music float from the pavement miles away into the sky, and from there it was blown by odd winds down the chimney, into the dining room at the castle.

I was not convinced.

7

Me gravat consciencia,
Terret in penitencia. *

—ANONYMOUS,
THIRTEENTH CENTURY

IT was the middle of March and I was trying to make a four-egg omelet in a dented two-egg pan. Michael had come in quietly, set his briefcase on the couch, and had crept off with the telephone to an inaudible corner of the room. I heard him dialing, then soft talk. The omelet drowned out the rest. I tried to flip it but it fell apart. He hated the look of uncooked egg. I tried to patch it, only succeeded in scrambling that which should have remained whole. The menu suddenly changed. I turned to a tomato, to help disguise the mess on the plate. Michael came into the kitchen.

"They're coming. Sunday at one."

"Who's coming?"

"Mother and Dad. I called them from the office today. Mother said she'd have to talk to Dad first. They said they could come on Sunday."

"You never told me anything about this!"

---

*May my conscience burden me
And frighten me into penitence.

[123]

"Gay, you've been wanting to have them over ever since we arrived. I simply thought to call them at work today, and Mum suggested Sunday. If it's wrong I'll ring them back and call it off."

"That only gives me two days!"

"Does it take you two days to cook one meal?"

I looked at the frazzled omelet in the pan. A good guerrilla tries overwhelming force against a weak objective; but I didn't understand what I was up against here. I wondered why on earth I had ever made such a rash suggestion to him. I was neither brave nor reckless; merely a young creature of convention, and one had to entertain one's in-laws, sooner or later. Sooner, it seemed. I let Michael eat the omelet alone, plate balanced on his knees in front of the television, while I lost my appetite making frantic lists of things to clean, groceries to buy. This was all new to me. I had to make a good impression. I hoped it wouldn't be my face in a plate full of mashed potato.

On Sunday they were early and I wasn't ready. I had to greet them from inside the bathroom, calling boldly through the door that I would only be a minute. The moment the words left my lips, I wished I hadn't said anything. There was no response from them, of course. That was one thing that England was teaching me: if in doubt about a social convention, do nothing. There was less to be ashamed of afterward.

I had agonized for hours over the menu: something that neither I nor the coal-scented oven could ruin; something that could be eaten gracefully, with knife and fork; something characteristically American to impress my exotic background upon them and so that Mrs. Jones would not feel competition on her own turf. In return, she could offer to teach me some of her English specialties and become a real mother. Chicken was out. Sloppy, and besides the English ones tasted fishy. Spaghetti was out, too. Un-American. I didn't have many more shots left in my clip. Steak was safe, I thought. Apple pie would have been nice if I had known how to make it. I found a Betty Crocker brownie mix in a gourmet shop in the Oxford market on Saturday. I seized it, even though it cost four times what it would have at home, bought the steaks, returned home on the bus to Warborough triumphant, having spent one week's salary. It would be so easy, so good, magnificently and impressively ethnic. I washed the walls in the kitchen, swept out the fireplace, stole a thick cluster of Phibbs's daffodils in the dark the night before. Perfect.

Never having experienced an in-law—being dewy-eyed and fresh to the business—I expected a benevolent old couple who would embrace me as their own dear daughter. Never mind that our first inauspicious meetings—the dark January drive from Heathrow to Warborough with Michael's father, and five minutes in their garden once on our way to a late dinner appointment at Cadfor with Richard—did not elicit tears of recognition and joy: this dinner would be different.

I had badgered Michael about having them over, but he never seemed to respond much, which made me badger all the more. I had so suddenly been deprived of parents that I was covetous of them once again. It was difficult to appreciate parents when they were always there, all-pervasive. Just the summer before, my entire social and family life consisted of parents. They were both so much alive and omnipresent; I felt their hands, their breath everywhere, without really being conscious of it. Without Michael around they were all I had, yet at that time I didn't really think of it that way. They were just always *there:* immovable, irreplaceable, it seemed. I did not think then of *love* or *need* or *nurturing:* they were simply appendages of myself, and it was all a bit incredible to me, seven months later, that both those appendages had been severed, and the wounds healed, almost as if they had never been necessary in the first place. Vestigial appendages. Like baby toes and little fingers and wisdom teeth.

But even when one had grown up it still *mattered.* It *matters* what your mother thinks, even if you are four thousand miles away and twenty-two years old and married and grown and gone from home. If Mother has told you never to eat raw cake batter because it will give you worms, you will remember that whenever you bake a cake and are tempted by batter. If you write and tell Mother that you have bought a used Volkswagen and she writes back to say that small cars are dangerous, you will not feel good when you drive the Volkswagen. No matter how far away she was, no matter that Daddy was dead, they were both still with me, like phantom pains from amputated appendages. I missed them. I could not bring either one back to me so that is why, I suspected, I was so persistent in asking Michael to bring his parents to me.

I had frequent letters from my mother, politely addressed to "Mr. and Mrs." but really only meant for me. Michael stopped reading them after a couple of weeks, since they were full of family news and homey chatter that only a daughter could appreciate. The letters bore no indication of current loneliness. She had moved into the same apartment building as her younger widowed sister, and the two of them kept busy, apparently well satisfied with their lot. Aunt Dorothy, an experienced widow of ten years, had already coaxed her into a tour to Las Vegas in February. They were planning to spend most of the summer up north in the cabin together. After the Las Vegas trip, her letters started getting shorter, less frequent, more vague. There was less talk of Dorothy and her canasta club and lunches out, more talk of weight loss, new clothes, theater. That Saturday, returning in triumph with Betty Crocker and red meat, I found a letter in the box telling me that she was moving out of the apartment in less than a month. Into a house. No mention of Dorothy. And that was that.

I sensed betrayal. Away less than three months and there were suddenly terrible secrets. I wanted my mother-in-law. I hated being left out, left alone, orphaned. I wanted Michael's parents to see me as an adult. They hadn't changed my diapers, seen my eight-year-old teeth burst forth like misshapen yellow dice, held me by the scruff through a rocky, pimply adolescence. I was delivered unto them whole. They would love me, of course. I would love them, too. They would be my adoptive parents. I told Michael that I was going to telephone my mother that night after they left. I had a mystery to solve. Into a house, indeed. Whose house?

When I emerged from the bathroom Michael was holding court before the fire, mercifully smokeless that day but still appallingly ineffective. It was ready to rain outdoors, otherwise I would have opened the windows: it was dryer and warmer out there. I turned the oven on, lobbed in six potatoes to bake, and went to greet them.

I should have taken it as a presentiment of disaster that Michael had to physically shake his mother's arm to get her attention away from the fire to introduce us again. I shook her hand, warmly I hoped, but hers was cold and limp and dry and not willingly extended so that I had to wrench it up from her lap. "Yes, dear" was all she said, viewing me with a single alarmingly upraised eyebrow which remained, almost miraculously, upraised for the entire visit. Michael's father had a slightly astonished expression that I did not remember from our two previous meetings. Neither parent seemed particularly eager to initiate conversation. Michael stood as a buffer between us, volleying questions and answers. I hoped to God he wouldn't have to leave the room. If he did, I would go with him. Mrs. Jones turned her eyebrow back to the fire.

"Can I get you a glass of sherry?" I said, edging back toward the kitchen. Sanctuary. No response from either front. Michael grinned like a stone gargoyle, regarding me with glazed eyes. Shocked, his father looked in the direction of his immobile wife. His wife scrutinized the fire with that predatory eyebrow. "Yes?"

"What?" Michael said.

"Sherry for anyone?" I repeated.

Michael turned to his father, as if to interpret. "A glass of sherry, Dad?"

Mr. Jones shook his head violently. For a second the look of astonishment vanished; it was replaced by one of benign, polite, and total refusal. I marveled at his theatricality. Michael turned the question to his mother, who seemed not to hear. He repeated it. She turned her head sharply, to look at me. I felt like I was being eaten. Shock. Eyebrow rampant. "I'd love one, dear." Safe exit. I poured for three, drank mine down, refilled my glass, delivered.

At first I had thought of two o'clock dinner. That gave us an hour to chat, an hour to eat, another hour to spare before they would have to leave. Michael said that they would not drive after dark. The sherry did not seem to improve Mrs. Jones's attentiveness. She continued to regard the fire suspiciously, looking befuddled and aghast. I had not remembered that expression of hers from our first, albeit brief, meeting. I groped. She did not seem to hear me until Michael repeated most of my questions to her. Filtered through his lips, they sounded feeble, useless, desperate. I thought that perhaps she couldn't understand my American accent. I went back into the kitchen and turned the oven up hotter. Hurry along the potatoes. One-thirty dinner seemed to make much more sense. I wasn't hungry. I had set the table the night before with virgin bone china. I had bought the plates at Debenham's department store one at a time, as I could afford them: a spectacularly gaudy turquoise Wedgwood with dragons. All I had were four dinner plates and four teacups and saucers. I planned to serve the brownies on napkins. I put the steaks on the grill, turned up the peas and carrots, refilled my sherry glass, and returned to the arena.

I was reconciled to listening to Michael do the talking for all of us. Fifteen minutes must have passed before I was distracted from his conversation. I wasn't quite sure what had happened to distract me, but I sensed that something was very wrong. I tried to convince myself that it was mere nervous imagination. If Mrs. Jones hadn't, startlingly, turned her brow to me and blurted, "Do you have a coal fire somewhere in the house, dear?" it might have been too late for the whole dinner. I ran into the kitchen. It reeked like the fires of hell: coal smoke and brimstone and brownies. As it turned out, only the brownies were scorched beyond recognition. I forgot that they had been in the oven with the potatoes when I turned it up. No need for dessert plates after all. Dinner was on the table before one-thirty.

And again if only I had had the self-control and composure to remain silent, they might have eaten well enough, and left with a quiet but at least a positive impression of their new daughter-in-law. At the table, I tried to relieve Michael long enough to allow him to eat. As it was, the parents both chewed slowly while he chattered nervously. I had to burst in to save him from starving. His food was getting cold, congealed. "I'd love to have some English recipes from you, Mrs. Jones. About the only English thing I can do to make Michael feel at home is to set the table with Wedgwood!"

She smiled. It made the eyebrow arch even higher. I half expected a comment. But no. She stabbed at a carrot.

"I fell in love with this pattern when I first saw it. Florentine, they call it. If they don't keep raising the prices, I might have a whole dinner set put together in a couple of years." I hoped they'd admire my frugality. "What sort of china do you have, Mrs. Jones?"

She kept chewing, staring at her plate. She swallowed. Hard. She pursed her lips momentarily. I felt a sudden gush of faux pas. Perhaps they couldn't afford china? Had I been a boorish American braggart? Cover my tracks. "It never occurred to me to invest in fine china until I got here and saw how inexpensive it was."

"I used to have a lovely set of Spode," she said, regarding her water glass like a frog watching a fly in its immediate proximity. I guessed right. She darted for the glass as if to escape further conversation, drank, replaced it, went for her fork again. "But it was broken." She stuffed some steak into her mouth.

"Oh, how dreadful! A whole set broken? How did it break? In moving?"

She looked at me then as if I were not there, but somewhere over my left shoulder. The eyebrow was focused on my face, but her eyes were elsewhere. I had no appetite for this. I wished Michael would butt in. But he didn't, busy chewing himself. "Someone broke it. By accident, I'm sure."

"Someone broke it! My God! If someone ever broke my Wedgwood, even by accident, I think I'd arrange to have him run over by a Mack truck!"

A fork clattered to the edge of a plate, toppling onto the floor. Michael stopped in mid-chew. Mr. Jones cleared his throat. The astonished expression was gone, replaced by one of sheer, naked disbelief as he stared at his wife. I heard a low whine, like a jet engine heard testing from inside the air terminal: a whine that became an unintelligible word, and then a terrifying, lowing lament. Mrs. Jones slumped back into her chair. Her husband reached across the table to grab her arms, to keep her from sliding onto the floor. He upset his plate and sent it crashing to the floor.

"Michael! What's wrong with her?" I kicked my own chair over backward and awkwardly ran around to hold his mother's shoulders up. She stopped moaning. Her eyes were shut, but the eyebrow did not budge. We guided her over to the couch, where she sat down, stiffly all of a sudden, and turned all her attention back to the fire. I ran to meet Michael in the kitchen, privately, while his father attended to his wife.

"Should we call a doctor for her? I'm scared."

"No." He said it flat. Dull. No edge or expression at all. Final. Full stop.

"But what's wrong with her? She's not at all like she was the last time we met."

"She's fine. She gets these spells."

"What spells? Is she ill?"

"No." He left the kitchen. It stank of coal-toasted brownies and overbroiled meat fat. I looked at the brand-new teacups, lined up ready to do battle. A nice cup of tea. That was it. I put the kettle on. When I went back into the living room, they were standing there in their overcoats.

"Thank you for the lovely dinner, dear, but we really must be rolling along now," Mr. Jones said, reaching for my hand. I seriously wondered if either of them knew my first name; they kept calling me "dear." He caught my hand off guard, waggled it, let it drop. "The wife isn't feeling well, and we won't be a bother to you."

"You're no bother! I've just put the kettle on. Can't you at least stay for tea?" I looked at Michael for help. He turned his back to me, jabbing at the fire. It had started to smoke.

"I'm afraid not, dear. We do have quite a long drive ahead of us, and the weather seems to be turning foul." With that they turned to Michael, wished him good day. He walked them out to their car. They stood there talking for about ten minutes. I watched. Even his mother was talking. I could see the eyebrow jerking with her expressions. Michael gave them each a cursory hug. They got into their Land-Rover and roared away. It was just as well. They were gone by two. I felt as low as worms, drunk on sherry and bitterly alone.

Michael came back in and went right upstairs. I heard the bedroom door click shut, the bedsprings creak. I cleaned the kitchen until four, when I thought it would be a reasonable hour to telephone my mother: ten in the morning, her time. The international operator put me straight through. I heard a familiar dial tone, a familiar ring: gentle burring, unlike the brash English *beep-beep*s. It rang seven times. Her apartment was small. She was either at church, or in the shower. She finally answered the eighth ring, breathless.

"Mom?"

"Gay?" Her voice was gravelly with sleep.

"How are you? Did I wake you?"

"Gigi! What a surprise! You didn't tell me you'd be calling!" I heard a rumpling noise: palm over the receiver. She came back on. "Is everything all right?"

"Everything's fine. In fact I called to ask you the same thing."

"Oh, of course! Everything's just fine! How's Michael?"

"Michael's fine. How's Dorothy? I haven't heard much about her lately."

"Oh?" She hesitated. "Dorothy's just fine! She's going to New York next week to shop and see some plays."

"Are you going with her?"

"No, I don't think so. Not this time."

"I suppose you're busy packing?"

"Oh, yes! Real busy!"

"Well, aren't you going to tell me where you're moving to?"

"I thought I told you? To a house. I kind of miss living in my own house."

"I thought you might. Did you buy the house?"

"No. You know our old farmhouse is gone now?"

"Both of them?"

"Yes. The developers took them both down just last week, and the rest of the barn too."

"That's awful. I'm glad I wasn't there to see it. They were perfectly good houses."

"Yes. I was even a little bit sad to see them go, but they really didn't blend in very well with the new development."

I held back a sarcastic comment. It would be like whipping a puppy for pissing on the carpet. No satisfaction, and the puppy would just go back and piss on it again. "So you're going to rent a house now?"

"No."

"You *are* moving, aren't you?"

"Yes, honey, but I'm moving in with someone else."

I could almost hear the satellite twirling our crossed messages through the vast grayness between us, our breath echoing off the stars. I was caught for a second fat-tongued and suspicious, wanting to ask without wanting to know the answer, without knowing how to ask. Hell.

"Anyone I know?"

"No."

"Well, who is it?"

"I wasn't quite sure how to explain it to you, Gigi. It's someone I met in Las Vegas. On that tour Dorothy and I took a couple of months ago."

"Male or female?"

"Oh, Gigi!"

"Well?"

"It's a gentleman. A widower. He was a business acquaintance of Daddy's. We've known him for years, but you probably never met him."

"So you're moving in with a man?"

"Well, at my age it doesn't make sense to waste time, does it?"

"I suppose not."

"Do you think your old mother is going senile?"

"No. You're old enough to know better. What's his name anyway?"

"Arthur Brekkestad."

"At least you're keeping the bloodline pure."

"What was that, honey?"

"Nothing. Are you going to get married?"

"Arthur wants to. But I'm not too sure yet. I'll write you a long letter now, Gigi. I just didn't know how to tell you, and it's kind of hard to talk about now."

I didn't ask. I felt Arthur hulking over the wires. A sixty-five-year-old Romeo. I felt betrayed all over again. Orphaned, battered, abandoned by two sets of parents, all in one day. The only faithful one was Daddy, and he was past caring. I heard my voice echo into the bottomless receiver. I hated telephones. Voices were not real. You could not touch them, taste them, smell them, believe in them. We dig our own graves and lie in them alone. Michael was upstairs. Mom was with Arthur. I had driven the Joneses out like some dreadful harpy and Daddy was dead. The world had forsaken me. Out of self-defense, I had to turn steely, block off the babyish hemisphere of my brain, be cold and adult and uninvolved, lest I be squashed by despair.

"Sure, I understand. Is he rich?" I couldn't help myself.

"What a silly question!"

"Well, is he?"

"Better off than I am."

Of course she would say that. "That's good. It helps."

"I'll write you tonight, I promise. With our new address. Arthur says he'd like to visit London next spring."

"We don't live in London."

"Oh? Is it far?"

"No. Not far. We'll be glad to see you both."

It sounded hollow. I was shocked, and she knew it. She had seen it coming, but it was done now. I hung up. Didn't even want to tell Michael. He was probably busy suffering quiet embarrassment himself over his mother's "attack," his wife's inexplicable behavior, the burnt food. I still didn't understand what had gone wrong after I mentioned the china. I sat down in the living room in front of the cold, smoky fire with the bottle of sherry, three-quarters full. I finished it, feeling like I had been out in a hurricane. As soon as the wind kicked back up, I'd probably head on out again, reality be damned. It was only what you imagined it to be anyway, and just then I preferred not to imagine anything at all. I thought that I had learned a lesson, taken another step up—or possibly down—the ladder of life. I didn't realize until later what that lesson had actually been about.

A deceptive day; the rain hid behind a bad late March English joke of warmth and dryness. I abandoned my overcoat on the sofa and rode in to Oxford unencumbered. I really should have known better by then, but I didn't want to see what was before my eyes. Not even the old dears with their plastic rain scarves and the young shopgirls in raincoats with collapsible umbrellas fazed me: I stood alone, like a big cheese. The lone, ugly American in my short shirt-sleeves and Bass sandals. The BBC weather had said "changeable with sunny periods," but it said that every day. For once I was determined to accept the day at face value. Michael had advised me to carry a sweater, at least. All I carried was a white plastic shopping bag with a book in it—Salzman's *English Life in the Middle Ages,* pinched from the office—a peanut butter and jelly sandwich, two oranges, and a Curly Wurly.

The office was centrally heated, if fitfully. Barnes gave me another two thousand words of his Lacy essay to type, to add to the existing pile of fifteen thousand that was growing in a locked drawer of my desk. He never asked what became of the master's work once it was funneled out onto my desk and translated into type. One assumed that the dons were harebrained and eccentric. One assumed that one's secretary had the presence of mind to accept full responsibility. That was one of the greatest annoyances I felt about England: one had to *assume* almost everything because it wasn't polite to discuss it. The problem with Americans, I found, was that we were forever bringing up forbidden topics that one should have made assumptions about instead. Like the china at dinner. And the footnote on page 86. Barnes had cited *The Lacy Family in England and Normandy, 1066–1194,* page 985, but it did not seem likely to me that that book—a 125-year chronicle of a single baronial family— would fill up almost a thousand pages. Knowing English scholars, as I thought I did then, it was entirely possible that the author had managed to wring over two reams out of the Lacys. But I was in a carping sort of humor that lovely day. Barnes had only come in to deposit the two thousand words on my desk, and I knew there would be no more work from him for several days because he was off to Wales to do more research. I needed an excuse to get outside, so I jotted down the relevant information about the Lacy book and walked in the sunshine over to the Radcliffe Camera to verify the page number with his sourcebook. After two months of Lacys, I was vaguely interested in having a look at this book as well.

The library was almost empty that morning. Students were not yet anxious enough about exams. The signs outside barring entry to tourists were ominous, particularly if one had an American accent that would not heal. I groped for my reader's ticket, found it. Fortunately Barnes had cited the book's call number in the margin and I was spared a trip to Duke Humphrey's library to seek it out although I might not have minded the distraction that day. It was hard enough to concentrate when the weather was warm and clear and fine, but Michael had burdened me with some very troubling information the night before.

He spoke mercifully little of his parents, especially in the wake of last Sunday's disaster. In fact, it was easy to get the impression from him that his friends and colleagues were all who really mattered in his life, and after his mother's strange behavior, I pitied him a little, and thought I understood better.

I had met his parents, in daylight, together, only once before the dinner, and thought them an artless, bland, middle-aged pair. His mother wore a dirty white apron with embroidered strawberries, had her hair done once a week, prattled on about the Women's Institute over a hasty cup of tea; his father wore Wellington boots, read the *Telegraph,* and pottered in the garden with the roses and the runner beans. Not the sort of people I could imagine trying to avoid as fastidiously as Michael tried to avoid them, and I had bothered him about that a lot. "Why don't we see more of your parents?" and "Why don't we have them over to dinner?" My nagging had rolled off his well-oiled, knowledgeable back until the week before, and I was sorry now that it had sunk in at all. Another lesson in keeping quiet. Tread lightly on foreign soil. Listen to the experts.

The little I knew of the situation the less I liked it, but they were, I reasoned, in-laws, and the ways of other families are always mysterious and noisome. I did not ask him about his mother's behavior, and he did not offer any explanation for over a week. It came unexpectedly, in bed. I was reading Giraldus Cambrensis, a translation from Barnes's library. Michael was not reading anything.

"Gay, may I interrupt?"

"Sure." I knew he was not relaxed. If he hadn't spoken, I might have suggested that he go back downstairs and watch the television until he was tired enough to sleep. I detested fussiness and fidgeting in bed, but I was glad in the end that I had not banished him to the horrid smelly green couch.

"Is it good?"

"Is what good?"

"The book."

"It's all right. I just read about some poor preacher who listened to his parishioners singing and dancing in the churchyard all Saturday night, and then first thing Sunday, at early mass, instead of saying *'Dominus vobiscum,'* or whatever it is they say, he said *'Swete lemman dhin are.'* A verse from one of their bawdy songs. The bishop forbade churchyard fêtes after that."

"I see. How embarrassing."

"Are you all right? You don't seem to be very tired."

"I'm not. I thought I was, but I'm not after all."

"Something on your mind?"

"I suppose, yes. Did I ever tell you about my brother?"

"No. What brother?"

"I didn't think I'd told you. His name was John."

"Did he die young?"

"Yes. He was seven. I was nine."

"Why didn't you tell me about this before?"

"I don't know. Yes, I do. Because it's not a very pleasant memory. I was with him when he died."

"Michael! I wish you'd told me sooner."

"Yes. When I was eight, my father signed up for a two-year posting in South Africa. He wouldn't take us along because he said that the schools were not very good in South Africa. Nor did he want to send John and me to boarding school, so he insisted my mother stay behind in England with us, and they sent us to the local junior school, within walking distance of home. I think he had a mistress there."

"Your father? In Africa?"

"Yes. That's why he was so insistent about leaving all of us behind in England."

"He doesn't seem the type."

"No, of course not. Not now. Anyway, Mother fussed a lot over John while Father was away. I suppose she thought I was the big brother, well adjusted, and could fend for myself, but poor little John needed more parenting since his father had left him at such a critical age. I don't know. But she certainly spoiled him."

"Are you sure it didn't just *seem* that way? I wouldn't know about such things, but isn't it normal for brothers to be jealous of one another?"

"It might be. But there was still no question that Mother favored John." He spoke with acid in his voice. I didn't like it. Michael never said much about his mother. I thought I understood why. Even now, almost twenty years later, he was still accusing her of loving a dead boy more than him.

"Why do you think she favored John?"

"God knows. It was incredible what she'd tolerate from him. I would never think of doing all that he did. If John didn't like the food on his plate, he would throw it at Mother, and she would just smile, mop it up, and serve him something else. He fought back, too. She couldn't punish him. He was always kicking, slapping her, trying to push her over, and the amazing thing is that she *let* him."

"That seems unbelievable."

"He was a lot like my father. He was charming at school, and in front of friends and relatives, but at home he was horribly spoiled, mean, sullen, fussy."

"I don't believe that any mother would tolerate that kind of behavior." I thought of the poor horsy woman in aprons.

"I was surprised, too. I still wonder if it's my fault he died."

"What happened?"

"He was crushed by a lorry on his way to school one morning."

I was mortified. To my soul. What had I said at dinner that Sunday afternoon? The unspeakable. Unimaginably gross.

"I was supposed to be walking with him, but I was angry with him again that morning for some reason. I was always angry with him for some reason. I was walking about a half-block behind him. I saw what was about to happen, but I couldn't call out or run ahead fast enough to prevent it. Instead I just watched. Mother never forgave me. She said that I could have saved him if I had called out. I don't think I've ever really forgiven her for saying that either. Father returned from South Africa then. He was changed after that. Not so mean to Mother. We moved right away, and Mother had a series of miscarriages in an effort to replace John. I felt to blame. She refused to buy new china after that."

"Why?"

"Because of John."

"What does that mean?"

"John smashed all of her Spode in a fit of jealousy on my ninth birthday. She had bought a toy train for me, and none for him. She promised him an outing as his reward for smashing the china on my birthday. You see, he had sulked when she stopped him smashing it, and she had to make it up to him somehow. I begged to be allowed to come along. We went to South Wales, to Bryngessy. He was killed the Monday after we got back."

Suddenly, it all made horrible sense to me. I was too gagged by my own stupidity and big mouth to cry. I supposed the woman had treated John as she would have tolerated her husband's similar behavior. It sounded to me like it was a good thing that that lorry came along when it did. But coping with a story of such unprecedented trauma and guilt was another matter altogether. I fell asleep beside Michael that night wondering who I had married, how he could have endured my idiocy of the week before with such silence, until that night. I wanted to die for shame, but knew better than to do or say anything else in front of him just then. One had only to assume.

I left for work early all the next week, and spent more time than I had to combing my typing for errors, reading and rereading Barnes's work. After his confession, Michael seemed just as unwilling to say any more about it. We both arrived home late, ate out, seldom together, both doing battle with separate guilt. I wanted him to unburden himself on me, but I didn't quite know how to bring up the topic gracefully. My feet did not taste good, and they did not fit inside my mouth very well anyway.

Back in the Radcliffe that sunny morning without a sweater, the book I sought was on the upper level. I climbed up a convulsing, delicate metal stairway and made my way in the circle around the top floor of the library until I found it. I quickly chose a seat nearby, left a pink slip in the vacated stack, and sat down at the empty table with the book. I had a suddenly wretched sensation of hunger. My stomach rumbled menacingly. I had not brought my lunch. I dug into my purse for succor: a Turkish toffee emerged. It had practically cemented my jaws shut when a nice-looking young man came walking along with his chin up in the air, his legs spread wide apart, taking long strides with eyebrows furrowed as only male English students can do. "I say," he said, whispering, redundant, "may I sit here?"

There were vacant tables all around us. I mumbled something through teeth thick with chocolate and epoxy-like pink goo which he, miraculously, seemed to understand. He walked away and I returned to the Lacys, having already discovered that the book had considerably fewer than 985 pages. By the time he came back with his books and sat down, I was engrossed with mine and I hardly noticed him, except for a peripheral awareness that he was clearing his throat, moving pencils around aimlessly, obliquely trying to attract my attention. He finally lapsed into fits of frantic note-taking in a fountain-pen script that was very clear, very upright, very English. I went back to my book, hoping to bring some insight to Barnes's work. I ignored the student, except for those moments when I was aware of his eyes on my face, my hands, my chest.

There was nothing inherently interesting about the Lacys, except that they seemed to have been everywhere in England at once, until one sorted the Ilberts from the Walters from the myriad Rogers. I wasn't sure how I kept on reading the book without falling asleep or being distracted by the student. Perhaps it was two months of exposure to the Lacy name. Barnes's paper was all about Walter de Lacy's connection with a William fitz Osbern who, after the 1066 invasion, was given complete palatine authority over Wales, including the Marches. Barnes was mostly concerned with the hows and whys of their subsequent castle-building and their relationship with the king. Having read and typed the names so many times made me feel some kind of affinity with them. It was interesting to read in the book that poor Walter, builder of Ludlow, Stokesay, Eardisley, Weobley, and many more castles, veteran of Hastings, fell from a church tower and died on the 27th of March, 1085. I had a soft spot for him, even though he was probably pushed, and rightfully so, after he, his eldest son Roger, fitz Osbern, and King William almost completely wiped out the population of the north in 1070, trying to establish control there.

Walter and fitz Osbern were really very shrewd fellows. The king gave them a great deal of land after Hastings: the holdings of more than two thousand Saxons were redistributed to about two hundred Norman barons. Walter's estate, therefore, was considerable, including demesne lands scattered over the fertile Herefordshire plains, up into the hills of Shropshire, across the turbulent Welsh Marches, into the Severn Valley and even parts of the Cotswolds. The Lacy fee encompassed over ninety miles along the central and southern Welsh frontier, which was far from being immediately profitable territory. Walter's wealth derived mostly from the lands on the plains and east of the Severn, which divided his holdings.

His headquarters was located at the castle of Ewyas Lacy, which watched over three rivers: the Monnow and the Escley to the east, the Olchon to the west. The mountain range nearby ran roughly to the northwest, with peaks rising from about four hundred feet at the level of the castle up to almost two thousand feet. Michael and I had driven by there in January. I remembered looking at the Ordnance Survey map as we passed through Longtown. The ruins of Ewyas Lacy were at the far end of town, overlooking the cliffs of Black Daren and Red Daren, standing ghostly against the sky that never seemed to be the same from one glance to the next. To the northwest the view was horrible and still beautiful: nothing but stark mountains, stippled with green in the summer, I imagined, but as I saw it dusted with snow in the winter—bleak and raw, mute and terrible. You could see nothing over Black Daren, beyond which sprouted Loxidge Tump, according to the map, overlooking the Afon Honddu that cut like blunt little scissors through the Vale of Ewyas, fed by mountain streams to the north and the Nant y Bwch from the west. On a clear day they could probably pick out the pimple of the Ysgyryd Fawr to the south which was close to Abergavenny.

I peered up over the top of the book, surfacing for air. My jaw was sore from doing battle with the Turkish toffee. I'd never buy that crap again. At least it had succeeded in gluing the sides of my stomach together so that it wouldn't roar out of turn in that hallowed place. The scholar across the table appeared to be rapt in note-taking. I averted my eyes, not wanting to distract him. I wanted to read more about Walter and his associates before I called it quits and went back to the office.

Walter had three sons and a wife named Matilda, according to the family tree at the back of the book: Roger and William and Hugo. I remembered Barnes referring to Roger—he had committed some kind of treason later, against William Rufus—but I had not read anything about this William before. Probably an idiot son.

Fitz Osbern dies in Flanders in 1071, succeeded in England by his son, Roger de Breteuil. Breteuil plots, in 1074, to overthrow the king. Breteuil ends up in chains, permanently, and a lot of his land goes to Walter. In 1085 Walter dies, plummeting from the church tower, and son Roger inherits. In 1086 son William marries a daughter of Sir Mortimer de Mauro, identified that way in the tree. The lady's name is either lost or insignificant to the historian. The book went on to catalog the Lacy fee in 1086 for Domesday: £234.18s.1d, with tenants' manors valued at £162.17s.11¼d. Roger plots against William Rufus (sodomist, lover of young boys, devil worshiper) along with Odo of Bayeux, Roger Bigod, Robert Mowbray, William of Eu, Geoffrey of Coutances, and others. They are caught and pardoned. Like all good and indefatigable traitors, they just turn around and do it again. Roger is lucky: he is banished in 1096 (others are blinded, castrated, imprisoned) and the estate passes to Hugo, now Third Baron Lacy.

I stopped reading. This was not right. Hugo was the youngest son. According to the tree—I paged ahead—William was six years older than Hugo, and he survived to 1137. William should have been the next in line in 1096.

I checked the index for all references to William. There were three: birth, marriage, death. I had covered them all. Poor William, not only disinherited for some unspoken reason, but also shoved into murky obscurity by his baby brother. I didn't think that was very fair. As the second son of Walter, he deserved more recognition than three sentences in a book about his own family. After all, he must have been of sound mind and body to have married, and lived to age (hasty subtraction) seventy-seven. A veritable Norman Methuselah.

I set the book down, closed it, stared at the stacks to my left seeing but not seeing, instead thinking about William de Lacy. Unceremoniously shoved aside by a prancing, traitorous brother who slaughtered innocent northerners and had the balls to imagine he would reconquer England. And even this Hugo, his younger brother, famous for founding churches, but otherwise a bore. Hugo's wife was barren, according to the tree. Hugo was probably a wimp. Some fellow named Pain fitz John inherited when Hugo died in 1120: not William, who was still very much alive then. Passed over three times. Funny how none of the sons lived up to the father. Roger died somewhere en route to the Holy Land, probably slavering to cleave a few more skulls. The book didn't give any details of Hugo's death, or William's. Funny how mysterious it still was. We think we've come so far, and then it all ends in a mystery. Everybody has to go, but nobody knows for sure what it feels like. I wondered about William. He must have died happy. I thought of Thoreau: *"A man is rich in proportion to the number of things which he can afford to let alone."* No cares or worries, no inheritance, estate, title. I started to think about going back to the office.

"I thought that Americans preferred paperbacks because they could mutilate them as they read."

I rose from my brown study. I had heard something ugly. The

voice was English, Etonian, somewhere off Essex way. "What did you say?"

"I said that I thought Americans read only paperbacks."

"Why?"

"Because they're disposable."

I tried to smile as he laughed, but it really wasn't very funny and I was getting sick of American jokes. What was worse was that I was beginning to believe them.

"What have you been reading so intently?"

I held up my book for his scrutiny. It was sufficiently erudite to spare me any embarrassment. He was sitting in front of the window and there was a glare. He appeared as a large shape, tall, broad-shouldered, fair-haired. There was a stack of six or seven books on the table in front of him, but I couldn't read the titles. I felt exposed, inferior, Midwestern. "History, eh?" he said. "Which college?"

"St. Anne's," I lied quickly. I couldn't force my mouth to shape the word "secretary." He was too handsome for that. "You?"

"New College. PPE."

I dared not ask for a translation. I could ask someone at the office later. Real life began trickling back, a drop at a time. The smell of deceased leather and old, bleeding paper. That unnervingly dull light from outside, and my short shirtsleeves. The heavy pile of indigestible toffee lying in the pit of my stomach. The telephone in Barnes's office sitting unanswered for the past—I checked my watch —two hours. I smiled a blank American smile at the New College man and let him assume my poor Midwestern liberal arts background. "I say, would you like to have some lunch? We can leave these things just as they are." He motioned broadly over the tabletop.

"I'm finished anyway, thanks so much," I said, realizing as I said it that I had accepted his invitation. I was hungry. But I doubted I could eat and maintain my lie about St. Anne's simultaneously. He made me nervous, and I had never even met a woman from St. Anne's, let alone crossed over its hallowed portals. I could see that the weather had turned from glorious to obscene. March. Fortunately he had an umbrella, but half of me still got soaked. I rolled down my shirtsleeves as far as they would go, but wet cloth against cool skin felt just as bad. We walked rapidly to George's Cafe in the market, which wasn't far. The food was nightmarish, but I had learned to order the least inventive items in English restaurants. Tea and toast were usually safe because they were difficult to destroy by either fire or grease or close proximity to a dead fish. Colin—that was the New College man's name—had a cheese and tomato sandwich.

"Unusual name, Gay," he said after we sat down. There were two other men at our table. Student types. One reading a Marxist newspaper, the other reading the muck left at the bottom of his coffee cup. They served Camp there, not proper coffee. Horrid, gummy rot.

"An unfortunate name," I added. The toast went down easily and I gloated secretly, watching Colin drop bits of cheese and tomato out of his mouth as he maneuvered his way around the sandwich. He was awfully good-looking in spite of his eating habits.

"Is it English?"

"I'm not sure what it is other than an embarrassment most of the time. My parents never explained it to me. They're Norwegian," as if that was a reason. Colin nodded, understanding Norwegians, with cheeks full of sandwich. Most English people had horrible table manners, I had arrogantly noted. Even eating chicken with my fingers at Richard's castle did not rival the way Colin was wolfing his sandwich.

"What brings you to Oxford, then?" He pronounced it "Awks-fud." I decided to lie again. It had something vaguely to do with Michael's confession. I wished that he had told me about his brother months ago. I hated secrets, especially big ones like that. It felt as if he had yanked a big rug out from under me. I was hurt, betrayed. He looked different to me the next morning. I felt as if I had to get to know a new person. I also wanted a secret of my own.

"This," I said and I waved my notebook at him, trying to change the subject by sucking up to the snob inherent in every Oxford man. "Can't do this sort of thing properly in the States. I'm working on a paper about the Lacys of Herefordshire." I hoped to God his surname was not Lacy. If Barnes could have heard me. My heart shriveled. I did hate lies.

From there we descended into platitudes from which I found it necessary to ascend several minutes later. I had been absent from the office since ten that morning and the ensuing guilt put an uncomfortable pressure on the sides of my head. Besides, I wanted my peanut butter and jelly. Colin pursued me as far as Cornmarket, where our paths diverged. He asked me if I was free on Saturday.

Michael was, reluctantly, going off to Gloucestershire for the weekend to help his father mix and lay some concrete on the driveway at the farm. I didn't have to go along. I was not asked to, either. I gave Colin the address of the cottage and told him to pick me up there around ten. I ran back to the office where the central heating was not on. I was wet and cursed myself again for trusting my eyes that morning.

He was precisely on time, arriving in an old MG. Looking aristocratic in cashmere and corduroy, down to his leather boot strings, and very handsome, he helped me down into the passenger's seat and we rumbled off to the northwest. It was just getting into tourist season and he wanted to avoid the crowds of Americans and Japanese at places like Blenheim, so at first we visited the reportedly haunted ruins of an Elizabethan manor house at Hampton Gay. Few tourists would be there, he assured me: one had to jockey about six turnstiles, three long fields full of unreliably sullen bovines and mushy fresh cow pies to reach the ruin. It overlooked a field where a village had once stood, wiped out by plague in the fourteenth century. The rippling medieval plow lines were still visible in the meadow. Colin stalked up to the front entrance of the ruin, destroyed by fire about a hundred years before. I followed timidly, suffering nettle burns on my bare ankles in saintly silence.

"Do you have any idea why I was attracted to you?" he called over to me. I was trying to limit our conversation by keeping back a good distance. I did not want to encourage any more lies.

"Not really."

"I knew you were foreign."

"Mata Hari." He had stopped in the middle of the path, near the front door.

"Silly. No. When I realized that you were American, I was astonished. I never would have guessed. I've never met such a stoic American."

"Me? Stoic?"

"It was bloody freezing that day we met. And you in your shirtsleeves, uncomplaining. You're not like the typical American girl at all. I like that."

If he only knew, I thought, ashamed. He climbed up a shapeless pile that might have, at one time, been an elegant porch. "Do you believe in ghosts?" he asked, straddling the threshold that seemed to lead only into a collapsed mass of blackened timbers.

"Oh, I don't know." I couldn't decide just then; but since I couldn't be honest with myself or with Michael about that particular subject, why, I reasoned, should I be with him? "I suppose not."

"Have you ever seen one?"

I didn't know what to tell him. He didn't deserve honesty from me, I decided. "No."

"You've never seen an atomic bomb blast. Do you believe that they exist?"

"You ask some pretty silly questions, Colin. Are you trying to tell me that you believe in ghosts?"

"I don't rule out the possibility." Michael would never have said anything like that, I thought. He was too earthbound, too self-conscious, too realistic. Michael had read geography; Colin was reading economics. I decided that I preferred older geography scholars. Colin's attitude was dangerously close to being silly, trendy. I didn't like people who thought too much like me. It was safer to be with Michael because I didn't *have* to think about such things. With Michael, they didn't exist. He called them nonsense, and so they were.

"What's the story of this place anyway?" I asked him. The walls of the house were still standing, for the most part. Some of the stonework had been despoiled to build surrounding barns and houses. The lower rooms were filled with dampened ash and partially roasted wooden beams. I thought that it must have looked much the same one hundred years before. You could still smell the smoke: a bit spectral, but nonetheless there, lingering like a sad spirit with no place better to go, up or down. In the rooms where you could actually squeeze in around the rubble and move about, traces of the original paint and decorated plaster work were still clinging to the walls in a pitiful state of deterioration: flaming, despondent, reminding me of those trees back on the farm that were now probably gone, neatly stacked in some suburban backyard, logs curing for the next winter's pretty, useless, party-time fires. The outline of a magnificent stairway was suspended in the center of the house just beyond the main entrance. It must have been built of wood. Only a shadow of where it had been built into the stone walls remained.

"Do you remember that railway line we walked over?" Colin waved his hand back toward the fields. I nodded. It had said DO NOT

CROSS THE TRACKS—DANGER. But we had crossed them anyway. "Well, there was a terrible train crash there about a hundred years ago. One of the survivors dragged himself over to this house to seek help. The owners refused to give it. They didn't want to get involved. They wouldn't let him in, nor would they go for help elsewhere. He died, and in dying here on the doorstep, he laid a curse on the house and the family. It burned down shortly after that; they never bothered to rebuild it."

The lead between the panes in the windows was still there but the glass was long gone. The place felt utterly benign to me. "I don't believe it's haunted now," I said, and was immediately embarrassed by my foolish attempt at clairvoyance, as if I was masquerading for him as some kind of a seer, a mystic. To ease my nettled anguish, I muttered something about looking for dock leaves. He changed the subject back.

"Did it ever occur to you that that feeling of yours might stem from something tangible? For all we know, this place could be emitting rays, or waves, or something else we can't see, but we can feel, distinctly."

"I believe what I see, not what I feel."

"Ah, a skeptic. If the temperature drops twenty degrees, do you believe that it's colder?"

I thought of the hall at Cadfor with the music. "That's different."

"Is it? Did you ever have a dream that was so real it stayed with you for days?"

"Probably not."

"I have. So have a lot of other people. How do you explain something like that?"

"You let your defenses down when you sleep. You're more vulnerable. Your subconscious is allowed to run rampant."

"You don't believe in possession?"

"Devils or capitalism?"

"Funny. Not necessarily devils. Any soul can possess another. Since the subconscious has such a tremendous will of its own, don't you suppose it has the power to grasp someone else's subconscious and either monopolize it, or augment it?"

"Too abstract and creepy for me. I can't accept that." I heard Michael talking. I suddenly felt a chill, but I didn't want to say anything. Not when he thought I was a stoic.

"What's a ghost, then, but misguided energy that doesn't know how or when to die? A soul that has lost its conscious mind, its controller."

"You ask too many rhetorical questions, Colin. I don't know the answers, and I'd rather not discuss this anymore."

"Scared?"

"No. Just out of my depth."

I tucked my hands up under my jacket when he wasn't looking as we picked our way back over the fields and went on to visit a few more obscure sights that Colin found on his Ordnance Survey map. I wanted to ask him to put the top up on his car, but I was still influenced by his comment that I was uncharacteristically tough for an American. I clenched my jaw and froze in stoic martyrdom. We ended up that night at the Trout, just outside of Oxford in Wolvercote. It was early spring but the place was already crawling with tourists. Peacocks were perched picturesquely atop the roof of the pub screaming their guts out, and there were big carp whirling in the boiling stream below the dam. Colin decided that it was not romantic enough there with all of the scurrying children, snuffling dogs, and strange foreigners with heavy coats and expensive cameras, so we drove farther on, to the White Hart in Wytham. I was anxious to get inside, but he insisted on sitting outdoors. I had my usual half-pint of lager to his pint of bitter while we sat talking in the courtyard in the waning rays of the cold springtime sunshine. I felt a cold coming on.

Colin was extremely good-looking by anyone's standards, with thick, dark blond hair well cut and casually brushed aside, an intriguingly hairy chest peeking out from beneath a partially unbuttoned shirt. His face was perfect: straight nose, blue eyes, long lashes, the lips of a god; his body was in excellent condition from all the tennis he played. He was certainly very clever, at least academically, but there was still something wrong, something very cold and detached about his approach to seduction. I blamed it at first on my nationality —a cultural and intellectual gap existed between us that, undoubtedly, accounted for the distance I felt as we talked: a growing awareness of certain subjects that I could never broach; unspoken limits to our affair rising up like a wall around the periphery of our conversation. We discussed Oxford, America, automobiles, everything but what we were doing together, as if it were just a jolly day's outing of brother and sister. He must have at least suspected that I was married; I had been wearing my ring the day we met. I suspected that he collected women like postage stamps. Men who looked that good and behaved with such insouciance in front of a new woman could never be constant.

We ate a light meal at the pub. Colin had asked me earlier on if I wanted a "bass neck." I didn't know what he meant, so I said no. When I got hungry, I asked him if bar snacks were available and he gave me a funny look. I assumed that that was what he meant by a "bass neck." I had two pints of lager altogether: enough to set me reeling. By nine, when it was good and dark, we were both off center and punchy. Colin drove me right back to his flat in Jericho in the MG with the canvas top still down, the moldy but sweet Oxford springtime air washing over my drunken face like a stream. I knew exactly what to expect there but in my drunken good humor, it seemed like a game: an unreal, titillating joke.

Colin maintained his rather hard approach all the way into the bedroom, discussing his thesis on some obscure aspect of agricultural economics, his family's country estate in Essex, undoing his necktie and shirt buttons while chatting about the new generation of hedonists at the university. He leapt on me with the suddenness and ferocity of an Alsatian guarding a petrol station. He bit my lips and squeezed my breasts so hard through two layers of clothing, that I actually cried out in pain, which hardly dissuaded him. In fact he seemed to like it. He was hiking up my skirt with all the subtlety and speed of a dustbin collector late on his rounds when I managed to wriggle out from beneath him and run for the door.

I moved like a locomotive all the way to the street corner and only stopped then to look back: no Colin. He wasn't the type to pursue. I checked my watch: 1:00 A.M. The buses had stopped running hours ago, and I was a good ten miles from home. For a second I toyed with the idea of going back, until I regained my feeble sense of honor, integrity, marital fidelity, all still secondary to mere disgust at the way the wretch had bitten and squeezed me. I held a tissue to my bleeding lips and agonized: I had to go somewhere, but it was one in the morning and my options were severely limited. Michael had plenty of friends scattered about the city, but any explanations I tried to give them (turning up in the wee hours with a bloody lip) would have to be ugly ones, and they would eventually get back to Michael. He would never believe them. Out shopping late, then to a pub (alone?), where I cut my lip on a broken glass and time just slipped by. Sure. I had no excuse, and the truth was too horrible to repeat. Bitten by a mad scholar and driven out into the dark night. I suddenly recalled that there was an all-night taxi service in Oxford. I dug into my handbag fiercely. Colin had asked to borrow some money earlier in the evening. I had had at least five pounds which I had foolishly let him grab while I went to the toilet in Wytham. Of course. Seventy pence left, and there wasn't any money at home either to pay the cab driver. Couldn't even make a phone call and still pay the bus fare with that. It was either walk the ten miles back in the dark, or else find a convenient sewer to hide in until a respectable hour, when I could catch a bus.

By the time I had ultimately made up my mind to go to Binsey, I was a good distance down the Botley Road, past the train station. Michael and I had driven to Binsey Church only once before, but I remembered the way even though things often look different on foot at night. I thought of the Skinheads as I walked. Vicious, bald creatures with razor blades embedded in the toes of their boots, who beat innocent people into asexual blobs. I wished I had worn rubber-soled shoes. My wood-and-leather bottoms were shatteringly loud in the dark. The village of Binsey, my destination, was just a mile down the chestnut-lined lane from the Botley Road. It was sort of a minuscule island bordered by Port Meadow, the ring road, and the city itself. You could hear all of this activity buzzing around you at Binsey, but, thankfully, none of it was visible. I remembered the churchyard as being very green, the grass very long and cozily unkempt and soft, and the church very quiet and ignored on the edge of the village. Inside, it smelt nastily of urine in one dark corner: testimony to its remoteness, if someone felt secure enough to pee there. Good place for transients. I hoped I could barricade the door behind me and at least have some peace until dawn, when the buses would be running again.

The chestnut trees blanked even the faint glimmer of a clear, moonless sky from the road. My shoes made munching noises on the gravel along the side of the road. I stopped once to listen for Skinheads, sucking my wounded lip, tasting blood. Nothing. Not even the distant nasal noise of the ring road. The wind must have been blowing from the other direction. I was not at all apprehensive about spending the night alone in an old church, until I actually reached the lych-gate. I groped for the latch, let myself in, secured the gate behind me. An immense yew tree glowered over the graveyard. Small comfort: yews kept the devils off. I listened again, for footsteps, whispers, slobbers from a drunken hobo who might have reached the sanctuary before me. My stomach felt tight, shriveled, dry. Too much beer, not enough "bass neck." I needed some water, some good food, but the only water there was an open well, out in the graveyard—St. Margaret's Well, miraculously created ages ago to cool off a fellow eager to enjoy the saint's pleasures without her consent. They said it cured blindness and barrenness. I was not tempted to drink. The water issued from whence many bodies had been planted. To me it held the same vile qualities as the water back in Arlington Cemetery where Daddy was buried. I did not like the idea of drinking body rot: water filtered through bones.

The church was, predictably, open. Everything worth stealing had already been stolen. I felt uncomfortable for the first few minutes. There was no electricity in the church, and until my eyes adjusted, and I was reasonably satisfied that I was alone in there, I did not venture out into the nave. I finally went to look for either an oil lamp or a candle and matches. In moving about I found that each pew had a candle mounted on a stand at the end. I chose to light one in a protected corner, to avoid having the light shine mysteriously out one of the windows and scare some poor passer-by. By its light I was able to bolt the door from the inside, and collect enough kneeling cushions to make even the ancient wooden pew reasonably soft and comfortable.

I blew out the candle, but I couldn't sleep.

Beer and bites and adultery. The church smelled of it. Accusing, condemning. Why had I let it happen? Why hadn't William inherited Ewyas Lacy? The questions of the ages. I was still very drunk. When I closed my eyes the darkness plunged, rose, wobbled. I sat up and pulled my coat tighter around me. Damp and horrid. I had not felt warm all day. Pride. It had seemed a nice little spot on the sunny March morning when Michael and I had been there: innocuous, ivied, nettle confined to the stream area below the graveyard. At least the urine smell had vanished. I thought about lighting the candle again to look for a blanket—an old choir robe or something that would at least psychologically provide me with some protection from the loneliness and chill. And guilt. It was silly to keep thinking about an adultery that didn't happen. I was blameless. Almost. I reached for the matches. Before I could even touch them I heard it.

A rustle. That was all it was. That was enough. I was not alone. My heart shot through into my mouth. Locked in the church with a rustle. I thought I'd die of the pressure pounding in my upper chest. My head ached. Thrombosis. A rustle. Oh God. I thought of the fingernail file in my purse: a small blade, self-defense, but I was too scared to move for it. And besides, what protection was a small blade against the unknown *rustle*? It was the devil. Cowls, robes, winding sheets. *For God's sake, a rustle!* I was bolted inside a church with a ghost. I deserved it. I would die of fright, I knew.

But I didn't hear it again, which was worse, knowing and not hearing. I sat like a stone, half-dead, hardly breathing, hoping to die completely rather than face it. The dark was like a concealing, smothering blanket over me. I couldn't move myself without making noise. But I also could not continue to sit there the rest of the night, ignorant, in that same position, waiting for another rustle. I had to light the candle, bring the situation to a climax. I did it as quietly as I could.

And it rose the devil. As soon as the match struck, there was the most satanic screech I had ever heard, and all hell's wrath came raining down from the roofbeams. I hit the floor and groveled underneath the pew, too scared to think of a better place to hide. The candle's light flickered dangerously each time the devil swooped by, trying to extinguish it with his big black wings, all the while screaming this unearthly, monotonous, high-pitched noise. It soared from the belltower to the apse, back and forth across the nave like a DC-10, judging by its immense shadow and the effect it had on the flame. I almost hoped it would succeed in blowing it out; at least then I could lie prostrate, undiscovered, in peace until it was daylight when creatures like this one had to crawl back into their tombs. But I had no such luck. It dove and it shrieked, to no avail, and finally it seemed to settle back into wherever it had come from. I could hear it rustling, pacing. I peered up over the top of the pew. Something large, dark, was jerking fitfully back and forth across the communion rail. I stared at it. It was a bird. A raven, or the equivalent in another species: immense and very black.

I thought we might be able to coexist, the bird and I, if the candle were out. I moved slowly toward the flame. I saw it flaring red in the bird's big black eye. It stood on its toes, extended its wings in an exasperated, huffy posture, but it did not fly out again. I quickly snuffed the flame. The bird flew off, to the other end of the church. I heard more intrepid rustlings, then nothing. My chest ached. In that haunted guide to England I had read about churches plagued by big black birds. The devil incarnate, it said. I wondered if I might be better off walking home to Warborough. I thought of the dark roads, Skinheads, the Ripper. I was better off there, even in the company of Satan himself. I lay back in the pew, wrapped my arms blanketlike around my sore chest. I heard some flaps high up in the roof, some more settling noises, and then it was quiet. I did not sleep.

I tried to think of nothing, but something kept creeping back into my thoughts. I began to wonder about myself, my own sincerity; if I had the capacity to love Michael apart from what I associated him with. The news about his brother had affected me more than I had at first suspected. Michael had been somehow characterless before that revelation: a compendium of neckties, foreignness, sweet words in the dark, and familiar smells. But now there were proper shadows behind the common nouns. He was showing me his scars. And I wasn't sure that I liked it.

It was something I had not thought about before: Michael's problems. He seemed never to have any, until now. He had been more attentive toward me than ever on that side of the Atlantic, which might have provoked me to take advantage of it, to test it. Colin had caught me at a vulnerable moment: still mortified by my own social ineptitude, the way I had behaved with Michael's parents, even in ignorance. I was not actively seeking adultery; but Colin had triggered some unpleasant mechanism inside my head that started me wondering, worrying, fantasizing, grinding over the details of my life and marriage. I was worried that all my speculation might only belabor honest love to a curious pulp.

When Michael came home the night before—Friday—I had analyzed him microscopically. What was it, exactly, that had attracted me to him? A curve to the eyebrow, a brownish tooth I had noticed before but never really *noticed*, a bony shoulder, a hairy hand, a series of sports jackets and very English expressions administered at just the right moments. An amalgamation of details: the way the chin moved as he chewed his food; eye avoidance, eye contact; it all boiled down to a foreigner that I called my husband. I wondered about the essential differences between our souls. Could I have loved Colin as a husband? Could I learn to endure his waxy ears? Could it be so with anyone? Were all souls made of the same bright essence that, given half a chance, could merge with any other and come out the other end in a state of connubial bliss?

[151]

It was no use. I was a victim of my subconscious—and beer. At least Colin had been right about that. There was power there. Uncontrollable power.

"What are you staring at tonight?"

"Your fingernails. I don't want to forget what they look like. I tried to remember them today, at work, and I couldn't."

"Why? Are you planning to take a lengthy trip?"

"No. Don't be silly. I just never noticed your fingernails before, that's all."

"An hour ago it was my teeth, now my fingernails. What next?"

"Your exoskeleton, I expect. Just making sure you're getting enough calcium."

"Why not let me worry about that? I am a big boy now, after all. So long as I render effective and reasonably frequent stud service, it shouldn't matter to you."

"What about the others, Michael?"

"What are you talking about?"

"Don't be so deliberately obtuse. Why do you ask when you know exactly what I mean?"

"You know all about the others."

"So you say. But with that last one, what was the quality of the relationship?"

"I told you all about that. It lasted about nine months and that's that."

"But who dumped who? And why? And in the beginning, when it was all rosy and exciting, did you ever notice her fingernails?"

"You're being a silly girl tonight. I can't remember any of that nonsense. She was just a nice girl who wanted to get married too soon. I allowed her to 'dump' me by not giving her the answers she wanted to hear."

"But why me, then? I wanted to marry you, too."

"I suppose you had more control over that female weakness. You behaved unpredictably badly at times, but you never allowed yourself to propose to me, or to pressure me into making statements about my feelings that had never occurred to me."

"Why couldn't you have married her?"

"I wasn't ready."

"It was just last year!"

"I just didn't want to, all right? She was potentially very boring. She wanted to be an accountant. Can you imagine being married to an accountant? We had none of the same interests either. It never would have worked."

He had said it, in so many words, so it must have been true: that there was something missing there, that there must have been something in the soul that was a mismatch. It was more than the study of fingernails and eyebrows; an intuition only the soul itself could provide, or refuse to provide. I wondered how many potential matches there were in the world. There surely had to be more than one.

I could have been in love with Colin, I thought, if he hadn't been so ferocious. He had all the essential requirements: a lovely accent, a background much more exalted than Michael's, an Oxford education. But there was that chemical lacking. Perhaps the chemical was lacking within me. Not enough bridges crossed, or mountains climbed. I wondered if I had ever really loved anyone, or could. Or was human life, marriage, love, just a series of nasty delusions of togetherness, of trying to forget that we were really all alone? It was an ugly thought, a frightening thought, and I did not let myself dwell on it for very long.

"Gay, before you get dessert, I've been meaning to ask you something." An ominous push of the plate outward, a leaning back, presaging unpleasantness.

"Shoot." I blew my nose hard. A vile cold had set in.

" 'Shoot'?" He practically picked the word up, with his tone of voice, and dangled it before me like a piece of cloth soiled with birdshit.

"Go ahead. Ask me."

"I was just curious to know where you went Saturday night."

My spleen froze. I remember making some kind of a primordial grunt as I rose from the table, taking my plate to the sink, hiding my eyes, frantically searching for the most perfect, gracious excuse ever conceived by man. Woman.

"Nowhere."

"That's odd." Fork taps plate. The noise stabbed at my temples. A flashback, four thousand miles. Something yellow, a jiggling pencil, guilt. Women were all the same. "I tried calling you about six times, and there was no answer."

"Phone must have been out of order. That's not unusual." It sounded too eager, contrived. I was not an effective liar.

"Um."

I was condemned. He knew. That "um" said it all. I had to change the subject, catch my breath, erect a blind. "What would you think if I switched jobs, Michael?"

He didn't answer for a few seconds. I thought he was going to ignore me. "That's up to you, not me. What's wrong with your job anyway? Barnes overworking you?"

"No. Quite the reverse, actually. I'd like to be busier."

"You're a rare one. Most people I know would rather be paid to sit back and do nothing."

"It's such a waste, though. My father always told me that it was a crime to waste time. I'd like to look for a job that demands more, pays more . . ."

"Oh? You mean a *challenge?*" He made it sound incredibly stupid, feeble, infinitely and hopelessly female.

"No, *not* a challenge. That's a dumb word, Michael. Barnes *is* a challenge; I just want to feel useful and get more money."

"Have you been looking for something else?"

"Not yet. No."

"Then isn't it a bit premature to talk about quitting?"

"How am I supposed to look for a new job if I'm stuck at the old one all day?"

"People do it all the time. You mean to say that you planned to quit first, without securing another job?"

"Of course."

"Can you afford to do that?"

"Daddy did leave me a little bit of money."

"What about our cottage? The downpayment?"

"I'll have enough by the time we find it, Michael. I'm just sick and tired of treading water and wasting time. There's got to be more to work than punching typewriter keys two hours a day, and reading old history tomes the rest of the time."

"A *challenge*, you mean?"

"Quit saying that."

"Dear Lord, every woman's fantasy: a challenge, but a husband to back her up in between forays into the unknown."

"It's not like that at all!"

[154]

"Do what you will, Gay. Just do me a favor and let me know when it's all over."

I suppose that was the beginning of the unspoken rift. A crack appeared the afternoon his parents came for dinner. Other cracks appeared as offshoots of the main branch in the subsequent days of silence. The crack widened when he told me about his brother, and the block almost split open after the date with Colin. It hung on a thread there, though, and didn't budge one way or the other—but there were definitely two separate sides, joined at the bottom. The bed was always neutral territory, but at table, on the couch, everywhere else in each other's company, we were strangers. Not quite enemies, but foreigners viewing each other suspiciously over the invisible boundary wall.

Given increasingly frequent weekends to myself, when Michael would be off on his own business, I started to ride my bicycle, thinking it was somehow an *English* thing to do. I rode the bicycle to the bus stop in Stadhampton every day and hated it like thunder. Sweating and pumping and cursing through the rush hour traffic, I rode downhill to the stop, uphill back home. My skirt always got wound up in the spokes and greasy chains, and I was perpetually in the wrong lane. I had to keep looking over my shoulder, wobbling precariously, and even then the lorry drivers blasted their devilishly loud and shocking horns at me, making me feel American. English bicyclists never seemed to have such difficulties. I lurched forward with the utmost gracelessness, blinded and drenched by rain, hated by bus drivers, loathed by motorists. But it was too long a walk to the stop, walking bored me anyway, so if I wanted to work in the History Department the bicycle was the price I had to pay for that privilege.

On weekends it was different though: I could direct the bicycle wherever I chose to go, and the traffic was never as bad. As much as the bicycle yearned to head toward Stadhampton, its master coaxed it elsewhere, to places with wonderful names like Watlington, Ewelme, and Chislehampton. Sometimes I would ride it along the lumpy but level paths beside the River Thame, or up onto the bus into Oxford and then through Port Meadow. I rode the bike into the city center sometimes, along Cornmarket, Broad Street, the

Turl, High Street, or on the bone-rattling cobbles around the Radcliffe Camera. It might have been the same old bicycle, but I was a different person on my days off. I was my own master. I was free. When I rode the bicycle I did not have to talk to anyone or think about anything.

Yarnton is a little village about six miles north of the city center. I took the bus into Oxford, then cycled up there one damp April day, just as the sky was clearing, and I found some stained-glass windows.

By 1975, parish priests had begun locking their churches to save them from vandals, yet Yarnton was still open. I pedaled up the A34 that morning thinking to touch upon Yarnton, Bladon, and Woodstock before nightfall and the last bus back to Stadhampton in an ambitious fifteen-mile circuit. I turned left at an old but tarted-up pub called The Grapes, and made my way along a country road to an old school, turned left again onto a narrower lane. There on the right was the Norman church I had expected to find: St. Bartholomew's, peeking out from beneath the big old yew trees in the graveyard. Confetti from a wedding had been trampled underfoot at the gate, making an odd, gaudy contrast with the dull, wet flagstones and the smell of humus that wrapped itself around the air of the graveyard. The church was very small indeed, although it had been enlarged in the seventeenth century. Most of it was thirteenth-century work, according to the guide that was glued to a wooden paddle sitting on a table at the back of the church. There were only a few Norman remnants, such as the south aisle—probably the original Norman nave—and the doorway there with its round, chamfered arch and molded imposts. It was a charming, silent little church, swathed by its monstrous trees in the yard outside.

I knew from reading in Barnes's library that at one time there had been almost as many churches as there were wealthy families in England. The huge number of tiny, empty parish churches and chapels that still existed was testimony to that. I had asked Michael once why there were so many about, and he admitted that he did not know. So much for an Oxford education, I arrogantly mused. In my attempt to be Roman I read profusely at work, and learned that many wealthy laymen wanted the dubious prestige of founding their own churches and appointing their own priests. In villages where there was more than one rich family there was oftentimes more than one church. Whether the churches were built to buy the patron's way into heaven, or whether they were built to somehow expiate the sins committed during the Norman invasion, one never knew.

Architecturally, Yarnton was not an extraordinary church, although the rector and parishioners might have disagreed. What was extraordinary about it, however, were the windows. Wonderfully incongruous stained-glass windows depicting angels, virgins, cherubim, birds, brothel scenes, a massacre of the innocents, an Eye of God, cryptic messages in Middle English, and lots of other biblical characters and scenes. Perhaps four of the window panels were indigenous to Yarnton; the rest came from the collection of one Alderman William Fletcher whose tomb of 1826 lay at the rear of the church. Seen in a mid-afternoon sunburst of stained glass, the tomb was a masterpiece of Gothic revival *kitsch*—tolerable, though, in that his eclectic legacy of stained glass made Yarnton such a fascinating jumble of color and light.

Stained glass must be the Christian equivalent of the gods' ambrosia. Color is never so vivid as when the sun streaks through it. Pompeii and Herculaneum can't hold a candle to the reds and blues of medieval stained glass. Look at them long enough, these simple medieval windows, and the brilliant colors and primitive renderings become something else, taking on an existence independent of the church walls. It was such a pretty little church, I thought: in a way a shame to be there all alone. It was selfish. But Michael said he had a valuation to do in Newbury that day. I wasn't sure if I should believe him. I had no reason not to, except for Colin. Guilt breeds suspicion. I tried to immerse myself in Yarnton, almost vindictively.

And make god thy frende at thy last end. Greete, richlyng, greete (Woe, rich fool, woe), it said on one fifteenth-century window in oddly shaped, bubblelike scrolls coming from the beaks of little medieval birds: fascinating, beautiful, disturbing in their simplicity. Whatever could have made men think such things? A funny little bird wearing a fantastic headdress appeared on one panel, saying *Greete, richlyng, greete.* The artist had a terrible preoccupation with confession, repentance, heaven and hell. Could they really have been so much worse than us? Not being Catholic, I could not understand the necessity of confession. If one felt forgiven, wouldn't it be too easy to just go out and commit the same sins all over again with a clean slate? Yet on the other hand, if I could have confessed the sin of Colin to a faceless priest, and believed myself absolved, then perhaps these rifts and cracks might never have appeared between Michael and me.

I wondered how the *"richlynges"* could tolerate this rubbish in their own churches. Here they would be up at the front in their own personal pews, in their own church, listening to their own priests who were fed and clothed and housed at their expense, and they had to listen to this? The world might have seemed smaller then. Things were perhaps interpreted more literally; but if so, then I had to pity them. They did not have the benefit of higher education at a liberal arts college in the American Midwest.

Ye schal praye for the fox, said an owl on the same window. It was odd that birds should be saying that. After all, a *richlyng* had built St. Bartholomew's. Why should that be reason for woe, I wondered? As meager as my religious training was—two fitful years of Lutheran Sunday School when I was nine and ten years old—I recalled catchy little tunes and phrases like "Jesus loves me," and "Jesus loves the little children, all the children of the world." They told us that Jesus died for our sins because He loved us. That was that. It never made much sense to me, but the teacher said that so long as we loved Him we were okay; although I thought then that it would be pretty hard to love someone whom you had never met. Sure, God gave us the pretty flowers, the fuzzy caterpillars, the trees, the frogs. He made everything, but God never hugged me or came to dinner. Jesus never squeezed my hand and told me that He loved me. It was all so difficult to conceptualize at age ten.

The Sunday School teacher never spoke to us of hell, guilt, adultery. That was for the Catholics—the sinners—she said, and maybe she felt that we were all blameless little angels (spoiled suburban brats actually: greedy and cruel to one another), with nothing to worry about in the hereafter. News of hell would come later, from Catholic friends. I worried about hell occasionally, but I worried more about ghosts. They seemed more plausible.

Yet medieval men must have known about forgiveness. Even I knew that God was supposed to forgive me provided I was genuinely sorry for what I had done. Why the hair shirts then? Why sleep on broken glass, bathe in icy water and endure threats like the ones uttered by the stained-glass birds in the windows? Why starve when there was plenty of food to eat? Surely feeling sorry was penitence enough. Were things really so bad then that salvation was not to be had without extreme self-mortification? It seemed so ignorant, so unnecessary.

I was not very happy about some of the things I had done in my life: the fornicating, the lying, the laziness, even wearing rouge and mascara bothered me at times, but my conscience usually punished me enough. Although I continued to sin most passionately (the flesh is weak, and I believed I was hurting no one but myself), I also continued to regret it. Living with Michael before we were married, even briefly, had been a sin. Buying expensive creamed corn and kidney beans instead of cheap pork pies and tripe was a sin. But if I decided to spend the rest of my days walled up somewhere, encased in hair or stone or metal, weeping and bleating out my transgressions, that would be downright selfish, and I wouldn't be doing anyone any good: not myself, not God, not my mother—that much I had learned from Michael's forefathers. Best just to feel sorry and try harder next time. Easier that way too.

Poor sods. It couldn't have been very nice going around hating yourself all the time. I thought of Colin and my thwarted adultery only fleetingly now. Michael and I did not actually argue, so our cold war was not too apparent. It was easy to ignore, like well-deserved guilt. Still, as I sat there in a pew at Yarnton, I thought that when your wife and your children could curl up, die, and rot before your eyes in a matter of hours, life was balanced on a tightrope much thinner than today. When digging a grave for them you might accidentally overturn Grandma and Grandpa's bones and unleash plague again in the process; when the ends of the earth went no farther than the shire boundaries; when death was upon you with an evil wink of the eye without leaving you the time to confess, to do a few more good deeds, then perpetual readiness was the only answer, the only sensible approach.

Perhaps things hadn't really changed that much. I could get squashed by a truck cycling home that night, and where would that leave my eternal soul? The world was a little bigger now, heaven and hell were perhaps less tangible above and below. Perhaps those smarmy, slick morticians shielded us effectively from exposure to physical corruption—but wasn't it still all the same? Birth, life, adultery, death—the past, the present, the future; here today, gone tomorrow; the same basic functions?

The difference was, I thought, that their lives mirrored the seasons and were subject to the seasons, where we are protected from the seasons. They were conscious of themselves on the middle earth, with the heavens above, the demons below. We see ourselves as a rotating pinprick in an ever-expanding universe. They touched God with their simplicity. We avoid God in our sophistication. Their year began in April; ours begins in January, not with a rebirth, but with the frozen hands of winter clutching at our throats.

I remembered from David's class that their vocabulary mirrored nature, too: full of homely, fresh, lively words. An old man who had lived beyond his useful years was a *fulle-flet,* or "one-who-fills-the-floor," rather like I was in Barnes's office. He was not a senile octogenarian, or an institutionalized senior citizen. If a man was *mete-less* he had no food; if he was *undeadliche* he was still alive. They seemed to move more with nature, while we try to fight it, triumph over it. They could speak of *iolyfte, merthis, gale, gomenes, murthe,* and *gleowes.* We speak of having fun. Rather than expanding our vocabulary along with our technology over the centuries, we seem to have reduced it. Their satisfaction was in mere survival, or, for the upper classes, the meanest quality of that survival. We survive regardless of drought, heat, flood, or cold.

The standard of living is only a function of the times, I realized. The poor were only as uncomfortable as the rich were comfortable, and the differences between them were much fewer than they are now. For the wealthy then life was easier, but there was less overall difference in the way of life between the rich and the poor—hence, the society was probably more stable. Our modern satisfaction is not a function of mere survival; it is a multiplicating elaboration on a theme of survival. It is transitory, materialistic, unnatural. As our universe expands, our world contracts. Life has become epitomized by the ideal of urban—or even suburban—living, like in Towering Oaks. Where have the trees gone? What has happened to the smell of wood smoke? Where is birdsong? The relief of a big, warm fire after the cold work of chopping ice in order to draw a bucket of fresh water? The warmth of a true husband in a clean, guiltless, cold bed? Gone with our luxurious, sophisticated way of life. Made redundant by our high standards of living and dying. You couldn't even build a little hut these days without installing hot and cold running water, an indoor toilet and, if you could afford one at all, a tiny, useless fireplace that probably wasted more heat than it produced.

I was not sitting there in Yarnton church trying to idealize any nonexistent pastoral, idyllic way of life. There has never been a Golden Age in the history of man. In 1100 it was lice and fevers and war; in the 1970s it was the atom bomb and cancer and divorce. One could just better see the essence of life then without the modern haze of life-sustaining machinery, smog, and television.

I had heard somewhere that low-pressure weather systems have an obvious influence on human behavior. That women's cycles make them more accident-prone at a certain time of the month. That full moons make you anxious and randy. That men prefer sex in the summer, women in the winter. Was it possible then that what was happening between Michael and me was only cyclical? Rooted in the turning of the earth around the sun? That perhaps once we reached the solstice in June, life would resettle? We might then speak to each other easily, and go places together again. I used to feel very good when it stormed. An aspect of my animal self, I supposed. But it never stormed like that in England.

I fully realized that my perceptions of life in the twelfth century were based primarily upon the small amount of history I had managed to absorb at Madison and in Barnes's office: modern interpretations as well as translations of contemporary twelfth-century chronicles. Yet no matter how many different historians I read—Maitland or Stenton or even Giraldus Cambrensis—each one told me a different story, each one was totally convinced that his was the only correct way of perceiving the facts. And who was I to judge? A sometime secretary, an adulteress, a person who sat in churches and daydreamed; not a person who nose-dives into old accounting books with an academic vengeance. In order to understand, I wanted to know how it felt to be alive in 1137: what it was like to inhale wood smoke all day long in a house without a chimney, to rely on horses and mules for transportation, on leeches for good health. It did not help me much to know how many sheep were kept at Margam Abbey in 1225, or what the diocese of Llandaff was worth in 1312 in terms of parish church prebends. Tombs revealed twelfth-century skeletons exactly like twentieth-century human skeletons. Certainly all medieval men did not have unnaturally elongated, pointy toes, sunken dark eyes, grossly disproportionate bodies; nor did all women have tiny button breasts and bellies like overripened pears. They might well have been shorter, less well fed; but they were still Homo sapiens with opposable thumbs, ten toes—five per foot, with a bit of luck. And they had feelings. In their skins and in their hearts.

It was dark by the time I got back to Warborough from Yarnton. It had not been much fun weaving down the busy main road on a Saturday night with only the tiny, faltering lantern, which went out when I hit rough spots. I had already been bumped off the bicycle once in the dark that night by a slow-moving vehicle without lights on a small country lane near Yarnton, and the rear reflector had been smashed. I had also skinned my knee when I fell, it hurt like hell, and I was not keen to have it happen again. I pulled up to the front door of the cottage around eight. Thatch and roses, indeed. Michael's Volkswagen was parked on the road. Kindred spirits: we drove the same model car on opposite sides of the Atlantic. I could see the kitchen lights were on as I put the bicycle into the shed with the bottle collection. I was faintly annoyed. I had expected him to be at the Nag's Head. The house was very quiet, and cold, as usual, which made me even madder. At least he could have lit a fire.

Michael was sitting at the dining room table having a cup of tea and reading the *Financial Times*. I noted with disgust that the soggy teabag had been plopped rather unceremoniously onto the kitchen counter without regard to the resulting stain. Kitchen bleach was expensive, and I had to pay for it out of my tiny salary.

"Where've you been?" His eyes read the clock accusingly. I had a fleeting sensation of déjà vu.

"At a Lupercalia." I dropped the teabag into the trash and wiped at the stain furiously, making a great show of disgust.

"You've been around classical scholars too long. Be careful of the drinking vessels in that department."

"Where've *you* been? You were supposed to be in Newbury today." I saw that he had had supper. There was an empty packet of biscuits in the trash, on top, and telltale crumbs on the table. I was peeved at that. If I didn't have to cook for *him*, I wouldn't bother to cook for myself. He had, unthinkingly, piggishly, condemned us both to a supper of crap. I opened the refrigerator to forage. Nothing. One pickled beetroot, shriveled. Some raunchy cottage cheese. A mutilated handful of watercress.

"Appleyard went instead. I stayed here, pottering in the garden all day. Did you notice that the shed was cleared out a bit? I talked Phibbs into parting with a fraction of his bottle collection so that you'd have more room for your bicycle."

"Um."

"Where were you all day?"

"Out. Touring."

"We could have gone together. You were gone by the time I came back from the office this morning."

"I didn't expect you to come along. And besides, I thought your bike had a flat tire."

"I could have repaired it easily enough."

"I thought you wanted to work in the garden. You've been making noise about it for weeks."

"You could have stayed to help. It's a mess out there. All Phibbs has ever grown are cabbages, broad beans, and weeds. I swear he never saw a tomato or a lettuce in his life. Where did you go?"

"North Oxford."

"Good Lord. What's up there?"

"Volvos. Big red brick houses. Big Chewder semis all in a row."

"Until eight?" I ignored him and his insinuating tone, and dug into the cupboard. Two ossified slices of Mother's Pride. I turned on the oven to toast them. It still stank distantly of coal.

"I went up to Yarnton."

"Oh. It's nice up there. You should have told me. I haven't been up there in years. I used to live on the way up there, just off the Woodstock Road, on Polstead Road. In a room in one of those ghastly red-brick houses."

"With gravel front gardens. I'll bet they're cold as hell in the winter." I buttered the toast and dropped a spoonful of strawberry jam onto each slice. I could never tolerate marmalade. Not even Cooper's, which Michael said was the best. Too bitter. Of course strawberry jam cost more, but it seemed like an innocuous luxury. No one ever went to hell for eating strawberry jam anyway.

"I thought we might head west again tomorrow," he said, as if anticipating some negative response from me. His tea was gone, and the newspaper was suspended in an unreadable position over his left knee.

"But tomorrow's Sunday."

"I know. But I've got to see a property near Bristol on Monday, and we could stay the night at the castle with Richard tomorrow. You can get off Monday, can't you? Make a day of it with me? Barnes can spare you one day, surely. I can call Joseph tonight and have him pass the message along to his father if he's not in."

I wasn't about to argue with that. While Michael telephoned Joseph Barnes I took my toast and milk into the sitting room, switched on the electric fire, and plopped down onto the green abomination that Phibbs referred to as a sofa. I had located one electrical outlet in the room, and we had one lamp. There was a new television set as well, but it was an either/or situation since neither of us had gotten around to visiting an electric supply store for a two-way plug. I had finally found an outlet in the bedroom, too, but we had no lamp for that room anyway. Bedtime meant bougies in an old brown cider bottle. I shuddered to think of what I might discover up there by the cruel light of a forty-watt bulb. Our spider had, magically, disappeared. I didn't tell Michael that it was stuck to the rubber sole of my left sneaker.

"No problem." He came in and plumped himself down in the gold easy chair. I hated that chair, almost as much as the couch. When you sat in it, it exhaled damp, putrid breath. I never Hoovered underneath it because of that smell. I was afraid. In three and a half months of habitation, all I had added to the cottage walls were two eighteenth-century copperplate engravings of an Australian frog and some nameless greenish lizard with tiny arms and legs, both gaudily painted at some point within the past two years. Other than the items that came in a package with Michael, I had bought only one battered old brass candlestick—for guests—to spare us the embarrassment of cider bottles, and a basket full of knitting wool which I hoped to transform into an Afghan to hide the nauseous green couch.

"I didn't realize that you would be so dispensable."

"On Mondays I am especially. Barnes has tutorials all day and doesn't come in until Tuesday. Why don't you light a fire so that I can unplug the heater and turn on the television?"

Michael dutifully went into the back hallway, where we had relocated the woodbox, and returned with an armload and some old newspapers for kindling. "What is Barnes writing these days?"

"An essay for *Archaeologia Cambrensis*."

"Sounds dreary."

"It's not so bad. It beats typing letters of recommendation and lecture notes."

"What is his subject?"

"Something about the Lacys of Herefordshire. Lots of names and dates and battles. Some of it is fun. Bastards and nutters and that sort of thing."

"Redeeming characteristics of any family, I'm sure. My grandmother was mad. She forgot how to cook when she was forty-five

[164]

and stopped talking at the same time. The silence was fine, but my grandfather committed her when he got hungry. I suppose nowadays they have estrogen, and fewer women end up in asylums."

"You're horrid, Michael. Remind me to make fun of you when you go bald and impotent." I went back into the kitchen for more forage, but I couldn't face the rancid cottage cheese. I tipped it into the trash and made myself a cup of tea instead. When I went back into the sitting room Michael was watching the "Match of the Day" by firelight, slumped deeply back into the chair. I just couldn't face the sofa again. Sitting on the gritty carpet was even better than the sofa. I settled down at Michael's feet, but he seemed not to notice. Soccer bored me, but I was too tired to watch anyway. I sipped the tea in silence, getting drowsier, mesmerized by the bluish jiggles on the screen, darting over the walls and ceiling like lost little spirits, until I could not keep my eyes from crossing. I leaned my head back on Michael's leg, but it fell away, limp. He was already asleep.

The daffodils passed their prime, then the tulips, too, and it was May. I missed Wisconsin thunderstorms—violent weather, that brought out the baser mammal in me. In England the weather was always the same. There were never those exhilarating extremes that created thunder, lightning, tornadoes back home. I wondered for a long time about what it was that I was missing that spring. I finally realized, partway through May, that what I missed was *noise* and unexpected violence. Electrical charges from above. English spring was annoyingly *quiet,* and utterly predictable.

And so was Warborough. Except for occasional forays to Cadfor, we had got used to spending most of our free time apart, although, as usual, this occurrence was never explicitly discussed. Michael just seemed to be much busier elsewhere. He was laying concrete or fixing roofs for his father, or working at the office most weekends. Mercifully, he did not pressure me to go along to his parents' with him, although he did, occasionally, ask politely if I would like to accompany him. I always declined, for their sake as well as mine.

If Michael was away he took his car, leaving me with the unenviable choice of either bicycle or bus for my leisure transportation. I sat thinking about that one warm May Wednesday afternoon in the office with nothing to do but leaf through musty tomes once again. Barnes had not been in for a week and the telephone had rung three times. I had written six letters to my mother, and might even have abandoned the office altogether if it hadn't been for a tattling harridan in the next office with the unnerving habit of popping in on me at four-fifteen several times a week. She discovered my desk empty often enough, in the beginning at least, to have reason to say something about it to Barnes. Of course he repeated the gossip to me, I was duly mortified, and thereafter stayed put—in bored torpidity much of the time—until I heard the four-thirty bells.

It was about three that Wednesday afternoon when, fidgety and sore, I summoned up the courage to telephone Richard at Cadfor, to ask him if he would mind me coming alone for the weekend. Michael had a property to value in Birmingham, and I did not especially want to go along. Nor did I want to waste a potentially warm May weekend alone in Warborough, still thinking of Colin, hoping he would not drop by the cottage again, and when he didn't, rather wishing he would. Richard probably needed a good meal more than anything, so he agreed to meet me at the bus station in Chepstow late that Friday night.

I was embarrassed the whole way there, thinking that I might have acted rashly in inviting myself to the castle alone. After all, Richard was Michael's friend, not mine. That was abundantly clear in the way Richard skirted around me when I visited, and in his constantly deprecating references to Americans, although he was never straightforwardly rude to me. When the bus halted in Chepstow I was almost loath to get off; but I did, and Richard was too sleepy to be anything but distantly polite.

When we got to the castle about midnight he crept off to his own pine-paneled master suite on the first floor, leaving me to my own devices. I took a long, luxurious, hot bath in his oversized tub, and then squeaked up three flights, past the wretched manikin poised to attack, to my room on the third story. The same orange sheets had been on the bed since March. I had no idea how many bodies had tossed in them, nor did I care. I fell asleep without inhaling too deeply.

Richard had retained his evangelizing distaste for Americans throughout our five-month acquaintance. He made fun of spray-can cheese, useless kitchen gadgets, wastefulness. As long as I kept out of his way and didn't ask too many questions, he could tolerate having me around. It really didn't matter how intelligent my questions might be: uttered in an American accent they all sounded moronic to Richard. When he wanted to mimic an idiot he invariably used an American accent. When I visited, our paths were mutually exclusive. I was either in the library or the kitchen: he was either in the keep or the Great Hall. We kept well away from each other.

The kitchen in the keep stank worse than ever with the warm weather coming on. Rather than relax on the croquet lawn with a book that weekend, I decided to attempt to redeem my reputation and spend it scouring and scrubbing. If I could not talk or think, at least I could work like a dumb mule. When I got up around nine on Saturday morning Richard was already gone, leaving a series of notes scrawled on the kitchen chalkboard: *RAYBURN. CATS. LOO. GONE TO CARDIFF. BACK FOR SUPPER.* He had remembered to change the date on the wall calendar, and there were two pints of milk waiting on the other side of the drawbridge. I brought them in and shut the gate snugly behind me.

The old kitchen in the keep was more than unkempt: it was like Armageddon. Dark cobwebs hanging in dismal strings wafted on unseen breezes and drafts of cold air. Water had leaked through and the plaster from the walls and ceiling was coming down, forming hard piles on objects underneath. The one glass window, set at the distant end of a six-foot-thick tunnel cut through the solid stone walls of the old keep, was opaque with dirt. Dextra and Sinistra, fixed and fat like two old capons, had succeeded in turning the flagstone floor beneath and around the butcher-block table where they were fed into a veritable charnel house. A black plastic trash bag about five feet high and just as wide bulged out from between the sink and one of the cracked marble counters that Richard had filched from an old butcher shop gone out of business. It looked as if the bag would tear right through if I tried to pick it up.

First things first, I thought. I fed coal to the dying Rayburn to ensure enough heat for a bath that night and a hot supper. I fed the cats, and dumped disinfectant into the upstairs toilet, letting it sizzle and stew. From there I returned to the kitchen, the room in by far the most dire need of attention, and started by slowly removing the garbage bit by bit. Once that was cleared out I could sweep the floor, then climb up a small stepladder and sweep the ceiling. That accomplished, I washed and stuffed a chicken for supper and started to clean and dry a month's worth of dirty dishes, setting them back into the cupboards. I had already started in on the pots, most of them covered with old, flaked plaster, when I heard a tapping noise coming from the direction of the gatehouse.

Ghosts have an annoying habit of appearing when and where they are least expected, and when they are least wanted. We are not aware of the rules that govern their dimension: some ghosts are manifested as sounds, like the crying I heard at Cadfor in early February, and the music in the hall later that month. I had actually felt the hall go cold that night, seen the words scratched into the plaster, heard them moaned later, but I had never actually seen anything that could be construed as a *ghost* there. Which is perhaps why the tapping was not an alarming noise. I wiped my soapy hands on my jeans, unruffled.

Richard would not have been back that early: it was just gone three. As far as I knew I was alone in the castle, so I suspected that it might have been a dove caught in the eaves. I left my pots in the sink and went out through the courtyard to check. Richard was not fond of the doves. If Dextra and Sinistra had been trainable, he would have taught them to attack and eat them; but I still had compassion for them, even the ones that had crossed with pigeons and came out with ugly spots looking like large carp in murky city ponds. I could not bear to see them suffer.

The gatehouse door was still shut. Sunlight streamed in through the holes left by missing slates on the roof. There were no birds in there. I felt curiously uneasy, almost as if the temperature had dropped, or the humidity had risen all around me. It felt like I was being watched. Carefully watched. My spine tingled. It was a bad omen. I should have gone out into the garden then, until the sensation passed, and I did in fact try to turn the handle on the gatehouse door, but it wouldn't move. It was temperamental. But what nonsense. I had to finish the pots, I knew, before the water got cold. There wouldn't be any more hot water to spare until late that evening, when the Rayburn would be cooking bravely once again. I went back into the kitchen.

He was standing in the corner by the cupboards, dressed only in a loose whitish shirt that hung to mid-thigh, unlaced all down the front. I didn't really see him until I had securely shut the courtyard door with its two latches and was within fifteen feet of his face. By then it was too late. He was saying something to me that sounded more like an echo, the words reaching my ears after he pronounced them. I could not understand a word of it. It sounded as if he was speaking French, but I couldn't be certain. His words were clipped, guttural, the only ones I recognized sounding marginally like *femme* and *vienne* and *Dieu* or *Jésu.* He was so close to me that he did seem quite real, no matter what I thought later. He was not composed of little bubbles, or static lines, as people have variously described ghosts. I was only taken aback by the suddenness and strangeness of his appearance. His voice was distant, though, and he seemed to be looking *through*—or just beyond—me. His features were rather indistinct in the darkness of the kitchen, the only window nearby obscured by filth and the approaching sunset.

Whatever could I say to a strange man wearing only a loose nightshirt and speaking some odd language? Enough inexplicable things had happened to me at Cadfor in the past five months that I wasn't overwhelmed by this. For all I knew, Richard was playing a trick on me with one of his actor friends from "Everyman," crawling out of the woodwork when my back was turned to deliver a soliloquy and frighten the American underpants off me. I would have been faintly irritated, embarrassed to be the brunt of the joke, if I wasn't, just then, completely horrified by what happened to him.

The man was reaching for my arm, his face slowly coming out of the shadows in the corner until I could see the dark hair, the same deep, dark eyes. Then suddenly his face seemed to turn into that of a much older man, bald, almost completely toothless except for a couple of oddly spaced, uneven, blackened fangs in front. I hardly had time to back off. A lecherous, terrible sneer spread across his suddenly ugly features, and then just as quickly that awful face faded and it was the young man once again. He took a step toward me, a look of determination, almost anger, in his dark eyes.

I turned back to the courtyard door but did not have the presence of mind to manipulate the two latches at once. My spine was crawling, every muscle of my body wanted to scream, to fly. I dove for the other door, into the newer wing of the castle, and rushed through the blue sitting room, upsetting the cats and the chairs, leaving a wake of flying newspapers. I ran all the way up six flights of stairs to the library at the top. I sat there like a granite stone in the window seat, listening, my back to the light of the window glass, thinking, terrified, wondering about my sanity.

I sat there until it was almost dark and I saw the comforting lights of Richard's Healey come winding up the hill. I couldn't possibly tell him. He would either laugh at me, his opinion of silly American girls even further reduced, or come up with an inadequate, lamely logical explanation: some local jokester, a prank, a dream, the wind. I had sadly discovered that it was best to keep such nonsense to myself rather than suffer his abuse. Maybe I *was* going mad, like the poor young wife unhinged by an electrical storm: a story that my friend Cynthia had once told me back at college. The woman battered her baby to death on the hearthstones in self-perpetuating terror. If so, Dextra and Sinistra had better not do any howling on stormy nights when I was about. I was a menace, or a potential one. I did not *want* to witness any apparitions. I did not *want* to be singled out for some spectral assault, or any practical jokes; I was not strong enough for that. I was not good prey. The whole nasty business had left me sick, weak, my stomach in a knot, my bowels grinding ominously.

With the comfort of another living person now so close, the whole incident was rather reduced to a gigantic embarrassment. Of course it had been a prank. It was not as bad as all that, or what badness there was faded when I heard Richard slam his car door. I had probably reacted exactly as the prankster had hoped I would. Richard had met him at the pub down the road to have a few pints and some good yucks over the way they had scared the jeans off that ridiculous American girl. Now that it was over and Richard was actually there I was feeling supremely mortified. I would never admit my fear to him; he probably already knew anyway. I had to retain some honor. I had a violent desire to leave right then and there and never come back, run back to Oxford and bury my red cheeks in the mothball-scented coverlet of our bed, never telling Michael what had happened. He would be so ashamed of me. Silly enough to be frightened by a white sheet. My heart was tapping in an unpleasantly palpitating way. Like everything else in my body and soul, it was trying to get out and run away.

It was so damned difficult being human. Who needed hell after life? What had I done, anyway, except to be born an American? I scrubbed his pots for him. I did not steal things when I left. I always sent a limpid little *thank-you* note after each visit, but I was still American. Unavoidably, unforgettably, uselessly, loudly, midwesternly American. I was doomed.

I heard Richard start ringing at the gatehouse bell. The door was probably still jammed. I leaned out of the library window and

called around to him to force it, trying to sound assertive and composed. I heard him thumping away at it, and soon enough he had
managed to get inside the keep. He was banging down the lids of
the Rayburn's burners to check if it was hot, doubting my capacity
to stoke it. I heard him come stumping up the wooden stairs after
five minutes. We met on the second floor landing, the halls lit up like
sunshine behind me. Artificial lights gave me great comfort at uneasy
moments.

"No supper yet?" Richard demanded. Men were all distressingly alike.

"Sorry. I got to reading and forgot all about it. It'll only take
a minute." I tried to say as little as possible to Richard, although I
heard even those few simple words calling out my nationality and
all the ugly things he associated with it: Buicks, ranch houses, moronic wealth. Richard switched off all the lights, muttering to himself
about "waste" and "being spoiled." My ease evaporated with the
ions of light.

"I'll give you a hand with dinner," he said. I was relieved, if
only to have company with me in the kitchen. He followed me down
the stairs, through the sitting room, where I stopped to right the
overturned chairs.

"Cats must've knocked them over," I mumbled. Richard just
ignored me and went into the kitchen where he silently started
mixing up some custards for dessert. I hoped I could get drunk so
that I could at least talk to him over the meal without feeling conspic-
uous, brash, cretinous.

"What's this on the chalkboard, then?" he called over to me.
I set the newspapers in a neat pile beside the fireplace, to use as
kindling later, and took a half-empty bottle of sack from the corner
cupboard. I poured myself a large glass.

"Just your orders, sir," I called back, "duly completed." I took
a good gulp of the sack. It went straight to my ears. A good feeling.

"Deus ait mercit de t'aneme?"

There was a sudden chill in the room. I switched on the overhead light, bugger what Richard thought, and the feeling seemed to
fade a bit. In the kitchen Richard was busily beating up his custard
at the sink, still full of dirty pots. I went in and looked at the
chalkboard. It was a strange, spidery script, almost illegible, very
faintly written slantwise over Richard's notes of that morning. *Deus
ait mercit de t'aneme,* it read.

"What does that mean?" I asked. Richard stopped his furious beating for a moment and looked at me strangely. Or at least I thought it was a strange look; maybe it was exasperation with yet another silly question.

"You wrote it. You should know."

"I'm sorry, Richard, but I did *not* write that. Someone must have come in and written it while I was upstairs. Do you know what it means?"

He raised his eyebrows, sort of grimaced at me, and added vanilla to his bowl. "Nobody could have gotten in through that jammed door without knowing its idiosyncrasies," he said. He went back to his beating.

"Well, apparently someone did!" I had to holler above the noise of the eggbeater. I turned to the refrigerator and removed the chicken that I had prepared that morning.

"Don't you know Old French when you see it?"

"Of course not!" My scalp began to bristle. Maybe it was the sherry. Richard was standing exactly where the man had been that afternoon. I set the chicken in a terracotta brick and thrust it into the hot black mouth of the Rayburn. "What does it mean anyway?"

"It means 'God have mercy on my soul.' "

8

"Say me, wight in the brom,
Teche me how I shule don
That min house bonde
Me lovien wolde."

"Hold thine tunge stille
*And have al thine wille."**

—CAMB. TRINITY COLL.
MS 323, f. 28, c.1275

OBEY thy husband, the Holy Church said. My mother had. The husband is the head of the wife, as Christ is head of the church. It was nice to believe that. It was certainly a comfort at times. It was, however, discomfiting to think that Michael did not believe the same things. Sometimes he joked about *the wife,* conjuring up pictures of a creature in blue plastic specs with spreading thighs; short, thin hair; a nasal voice; armed with a box of chocolate Dainties and a television set. Words said in jest are oftentimes truth in disguise. "I don't have to impress you anymore," he would joke, and I would accept it seriously. "You're a *wife* now," uttering that evil, ball-cutting word as if it were synonymous with "dog pile" or "breaking wind."

Personally I quite enjoyed the word, the traditional concept,

---

* *"Tell me, creature in the broomgrass,*
teach me how I am to behave
That my husband
will love me."

"Hold your tongue still
and have all your will."

[173]

and the reality of a husband. It meant that there was someone in the world who *wanted* to have me around, someone to protect me—at least metaphorically—to provide comfort both physical and emotional. It was someone who would keep me warm and unafraid at night, and scare away the ghosts. It was even someone to wash clothes and cook for, someone who needed me and appreciated me, even at my lowest moments. Without a father to defend and protect me anymore, without a conveniently located mother, having a husband around—at least sometimes—gave me a certain medieval, perhaps foundationless, security.

Sex was perhaps less of a novelty to the twenty-six-year-old Michael, who had had his share of quantity and variety before he met me. Very early on he had admitted that his first encounter was at age thirteen, with the schoolgirl next door. He said that it never bothered his conscience much because they moved a month later and he never had to see her again. I recalled that at age thirteen I was still playing with rag dolls. When I started to associate with boys at seventeen, my mother went to the public library and withdrew three books on "growing up." They were published in the fifties, full of Walt Disneyesque pictures of mysterious things called ovaries and vaginas, yet they never actually explained how A went into B resulting in C. It was all a terrible mystery to me until I once saw my college roommate Tina and her boyfriend Alan naked as fishes undulating with the tides in our room and, afterward, Tina sat down with me and explained a few things that the book never even hinted at.

Sex was still naughty to me, and I rather enjoyed that. When I was twenty my mother went so far as to tell me that sex was all that men wanted from women, and when Michael's demands did not meet my exacting standards for "all," my insecurity mounted. I thought it might have been because of my past experience with Robert, or maybe it was just Michael's great age and his upbringing in that damp, chilly climate. I reasoned that he might have better things on his mind every night, like sleeping, or working, or other women. Perhaps I had read too many cheap novels, and expected superhuman efforts from the poor man. It wasn't that I wanted or needed daily sex; I was simply led to believe that he wanted it, and when he didn't ask, I worried.

Michael had very little reverence, if any, for birthdays, anniversaries, and holidays. My world had virtually pivoted around the excitement and sentimentality associated with those days, when I

[174]

could capture my parents' unadulterated attention. Michael was unimpressed with the elaborate cake and the gifts that materialized on his birthday in March. When my birthday in April slipped by without even a card, I sunk into a fathomless depression. Or so it felt. A fantastic gift—an expensive wristwatch—appeared some days later, called a "birthday present" by Michael, but somehow it never meant as much unless it was delivered on the proper date—the day that you were special—accompanied by cakes, kisses, and candles. "A typical man," my mother said in one letter in response to my laments, but I still did not have the slightest idea of what that might be. I did not want to lose my childish excitement over holidays, but it seemed that if I wanted to live successfully with Michael I would have to.

He was so *adult*. It wasn't that he was hard-nosed or boring; he was just mysteriously *mature* about such things. I felt embarrassingly childish in his presence sometimes. Almost inadequate, mentally deficient, burdensome, a nuisance; but upon close examination, it wasn't Michael *making* me feel that way. It was my own fault; a perception of myself with an undeserved Michael, lurking in the shadow of his greatness.

We began having bitter fights over the most insignificant things, instigated, for the most part, by me, unable to make sense of good English frugality. One involved the cheap fan heater.

"Shut that goddamned thing off. I'm roasted!"

"Well, I'm *freezing*," knowing perfectly well that it would toast my skin into little white flakes and shrivel my sinuses like fresh figs in a hot oven. Then a giant leap out of the bed, a cold blast of damp English nighttime air scented with mothballs coming in under the dislocated wool blankets, *thud-thud-thud,* the unfeeling one crossing the polar linoleum floor and switching off my savior, wrenching its sweet three-pronged plug from the wall outlet and dropping it with a distasteful clatter. My nose went immediately solid with frozen mucous membranes at the mere thought of the heat stopping.

"It doesn't really heat the room anyway. See? It's cold already. It's just a bloody waste."

My feet turned into cold, unliving potatoes at the lack of psychological warmth. It would be another sleepless night, thrashing with the cruel realities of life in a country where the standard of living was reasonable. An even worse battle ensued when the first quarterly electric bill arrived.

"Look, it's *our* house and I'd normally pay half, but if you insist on eating up electricity like candy with your bloody fan heater, then you can bloody well pay three-quarters the bill!"

"But that's almost a whole month's salary for me!"

"Well, what if you were living alone and had to pay the whole works? What if you had to keep feeding shillings into some bloody meter all day just to keep your bloody heater going?"

"But we're *married*," I whined, the worst possible argument I could have used. Married in name, married in bed, but separated when the bills came. I had never been so cold back home, not as far as I could remember. If it was cold, there were always rooms where it was warmer. The existence of accessible warmth made the cold more tolerable; it was never painfully, perpetually cold, like this, with one room as bad as the next. Even though my parents, with their raw Norwegian blood, had kept their house thermostat at sixty-five degrees before it was fashionable or necessary, our house was still warm and comfortable.

In England you had to keep moving all the time just to stay alive. In England you could see your breath condense in the frosty air when you woke up in the morning, even once spring came, even with the fan heater going. The first time that happened, soon after we moved in, I thought that it was just a bad dream: a ghost hovering in the dawn air over the bed, a will-o'-the-wisp chasing fantasies out of my sleepy head. It dawned on me, knees up in the tiny bathtub ten minutes later, that it wasn't a dream at all. I was wide awake then, semi-immersed in six inches of tepid water—the maximum output of our minuscule water heater—and I could still see my breath condensing. Certainly it was chilly in a house without central heating, but condensed breath belonged *outside,* not inside, especially when you were naked and wet in the bathtub.

Then there was the issue of grocery shopping. Michael didn't believe in going with me. It was evidence of being henpecked to be seen in a grocery store with your wife, he said once. It wasn't like back home either, I almost hated myself for thinking. There I could drive my car into the tidy, suburban shopping center, buy two weeks' worth of food all under one roof in an hour or less. I could then back the car up to the door, load it in, take it home, freeze half of it for the next week, and be done with it. Here I had to go to four or five different shops and stand in long queues every day since I could only carry enough on the bus, or on the bicycle, to feed us for a day or two at a time. I did not have strong arms to carry heavier loads, and the little refrigerator could not accommodate any more than a day's worth. I had tried to buy four days' worth of food in a single, crazy spree once, but all I succeeded in doing was to smash a half-dozen eggs on the pavement when the bicycle tipped under its unreasonable load. I strained both my patience and my leg muscles trying to pump uphill carrying all the overloaded plastic sacks. I ended up walking the last half-mile to the cottage pushing the useless bicycle. By the time I arrived my arms felt like frayed rubber and I could not lift a hairbrush for two days.

I was also at the total mercy of Michael's car. I did not harbor much love or respect for my bicycle. He drove his old Volkswagen to work every day and refused to drop me off because it was two miles out of his way, and because of the heavy traffic into the city center during the rush hours. I sensed that Michael interpreted heavy traffic as a personal insult: I also thought that he viewed delivering and retrieving me from work as another sign of being henpecked. No matter that I got wet, bumped, greasy, and cold riding the bicycle to and fro. He stayed warm and dry. No matter that once I was squashed by a blinded, rapidly moving Fiat at a roundabout and ended up at the Radcliffe Infirmary with green, blue, purple, yellow, and black legs that I could not walk on without pain for three days. Let her eat fumes and cement. Who wants a fat, complacent wife anyway? One of Richard's fleeting girlfriends—a German woman—had once told me that all Englishmen were like that. Never having married or met one before Michael, I accepted her prejudice without too much argument. All husbands were probably tyrants at heart. I remembered that my father had never let my mother wear trousers. It was women's lot to be pushed around by men. And besides, living in England on £25 a week, I could not afford to buy my own car.

Yet on one momentous occasion Michael actually did deliver his car into my inept hands. He must have been feeling pangs of guilt that early June weekend. I had arranged to take Monday off work, and he had promised to take me to Cadfor. But then, on Friday night, he decided instead to stay in Oxford and tinker with an old car that his friend Theo had just salvaged from a junkyard. He had let me drive his Volkswagen before, but it had never been a great success. He sat like a stuffed dummy wearing a horrible, scowling Chinese mask in the passenger's seat, holding onto the dashboard, gasping like an old bellows every time I changed gears, stopped, started, or passed another vehicle on the road. On every occasion I relinquished the keys after a few miles. I was afraid for his heart, and it always disturbed me to hear him muttering unintelligible execrations under his breath, especially when I knew they were directed at me.

It wasn't as if the Volkswagen was such a gem either. It was twelve years old, with over 113,000 miles on the same engine. Michael took good care of it and it ran like a happy little bird, but it still had some serious fundamental problems. For one thing, the heater would not turn off. This pleased me to no end, for I soon learned that summer was oftentimes as unpleasantly damp as winter, but it made Michael very unhappy. The red color had aged badly, too. It was a dull, flat, rufous shade now. I wasn't sure about what went on inside of it, but I knew that its days were numbered. Michael seemed to be changing the oil all the time, and he watched over its squeaks, pings, and rattles like a mother hen.

Entrusted with the sacred ignition key, I listened as patiently as I could to the same old instructions before pulling away from the cottage and heading westward. My plan that weekend was to go to Cadfor alone again. The day after the incident with the man in the kitchen had been blissfully uneventful. Richard had seemed actually to appreciate my services: the cooked food, the cleaned kitchen. One female who was not out to trap him? In any case, that Sunday had been pleasant in his company, so I was not as apprehensive about returning by myself once again.

It was nice not to have to ask Richard to pick me up at the bus depot, or ask Michael to drive me there. It was nice to be independent. I had almost forgotten how it felt. I was sure that I knew the way. We had driven it so many times before, but unfortunately I had never been behind the wheel. Once I found the A40 out of Oxford, everything suddenly looked strange. I recognized some of the names on the road signs, Witney, Burford, Northleach, but between signs I felt animal terror stirring inside me. I was not a geographer like Michael. The skill of map-reading had eluded me throughout my life, and the middle of the road looked vastly different from the scenery I was accustomed to watching in the fields on either side.

I made it as far as Cheltenham—another familiar name—but became utterly lost there for over an hour, going in circles and not realizing it until I had made at least three circumnavigations. By chance I finally ran across a sign that read GLOUCESTER (A40). I did not know why the A40 was in parentheses, but the word sounded right so I headed in that direction. Before long I was, in fact, in or near

Gloucester, cleverly bypassing the city center on a clearly marked A40. It wasn't until I was about seven miles outside of Gloucester that I noticed the road signs all reading ROSS-ON-WYE. I didn't *want* to go to Ross-on-Wye. That was miles from Cadfor. I wanted the road to Chepstow. Cadfor was on that same road, but what road was it? For lack of a map and anything better to do, I carried on toward Ross. The road forked just outside of town and I bore to the left along the old A40. It seemed like the right direction, but by then I knew my instincts were about as accurate as a dead mole's.

The scenery that I tried to glimpse was spectacular. It was marvelous to be behind the wheel for once, mistress of my destination. The scenery was only attributable to me because I had driven myself there. Even though I was lost, I was still proud of myself. The road passed through gently sloping cultivated fields for a while, then steep drops into green valleys on one side, rock escarpments rising up on the other. I drove past clean, fast-moving rivers and streams, through poor little villages with odd names like Ganarew and Weirend. Not far outside of Ross the signs began to read MONMOUTH. That was comforting. I had been to Monmouth before, with Michael, and I knew that it wasn't very far from Cadfor.

I was quite pleased with my driving up to that point. At first I had been overcompensating, pulling too far to the left in my fear of being too far to the right. But after a hundred miles it seemed to fall into place: the left hand on the gearshift instead of the right, making easy left turns instead of easy rights. It didn't take very long to unlearn six years of right-hand driving.

As I approached Monmouth the road started to twist and wind. I slowed down. There were road signs all along the way warning of falling rocks from the steep rock faces to the left. Monmouth, I hoped, was just visible through cracks in the trees at the bottom of a green valley to the right, somewhere to the remote south. A lorry barreled past me down the hill, taking the corner up ahead very fast and wide. I figured that the lorry driver probably knew the road better than I did and that it might not be such a sharp bend after all. I was running lost and late. Putting my faith in quicksand, anxious to reach Monmouth because it was already three and I didn't want to admit to anyone that I had been lost ("Oh, I just stopped awhile to shop in Gloucester") I depressed the gas pedal and took the corner at about forty, clinging further to the left than the lorry had. It was such a shame.

The old red Volkswagen, Michael's precious, coddled, senile

baby, 113,526 miles old, victim of only one negligible dent to the rear right wing, made a terrible noise. It was a noise like the sharp cracking dirge of a tall ancient tree falling, snapping off the branches of surrounding trees in its plummet toward eternity, never to rise again. The car lurched forward a few hundred frantic feet down the steep hillside around the deceitful corner. It shuddered and it stopped. Dead.

I had done it. The oracle had come to pass. Whatever had happened to the wretched motor—a simple, unavoidable mechanical failure or a total clapping-out—did not matter. What mattered was that I had been behind the wheel when it happened. I sat there numbly staring at the instrument panel, watching the little red indicator on the petrol gauge move back toward R, watching the clouds scuttle in front of the sun. No doubt it would rain. It had had to happen. That was the way life always was. You never knew until it was too late, death sneaking out from behind dark corners like a thief. Then you kicked yourself, if you were fortunate enough to be alive, for your stupidity, for letting your defenses down just that once. The way Michael had cursed and strained whenever I drove his car with him had been an omen. His refusal to take me grocery shopping, or drive me to work in it, were more bad omens that I should have heeded. And now I had done it. Really done it.

I remembered to take my foot off the brake pedal, pulled up the emergency brake and stepped out of the car. I saw that I had stopped a little bit too close to the fateful corner and decided to roll forward a little farther so that vehicles coming around the blind bend could see me in time to avoid me. I let up the brake and the car lump-bumped agonizedly down the hill about fifty feet, moving as if it had square wheels. I yanked up the emergency brake again and got out, checking to see how close I was to the left side of the road. I saw then that both tires on that side had been shaved to ribbons.

I looked up the road to the corner where it had happened. Those falling rock signs, of course. I walked up the road, around the corner, and there they were sure enough, scattered everywhere now, sharp and wicked. Damn them. The lorry driver *did* know what he was doing when he took the corner wide. So it *was* all my fault. Of course. In my helplessness and feeble rage I heaved the rocks to the verge of the road to prevent any other poor sods from shredding their tires.

I waited there miserably for more than an hour in the drizzle before a benevolent motorist stopped. I was too proud to wave down any of the cars that passed; the woman in the Ford Cortina stopped of her own volition to ask me if I was in distress. I was more than distressed by the time she stopped: I was livid with myself. I swallowed my choler, trying not to blame her for everything, and told her that I needed one more spare tire since I had managed to blow two, and a tow into Monmouth. She took pity on my American accent and drove off to the closest garage.

Of course the miserable old car would take only expensive tires: Michelin ZX's, and nothing less. The other two tires were irreparable, hanging in loose, rubbery strips like fingers on a dead man's hand. I could have spat on them as the shifty-looking Welsh mechanics carried them out of the garage into the rubbish heap. It wasn't as if spending over £40 on new tires could make up for the damage done either. I had to explain the accident to Michael, who would never believe that it was an accident, who would rather accuse me of incompetence than accept the fact that God had placed those rocks there, and not me. He would certainly find some additional damage to the car that could, remotely, be related to this. He would probably notice the new tires as soon as I turned the car into the road, or sooner. And he would probably complain that the new tires were not as good as the old ones. The men in the garage let me use their phone to call him, long distance. It was Saturday, six o'clock. The pubs had just opened, and I hoped to God he'd be home.

English phones have a harsh, rude way of summoning you. I was usually in a bad mood by the time I answered. He was home—cheerful, surprised to hear from me.

"Michael, it's me." Sometimes I think I tried to live up to my moronic image of myself.

"Yes. What is it? Are you at Richard's?"

"No. I'm afraid I've got some bad news."

The line was as silent as a ghost's footstep. Even the operators waited, breathless.

"Well? What have you done to the car?"

"You don't have to sound so smug about it! It's not as if I did it on purpose!"

"No."

"Jesus, you're always so self-righteous. I swear you make me so nervous it's no wonder it happened. It was a self-fulfilling prophecy."

"Yes."

"Is that all you can say? My God, you're as much to blame as I am! Here I've been shocked silly and now I have to listen to your silent disgust? I already paid for all the repairs, Michael, so don't you worry about it. It won't cost you a cent. It was more than a half-month's pay for me, too." I exaggerated. I was mad. I wished I could control it, but that would not have expiated enough guilt.

"Yes."

"Are you furious?"

"Why don't you tell me what happened first?"

"I did!"

"No, you didn't."

"Don't play games with me Michael. I'm sure I did. You're just trying to rub it in! Look, I'm sorry, it couldn't be avoided. I'll never drive your car again, as long as I live, I promise. I couldn't stand going through this third-degree again. I'm sorry! You can just hitch-hike out here and take it back yourself, okay?"

"Yes. But what happened?"

"Nothing! It was just an accident!"

"Then why are you calling me if it was nothing?"

"I thought you should know. After all, it's *your* car. You have to come and get it. I refuse to drive it anymore."

"Where are you?"

"In Monmouth. At West's Garage. I took a detour for a change." I couldn't admit that I was lost. I still had some pride.

"Will the car run?"

"Of course it will run! It was only the tires."

"Well, why didn't you say so in the first place?"

"I did. You just weren't listening."

He sighed, but caught himself. "Do you still plan to go on to Richard's?"

"I don't know. I wanted to hear your reaction to this first."

"How about if I meet you halfway? Can you find your way back to Gloucester?"

"Of course I can." My hands started to sweat.

"I'll catch the next bus from Gloucester Green and meet you in front of the cathedral at nine."

By the time they finished changing the tires and charging, then overcharging, me, and by the time I found the cathedral in Gloucester, which was ridiculously well signposted but defied me anyway, it was nine-thirty. He was waiting there, cool and efficient, with his overnight bag. I expected him to wrest the keys from my hand and take over the wheel, but he got in the passenger's side, pecked me on the cheek, and started to tell me the way to Richard's. We were there by eleven, ensconced in our usual room by twelve, the sheets yet unchanged.

The drive had been almost shockingly uneventful. Michael never even asked me which tires had burst. He told me about the ancient Morris he and Theo had exhumed from Crummy's Salvage Yard, about Phibbs weeding out two of our tomato bushes before he could stop him, about the letter from my mother in that day's post. It had been a full day for both of us, yet once we were nestled into the lumpy rope bed, neither of us could sleep. The full moon might have played a part in it, coming in through the two unshaded nine-over-nine windows so that the room was full of cold shadows. With Richard being alone that weekend and sound asleep two stories under, the rest of the castle was as hushed as winter twilight.

"I can't sleep," I finally said.

"Something's on your mind."

"Guilt."

"Why?"

"My mother used to leave money for the milkman in a bottle in the garage. I stole it twice. Maybe more than twice."

"We've all stolen from the milkman. There's no reason to lose sleep over it."

"I ruined two of your tires. It was all my fault."

"But you fixed them."

"That's another problem. The car is so old, it doesn't really deserve brand-new tires. What happens if it croaks tomorrow?"

"Don't use such language. And if it claps out, we just graft the new tires onto a new car."

The criticism of my language humbled me, and I lay there a long time on the long, narrow, rolled pillow, hating its hardness and the lumpy mattress. I wondered how Michael could be so kind to me after I nearly ruined his car. We could not afford a new one; we could not even afford a used one. He seemed to be making extraordinary efforts to be kind, but then I had never been so naughty before. Perhaps this was a normal reaction. Perhaps he knew that my own conscience would punish me more than he ever could by berating me for my stupidity. The worst thing I had ever done before that was the evening with Colin. Suddenly all the guilt rolled back, compounded, black and sticky, all over my soul. I had to talk, to keep from being overwhelmed by my own vileness.

"You've taken it very well. I'm glad you aren't angry." My voice was clear and loud in the black and white room.

"No point. It wasn't your fault, I'm sure."

"Why are you trying so hard? What did I do to deserve this?" I rolled over on my side and threw my left arm over his bare chest. He always lay on his back when he couldn't sleep. I could see his eyes were open, staring at the yawning black hole that was a fireplace on the far wall.

"I'm not aware that I was trying hard. It just doesn't make sense to argue over small things. My parents always did, especially after John died. I remember wanting things to go smoothly so badly that I cried myself to sleep whenever they fought, which seemed to be almost every night. It was so senseless. They could have been happy, but instead they argued. They fought so bitterly. They slapped each other, and said things that could never be forgiven and forgotten. It was a terrible thing, a terrible way to live."

The moonlight made the face of a great wooden doll propped in a highchair in the corner glow as if it were alive. It looked as if the yellow-shot pupils of its glass eyes were moving, staring at us stupidly, like some animal. I almost envied its brainlessness. No pain. No memory. The branch of an oak tree in the garden swayed slightly; the leaves rustled like running water through the open window and reminded me that it was summer. He had tears in his eyes, and I just couldn't think of anything else to say.

"You're right. Thank you, Michael."

He was quiet, and I think he cried himself to sleep.

The moon had moved. A footstep in the hall, bats in the roof beams, or perhaps a blanket gently pulled over bare skin woke me. My face was in Michael's back, almost smothered in pillow and rank sheet. I didn't know how long I had been asleep. I could just see the top half of a grisly Victorian insect diorama on the wall over the washstand. I wondered if I would be able to get back to sleep again. I rolled over and my movement roused Michael. Almost instinctively, but still in a dream, he started to pull up my nightdress. I was in no mood to resist; in fact I thought it might help both of us to forget, relax, sleep more soundly. He was usually very particular about making love away from home, worried about creaking bed-springs and our own heavy breathing. But he must have realized—or been too sleepy to care—that Richard was asleep, and we could relax.

I let him have his way. I buried my head between his neck and his collarbone and kissed it as he moved over me, almost in a trance, eyes still closed. It felt warm and good to be so close again, in the moonlight, without having said anything, even in the smelly old bed. I closed my eyes and tried not to feel the hardness of the pillow, the bed cleaved, sinking toward the middle. I concentrated on Michael moving thick and slow in his dream. I only opened my eyes in response to a movement I sensed.

I thought I saw something foreign in the darkest corner of the room then, near the bed. I stared, but it only grew blacker. Clouds over the moon. I did not disturb Michael's rhythm, but held on to his back and kept looking into the corner. I looked away, hoping to see whatever it was in my peripheral vision. Michael started to kick off the blankets. I was distracted. But when I looked back at the corner I could have sworn that I saw two dark eyes shimmering with tears. I saw them only a second, and the palest outline of a man in dark clothing. When I blinked they were gone. I didn't tell Michael, but he was curiously sleepless the rest of that night. The corner was empty, save for one cobweb, the next morning.

The next morning, Sunday, Michael talked Richard into going over to his parents' house for the day, to help prepare a spot in their old, crowded, stone barn on the hill for the pieces of Morris he had found the day before. Fortunately I was able to stay behind. It would have been only my third visit, even more unwilling, though, than the previous two.

The couple did argue a lot, augmented by Mr. Jones's deafness, I feared. On my sole visit to their house since the March debacle, Mrs. Jones was more animated than I had ever seen her. But she was easily irritated by her husband's smiling lack of response to even the simplest questions unless they were shouted. Pride kept him from wearing a hearing aid, Michael said. Simple conversations invariably turned into shouting matches, and I was relieved that my previous visit lasted only half an hour. The deafness had come on suddenly, in the last three years, Michael told me. I could see him flinch when his parents started in hollering. Even though the topic was usually harmless—"More tea?" or "Shut the door"—the fact that their voices were always raised seemed to hurt him deeply. He became very withdrawn in their presence, and often stayed that way for days afterward. The subject of parents became another one relegated to the realm of the unspeakable.

The elder Joneses had owned their house for thirty years, rented it to unsympathetic tenants for over twenty, and had been living there themselves for almost nine years. Yet the house had hardly been touched since the initial gutting soon after they moved in, nine years ago, in anticipation of redecorating. An Elizabethan house does not exactly lend itself to massive gutting. In the upstairs toilet, for instance, one could see clear through into the kitchen through the gaps in the floor boards since the linoleum had been removed. The parlor floor on the first story had been completely removed so that you could look up through the beams from the cellar into the attic with all of the fireplaces in one wall dangling feebly in midair. The Joneses did not seem too put out by their house's arrangement and condition. They had not yet unpacked, but after nine years it was home, no matter how it looked to an outsider.

The chimney in the kitchen was dangerously close to collapse, buckling out at the base. The roof lacked so many slates that the attic was more like a solarium. All of the bedroom ceilings leaked. Rats and mice thrived in the kitchen walls, coming out to dance in the butter after dark, and the hot water heater above the bathroom periodically exploded, drenching all the rooms beneath it with rusty lukewarm water. The house suffered from dry rot, rising damp, deathwatch beetle—everything in the book. Yet the Joneses seemed content with it, if not with each other, feeding their pet pig and cow, tending to their small flock of chickens, weeding their garden, visiting with their neighbors. They stayed outdoors as much as possible. The house reeked of Cuprinol—a woodworm killer that Mr. Jones had used to treat some of the rotten beams in the building shortly after moving in. The prospect of spending the night there was not very appealing, particularly since the elder Joneses were not inclined to speak to each other during the day, let alone to me—their only son's gawky, nervous, albino bride who was not yet pregnant.

I had been invited to stay only once, but I had declined and the invitation was not repeated. I did not relish the idea of being at the mercy of Mr. Jones's taciturn deafness, his wife's greasy breakfasts, their combined scrutiny in the noisome house, and Michael barreling from garage to barn to pub to garage, avoiding them and their shouting.

I was greatly relieved when Michael told me that Richard was going with him, and didn't mind if I stayed at the castle to feed the cats, wind the clocks, and stoke the coal fires, in case they decided to stay over that night. It was not a difficult decision for me to make. Probably as anxious to be rid of me at that point as I was anxious to be left alone, Michael and Richard drove off on Sunday morning in the Volkswagen.

It was high June: summer in England lasts about six hours, and no one ever knows when it will happen. Yet the weather never really bothered me unless I was cold and out of the range of a fire. When it was overcast I felt cozy, as if I were encased in a fluffy layer of goosedown. Being outdoors was like being indoors. I preferred the drizzly, dun, overcast days to the sunny ones. When the sun was shining I felt slightly guilty that I was not outside working. It made me think of the neglected garden at Warborough. Having spent over ten pounds on exotic garden seeds that spring, it was rather tragic that I never took the time to weed the garden properly. Barnes kept me locked indoors during the week. I looked as white as the underside of a dead carp.

I had my sewing to keep me content indoors at Cadfor: a simple little sampler that I would have stitched at age twelve, had I lived a hundred years earlier. Richard's library would also keep me amused. After they left I fed some coal to the Rayburn to keep the water hot and the stove warm enough for cooking. I fed his fat, voracious cats, who returned the favor by delivering disemboweled mice and rats to my feet that afternoon as I sat in the blue sitting room. They curled up picturesquely before the hearth as I enjoyed the fire, sewing, listening to the television but not watching. This was a proper weekend away, I thought to myself as I savored the quiet, for once luxuriating in the feeling that there was nothing in the world that had to get done before Tuesday. All I really had to do was to feed the Rayburn, and the cats, wind the clocks once, and stay content. Peace. Blessed, temporal peace. Why can't it ever last longer than the wink of an eye?

Richard had left the keys in his old Rover, but there weren't any shops open that day anyway, so I would not need it. Besides, the thought of another person's car spooked me. Only one group of sightseers materialized at the castle gates by three, and I let them poke around the older, unimproved bits by themselves with a little brochure Richard had prepared describing the castle, glued to a wooden paddle. As usual I was embarrassed by my accent so I didn't say much to the tourists. They paid me forty pence each for the privilege of looking and reading the paddle, and then they were gone.

Richard and Michael called from a pub in Cinderford, near his parents' house, to say that they would be staying the night, and to expect them back early Monday. Richard gave me a few more instructions on certain idiosyncrasies of the older clocks, and then Michael came on to ask how I was doing. He sounded almost confused, or maybe it was hurt, when I told him that I was enjoying the peace and solitude so much. He was eager to affirm that they would be back as early as possible on Monday, and we could then return to Warborough to spend the rest of my day off in the garden together. The prospect did not thrill, but I didn't say anything about that. I wished him good night, and he rang off. There were still two good hours of daylight left; in June, you could see light in the sky until nearly eleven.

I had had time alone like that once before. It was in the winter, caught in a deep snowbank in that college town on an Easter break, between endless January and April thaw, when the climax of the day was a trip into the empty student union for a soda. I was not the sort of person to go mad under the pressure of nothingness; in fact, the fewer demands life placed on me, the less I felt I could tolerate. When vacation ended and classes started again, the shock of actually having something to do sent me reeling in desperation until I had gathered up enough momentum to properly adjust to the new schedule.

That past winter in England had been full of many firsts for me. I was living away from home, but it was not the same as it had been at college. I was *living* here: not existing on parental relief. In fact it was the first winter of my life spent without any parents. I thought of all sorts of useless analogies that did not really apply: a fledgling, trying out my new legs. It hardly felt odd, and I was not homesick. When I thought of my mother and her aging cohabitant, portly

Arthur, I felt sadly alienated. That was not the mother I knew. She had died with Daddy in the autumn, and I was an orphan that winter, for the first time. I wondered what sort of thing love was if it could vanish so rapidly after the death of the loved one, or if, after twenty-eight years of marriage, my parents' love had been worn thin, and erased utterly by the disappearance of one partner. It made me despair a bit of the eternalness of marital love. I saw myself turning cynical, withdrawing a bit from my former romantic self, viewing Michael as almost a passing fancy. No more than a roommate to be tolerated. A body to pay half the utility bills. It was not nice, I knew, but I still wondered if it was inevitable.

I cooked, tried to behave like a wife, and, for the first time as well that winter, exchanged my precious time for subsistence pay, no better than the meanest serf. One day off, alone, and I wondered why I put up with it. The work was not unenjoyable, but in the summer there were just too many times when the work ran out, when the day was so fine that I could have cried that I had to see it from behind a sooty windowpane. My backside seemed to be increasing in size from all of the sitting, too; Michael even commented on it once. Since he took the car damage so well I wondered if I might test his benevolence further by quitting the job. I decided that I wasn't quite ready to try that.

I could never quite understand why people did things that they knew were wrong. Plenty of people did things that were wrong, but they didn't realize it; even more people did wrong things in spite of themselves. Like me. On my salary, I knew that it was wrong to buy an expensive pair of boots. But I bought them all the same, loving the boots and hating myself at the same time. I knew that it was somehow wrong—a violation of the laws of nature—to fly in airplanes but I did it anyway. Once, when I was very, very angry at Michael for complaining that the room was too hot when in fact I was very cold, I had smashed a drinking glass on the kitchen floor. That was wrong. Although it felt marvelous at the moment of impact, I regretted doing it almost immediately. Anger turned to guilt, and I swept up the shattered pieces, rightfully cutting my hand in the process. I even bled on a white blouse, a stain richly deserved. I felt this urge come over me as dusk settled that Sunday night at Cadfor. I was in Richard's library scanning the shelves for a respite from sewing when I came across something very wrong. It was a book about haunted castles and abbeys in Britain, written some time in the nineteenth century. I knew that a Victorian ghost writer could be merciless.

An earthquake would not have stopped me from taking that book off the shelf. My brain called out that it was wrong, but my arm kept moving toward the wretched book, slave to an unnatural, foreign lust deep within me. The book securely in hand, I went downstairs with it into the blue sitting room, rekindled the small fire in the grate, and settled back into a rocker with a sigh of masochistic pleasure. My spine was tingling before I finished reading the introduction.

I read with horrible delight of ghosts who paced long galleries, crying; of ghosts who screamed in nightly agony; of ghosts without arms who stood at the foot of the stairs grinning diabolically; of headless ghosts and ghosts without feet; of spectral, faceless monks who walked through walls, or ugly nuns who showed their faces and drove the unfortunate witnesses mad. I read of laughing ghosts, weeping ghosts, bleeding ghosts, dancing ghosts, ghostly lovers; the writer's imagination was limitless.

But was it all his imagination? The wretched book actually quoted real people, noble people whose families still lived in these haunted castles, and clergymen who worked at the sites of old monasteries and churches. As much as I wanted to hear at least one denial, I wanted to read a hundred affirmations. I felt the dragons tugging inside my head. Put it away, open it up. In the end I thought it was best to let them fight, let them sink into a silk sheet in a pit full of mead, drink their fill, and then lock them away in a stone chest for all of eternity. If it had only been so simple. If only memory could be locked away like that.

I poured myself a glass of sherry. It helped, and I turned back to the book. Now it is and now it isn't. Everything we know is in the past. The last sentence, the last word, the last letter I read is all past history. As soon as I imagine it to be the present, it is past, so why couldn't ghosts be real? If I look at a clock and say, "Five minutes from now it will be the future," what does that mean? That I am a ghost of the past? By the time five minutes is gone, it is past. Past, present, future; it is all the same. We are the ghosts of tomorrow, the unbelievers of today.

I was partway into the seventh chapter when I read it. It was like discovering that your husband had lied all along, had been unfaithful for the past five years. When you thought that he was working late every night he was really in bed with your best friend.

> *. . . this case was similar to one reported by a former owner of Cadfor Castle, a twelfth century edifice threateningly perched on top of a foreboding rock face in the South of Wales. One winter evening upon retiring, this owner claimed to have seen a spirit in the ruins of the Norman Keep, apparently carrying on a heated discussion with someone. This owner did not linger long enough to hear and understand what the ghost was saying, yet he understood the language to be French. On yet another occasion, this same owner purported to have heard pitiful cries and groans emanating from the darkened bailey: cries which turned his blood to ice, accompanied by the sensation that he was being carefully scrutinized by a hidden viewer. It was shortly after this second incident that he promptly sold the property to a local farmer, stating that it was too horribly haunted to be habitable. The farmer turned the ruins of the castle into a cattle fold. The presence of the cows seems to have deterred the ghosts, for we have heard no more stories of the tortured spirits of Cadfor in recent years, apart from the farmer's comment that, on rare occasions, he would hear music in the ruins, drifting down the chimneys. The previous owner speculated that certain bloody incidents that had taken place when the de Mauro family built and lived in the castle might have been responsible for the hauntings, and he linked them to similar manifestations reported at Bryngessy Priory, in that same shire. This owner also believes that Cadfor's ghosts have not yet departed its mossy walls, judging by his own preternatural intuitions at a recent visit to the castle.*

Of course. I had known it all along. One should always trust a woman's intuition.

De Mauro. I had heard that name before. Had Richard mentioned it? Had I read it in an inscription somewhere? I set the book down and flogged my brain. I got up, poured myself an orange juice in the kitchen (with long looks to both sides, but he was nowhere to be seen), went back to the sitting room and stared down at the book in its harmless blue leather binding. It was just a hunch. The de Mauros built the castle in the twelfth century. My madness prevailed. I walked back upstairs to the library and searched the shelves for one of Richard's old histories of Cadfor. I knew that he had some. He collected anything with the slightest connection to the castle, and had recently referred to a particularly good find: a book, hand-printed on vellum in the early seventeenth century, giving names, dates, places, and tales about Cadfor that he had never found reiterated elsewhere. It was a freakish book, compiled by an old woman who lived alone at Cadfor after her husband's death. They were the ones who had built the "newest" wing—the last addition to the entire complex. Richard had let me glance at the book once. He probably figured it wouldn't interest me. I vaguely remembered a light-colored cover with red lettering.

It was there. Protected by a clear plastic jacket. I recognized the red letters on the binding. *A Report on the Principal Families of Cadfor in Striguil with Divers Tales of Their Historie.* I opened to the first page and hardly needed to go any further. There was a delicately drawn, fragile-looking tree, carefully sketched in an old lady's hand. At the base of the tree it read "Sir Mortimer de Mauro." His wife, Eva St. Pol; sons Henry and Bernard; daughters Matilda, Agnes, and Gaie.

Gaie. Gaie de Mauro. Gay Mortenson.

I set the book down, went to the window, sat in the cushioned well. It was not so much fear and apprehension as a feeling of soaring accomplishment. I wanted to tell someone. My own personal discovery. I had read that there had been so many Viking raids down in Normandy that the Normans were really in part Scandinavian. Had my ancestors donned horns and flooded south to rape French ladies? Did I have some remote claim to Richard's castle through a woman whose name sounded a little bit like mine? Hardly. It was still an exciting idea, though. I went back to the desk to see if there was anything else about Gaie de Mauro in the book. I looked at the tree again.

Born 1070. Married 1086. To William de Lacy. Died 1087.

Oh, Lord.

I started paging through.

It was very hard to read the old lady's spidery, florid hand. Half the words I had to skip over because they were simply undecipherable. The first part of the book, strangely, was all about the author's grandfather, who had been a trader living in Bristol. I got the distinct impression that she had sat down and written whenever the fancy struck her. There was no logic to the way the book was organized, and certainly no index or table of contents. I had to scan each page, looking for the names I wanted to read. I found them in the third chapter, and then just enough to tantalize and frustrate—hardly enough to satisfy.

Gaie had died of unknown causes "to the north." Stricken with grief, William retreated into the wilderness and became a hermit. According to legend, he had visions of the devil, disguised as a beautiful, white-haired young woman, who looked like his deceased wife. He was prone to lascivious apparitions his whole life.

So he *was* mad. Sort of. That explained why his younger brother Hugo inherited the entire Lacy fee from his father, Walter, while William was still alive.

But a white-haired she-devil?

No. Life was not like that. Not anymore. Life was brushing your teeth three times a day and growing carrots and taking the bus to work. I closed the book. The de Mauro chapter ended there. The next one was concerned with some cousin of the old woman's who was cabinetmaker to the king. I looked up on the wooden mantel at the clock, ticking tidily on the downswing of its thirty-hour span. It was a pretty, plain, little ogee shop clock, no older than the 1890s; Richard claimed that he never spent more than fifty pence on anything. I remembered that I would have to wind all of the clocks before bedtime. Against my better judgment, I went back downstairs and picked up the Victorian horrors book. I felt as if nothing could scare me after what I had just read. I felt suspiciously eternal, with skin and heart like metal.

I heard the cat-door flap open, swing shut as Sinistra came slinking into the sitting room. He was the official resident patriarch at Cadfor, huge and black and sexless with a cleft nose. With his position unchallenged for so long, his wits were getting a little bit dull and it showed in his eyes; they were as yellow as harvest moons, as clear as wells, wide, disconcerting, and stupid. His life consisted of begging, eating, walking aimlessly around the castle, and frequenting especially comfortable and warm places reserved for him alone. Dextra knew his turf. The Indian throw rug before the hearth in the sitting room was one of those special places. Dextra had to curl up on the overstuffed couch behind him where there were drafts.

Murdered lovers, suicides, unhappy spinsters. I sat down again and kept working on the ghost book. The list became longer. Still, it wasn't scaring me anymore. I was thinking about that other book, searching for the arc that might complete the circle. Who were the ghosts of Cadfor? I knew then that I would never sleep that night, listening for them. It was already eleven and my nerves were on a sharp, raw edge with more than a quarter of the book yet to finish. I remembered that I had not yet bolted the gateway door. Richard had emphasized that to me several times. I felt a flush of guilt, incompetence. I set the book down on the seat of the rocker and ventured out into the courtyard.

The sitting room and the kitchen at Cadfor were originally part of the lower storage rooms of the twelfth-century keep. They had not been significantly altered since, with the exception of a few minor creature comforts, like a window, some rudimentary electric wiring, and a solid fuel cookstove. Almost all traces of former occupation by cows had been removed by the owner prior to Richard. The lower part of the fifteenth-century wing was still full of hay, troughs, and stall partitions. Richard was slowly removing all traces of farm life. Gradually, as he worked, pointed arches became visible. Stone lintels over blocked-up fireplaces and other architectural details formerly covered by dung and mud and plaster were seeing the light for the first time in centuries.

I had to pass through the courtyard—formerly the bailey—in order to reach the gateway. I shut the door, drew the old iron bolts across it at the top, bottom, and side, and listened to a distraught dove flap her wings and raise dust in protest in the musty darkness above. When I turned back toward the kitchen door, I heard the most incredibly loud clattering.

It seemed to be coming from every corner of the courtyard at once, echoing off the walls which in turn made it louder, and louder still. It sounded as if a hundred horses with loose iron shoes were galloping at breakneck speed across that tiny enclosed space, their hooves smacking the flagstones like gunshots and echoing enough to deafen a person, or to drive him mad. They seemed to be tilting toward some unmarked point in the center, clashing there terribly. The cats inside the sitting room set up a woeful caterwauling and the doves suddenly flew out from under the eaves and began to swoop through the bailey like white bats in the darkness, cooing and clucking in a frenzy of their own.

As if this wasn't enough to rival anything that I had ever read or dreamed of before, the church bells next door began to ring the changes. Not having had the good sense to turn on the courtyard lights before I left the kitchen, I clawed crazily in the dark for the iron bolts on the door. The horses, cats, doves, bells were creating a hellish bedlam symphony that enclosed me like a smothering blanket in the dark, too unreal to be real, too loud to be unreal. But then, just as abruptly, it stopped—just as the bird had settled onto the communion rail, just as the man had vanished in the barn.

I turned around, plastered my back to the hard, immovable door, and held my breath. This was madness, I thought. I was walking on hot coals. There was a perfectly logical explanation. Something fell—meteor? airplane engine?—frightening the cats and the doves. Some nerd was practicing the changes for Sunday because no one could hear and be disturbed way up on the Cadfor Castle crag. I was just stretched taut, on edge after what I had read. Best to go inside, have some warm milk and biscuits, sleep with all the lights on and a shovel at my side. I waited for the last dove to flutter back to her roost, waited for the strength to return to my rubbery knees. I felt one hand was bleeding, smashed over the knuckles on the door studs. I lurched, as quietly as I could, back into the courtyard, hugging the stone wall of the keep.

There he was again standing just outside the kitchen, as clear as day in the light cast out from the open door. He looked as though he were on his way to the loo or just out for an evening's constitutional, with a perfectly vacant look on his dark face: just another she-devil here, looking at him, all dressed in his armor and mail and rough leather boots.

"Oh, God. Who are you?"

He stared at me. The wretch just *stared.* He didn't reach out as he had in the barn and in the kitchen that day. He wasn't crying this time, and it looked as if he didn't even plan to speak to me. It was just a stare this time. That's all.

I blinked, tried to break the spell. "I'm sorry, but this is private property and you're trespassing."

Nothing. He sniffed, I think. His nose twitched. A finger moved on one hand. He blinked back.

"I'll call the police if you don't leave quickly." Stupid. He was blocking the way to the telephone. I remembered the gateway door behind me, bolted. Trapped.

"Who are you, sir?" A rising note of terror.

"Gaie, c'est te?"

That's all he said. That's all he had to say. I turned around and raced back to the bolted door, heaving against it with all my strength, tearing my blouse all across the front. I tried madly to unlatch the iron bolts, not without further damage to my already bloodied hands. I did it, and clambered across the makeshift draw-bridge barefoot to Richard's car. I thanked God for his trusting nature. Even with an American around, he had left the keys in the ignition. Just before I slammed the door I hesitated. I thought I heard something else behind me, something like a horrible, low-pitched moan, but I couldn't—wouldn't—be sure. It might just have been the cats. I wasn't about to stick around to find out.

I squealed off the cobblestones and tore away like lightning, flailing down the narrow lane and around the steep rocky crag onto the main road. I flew like hell to Newport.

Why me? I wondered, my spine still tingling in the speeding car, taking quick peeks in the rear-view mirror into the back seat. Why couldn't I just have been allowed to read those books in peace, content that someone else had seen the ghosts? Why in Christ's name always me? It was an embarrassment. No one would believe me. I hardly believed myself. God only knew, I wanted nothing to do with the bloody de Mauros or this crazy William, who had married my namesake. I had read about the Ratchet in one chapter that night—the sound of the seven horsemen and their dogs—but that was supposed to be a Yorkshire phenomenon, foretelling doom for the person who heard it. I hoped that that was not what I had heard.

I didn't feel half right until I had checked into a cheap small hotel in downtown Newport and was safely ensconced in a stark, modern room with lots of light bulbs that all worked and lots of people jarring the thin walls in the rooms on either side of me. I had babbled something to the night clerk to explain my shoeless state, my torn blouse, the bloodied hands and no suitcase. He just glared at me like any other stupid Yank with more dollars than sense.

"Honest! I just got scared right out of a haunted castle! My clothes are fifteen miles up the road . . ."

He smiled a bored, enduring smile, handed me the keys to his cheapest room, and directed me to the lift. I felt like a fool. But I was getting used to that.

I never slept that night, expecting him to have followed me. I waited to hear him start up his bashing and yowling and moaning in the street outside. In my fatigued state I developed a very convinc-ing theory that Richard was behind it all. I sat there the whole night with all the lights on in the room thinking about that, staring out the window at the lights of the city. As soon as the sun was up soothingly high on Monday morning I showered and checked out, paying with a convenient five pound note I had stuffed into my pocket from grocery shopping in Chepstow.

I drove, this time much slower, back to Cadfor. It wouldn't do to have Richard and Michael return to an empty castle with the front gates swinging open, but I didn't expect them that early. I inched up the narrow lane and gingerly parked the Rover a good distance from the front gate. The gate was closed. I felt sick.

They were back. They would have found all of the clocks stopped, the cats ravenous, the Rayburn gone cold. Worst of all, they must have found the front gate wide open, and Richard's old car gone. Not that I ever cared to stay there again, nor would I ever be invited back, but it would be embarrassing and poor Michael would be very ashamed of me. No one would believe my crazy story either. I was just as well off to forget it, admit my incompetence. I could point to that passage in the horror book, but they would call it romantic nonsense—blown out of proportion by a silly girl getting her period or going through early menopause or nightmares or something. Slates falling off the roof had crashed in the courtyard. That was all it had been. I was tempted to run back down the hill to the main road and hitchhike back to Warborough rather than face them. But my suitcase, the rest of my money, my house keys were all inside. "Cadfor is a happy castle." Bullshit. Might as well say that marriage was sacred.

But there was no immediate ordeal to face inside. They were not there. The atmosphere was quiet, calm—a sunlit, warm, June morning. Inside the kitchen the Rayburn was burning bravely. Dextra was curled up in a basket beside it, enjoying the heat, while Sinistra wolfed down a dish of fresh cat food beneath the butcher block. The empty tin was sitting in the sink. Since when could cats use can openers?

The clock in the sitting room read eight-fifteen. So did my watch. On the quarter-hour the grandfather clock in the foyer chimed once. The clocks had all been wound. I went back into the sitting room. The horror book was gone. Of course. And it was probably back in its place on the library shelf. I went upstairs to check, and it was. Either I had a very poor memory, or Richard had a maid come in on Mondays. I quickly stuffed all of my belongings into my suitcase, dragged it downstairs, and then outside. I sat on the garden wall and waited for Michael. They were early. Ten o'clock. I said something about being anxious to get home.

He didn't confront me with anything until we were home. I expected massive abuse, or an interrogation at the very least, especially compounded by Saturday's disaster with the tires. But instead he was quiet, grim. He pointed the car toward Warborough, did not stop once, driving at top speed. I figured that if he wasn't going to ask, I wasn't going to tell.

He finally said something when we were out in the garden squashing cabbage worms. He was always asking me to do this unpleasant job, but I avoided it effectively. The only pesticide he let me use was rainwater steeped with salt or nettles, and like most organic compounds used by nonbelievers, it never appeared to do much good. So I had gone out and bought a small bottle of Malathion, blasting the cabbages and brussels sprouts when he was gone; but the worms had come on in full force after that. Even twice the normal dose of Malathion did not seem to budge them so we resorted to plucking and squishing them by hand.

"I don't even *like* cabbage," I said, trying to start up innocent conversation with him. "It gives me terrible gas." But he said nothing. "I think I'd rather thin out the carrots." My fingertips were all green and slippery, and the worm juice made my ravaged hands sting. It was a job one had to do blindly, because if one thought about it too much it was very easy to get sick.

"This needs doing more. This, and then the aphids on the rosebush."

I had tried spraying the rose, too. "Can't we just hire a neighborhood kid to do this?"

"I'm sure they're all doing it for their parents. I'm still puzzled over how we got so many all of a sudden. Perhaps a change in the wind . . ."

I didn't venture any confessions but, placatingly, kept popping the green bodies between my thumb and index fingers. I had brought on a plague of worms.

"Do you mind if I ask you why you left the castle in such a shambles this morning?"

"What do you mean? It looked fine to me."

"That's only because we got back before you did. We went back into Chepstow for some breakfast after we cleaned up."

I wasn't ready for this. The tires had been bad enough. He would have some maddeningly logical explanation, thoroughly unacceptable to me. I had already shaken his faith once that weekend, and once was quite enough.

"You can ask, but you wouldn't believe me anyway."

"Try me."

"I got scared. That's all." If he didn't realize that I had left the night before, I wasn't about to volunteer the information.

"Scared of what? Spiders? There's nothing else there that could frighten you."

"Richard does. He isn't exactly the world's most comforting person, particularly if you're American. I mean, he doesn't think very much of me, does he?"

"He let you stay there alone."

"One night. Big deal. And look what happened."

"Whatever it was, it was more your fault than his, I'm sure. What did happen anyway?"

I didn't want to get my feet irretrievably stuck in my mouth. "Just noises, I guess. Orchestrated by Richard, perhaps. I had a real bad night. Does he say wicked things about me to you?"

"Of course not. I'd be the last person he'd say such things to."

"Some comfort. He must have said something at some time. Can't you remember?"

"You're too sensitive, Gay. You can't let these things bother you so much."

"Think real hard. Has he never said anything about me?"

"I really can't recall. We don't talk about you when we're together; we talk about castles. Maybe once he said something. I think he said he didn't think that you were very nice to me. And another time I think he said something about you pretending to be some kind of a clairvoyant. It was after that traffic noise we heard last winter in the hall. You thought it was music, or something. He thought that was a good laugh. That's all. Honestly."

"That man really doesn't like me."

"I wouldn't go so far as to say that. You always exaggerate."

"Do you know if he's been doing anything in the courtyard lately? Like fiddling with the roof slates on that side?"

"I don't know. Last I knew he was ripping out a floor in the Great Hall. We got there so late on Saturday I didn't notice. Why?"

[199]

"No reason. It was just some noise I heard out there on Saturday night. Slates falling, I thought."

"I doubt that, unless some rats had dislodged something in the keep. There was almost no wind on Saturday night."

"I'm sure you're right. Or else Richard had it all planned that way to scare me again."

"Don't be ridiculous. What would be the point of doing that?"

"Indeed." I thought of Fred Schmidt all of a sudden. Why would he have scared two eleven-year-old girls in the north woods that August night so many years ago?

A big caterpillar had just eluded me, dropping to the earth. I squashed it with my foot—an exaggerated stomp. It was American to exaggerate.

"Actually, I'm afraid I didn't have a very good evening myself."

I tried to shake another, smaller one to the ground. It was neater to exterminate them that way. "Couldn't find a spot in the barn for your junk?"

"Not junk, my dear: a 1929 Morris Minor."

"Junk to me, my dear."

"Philistine. No, we got that packed away all right. I just didn't sleep very well."

"Guilty conscience."

"You're the one who should have a guilty conscience." He said it jokingly, probably afraid to be serious with me. "Insomnia, I guess."

"That's not like you. You're usually asleep in six seconds flat. Are you feeling all right?"

"I'm sure I'm perfectly fine. It was very odd, that's all. I'm almost ashamed to admit it."

"Admit what? I love confessions." I had almost had my fill of little green worms.

"The dream."

"What dream?"

"I dreamed it again. You know—the sky, the clouds, the green mountains, the weight on my chest. It was the same dream, but—funny—it was at night. Everything seemed the same. I mean, it felt the same, but it was night, and I couldn't see the mountains. I knew, though, that they were there. I just knew it. Silly."

"Not silly. What happened?"

"Nothing. Nothing at all. That's what was so disturbing. I kept expecting it to happen and it didn't. Absolutely nothing happened in the dream, but I woke up groaning. I woke everyone in the house up with my wretched groaning. It was very embarrassing, really. I stayed up and tried to read then, for fear I'd nod off and start in again, upsetting everyone else. It was most disturbing."

I didn't know what to say to him. To console, to change the subject, say, "Yes, I understand, that *is* odd, but it will never happen again." Instead I said, "Maybe you're possessed," and I laughed. Callous, cruel woman. He gave me a hurt look, and then didn't say anything for a few long minutes. I wanted to comfort him, I really did. But rather than move and speak wrong, I stalled and remained silent. It was a mistake, but how was I to know?

"By the way," he finally ventured, studying some green slime that had spattered onto his T-shirt, "why did you take Richard's Rover out last night, and return this morning?"

"What makes you think I was out all night? What if I said I wasn't?"

"I'm afraid I wouldn't believe you."

"So what. I don't care. I'm going in now. This grosses me out." The last worm had been red, and my hands were covered with gore. I was scrubbing them at the kitchen sink with Swarfega when he came in and sat down.

"Why are you avoiding me?"

"I'm not avoiding you. I just didn't like the tone of our conversation."

"First there was that bicycle trip to Yarnton. Now you won't ever go with me for a weekend to visit my parents, and you've been so eager to stay at the castle alone. What's wrong? Do I smell? Am I unpleasant to be with? Do you have a lover?"

I dried my hands very well and rubbed some cream into them. They still stung fiercely. "Do you want a cup of tea?"

"You never answered my question."

"You didn't answer mine either."

"Yes. Give me a cup of tea."

I put the water on to boil, but I did not put the tea in the pot. I had been corrected on that too many times already; one first warmed the pot with scalding water, then added the tea. I stared at the teapot, my eyes crossing, almost talking to myself. "It's not you, Michael. Sometimes you're too good to be true. I suppose being alone is a novelty for me. I've never been alone like this before.

Robert stuck to me like a postage stamp throughout college. I never lived away from my parents, and from them I went directly to you. It's a novelty, that's all, but I'm developing a taste for it. Some women never really experience freedom until they sever the apron strings from their father and their mother, marry, and realize that their husband is a lot more malleable than their parents had been. I'm not scared of you like I was of them. I can earn my own keep now. Don't worry. You don't smell, and I don't have a lover. I could accuse you of the same, I suppose. I'm just starting to realize how easy it is to be alone, how nice it is to be grown up: no excuses to have to make for yourself and your behavior, no one to be accountable to. Does that make sense? Am I being a spoiled brat?"

I finished the tea and left it to steep by the stove. He was just sitting there looking down into his lap like a whipped puppy with the same glazed look in his eyes that I must have had a minute earlier.

"And another thing, Michael; I'm going to quit my job. I have to. I will. Next week."

9

Gay, gay, gay, gay,
Think on drydful domisday.

—BRITISH MUSEUM,
MS SLOANE 2593,
FIFTEENTH CENTURY

BRYNGESSY Priory. The Black Mountains of South Wales in the late summer. An old Volkswagen running without shocks. The past, the present, the future: walking on the tightrope between dimensions, the thin line of answers running like cat's eyes down the road through the thick Welsh mist.

"Surprise," Michael said. I hadn't remembered the way there, along looping B roads that followed the cleft of the Honddu Valley, so that it really was a surprise in the early evening dusk of a cloudy August day when Bryngessy loomed hazy before me, like a face from the past in a smoky room. The reddish stone arches of the thirteenth-century canons' quire and the Department of the Environment's perfectly groomed cloister were exactly as I remembered them on that winter morning months before. The cellar pub and dining room where the dormitories once stood and the tower beside the outer parlor rose up and up and around like a Welsh mist. We left the car on the gravel drive and carried our bag to the hotel porch beside the cloister. Michael did not appear flustered this time. It was as if he had purged himself of memories of his brother's blood, and this was the final step toward a lasting cure.

The man at the bar let us choose our room since we were the first guests there that rather damp week night. The east tower had been built in the twelfth century. In the eighteenth century the tower had been converted into a four-bedroom hunting lodge, incorporating the original Norman stone staircase into the design. The lower two rooms sat side by side and were closest to the hotel's only toilet. There were two more rooms up in the tower itself. One room was twenty-eight steps up from the comfort landing, the other one was fifty-two steps up. We chose the topmost room; we were young, fit, adventurous. The room directly below us was empty, so that we wouldn't have to worry about squeaky floors and intrepid dashes downward in the middle of the night. We had the entire tower to ourselves. All eight centuries of it.

The man led us through the vaulted priory kitchen in the former cellar (I dreamed as we walked of Barnes's library: of roasting cygnets, egrets, curlews, and capons; the butler, the carver, panter, chaffer, and parer waiting table; the cook in his cowl ruminating over the terrible question of musclade of minnows or eels in saffron sauce for the bishop; the fabulous odors that will drive the mind wild when it is fasting and dull it to the point of sloth when the fast is over) to the foot of the stairs. (Countless feet had passed that way. How many in pairs, like ours? How many alone? How many never walked down again?)

The stairs wound sharply up and around. The man went back to the pub, leaving us to struggle through the narrow, Norman stairwell, complicated by a large suitcase that had to be squeezed around tight corners. We hardly expected door-to-door service for four pounds a night, so we fought our way uncomplainingly to the topmost threshold. The room there was worth every step of the way.

It was a honeymooners' room, or a room where one could dream of resurrecting a dying marriage. The bed was in the center, with white curtains and a frilly canopy and four intricately carved posts. There was an eyelet-lace coverlet, feather pillows, and an eiderdown on the bed. Around the room, I saw two brass candlesticks for light, a small Victorian-insert fireplace for heat, and an old, finely lined Staffordshire pitcher and basin on the marble washstand. We found a wooden commode with a chamber pot sitting discreetly beside the bed, a wooden mirror on the wall, and wooden clothespegs set into the plaster: all the most basic elements for creature comfort. A single arched window cut through walls five feet thick looking down into the open nave of the ruined priory church. It was magical.

I leaned back onto the bed pillows while Michael rooted in the bag for his shaver, to quell the five o'clock shadow that always plagued him. We had gotten there in a roundabout way; I had thought, uncomfortably, that it was just going to be another day's outing westward, terminated by Cadfor. But he didn't turn south when he should have, when the sky was well advanced toward dark. I started to be suspicious then, when suddenly we were at Bryngessy. It was nice to be surprised like that, treated almost childishly. He had been trying so hard since June that, if such things could be at the mercy of reason, I almost felt guilty for not caring enough, or at least as much as he evidently did.

"This is really nice, Michael. What made you think of it?"

"I never forgot it. We were both so attracted by it last winter." Nice dodge. I admired his courage.

"You're so sweet you make me feel like an old bag of misery sometimes."

"That isn't my intention. Do you mind if I'm scruffy tonight? I don't seem to have brought the wretched shaver with me."

"Fine with me." I hesitated, not wanting to offend, or to tread on unstable ground. "Aren't you at all disturbed by this?"

"By this what?"

"This here. Remember your reaction to it last winter?"

"Oh, I've gotten over that. I was only bothered at not being able to remember when I had been here before." I sensed that he was lying. He was too brusque, the answer was too well rehearsed.

"It really doesn't bother you to be back here?"

"It wasn't a bad dream, Gay. Nothing horrible happened here. It was just the circumstance of my last visit, and what happened immediately after. It doesn't bother me anymore. The street corner where he was killed would bother me a lot more."

He sat down on the bed next to me then, staring at his feet. The rain had cleared away with oncoming dusk, and there was still enough light in the sky to discern shapes on the lawn below: column bases, odd earthen configurations significant only to archaeologists, casting their secret shadows over the turf. Now and then one could spot an ardent tourist darting through an open doorway leading into

[205]

yet another roofless, two or three-walled chamber, darting out again, stopping, gazing about, then vanishing from the framed screen of the bedroom window. It was too dark to read, too light to waste a candle, too warm to light a fire. There was a late summer rose in a small bud vase beside the bed.

"What's happened?"

"To what?"

"To us. I thought this would be such a good idea."

"It is. It's lovely here. It was a wonderful surprise."

"Not this. I mean coming back to England. You seem to have changed so much since we arrived. I'm really having second thoughts about us living here, yet you've never said that you wanted to go home. It's as if you're determined to be independent of me here. I don't understand."

"I'm not sure I follow you. How do you mean I've changed?"

He took off his wristwatch and set it on the bedside table—a prelude to sex, usually. He stretched out by my side, staring now at the pleated insides of the bed canopy, his eyes glistening in the advancing dark. "I don't know. Increasing distance, I think most of all. You never let me in on your thoughts anymore. For instance, when you quit your job it came as rather a shock. That wasn't fair. I hadn't a clue that you were so dissatisfied with it."

"I gave you fair warning, Michael, a couple of months before. You just weren't listening. I had so many small reasons that I couldn't think of any one important enough to tell you. You accused me of seeking a challenge. I was embarrassed. I didn't want to discuss it with you. I'll get another job before winter anyway."

"That's not what bothers me. If you need some time off, then by all means enjoy it while you may. What bothers me is your aloofness. Do you still love me, Gay?"

"You know I do."

"I wouldn't ask if I knew. Do you want to go home?"

"What's home?"

"Home is, presumably, where the heart is. Where the family is."

"Then I'd better stay right here."

He rolled over so that his left side was on top of me, and he buried his fingers in my hair and kissed me. I was thinking about the job I had left. There would have been almost nothing to do that summer apart from typing letters and odd bits of essays that Barnes was writing. It really hadn't been such a bad job. It was the feeling of entrapment that I objected to—a slave to the bus, to the bicycle, to the clock. I had been free now for almost two months. It was August; I had quit in June. But I had not yet reached the point where I took my freedom for granted. I would probably get another job, as I told Michael, when the winter came. Where, when, and what had not yet occurred to me. "Somehow you're not terribly convincing."

"What?" The room would have been dark enough for a candle if someone hadn't switched on some spotlights in the nave of the ruined church. It was just enough light to navigate around the room.

"I said you're not very convincing."

"What am I supposed to convince you of?"

"Your devotion to me."

"Do you want it in writing?"

"I have it in writing. I want it in actions."

"Sorry. I don't really know what you're talking about. I mean, what do I have to do to prove it? I haven't been unfaithful. I'm not overly lazy and fat. I wash and iron your clothes. I'm usually there when you get home from work. I cook. What am I doing wrong?"

"You're not talking to me. You're not *sharing.* You've got expectations that you're not telling me about. How are we supposed to get on together for the next forty years if I don't know what you want? Maybe *you* don't even know what you want yet. Perhaps I shouldn't have robbed the cradle."

I moved out from under him, stood up, and straightened my skirt. His tone of voice was unpleasant. I brushed my hair quickly, took up my purse and went to the door. He was quiet the whole time. "I'm going down to the pub."

"Wait up. We have more to discuss."

"I'll meet you down there," I said, and I left him in the darkness with the scent of roses.

As I descended the spiral stone steps, I forgot about Michael. I thought instead about words like "Dark Ages." They seemed misplaced outside of fairy tales and history books. The steps were much the same as they had been in the year 1200—perhaps slightly more worn. Why were they Dark Ages anyway? The words were stewing with visions of dirty yokel villeins dressed in ragged mantles and tunics with rusty hauberks who reeked of wood smoke. They had used hay for Kleenex then, hands for forks. I wondered if they would use modern cutlery in the restaurant that night, or if we might be served finger food on stale bread trenchers. I descended in a spiral, almost dizzily, thinking of the palmers, brewers, mummers, smiths, lepers, reeves, woodwards, cotters, parkers, and carters blindly obeisant to their lords, both temporal and spiritual. Michaelmas to Christmas, Candlemas to Easter, Hocktide, Whitsun, Midsummer and Lammas, on back to Michaelmas. Bringing in the May, the battering ram and boiling oil, tilting at the quintain. I descended, trying to keep Michael out, and past, present, and future in mind together. Wives were faithful then, because they had to be. Bryngessy Priory was there in 1109, it is still there today—only the outer configurations had altered slightly.

I bought a copy of the hotel guidebook downstairs for tenpence. Michael had still not come down. I ordered a glass of sherry and sat alone in the cellar pub to read it. There had been a Christian settlement there six centuries before the priory was built, it said. A primitive little hermitage was stationed beside the Honddu Brook, erected by St. David himself, the patron saint of Wales. Around 1100—exact dates were misty—a Norman knight and some of his men started to build the first church there: a simple little affair the foundation of which was now supposedly somewhere beneath the apse of the current parish church, located just outside the cloister walls. I read on, and stopped. A Norman knight. I skipped ahead a bit, skimmed the pages. His name. It was William de Lacy.

The mountains around the priory were steep and green and full of drama when the sun played with the heavy ocean clouds. The priory sleeps on the hillside, slowly turning back into dust, trying to erase a turbulent past. *Nos habebat humus.*

I toyed with my sherry while Michael, evidently, was sulking and taking his time upstairs. I tried to imagine how it was in the late eleventh century when William found it, after Gaie's death: a wild valley (strident female voices of the past, pigskin drums and bells of the Welsh princes passing through). The Christian community at Bryngessy had slowly disintegrated over five centuries and the small settlement left by the early hermits was now a ruin of untamed ivy, fallen roofs, nettles, and the desecrating rooks with their empty, cold cries. Time passed, more stones tumbled, and the rooks and adders were the only inhabitants of the settlement.

It was almost the new century when, one wintry day, the rare Welsh sunshine was teasing the earth, and this Norman knight, William de Lacy, kinsman to Roger de Lacy, Lord of Ewyas, lost his way during a hunting expedition (truth? legend? was he alone, seeking self-destruction?) into the thickly wooded and swampy Vale of Ewyas. He stumbled onto the ruins of the ancient hermitage and saw the fearful state it had fallen into; bleak and abandoned, the only sounds the wind and the swishing of the Honddu Brook.

It must have moved William in an unsettling way. He was convinced that he had to retreat there forever after, to erase a previous existence by rebuilding the little chapel of St. David and by spending the rest of his life there. According to the pub guidebook, legend had it that William de Lacy never removed his armor, but spent the rest of his days, as promised, at Bryngessy, clanking and squeaking over the rededication of the site in his mail and breastplate, suffering from dirty dreams. I felt goose bumps. History was mute on the reasons for both the armor and the dreams. Was it because of a self-imposed penance? Or was it due to corrosion brought about by the dank atmosphere of the valley? Only God and William knew. I wondered whether or not to tell Michael.

The guidebook went on to explain that by 1108 those same cellars, where I was sitting, sipping, reading, were there. And the reddish stone walls of an earlier priory church were growing with the enthusiasm and increasing numbers of newly admitted canons. Canterbury proclaimed it Augustinian (the Cistercians already had a reputation for miserliness, and the Benedictines were known as lazy and lecherous). The monks were known as Black Canons after the color of their habits, and Bryngessy prospered during the early part of the twelfth century under the patronage of people such as the Constable of England—Walter of Gloucester—Queen Matilda, and Hugo, Third Baron Lacy. William's brother.

However, the community suffered a setback around 1135 when King Henry I died. Wild Welsh tribesmen, always on the brink of attacking, heard of the king's death and of King Stephen's ineffective and disputed rule. It resulted in anarchy, slowly at first, getting worse as time went on. Many of the canons were driven out of Wales, seeking refuge with a former prior in Gloucester, where another priory, Bryngessy Secunda, was established. Between 1175 and 1230 the priory church and outbuildings at Bryngessy Prima were completed by the slowly returning canons, feeling guilty that they had abandoned their mother house before peace had been restored again in the mountains. The community once more increased in size until later in the thirteenth century.

I looked up from the guidebook long enough to rest my eyes in the dim light. The bar was lit with oil lamps, the only windows set into the doors up a flight of stone steps opening into the cloister. The barman had retreated into what I assumed was a kitchen since it emitted cooking sounds: sizzles, the noise of a belching pot, dish against dish, the clank of cutlery. The pub was not very busy. An ancient gentleman sat almost rooted to a settle bench next to the bar, every now and then raising a pint of very dark beer to his lips for a ponderous, appreciative, palsied drink. Three young men in Wellington boots and capelike green macs with hoods sat around a small round table near the door. They were unusually quiet, perhaps not wanting to protrude like disrespectful elements in the ecclesiastic atmosphere of the old priory's cellar. A couple of middle-aged people tied their Corgi to a post on the porch and came in, bringing with them a gust of warm August wind that had already blown all the clouds aside to reveal a nacreous moon. The barman emerged silently, like a trapdoor spider, to take their order. I asked for another sherry and went back to reading. It had been half an hour and Michael still had not appeared.

The Black Mountains were treacherous and wild then. The hills and woodlands were havens for outlaws and wayward noblemen who chose to rule their demesnes as tyrants. The people were, out of sheer necessity, lawless and self-aggrandizing. The canons at Bryngessy succumbed to the threat of all ages—greed—and they were forced to defend themselves against the overtaxed local population on many occasions. Mutual enmity prevailed, one group attacking the other, murdering, pillaging, up until the sixteenth century when Henry VIII pulled the carpet out from beneath everyone. Monastic life in Britain was given a stark pit to lie in and was covered over forever. On 10 March 1538 the Reformation claimed Bryngessy. It was no longer a house of God, but just another parcel of land on a remote Welsh hillside. The king sold it to Nicholas Arnolde, Chief Justice of Ireland, for the degrading sum of £160. Arnolde would not even live at the priory; instead he built a grand new house in the Tudor fashion at a nearby cross-roads.

I remembered the travel book I had read, furtively, before we moved, rife with legends of spectral monks that Michael had scoffed at: men who had lived simple lives, from boyhood to manhood to old age, within the cloister walls. Men who knew virtually nothing beyond the limits of their community, removed from the rest of the world by stone walls and the invisible grace of God. Matins, Lauds, Prime, Terce, Sext, None, Vespers, Compline and over again, with the same chores sandwiched between each trip to the chapel, whether it was weeding the community garden, plucking the chickens, or cleaning the cesspool. From boyhood, sometimes from infancy, the monk was shielded from daily trials by his religious community. He grew naïve, fat, and oftentimes helpless. In 1538 these monks were turned out of their lifetime homes without having been trained in worldly skills, without money. It was traumatic for many and they died both physical and psychological deaths. Some died sooner, some later, wandering mad, loathed or feared as Papists, alone for years before expiring shamefully, as beggars or lunatics. The thousands of inexplicable dark figures who still moved about the ruined cloisters of Britain were perhaps the remains of those who could not cope with the change, and returned to the familiar life within the cloister.

I thought of the ghosts at Bryngessy over my second glass of sherry. It seemed logical that if there were ghosts there, they would be the canons. Or, going back to an even earlier time, perhaps even William, in mail and breastplate. But I could not allow my imagination to dwell on that for very long. It was just coincidence that he had married a daughter of Cadfor, and founded Bryngessy as well, but it did make me a little nervous. I had been curious about Bryngessy ever since I read about its connection with Cadfor in Richard's haunt book. I wondered what "similar manifestations" the author had been referring to in connecting the two places. It might have had something to do with the de Mauro-Lacy marriage link. I wondered if it was common knowledge that Bryngessy's founding father had been a married man?

The dinner that night was every bit as good as Richard had suggested it would be the winter before. Michael tended to eat too much when he was upset; he had a snakelike tendency to gorge himself ruthlessly, then roll into a dead, obliterating sleep for twelve hours or more. I had pork cooked in cider along with the customary English staples: chips and brussels sprouts. Michael had a fresh trout baked in Pernod, sprinkled with blanched, slivered almonds. There was a potent rum tart for dessert with plenty of clotted cream, a fine bottle of burgundy, and tea served in the outer parlor afterward.

It was very quiet that night. We were alone, no other guests had turned up. Our stomachs were full to bursting. Although the meal had been inexpensive, Michael had left a five pound tip. He was very impressed with everything about the place, now that he seemed to have transcended his initial apprehensions, impressed enough to have been distracted from pursuing our previous conversation over dinner. I was still feeling upset with him. Wrong word. Not upset, but indifferent to his feelings. I wanted to tell him about William de Lacy, and his wife with the unusual name, but he had accused me of not sharing, not knowing what I wanted. It was a self-fulfilling prophecy. I would keep that tidbit of information all to myself for the time being. And would wait, and tell him later within the familiar walls of Warborough when the bad feelings had settled down. It was lovely at Bryngessy and our argument had done enough damage to that already.

A small coal fire in the poet Landor's eighteenth-century grate kept the late August chill from nipping. Michael did not make it all the way through his first cup of tea, perhaps overly anxious to escape in sleep from our disagreements. He had drunk quite a few pints of heady Penrhos porter in the pub before dinner while I daydreamed over my third glass of sherry. From a distance, I watched him toast Bryngessy's oldest inhabitant sitting deep in his settle, toast the barman, toast the cook invisible in her kitchen, not toast me, but toast anyone else who had the misfortune to walk through the door that night. The combination of porter, wine, and trout made him feel, and look, rather like soft lead.

He excused himself early and started the long climb up the sixty-three steps in the tower to our bedroom at the top—a sobering journey. I listened to him as he went up, shuffling step by shuffling step, foot against timeworn stair, hands balancing and sliding along the stone walls, groping around and around in the darkness with just the frail pinprick of the candle guiding. They were the only sounds there except for the grandfather clocks and an occasional clack of dishes being washed in the kitchen at the distant end of the pub.

I sat with the host's cat in my lap, a six-toed tortoiseshell tom, for a few minutes longer. I savored the loneliness, the rows of odd stoneware jugs on the mantel and the shelves around the room. There were brass and copper hunting horns slowly tarnishing over the doorway to the wine cellar. Two tall case clocks ticked to different time zones. A row of copper teakettles were turning green with age and lovely neglect above the fireplace. I looked over the polished surface of the heavy oak table with indentations where centuries of rude elbows had leaned, wondering why I loved him, if I still loved him. At last the open door to the tower was very tempting to sleepy eyes and unpleasant thoughts. I left puss on the chair and started climbing myself.

When I got to the top, after an intermediate stop at the loo, Michael was already asleep, as I had expected: snoring, twitching, hopeless until daybreak. There would not be any resurrecting of elusive marriages done in that room that night. He had left his candle burning and I set mine beside it on the bedside table. The sheets on the bed were a gaudy canary-colored nylon, a nasty English phenomenon. I had first encountered them at Richard's castle. They made me sweat, and I did not like them very much.

I crawled into bed beside Michael, leaving the candles burning. I wanted to enjoy the room awhile longer. I wanted to see the domed ceiling, the rugged wooden mantel, the old solid iron bolts on the door. I wanted to see everything worth seeing and remembering in that remarkable room. I wanted to pretend that it was three hundred years ago and that I had just been ravished by a handsome, dark, itinerant tinker. I wanted to hear Brother Rhys swishing through the cloister on night watch, his ears tuned to the stables for sounds of marauding villagers. I saw the carved bedposts, the canopy, the whitewashed plaster walls, the image of two candlesticks casting shadows over the fireplace. It was nicer than Cadfor; there were no obligations. One paid for what one got. One did not have to feel guilty or obtrusive. One did not starve. I hardly felt self-conscious about my nationality. I saw the moon, full and white, pass behind the clouds, hushed and imperceptible past the window. I heard a dog baying in the hills, felt Michael's warm back against my side, and I was falling asleep just as the monks were waking up for Lauds.

Vita tua debilis
et mors flebilis
Quare non tristaris?
Nam per mortem transiens
et non reverteris,
fragilis ut glacies
et cras morieris. *

—ANONYMOUS,
THIRTEENTH CENTURY

We are as fragile as ice, and tomorrow we may be dead, I kept thinking, a sleep-inducing fragment from a song I had heard many times before going over and over in my head. As fragile as ice, our lives melting slowly all around us until we were nothing and no one but air and dust and memories and then nothing, never to return. Like ice, hard to the touch, but once touched, we disintegrate. Like bodies untouched for centuries lying in their tombs, but when the lid is at last lifted we do not rise up again like spring flowers, but rather, disintegrate at the merest tender waft of fresh air. Then we are gone, forever, the molecules redistributed perhaps, but the original essence gone: turned to puddles, or a box of dry old bones wasting space in some lovely verdant churchyard. Nothing is permanent but change; there is no tomorrow. There is no such thing as love, as fidelity, and marriage is a myth for romantically diseased women. As fragile as ice. The icicle fell that night and it shattered. It did not melt. It did not disappear. It simply shattered, and the atoms were scattered.

I lay there thinking about Michael and me. The failure of the past few months to concretize our union could not all have been the fault of my alleged immaturity—"robbing the cradle," he had said earlier that evening. We had not established our solidarity as a couple, with the gradual moving apart, the cruel silences, the leaving behind. There was no way for me to judge how my own strange behavior was really affecting him, since the metamorphosis into two

---

*Your life is frail
and your death is lamentable
why do you not grieve?
Now you pass through death
and will not return,
You are as fragile as ice
and tomorrow you may be dead.

separate entities had been so insidious and gradual. I flew off into rare rages and I sulked, as I suspected most women did some of the time. He did complain when I went away without him—to Cadfor, to Yarnton—although as time went on and the separations increased in frequency and duration, his complaints sounded more hollow to me.

I became reconciled to this mysterious restlessness. Was it me, I wondered? Was it what marriage had done to him, to us? Would it have happened this way with anyone he had married? Or with anyone I had married? I had fought the demons with their tempting scenes of lusciously disgusting infidelity. That was not what I was after. Michael did not bore me enough to drive me into the arms of a lover, although I believe I could have done it in retaliation if he had told me that he had taken a lover. Yet I wondered how much of his desperate clinging to what I smugly assumed was an impossible marital ideal was the result of my scorning it.

There was something very seriously wrong here that I consistently refused to face, had refused to face ever since we moved to England, and possibly before: that Michael was a good, honest man at heart, and I had all the potential for being a spoiled, selfish brat. Such an awfully simple explanation—my selfishness and his honesty —but wasn't that the essence of it? I did not try because I saw him trying until he was blue-faced and teary-eyed. He would not stop trying either, because he would not admit defeat. He loved me with more of his soul than I let myself love him with mine.

I didn't realize the limitlessness of such love. I set boundaries, for some reason that was yet unclear to me. Perhaps I wanted to avoid the responsibility of his love. I felt that I could have overstepped the boundaries, but I didn't want to just yet. Men give excuses for such behavior by saying that they want to be free to experience quantity and variety. They just aren't ready to be tied down, one person bores them; none of that was true for me. I think I just wanted to be a baby for a while longer. A free baby, indulged, cosseted, and loved to distraction. It was a curious withdrawal I had experienced. We could still lie there side by side without snarling and drawing daggers, so wasn't there hope?

The cold, clear sheet of ice that divided the bed in half was my answer. Melt that, touch a congenitally sickened heart, reshape an alien soul that resisted sharing for the same reasons that Michael wanted to share, and maybe we had a chance. A tiny chance. A compromise was still possible. I could take a new job, try to immerse myself more in his hobbies, forget my fantasies, try to be realistic for once, content myself with one man and a little cottage with roses. But at the same time I knew that a compromise was not possible until I had purged myself of something that clung to my soul like a tenacious sucker of ivy. Romantics die hard. They do not like to admit that some people are best left alone, even if only for a short time. They do not like to turn their backs upon what the Lord has joined together, even if the knot has slipped out, even if they are joined together only by someone else's word and not in their own souls.

The dilemma was very clear to me. It was plow or perish: dig now, or die. It could not be denied any longer, for wasn't it worse to be left than to do the leaving? The dead do not mourn. After all, I still had my free will, and it was time that I exercised it rather than waiting for the miracle that would unfreeze my heart, change my attitude overnight, and fill the skies with rainbows, candy canes, and bluebirds. I was being selfish, I knew—romantic, lazy—not inclined to do much about it just then, as long as I had Michael's devoted attention. I needed to be left alone, because young dreams die hard.

It must have been the peculiar translucent quality of the air in the Black Mountains that helped me make such clear sense of it that night. It has never since seemed as simple. The moon was full, a big cheesy harvest moon; the air seemed to be sparking with mystery, wisdom, life, death, love, loneliness. I had kept myself awake before, thinking hard like this. It would be a sleepless night, I could tell. Thinking should be done during daylight hours—not in bed.

One of the candles had guttered out but the other one was burning bravely beside the bed when I groped for Michael's watch. Two o'clock. Breakfast was at eight, and Michael had to leave early. He wanted me to drop him off at the station in Bristol to catch a fast train to London. It meant I would spend the next night alone in Warborough. Another long week of uninspired pottering in the garden, feeling some guilt for not earning money, yet not enough to spoil the luxurious feeling of the freedom of unemployment. I really had to get some sleep. I couldn't afford to be crabby the next day. I heaved over onto my side, turned the pillow over to where it was cooler, put my back to Michael's, and wished myself to sleep. But there was the candle.

It could have been a dripping faucet, or a dog barking irregularly, invisibly in the distance, or the slow but steady progress of a spider across the ceiling. The inaudible ticking of his watch could have been responsible, or even the wind rattling a loose hinge somewhere in the valley. I was not going to sleep that night. It seemed such a shame in that delightful room, when I needed the sleep so badly, when Michael would wake up refreshed and unsympathetic to my baggy, dark eyes and gravelly voice. But when the mind refused, its refusal was irrational and absolute—not to be seduced by the creature comforts of the mattress and the eiderdown.

There was a certain obstinate pressure directly behind the eyes on insomniac nights: a pressure that pushed inward rather than outward. It was a feeling of agitation in parts of the body seldom used. My stomach burned slightly and rumbled. I had to keep bending and stretching my legs, moving into awkward postures that would eventually, painfully, freeze up my muscles. My eyes felt as if they had dust or sand in them. My mouth was dry from the alcohol, and my nose tickled. Everything felt wrong. And all the time my thoughts were bounding through my brain, pushing it into a tight little ball, wadded up like a piece of cottony soft white processed bread in a wet fist. Nothing would relax. I felt I had so little self-control that night. Once I had succeeded in relaxing my knees, I realized that my diaphragm was tense. I could not even concentrate on one single set of insomniac ideas, tripping over the arbitrary dross of my mind.

I was reaching over to snuff out the offending candle, catering to the mind's irrational whim, when I noticed a flickering light weaving back and forth, up and down, in the tiny space between the bottom of the old wooden door and the floor. *Fire*, I thought at first in a second of panic, my aorta suddenly rising to choke me. Then I remembered that there was nothing flammable out there. The staircase and the walls were made of solid stone. I would have smelled the smoke by then, too, or felt the heat, or heard an alarm; and besides, this light was no more brilliant than the flame of the candle burning beside the bed.

Who would be out there on the stone stairs, sixty-three steps up from civilization? The wretched stairway led only one way, right up to our room, so that no one could have taken a wrong turn. On the other hand, a late arriving guest, a *very* late arriving guest, could have overshot the right level and kept on winding if no one had shown him the way. Yet if so, then why didn't he open the door and see for himself? I snatched my robe from the foot of the bed and walked as softly as I could over to the door on the balls of my feet. It wasn't completely shut, which surprised me. I thought I remembered hearing it lock, click. The latch was even ajar. I was about to put my ear to the door when I heard someone call my name.

"Gay."

I had heard that voice before, and it was not my husband's. Michael lay sleeping like a stone, his dreams gray, shapeless phantoms incomprehensible to me. I pulled the door open just an inch, and peered down into the stairway.

He smiled up at me, standing about two steps down, holding some kind of an iron hurricane lamp with a single candle burning in it. He was dressed exactly as he had been the autumn before, in the wheeling dust of the old barn, only without the armor breastplate and the mail. He smiled at me, a face creased and benevolent. Those wonderful dark eyes were like wells reflecting specks of gold and sunlight at the bottom. He had a crooked smile, I noticed. I had never been close enough to see it before; it came up higher on one side than the other. His hair was unevenly trimmed, very black, brushed carefully off his face, straight back, covering his ears. I smelled a spicy scent, perplexing and tart, like cloves. He held his hand up to me, as if to assist me down the steps, and I took it.

There was no hesitation this time—no spark, no lightning: just a warm, dry hand in mine, with an inviting, crooked smile. After all, he was almost an old friend. A woman could tell; I knew that he meant me no harm. If there was any harm to be done, I would be the one doing it. He seemed so vulnerable with that smile.

I was curious, too, but most of all I didn't care. Life with Michael loomed ahead like a great blank that I could not imagine how to fill without a lot of time spent alone pondering it. I would surely be eaten alive by doubt if I did not go with him, and Michael would never want that. My marriage was fading. What did I have to lose? I wanted some answers, but God never speaks to us directly unless we are saints.

I don't remember what I was thinking of exactly as I shut the door behind me and walked quietly down the steps with him. Perhaps I was wondering his name, why he was after me, what this odd attraction was that I certainly felt for him: a kind of pity and a physical attraction at least. I wondered, wanted to ask what he felt for me, how he knew my name, and where to find me at the strangest times. In retrospect, I felt as if something had snapped just then. Like a stroke, a numbing of certain parts of my body had taken place, and I no longer felt Michael. Something had collected around my heart: it stopped when I took the man's hand. Something had seized up in my brain at the same time, and I wasn't able to think about whether or not this was foolish or wise, to descend the stone steps with a strange man and a crooked smile. To think just then would have spoiled it. I might have backed off again or been unnecessarily frightened, although there seemed nothing to be frightened of.

I didn't believe in ghosts that were warm and hard to the touch. He was real. I supposed, afterward, that he might have been just a shy, devoted admirer who had followed me around the world with some very good magic tricks up his sleeve. He did not behave like a dream. He was no conventional spook: no cold, bloodless phantom wafting through a moonlit graveyard. He was no bogeyman hiding underneath the bed, whispering to me like low thunderheads. This was a man. Just a man. A kind, warm man whose black hair was soft and fine, his beard stubble stippled with salt-and-pepper, who smelled faintly of cloves and lettuce, whose hands were warm and dry and callused.

He squeezed my hand in his as he led the way cautiously down the spiral steps, holding the lamp before us. His leather boots clumped against the stone. He stopped once to brush a cobweb out of his eyes. He even turned to me near the foot of the steps, at the entrance to the dining room, as if he could not wait, and he put his lips to my forehead. They were warm, dry lips. He kissed with affection and sincerity, and it ran through me like hot oil, settling into the pit of my stomach, into my womb like moths batting around a flame.

The fire in the grate was glowing bluish-orange. In front of it, the cat was wrapped in a hot, tight knot where I had left him on the chair. He did not wake up as we glided past, undid the lock, and walked together out onto the porch and into the cloister. The sky was full of dim stars that were visible only in the corner of your eye. The moon was high now and yellowish over the mountaintops, giving off enough light to make the lamp unnecessary. He left it on the flagstones of the porch and motioned for me to follow him over toward the western slope of the hills—beyond the priory ruins. I was reluctant at first to go all that way; my feet were bare and the grass was damp. He was, after all, a stranger, and I am not inherently the trusting sort. He tugged a little at my hand. His eyes glimmered in the dark. His hair looked so soft and clean. He kissed me again, longer, on the mouth. I went with him.

He shinnied easily over the wall that separated the priory grounds from a green meadow; then he helped me over, awkward in my bare feet and long nightdress. He walked on up to a sort of grassy, treeless strip that seemed to run bare all the way to the summit of the mountain. We stopped at a place beside the wood which he had, evidently, prepared for us. There was a thick sheepskin spread over the ground, at least five separate skins all sewn together to make one very sizable rug, and a coarse wooly blanket on top of that. He sat down on the skins and tugged me down beside him. The moonlight felt almost warm. The man's arms were warm. He held me tightly at first, as if I were a wild rabbit ready to bound free. Then he held me loosely, but securely. I felt my face reflecting the moonlight and the stars. He said my name again, whispering it, lovingly. I noticed that he had something like a French accent, but not exactly. We had not had much opportunity to speak to one another. Logic prevailed. I tried.

"What is your name?" I asked slowly, as if I was speaking to a deaf-mute who had to read my lips. He shook his head no. I tried to remember the words in French, a language that I had not even considered since my last school examination some nine years before. It was worth a try at least.

"Appel? Nom? Ton nom?"

The light spread across his face and he said something very quickly that I could not understand. He laughed at me, stroked my hair, and then he said it again, slowly. *"Guillaume."*

William. I remembered that much French. It was familiar, perfect. So my lover was a Frenchman named William. How utterly romantic.

"Je m'appelle Gay Mortenson," I said in an ugly American accent, wishing that it did not sound so nasal and twangy. My accent sounded bad in any language. But he already seemed to know my name. He ignored me, interrupted me as he ran his hand down my cheek.

"Tei aim si sai ke te numes Gaie de Mauro."

I did not understand him just then, but that did not seem to deter him. Whatever he had said, it was sweet.

"Ne te peüsse oblier. Nule altre amer ne peüsse."

"Comment?" I could make almost nothing of his French, yet in spite of the language problem I understood that he was saying that he loved me. I basked in it. He was so gentle with me, so happy and warm. He held me in his arms like I was a little jewel, or a small sparrow. He ran his fine, long, hard fingers over my cheekbones, around my ears, down my neck to my shoulders where he pushed the robe off and helped me to wriggle out of it. It was not cold, and I did not fight him. He pulled the blanket over my shoulders, and he kept kissing me.

"Ne te peüsse oblier. Tant dolce m'est de tei li souvenirs."

We lay down on the sheepskins and I was only thinking of the mild spicy aroma of his hair, his wonderfully chaste, dry kisses, his warm and gentle hands working all up and down my body. He seemed so experienced, so generous, so content to just be touching me, as if by acquiescing I was giving him the most perfect gift a woman had ever given a man. He was so appreciative, so affectionate, and I held him close to me. I wrapped my arms over his back and I buried my face in his neck and I kissed him, too.

I held him with all my might because it was so good to be with someone who was no one: to undo all the strings and open up completely for a stranger in the darkness. "I love you, William," I said, not knowing if he could understand me. But I think he did because he said something back that I could not understand either. We pushed down on the soft fleece, deeper, and were almost smothered in it. I asked him not to wait any longer, hoping for him to understand. He rolled over onto me, into me, starting to rock gently above me in the darkness until I imagined he was everywhere around me at once: dawn, sunrise, dusk, moons, stars. His face was moving around on top of me too close to see without blurring the soft dark edges, to explore the lines etched around the tanned eyes. I tried to see his face as he pushed at me gently, my own body heavy with first despair and then guilt.

These emotions did not take long to turn into blind willingness, but then just as suddenly I felt a terrible urge to rush back to the tower to my husband. I had to see the moon shimmering in the early autumn sky and feel the cool earth free beneath my bare feet. I had to be free of the wretched guilt, and the horrible regrets that would surely come. But he kept me riveted, rocking gently, a contagious, slow rhythm, like he was approaching the center of the earth inside of me. As he came closer he sensed that he could not make it all the way so he increased the pressure just slightly with each slow thrust, frustrated by fleshly resistance. I felt his weight above me in the dark as a distinct mass, his beautifully proportioned body, visible in moonlight. The black symmetrical hair on his chest was rubbing against my breasts, his feet to the east and face to the west, aligned like an abbey church. I was too close now to see those melancholy dark eyes reminding me of the entrance to hell for the unfaithful wife, the pathway to heaven for the lover, the peephole to the soul.

His fingers wrapped through my hair, and I heard the delicious foreign voice saying something like *dieu* and then my name, over and over. I heard myself telling him not to stop, lascivious-sounding words, with devils and succubi and angels reflected in his dark eyes when he pushed up and looked down at me. My own guttural yesses were hisses like a snake's; they were sounds so distant that they were like another voice, disembodied, from a bystander who was translating all that I had felt when I saw him in the barn, at Cadfor, in dreams before marriage and after. I hooked my chin over his shoulder, to see his back sloping into the moonlight, buttocks with a soft furry coat of dark hair.

We had to prove that centuries were nonsense, that time was nonexistent. Death was cruel and unnecessary: we had to prove that I needed him and he needed me—to soothe one another, to wound one another, to love and to hate. Contrary notions, souls in the dark, where all things were possible and probable. *Dieu,* he kept saying, over and over, and other strange little words like tiny black swirling masses in the dark summer universe all around us, with no place to light upon, no person to hear and understand and absolve.

I had known it would happen, months ago. It had to. I had tried it with Colin and it was not time then. Colin had not been the right one, and even now I fought with silent morals, unable to cry out because I half hoped that he would stop all by himself and go away. But then I knew that it was too late, and I hoped that he would never stop. There were hidden ears and eyes everywhere in the wind, in the sky. My mouth was too dry then to cry out anyway as he buried his hands in my hair for one last thrust: one leg astride my thigh, the other hand stroking my breasts like they were made of thin porcelain, as fragile as November ice. *Deus ait mercit de t'aneme,* he said. Yes, I said, and the ghost became a man to me.

I had been a little bit scared of him. I had been scared of him even though he meant me no harm, and he never threatened me in any way. We tussled on that fleece for what seemed like an hour before we won each other and melted together finally: two human beings connected in flesh for such a brief space of time in the face of eternity. Then he was gone. Gone from my body, gone from the mountainside, gone from the priory, gone without a comprehensible word or some acknowledgment of the pain and the confusion and the regret that he had left me with.

We lay there for a long time afterward on the skins, both of us covered by the blanket, arms and legs intertwined underneath like creepers. Then he nudged me out of a dreamless dream, lifted me to my feet, helped me back into my gown, and walked me back to the priory grounds. He set me down on top of the wall, vaulting over it himself, then holding me all the way to the door of the dining room where his lamp still burned on the flagstones. He kissed me once more. Now I was the one with tears in my eyes, but there was nothing else I could do.

"A Dieu, Gaie. Tei aim. Deus ait mercit de nos anemes," he said, and like a dream he walked with his lamp across the cloister in the direction of St. David's—becoming fainter and paler and whiter until he just disappeared around the corner. I had a mind to follow him, but if that was what he had wanted he would have turned around, asked me to come along. There was an awful finality to the way he had left me. I turned around and quietly moved back into the sleeping darkness of the hotel tower. The cat was still there, its sides puffing in and out rhythmically like a bellows. The embers in the grate were still glowing a deep orange and blue, exactly as I had left them. I went up the stone steps, winding around in the dark alone like a fog, feeling my way against cold stone with my hands until I could see the light coming from underneath the door of our bedroom.

The candle was still burning. Michael was sound asleep. Nothing had changed, but me. I blanched slightly at the thought of climbing into bed beside Michael after what I had just done, but it was too late for moonlight confessions . . . and what could I have said anyway? That I had just laid a ghost? I didn't even know what had happened, or why I had allowed it to happen. It just had, and I didn't much care for reasons anymore. I blew out the remains of the sputtering candle and I fell asleep like death.

10

Al sal gon that man hier houet,
and al it scal bicome to naut. *

—BRITISH MUSEUM,
MS. ARUNDEL 248, c. 1265

ON Tuesday morning we left
Bryngessy. I took Michael to the station in Bristol where he caught
the first train for London. I drove back to Warborough alone and
packed that night while he was away. On Wednesday afternoon I was
back at Bryngessy. It was chancy, but I planned it so that I could bow
out gracefully. If they wouldn't have me, I could just plead temporary
insanity, pay for another day or two in the hotel, and return to
Michael with my face still clean. But I didn't *want* them to refuse me. I
was prepared to be a supplicant. By the time I reached the cloister
once again I realized that I had a lot more at stake than just my
humility; my pride was on the line, and my marriage. I had to do it.

A man with an eager white face came to the door. It was the
man who had been tending the bar when we were there. He had a
mild case of Dumbo ears and milk tooth, accentuated by balding,
wavy hair combed unnaturally to the side so that it stood up defiantly
over one ear. His name was Andrew, and he remembered me. He

---

*All shall disappear that man owns here,
and all of it shall return to nothing.

[224]

asked in his best hotelier's voice what he could do for me. I knew that it was plow or perish.

"Actually I was hoping to be able to do something for you."

"Oh, really?" The smile went immediately wooden, sensing solicitation. The great show of teeth was very nearly daunting.

"I was wondering if you could use any help here." I gestured unpersuasively with my elbow, since my hands held bags. "I mean, in the garden maybe, or in the kitchen."

"Help in the kitchen?"

"Yes. Or in the hotel? You know, I was so impressed when I stayed here that I was determined to come back and ask you. I'd even be perfectly content to work for room and board."

"Well, I really don't know about that. High season's almost over, and we've managed well enough so far. Perhaps next spring we could offer you something?"

"I really could use it now, though, and I'm sure you've got your hands full here most of the time. I was so much looking forward to this that I packed all my things for a long stay." I tried to raise the largest bag, but my arm was enfeebled from having carried it up from the road where my last ride had dropped me. "But I can't afford to stay for long unless I can earn my keep."

The man's grin appeared shellacked to his face and his chin started to recede into his neck, rather like a turtle. I thought that it was over, and started imagining with dread the unpleasant return and subsequent explanation, when a chubby blond woman in her late thirties thrust her head into the doorframe and said "Oh, hello." I repeated my entreaty to her, since Andrew didn't appear too eager to volunteer the information.

"Andrew, that's marvelous," she said. "Where were you four months ago, dear? Come on in and we'll discuss it over tea."

I pushed past Andrew with my big bags, fiscally responsible Andrew who evidently had not thought his wife was overburdened, and went with them into the priory kitchen. The woman—she said her name was Angel—put the water on to boil, chattering on about how impossible it was to do anything properly without help, admitting to unchanged sheets on some beds, unemptied waste cans, unfed cats, and carrots cooked in their skins, all for lack of assistance. Andrew sat sheepish and guilt-stricken in the corner, quietly polishing glasses. It was two hours until opening time at the pub, and I was aware that I shouldn't linger too long. I mentioned to Angel that I needed a place to stay, and that I could start working that very night if I just had a place to set my bags down.

"What's wrong with the cottage, Andrew?"

He turned from the sink with the numbed look of one who speaks but is never heard. "She wouldn't like that, sweetheart. No one's been up there in months anyway."

"It will be perfect for her!" Angel crowed. "A bit musty and dusty now, but you can sort that out tomorrow. Just open the windows and give the linens a good shake tonight. You'll have much more privacy up there. There, now I'll give you some fresh sheets to take up with you." I wondered why she assumed I wanted privacy. She must have remembered Michael. She seemed to forget about the tea, and hastened out of the kitchen in a distracted flurry. I felt obliged to address the sphinxian Andrew, polishing relentlessly, his eyes crossing and uncrossing.

"I hope I can be useful," I ventured.

He made a dispassionate "um" sound. I thought that was the end of our conversation until he suddenly whipped around toward me. His face had the expression of a pushy cartoon pig, his eyebrows wriggled like beached fish, his eyes bulged, his mouth went all askew. I was startled. I wondered if he might be having an attack of some kind, when he suddenly spoke.

"Oh, yes! I'm sure Angel will make quite good use of you. You must excuse me now. I have to set up for opening time." He nodded hugely, with a great monosyllabic laugh that said "HA" issuing from somewhere inside his throat. He was out through the swinging door into the pub just as Angel came back carrying a bundle of lavender-colored nylon, which she thrust upon me.

"It's quite a hike up. I'd go with you, but I have to get some chickens on for supper. I'd suggest you take only what you desperately need tonight, and Andrew can help you take the rest up tomorrow. Come on, I'll point you the way."

I rooted through my bags dutifully, transferring all items of dire necessity into a smaller sack, along with the sheets. Talking at an unflagging pace, Angel handed me a flashlight, steered me out of the kitchen and up into the hills. The path led roughly to the northwest along a cattle track. She told me to watch to my right for a fork, then to keep my eyes open to the left for the cottage situated just narrowly above the treeline on the hillside, almost camouflaged by stone outcrops.

Angel gave me the key to the cottage before abandoning me on the other side of the priory wall, in a meadow full of sheep. The sun was low enough to have caused a chill in the air, a breath of wood smoke and coal in the atmosphere. I carried on up through the meadow, through a wood where it was as good as night already, and over the treeline to the cottage. Surrounded by bracken and boulders, the cottage was tatty, cold, and unwelcoming that late in the day. Still, it was an acceptable end to a journey that had started out so uncertain.

It was small: one room, a beaten earth floor, and utterly unimproved. Angel had suggested I use the toilet in the pub as much as possible, only resorting to the outdoor one there in absolute emergencies. The water pump was installed beside a copper sink inside. Just to the side of the front door, piled underneath a simple wooden lean-to with a tin roof, was a pile of coal for the stove, which I gathered was intended to provide heat as well as a cooking surface. The furnishings were rudimentary: a table with two chairs, two kerosene lamps, a chamber pot, a box bed built into the back corner wall, one cupboard, a vestigial floor covering that might have been woven rags in some past geologic age, one plate, one cup, one fork, one cookpot, a broom, a stone hot water bottle, and a mirror on the wall that had lost substantially all of its silvering. There were two windows, both covered by drooping, yellowed curtains strung up on linen cords between two nails.

In two hours I had the cottage in slightly less depressing condition. I had a good fire going in the stove which would, with luck, be burning still at eleven, after work. The bedclothes were off and airing, fragments of moth and spider egg sacs vanishing in the cleansing wind that lashed over the mountaintop and made doleful sighs as it forced itself through the cracks in the stone walls and through the gaps where the window sashes had separated from them. The lamps were lit, the lavender sheets were on the bed with the hot water bottle warming them.

I washed myself, extinguished the lamps, and picked my way back down the hill with the aid of Angel's flashlight. The pub and restaurant did not appear to be too busy, but it was early—just gone seven—and she had said to expect the crush after eight. Angel was ladling soup out of a monstrous black speckled caldron when I came in. The smell was exquisite. I had not eaten since breakfast.

"How does it look up there?" she said, expertly stacking the filled soup dishes onto a platter.

"Just like you said, but I think I've made it habitable. I wondered if I could have a towel and a teapot up there?"

"Take whatever you need, but first could you take these soups out to the dining room?"

I had never been a waitress before. Time to learn. I pulled a plastic apron advertising Ruddles beer over my head, and served the soups. After that Andrew asked me to wash glasses, then to beat up some soufflés. I managed to eat between serving courses to a party of six, and after washing dishes it was nearly midnight before I felt guiltless enough to make noises about going back up the mountain. The prospect of fumbling through the dark, alone, did not enchant me. Angel detained me, without too much difficulty, with an offer of hot cocoa and bread. We sat, with Andrew grinning politely, slightly less opposed to my presence than he had been eight hours earlier, in the outer parlor. The fire was still burning, and all the lights were out but the one in the passageway that led up the tower to the hotel rooms. There were no guests at all that night. Andrew went across to switch off the light.

Angel was a short woman, fair, overweight. I guessed she was close to forty by the fragile, tenuous look about her eyes and the delicate lines forming there like hairline cracks on fragile, fine porcelain. She spoke with an accent that I could not identify, her *r*'s sounding like *w*'s, the rest of her speech hurried and windy so that one presumed her thoughts were correspondingly whiffling. She jumped tracks faster than I could follow her, and before Andrew returned to his Windsor at the fireside she had gone from clock repairmen to her niece's haircut to tomorrow's menu. I was too exhausted for conversation. I just listened, resigned, as did Andrew, thinking that it was nice not to have to go to work until late the next morning. It was a relief to be working there too, rather than in some stuffy green office in a city.

"I was just waiting in here for the phone to ring that night, getting awfully dozy, when I heard someone come in from behind," she said, having gone on to a new topic before exhausting the menu. I still wondered what I was supposed to buy in Abergavenny the next day, but I was too tired to ask. I supposed she would have a list prepared by the next morning anyway.

"And I got up from that couch," she pointed to a green velvet Victorian loveseat in an alcove by the door, "to see who it was, but the room was empty. We didn't have any guests then, as I recall . . . do you, Andrew?" He nodded and started to say something, but Angel continued. "No, we didn't. You see it was January and we close up most of the rooms then, but I was waiting in here for my mother to call from Devon, just nodding off over there under a coverlet when someone came clumping down the steps. Andrew was asleep next door in the farmhouse when it happened. We had closed the pub early because no one had showed up and I simply couldn't imagine who would be in the passage at that hour especially. So I called out to ask who was there, and as soon as I did that the door opened—I heard it, but I didn't see it—and then it slammed shut. I got up to peek, and you know there wasn't a soul there? Not a living soul! I couldn't figure that one out. I simply told myself that it was the wind, a draft, or some such thing, and I went back to my couch to wait for the call. But it happened again! Twice over—first these clumpy sort of steps coming all the way down the passageway, like someone's boots were too big for him. Then a pause, the door opens, the door shuts, but I watched the third time, and although I distinctly heard a door open and shut, the door there—by the passageway to the tower—didn't budge! It was the oddest thing. I always meant to ask Mr. Modgett about it since he seems to be acquainted with most of our local spooks. . . ."

Her voice trailed off for a moment, interrupted by a slumberous blast issuing from Andrew's nose and throat. His head was lolling over the back of the Windsor, his eyes half-shut and the balls rolling around grotesquely. His lower jaw wagged open, revealing three gold teeth and numerous silver fillings. "Oh dear," Angel said. "He always gets this way after a trying day. I think we'd best be getting on to bed, don't you? I hope we haven't kept you up past your bedtime, Gail? I am naughty, telling you ghost stories just before you creep out into the dark. Can you manage?"

I told her that ghost stories fascinated me. I tried to get her to go on, in spite of my fatigue, and Andrew's valiant efforts to drown out the conversation.

"Well, you know this spook nonsense has never affected me all that much. As soon as one moves into an old place like this, one always hears the wildest tales from the neighbors. And there are always guests with monstrous imaginations who come up with the most frightful stories of ghostly monks!"

"Have there been any recurring stories?" I asked Angel. "For instance, a ghost who appears to more than one person, more than once?"

"We did hear quite a lot about a thing in a cowl once, but that's to be expected in an old priory. I really don't think there's anything at all creepy about the old place, although Mr. Modgett does come up with some fine stories now and then, especially when he's had too much to drink."

"For instance?"

"Well, he likes to tell the one about the Welsh ladies prancing bare-bosomed through the frater when the monks were here. That was after Henry I died, in 1137, when there was a Welsh uprising out here and the local princes took over the priory for a brief time."

"That's pretty timid, really, compared with some ghost stories I've heard."

"I suppose so. There's also the one about the gravestone in the parish church. I rather like that one, but it's more of a mystery than a ghost story. I've never actually seen it myself. Mr. Modgett says it was reburied, along with the body, in the churchyard."

"What's so mysterious about a grave inside a church?"

"Well, you see this one was situated directly beneath the high altar, where one would expect to find some dignitary, and no one had a clue about who this lady was."

"A lady? Beneath the altar?"

"Yes. Curious, isn't it? Beside a priory, no less."

"Wasn't the stone marked?"

"Just initials, I understand. I really don't know much about it. You should ask Mr. Modgett next time he comes in. It happened when he was a boy, and he was there when she was exhumed, and reburied."

Andrew almost choked. He woke up with a massively loud gargle, lurching forward, amazed at the power of his own nose and throat. He looked right and left, gripping and releasing the arms of the chair. "Angel!"

"Yes yes, dear, it's time for bed." She reached over and patted his bald spot. He stood up, still not entirely sure of his whereabouts, staring at her like an obedient, but disoriented animal. "Will you be all right going up alone, Gail?" Angel said.

I told her that I would be fine, although I might really have preferred one of the empty hotel rooms that late at night. After taking the fifth best teapot from the kitchen, two towels from the warming cupboard, and a few more articles of clothing from my large suitcase, I left for the cottage with the flashlight. Michael hadn't called. I had left a note on the kitchen table, telling him where I would be, too. I had hoped he would call. Perhaps it was for the best that he didn't.

There were no stars in the sky, like I saw the night with William, and the cold smelled of autumn. The path was patchy with cow flop, but I was wearing rubber boots and it was harmless shit anyway— more mud and grass than real excrement. The wood was a solid dark mass to my right as I climbed Chwarel-y Fan, either a big hill or a small mountain, depending upon how short-winded you were. When I thought that I must be halfway up to heaven, I turned around to look over the valley. Below me, only infrequent spatters of light showed in the blackness. The farmhouse dimly visible beside the priory looked small enough to tuck into one palm, its lights undulating as leafy branches passed back and forth before my eyes. I turned the flashlight back on, and went on to my cottage.

If you continue to deny it, it does not exist. Or does it? Does it wait in the back of your mind, growing bigger and uglier like an unseen, unfelt cancer until it is too late to operate? Does it lie forcefully hidden until it is too late to deal with because it has gotten out of hand in your absence? Like the crowfoot and the quack in a neglected garden, or the dry rot left too long in a timber, once it is realized, the inside has already evaporated, the outer shell is just a dry sponge, a ghost of the former proud beam. If you try not to think about it, will it be forgotten, and go away forever? Or will it be larger than life on that unfortunate occasion when you do remember it, if only by accident?

No final words had been said, nothing had been concluded or resolved. That was the way it had been since we settled in England. I thought, maybe, that marriage would caulk the cracks, relieve me of some of my anxieties, turn me into a talker, a sharer. Then I thought that the moving would settle things between us, bring us closer together, reassure me of his conviction, and my own; but by that time I was getting accustomed to the way things were. Although I did not like what was happening, although I was, marginally, aware that I was blinding myself to our problems, I was resolved to them. Like winter. There was nothing anybody could do to hasten spring, or summer—no matter how hard you wished, hoped, and prayed. Winter eventually melted into spring. Spring blew into summer.

Summer faded into fall. Fall dropped back into winter. That was the way it was. There was no such thing as marital love, except in the first rosy idealistic months, and after that it was a steady progression toward winter.

I thought that by leaving it alone, leaving him alone, the problems might either self-destruct or fade of their own accord. But only the saints go to heaven when they die. Nothing was ever final for mortal men: not love or marriage or death. There was no sense in clinging to a premarital romantic dream that had started to dissolve months ago, I knew. If infidelity was so simple, there had to be something fundamentally wrong with the marriage. What had happened at Bryngessy had made that clear to me. The ice was still frozen, but it had shattered. Let it melt, evaporate, fall again as rain, refreeze. Perhaps in another form, in another place, it would be different and might work. Once reduced to adultery, though, there could not be much hope for returning to a pure and romantic footing, as it was in the beginning. The memory and the suspicion would always be there, a bit of soot that could never be scrubbed away. A scratch in the glass that interfered with the view. Sometimes that imperfection made a thing more interesting. Or it could make a thing worthless, particularly if it happened over and over again, even if only in your daydreams.

As if I didn't have enough agony, the mere word "Oxford" filled me with cold, hollow feelings of American inadequacy. Even his friends made me suffer stabs of inferiority: they had castles, they were sons of dons, some had titles. I had no friends there. They were all Michael's. He had a career as an appraiser, I was a housewife; and now I had my own bad behavior to reconcile with his utter goodness. I had no right to judge. Michael was simply perfect, except for the guilt he inspired in me by his perfection. And I was a worm, but reconciled to it, at least temporarily. It was akin to sticking my head in the sand. I ran away because it hurt less that way.

I shut the cottage door behind me and bolted it. The wind blew dust and leaves under the large gap between the threshold and the door. I stuffed a rug in the open space. The dark and the quiet expanded like a universe. Before I lit the lamps, the cottage's emptiness seemed boundless and eternal: space only to be filled by my own expanding chest—an appalling feeling of vacancy that wanted to come out, to dissipate, but the flesh was too strong and held it fast inside. The fear was there, too, as horrible as ever: of being widowed, of seeing ghosts alone, of being deliberately abandoned, all at once. Even though I had been the one who did the abandoning this time, it was mostly done out of fear that he would do it first. I lit one lamp. The walls, windows, curtains, furniture appeared. It all came back into perspective. I jabbed at the pale orangeness in the stove, threw on some more coals, and left the door open to watch the flames cast skittering lights across the floor as I got out of my clothes and into a flannel nightdress.

Not a word had been said of divorce, and it was just as well. I could not bear the thought of that kind of rejection just yet, and it was a small comfort that he did not (yet) have someone else. If he found someone else and said so, then I would quietly, bitterly, like a martyr, have my name removed from beside his on a legal document somewhere. St. Peter would have to pick up the crowns waiting for us in heaven and set them aside for another couple.

But I doubted that he would do that; once burnt, twice shy, and anyway he had been hard enough to capture the first time. He would probably get more satisfaction from torturing me with his goodness. He could put me away for unchastity, and perhaps I could divorce him for some equally nebulous reason, but that was not as easy to prove as adultery. I thought, though, that adultery was an awfully strong word for what I had done. The man might not have existed outside of my fantastic, idle, desperate dreams. But then I remembered that he had been warm, hard to the touch. I had gone with him consciously, willingly, deliberately, convinced that the other thing was lost forever. Whether with the living or with the nonexistent, I knew I had been adulterous. I had ruined my own romantic dreams, and now I was living alone for it, cloistered in my mean little cottage as atonement.

In the late summer dark, between slippery lavender sheets in air scented with dust, creosote, distant rot, I was so cold and alone that I could not sleep. I tried hard to think of what I might be missing back in Warborough. I was missing one half of myself, if not more. Strong arms, warm sides, someone who cared, wanted to touch me. I felt reasonably safe in the cottage. I had my stove, my coal, a cupboard full of tinned food that I doubted I would ever eat. If I wanted I could go for a week without seeing anyone except for the animals down the slopes. From my hillside they were as tiny as bugs and as far removed from me as moon creatures. It was so quiet there. My nerves were unusually calm, and I was my own master, subservient only to memories.

I weighed the alternatives again, for the fiftieth time, and decided that I was probably best left alone there for the time being—in spite of the occasional fits of melancholy I would inevitably suffer, in spite of the hole in my heart. The vacant spot in the bed, my betrayal, the wasteland that stretched from the Bryngessy valley clear across to a small cottage in Warborough, helped me make up my mind. I believed then that I was a hermit at heart, and hermits need something to suffer for, real or imaginary.

There were only my dreams to suffer with that night. Long, excruciating, exhausting dreams that I could never seem to waken from, but dreams that were, thankfully, just dreams. Michael was showing me pictures of women he had had. I sat there looking, waiting for him to come to the last picture—a picture of himself. That was the only picture I wanted to see. But the pictures of different women kept flashing before me, one after the other, endlessly. Michael did not recognize me in the next dream. His parents closed doors in my face, and threw fried tomatoes at me out the windows. Old Volkswagens broke down in vast rocky deserts. Michael sat at a restaurant table with a strange and exotic dark-haired woman. Women were making nasty faces at me, women I had never seen before. I had visions of Michael copulating with them on green hillsides in the moonlight. I could not exorcise the dreams even with the light from two kerosene lamps.

At some murky hour of the morning I got up to sit at the table, thinking, realizing with awful pain that I *was* alone, that we are all alone. No matter how the spirit may resist, we will eventually lie alone in that grave, if not in soul at least in body. I was afraid of that, and who isn't? I thought that life must only be a period of time set aside for the soul to spend reconciling itself to eternal aloneness. There may be souls moving beside or around us at times, but they will always drop away, sooner or later. There was no sense in fearing the obvious and the inevitable. It could only diminish the ephemeral, but very real, pleasures of clear sun, moonlight, lilacs; the pinching, stroking sensations of love. I knew that I had to believe in that to stop the pain. I had to find my strength in that.

There is a certain satisfaction in melancholy and self-pitying indulgence, as if that is how God intended man to be. Happiness and contentment could only be fleeting sparks. One worked to eat, to keep the wretched body alive. One worked to justify one's existence. It was the lot of all men to be melancholy for most of their lives, for without it we would all just waste and die and the world would end, uncaring, and uncared for. There was no such thing as peace in this world, I decided—not for anyone. All are dreams, and death is menacing. There was no such thing as solitude for the living. There were only memories. We live for memories.

I fell asleep soon after the sky exhibited a certain pinky evidence to the east that the dark was not going to last forever. There was great physical comfort in natural light. I woke when the sun was streaming full in the window. I groped, found that my watch had stopped. Rather than risk arriving late on my second day of work I got up, without much difficulty, since the *nuit blanche* had left me too tired even for sleep. The fire was out, but the stove was still toasty. The sun was warm enough so that I could dress without too much discomfort. I pumped some water out into the cookpot and tried to warm it on the stove, but the fire was gone. I washed cold and decided to use Angel and Andrew's shower before starting work.

I didn't realize that it was all that early until I was almost down the mountain. The quiet occurred to me like a sudden noise, odd for a weekday I thought. I should have heard the monotonous *nizz* of distant combines, muck-spreaders, tractors, seen more activity below. The sheep were in the same field as they had been the night before, the hotel was locked up tight. Angel had given me a key to the side door. I let myself in and smelled coffee. She was drinking it out of a glass pint mug, reading yesterday's *Telegraph,* her feet up on the kitchen counter.

"You had a phone call, Gail," she said. I was not yet confident enough of my position there to correct her on my name. She would see it in print soon enough and learn it.

"Michael, right?"

"Yes, I think that was his name. I didn't realize that he was your husband. He called last night as well, just after you'd left. Woke Andrew, he did, but Andrew can fall back asleep in seconds. He amazes me sometimes. I have to toss for a good half-hour before I'm ready. I really do wish I could drop off that easily. Just think of the time it would save! Did you have a good sleep?"

"You know how it is in a strange place the first night. You have to get used to it. Did Michael leave a message?"

"No. Just said he'd try again later. I didn't expect you up this early, I must say. Only reason I'm up is habit. There aren't any breakfasts to make this morning, but I've trained myself to get up at six, and it's not a good idea to muck up your schedule. This is the first time I've been able to read the paper in weeks; normally I'd be doing the last night's dishes, but we tidied all that up already. Fancy a trip into town today? We've got a full house coming this weekend and I'll be needing bags of things."

I didn't have a chance to answer her before the telephone rang in the outer parlor. She ran to answer it, and called for me. "I'll just start some cakes for the weekend," she whispered, leaving me alone with the call.

"Michael. Sorry I missed you last night."

"I think you've got some explaining to do. Shall we work from the present back, or vice versa? First tell me where you were last night. You leave me a note saying you'll be there, and when I call at midnight this silly woman tells me you've gone and won't be back till morning. What's his name anyway?"

"Don't be so silly. I'm staying alone in a cottage near here. I couldn't very well stay in their hotel for nothing, could I?"

"I expected you'd pay. Pardon me for presuming too much, but the note I have here says 'I've gone back to Bryngessy to be alone for a while, call me at the hotel.' From that I gathered you'd be staying at the hotel. What cottage are you talking about? Whose cottage?"

"Theirs. It's just a tiny little place up the cattle track—no electricity, no running water, dirt floors, very inexpensive."

"What do they make you pay for that, living like an anchorite? Sounds like you'd be better off in a tent, or back here."

"Costs nothing. Almost nothing. I'm doing work for them in exchange."

"You're *working* there?"

"Yes."

The line went quiet. He cleared his throat. I did not like the implications of that. "Dare I ask why?"

"I don't know. Go ahead and ask. I suppose I needed a change. Don't take it personally, Michael. I just haven't felt comfortable with you for months. I suppose ever since that fiasco with your parents in March. Everything we seem to accomplish here is due to your inspiration, your knowledge, your connections. I really need to prove to myself that I can survive here without you. I can go off on my own little sightseeing trips, be a successful tourist, get a job, feed, clothe, and house myself. Sometimes you make me feel like such a *dummy*. I'm just a drudge around you. I cackle and I sound like a stupid Yank. I look for *challenges*. I don't know how to make a trifle, I can't cook tripe, I can't even fill the car with gas. I don't know the difference between Labour and Conservative, I stick both my feet in my mouth around your parents. I even have a hard time dialing long distance here—all because in comparison you sound so good, you can do all these things effortlessly. I want to *learn*. I *want* to be as competent as you are. I *want* to be smart, but I don't like feeling like such a dummy in the process of learning. I feel like a spoiled brat sometimes, and not good enough for you. It's *my* problem, not yours."

"A dummy?"

"Yes, a *dummy*. Do you see? I'm not supposed to use words like that in front of you. I'm sorry. Would you rather I said a dunce? Is that better?"

"You needn't feel that way, Gay. That's nonsense and you know it."

"You see? You tell me that the way I feel is nonsense. If I feel that way, and have felt that way for eight months, it can't be all nonsense. And if it is, I mean to resolve that by putting in some time alone here to purge myself of it. It certainly won't happen in your company."

"Who have you been talking to?"

"Don't make accusations like that. Do you think I haven't got a mind of my own? You're as bad as my mother sometimes. What friends do I have here anyway?"

"I don't know. There was that Cynthia, and that weird girl in the bakery at Chislehampton. You were friends with Margaret at work."

"I had lunch with Margaret once. My accent must have offended her."

"I don't know what you might have done to offend her. Who did you go off with the night we stayed there?"

"What are you talking about?"

"You left the bed that night. You must have thought I was asleep. Where did you go? You must have been gone for at least an hour. Doesn't take that long to go to the loo and back."

"I don't know what you're talking about." The nasty edge of panic returned to my voice. He could tell. He pressed.

"Lying doesn't suit you, Gay. I saw you leave the room. Where does a woman go for over an hour in her nightdress at two in the morning in a hotel? Are you living with someone out there?"

"No, Michael. I don't even know anyone out here. That's the whole point."

"Look, I saw you go, all right? I can make the rest of the assumptions. There's no point in denying anything now. Whatever you did that night, it's done, and I can forgive you, because I love you—although I would still like to know some time why you did it, and what I did wrong. I suppose you met someone in the pub while I was upstairs. I can understand that. You were pretty upset with me, as I was with you, and that was your revenge. It isn't very nice to think that you have the capacity for that sort of behavior, but it is understandable."

"I don't understand what happened that night myself, so I don't see how you can."

"Just tell me this. Are you living with him?"

"Living with who? Of course I'm not! I don't even know where *he* lives. I'm not even sure that *he* exists."

"Truthfully?"

"Lord, yes."

"You mean I could come up and stay with you in your squalid hut any time, and I wouldn't find anyone else there?"

"Lord, no. But you aren't invited. At least not yet. Give me some time to catch my breath."

"Are you seeing him?"

"No, Michael. I *told* you, I don't even know who *he* is, and I'd rather not think about what I did that night. It's over, I'm sorry if it worried you, and I'm especially sorry that you had to find out, because it was no reflection on you or my feelings for you."

"I still find that rather hard to believe. If I was the perfect husband, why would you have done it?"

"Perfect husbands don't necessarily have perfect wives."

"Will we be together on our anniversary?"

I hesitated. He took me by surprise. I had forgotten all about our anniversary, and I assumed he had as well. "I don't know yet. Can you just leave me alone here for a while and try not to press me for any commitments? I know that sounds awful, but I really need

[238]

to be deprived of you for a time. Perhaps I'll come to appreciate you more that way."

"Whatever you like. But I want to see you. I want to talk, in person."

"We will, but not now. Loneliness builds character. I have to get to work, Michael."

"When can I call you again?"

"When do you want to call me?"

"Tonight?"

"No. Maybe next week some time."

"Till then. I love you. Be careful."

"Till then."

I hung up, offended that he had to tell me to be careful. In the shower I repeated the conversation over and over to myself. In a sense I had just reacted to his constant reassuring. He was so good that he made me bad. The chase was over, for me at least. I felt I had lost, even though he kept on pursuing the former pursuer. It was a little bit awesome. That morning I had felt lost and abandoned; now I knew that he wanted me, but that knowledge made me want him less. It was as if his pushing had shoved me further away rather than securing me, as it was intended to do. It was crazy.

Michael kept referring to *him* and *it*. The morning after, at breakfast in the dining room, *it* had never happened, as far as I was concerned. I could have had a vivid dream. There were no obvious traces of passion on me: no foreign dark hairs in private places, no sore bottom, no scratches, nothing like that. All I could really remember was the smell of him: lettuce and cloves. It was unusual to dream of smells. But that was all the proof I had to go by. I did not see *him* that morning around the hotel or on the priory grounds as we ate, paid up, packed the car. I remembered Michael's dream being so vivid that he said he could not shake the feel of it for days, or believe that it was only a dream. The morning after, *he* was no longer a feeling; he had been reduced to mere memory. The subconscious was subtle and powerful. He could have been real, or he might not have been; but adultery was the same ugly beast either way. Had he been real, I would have given in that night; and if he was real, then I did. I went outdoors and brushed my hair in the sun and warm breeze until it was dry. Angel gave me a grocery list and I drove Andrew's van into Abergavenny for the provisions.

After the two o'clock closing, in a tiny oasis between washing up and getting things ready for supper, I took a walk up into the hills, away from the cottage, hoping for some answers. I somehow suspected that he—William—could have told me all that I needed to know. But I knew that William no longer existed.

I went up the low southern slope and sat down in the dry green August sun. My eyes were scratchy with lack of sleep. It really disturbed me that Michael had seen me go that night. I had not even been certain of it myself the next morning, and I had almost made myself believe that what happened that night was a dream. But the fact that Michael was witness to it—to at least a part, if not all of it —made it indisputably real.

The man, William, had not felt unfamiliar to me: to kiss him felt quite natural. He bore no resemblance to either Robert or Michael, my only points of reference, so physical familiarity was not the answer. But nothing else could explain it, short of reincarnation, which was too far-fetched to even consider. The attraction was fierce, but short-lived. I thought of William distractedly now, as a milestone, a hurdle that I had stumbled over but managed to clear. I wondered how it could have happened that I was able to give myself so easily to an utter stranger—someone who had not and could not even talk to me. The attraction had to have been physical, animal, and nothing more, because we knew nothing about each other. I tried to imagine loving Michael without ever having spoken to him. I couldn't. It had to be a pitiful and a very lonely person who could fall in love with an image, an icon, because a person was the sum of his or her thoughts.

A passion like ours had spent itself in one fuck, and that was the extent of it. It was peculiar that it could have happened so suddenly, but perhaps I had been ready for it. My apprehensions about marriage to Michael had reached a peak; and I could not reach a resolution without such a push. It had almost come to that with Colin: a pretty picture of a man, but he bit, and I was not ready just then for the hurdle. It was unfortunate that some souls could confuse real love with physical love, to love something for only its sex and its veneer. I was not going to moon after something physical and unreal —a picture that conjured dreams but was not capable of fulfilling them—because I was awake more than I was asleep. The sensibilities behind the touch had to matter more than just the touch itself. William no longer existed. And I knew I would never find him again.

The historian's, the novelist's, the lover's, even the cook's goal is to find that missing link—the element that solves or completes the chronology, the story, the enigma, the recipe. Yet once that link is discovered, it is inevitably accompanied by yet another discovery: that there is more, always more, down even deeper. Once we reach the bottom, though, we have to stay there. Covered over with earth.

As I walked back to the pub I wondered if I would ever see him again. If desire could have its blind way, I would have; but there was no sense in it. He was not there, not for me. Even if he had been, I would not have let myself go with him again. That was all over. I paused on the edge of the hill called Chwarel-y Fan, the sheep keeping a respectable distance away from me. I looked up the slope to the barren zenith, up to the top where Offa's Dyke ran along the ridges. Michael had seen mountains like that in his dream. The sun was bending low over the west and I could not see more than a blasted outline of objects surrounded by a solar halo: hikers, cattle, boulders, crags. They had no substance. They existed, but one could not discern any details. They were like dreams, even though I knew they were every bit as real as I was. But I could not touch them, did not know them; and so they passed by me as particles unloved, unwanted, unreal. What mattered was the time and effort it took to comprehend the essence. The essence that you could touch, and would touch you back. Without that these objects were no more than ions of light, here and then gone in a blast of wind.

I went back to work, feeling irrationally hurt that Michael would not call. He did not call again for two weeks.

As luck would have it, Mr. Modgett was in the pub one night about a week later. Angel, uncharacteristically, had remembered our talk that first night. There were only two tables full in the dining room and I was loafing in the kitchen, idly picking at someone's leftover salad with my fingers, purposely avoiding the dishes, when she suggested I go in and have a drink with the old man.

I introduced myself and sat down in a chair across from the settle bench where he was stationed. My big plastic waitress apron put him off at first; he seemed befuddled, slightly surprised, staring at the big white letters RUDDLES THE COUNTY ALE. I repeated my introduction, spinning out some yarn about wanting to hear some of the marvelous, colorful tales of local history that he was so famous for. He settled back into the bench, and after savoring a sip of the dark stuff he was drinking in a pint jar, he launched into a story about the crazy poet Landor who had lived there in the early nineteenth century, and who had built the cottage where I was staying. Angel, or Andrew, had evidently told him something about me, but I was not bothered by that kind of gossip. He was so interested in local history that he would naturally want to know all about any newcomers to Bryngessy.

"Angel said something about a mysterious gravestone in St. David's."

"Ah . . . a young lady who enjoys ghost stories!"

"Everyone likes a good mystery, don't they?"

"To be sure, and that was a mystery to us all right. To this day it's still a mystery."

"How did you come to find the stone? Was it hidden somewhere?"

"I was just a lad then. They were redecorating the old church, thinking of putting tiles down before the altar, and removing the old, worn flagstones. They had just started, taking them out right underneath the altar first of all, when they ran into this stone there."

"Wasn't it inscribed? Wasn't there any kind of a church record identifying it?"

"Church records don't go back as far as that gravestone, but we did find an inscription on it. Not much to go by, though. It was Norman. We could tell that much."

"What did it say?"

"Just initials, and a short phrase. It was quite worn, but we had a professor from Cardiff come out and read it for us before we buried it again. I don't remember exactly what it said now . . . something in Latin like 'have mercy on my soul'—your typical funereal inscription. I do remember the initials, though, which are what confused everyone. They were G. M. We would have expected a prior, or a canon, to have been laid there, or maybe even a benefactor, but none of the men from that period of time had those initials. It was very curious."

I knew it then. It was all starting to fit. The final arc. I had the last piece to the puzzle, and this was the place to put it.

"Do you know the name of the priory's founder?"

"Of course. William de Lacy."

"He was married, wasn't he?"

"I believe so, for a short time, but that was well before he settled here."

"Do you know his wife's name?"

"I believe he married into the de Mauro family of Striguil."

"I know his wife's name. I found it in an old vellum manuscript at Cadfor Castle, the de Mauro's home. Her name was Gaie. Like me."

"Gaie de Mauro. G.M. Of course! It makes sense. The time is about right . . . but that means the old dog kept his wife here while his pals were celibate. How very clever of him, and of you!"

"You say she was exhumed?"

"Yes, in order to fix the floor. I wasn't present at the time, but I understand she was reburied, along with the stone, somewhere in the churchyard. Of course you can appreciate there wasn't much left to rebury. Just a few dusty bones, the baby's tiny skeleton, and some hair, as I recall."

"A baby? Hair?"

"Yes. That's what the workmen remembered best of all. The long, white hair, still soft, they said, surrounding the skull, and the tiny baby. A newborn. It sounds rather ghastly, doesn't it?"

He went on to other stories then. I could have been there until closing time, listening. The more he talked, the better he talked, and it was impossible to leave, because he was forever thinking of just one more short story. Finally Angel had to come in and physically separate us, pleading desserts to be served and dishes to be washed.

I left him, reluctantly. The flames were blue, but I was not scared this time. Imagination was always worse than the truth. I saw him bent over her grave, haunted by memories of her. I had a feeling that there was more, but that I just hadn't asked the right questions.

11

Iube domne silencium
et aures audiencium
ut possint intelligere. *

—ANONYMOUS,
THIRTEENTH CENTURY

I had never known such cold. I was colder than I had ever been after heaving myself down a snowy slope for hours as a child in a Wisconsin January. In a dawn dream, I felt conscious at first only of the thrill of the sweep down to the creek and the pleasurable shiver of knowing disobedience as I rocketed across it. My mother had told me that it might very well crack; a silly boy had once gone through and drowned there. How could she have known that the hill was steeper on that side, with two intoxicating dips that sent your bowels leaping into your lungs and made you oblivious of the cold?

But then, at the bottom, when the ride was over, you suddenly realized, with a miserable smarting in the extremities, that your socks were drenched, there was snow burning down your mittens, stinging up your arms, prickling down your neck, and chewing at your backside. Your lips would only move with the utmost difficulty. Your

---

*Lord, command silence
that the ears of the hearers
may understand.

toes ached in the throes of primary frostbite. You had to pee fiercely and you were fifteen minutes from home, and the sun had almost disappeared in the midwinter gloom.

It was colder than all of that in the cottage on the hillside, and then some. It was a cold without respite, a cold that came at you from hopeless, unexpected angles, a lonely, Welsh cold. It might not have felt so cruel if I hadn't had to get up, wash in it, and be at the pub in thirty minutes. It was the difference between the cold feet in a bad dream, and real, piercing, immediate pain. If October was this bad, I wondered if I'd survive a January there. I moved one leg, and it hurt against the unwarmed section of sheet. I vaulted out and over to the stove. There was a lame glimmer of life in its poor, cold, black belly. I gave up before even trying to relight it, and washed in cold water, holding my breath to keep from giving way to violent shivers.

For weeks, as I walked down the mountain to work, I had the sensation that someone had just seen me and had disappeared in a silent tither, with a gasp of recognition. Their scent, or maybe the smell of the cold, or a breathless, living quiet never quite left me in waking hours in and around the cottage. I felt it again that Sunday morning, walking down the mountain. There was no remote drone of a combine across the valley then, nor even the tinkle of a pony trekker's bridle, or the toylike whine of a Mini twirling along in the tortured depths of the thick green hedges lining the road. It was as if they had perked up at my footstep, and as soon as I fiddled with the latch on the cottage door they had sped away lightly, leaving nothing behind but the untouched, perfect dew, having uttered the faintest, barest, most spectral suggestion of surprise, which sounded to me like a breeze through dry leaves. I could almost feel their footsteps going before mine, the same prints, the same stride, the same speed, almost an alter ego in perfect tune with my own breathing. When I stopped, they stopped. Sometimes the sensation was so strong that I had to say to myself it was nonsense to think or to feel such things, because only men are real, and cannot behave like vapors in the dark.

I hated walking through the cows. I was certain that someone long ago had taught me that cows did not have horns: only bulls did. Yet these creatures that appeared on Sundays in the field directly below my cottage had horns and, incongruously, udders as well. They eyed me through thick, malevolent, inky eyeballs, looking too stupid not to be shamming, so they must have been plotting: flagitious minds behind the cud-chewing, ruminant veneer. I saw the horns and I hated them, especially the ones who moved swiftly in the corner of my vision, the sudden thump of a hoof shaking the turf, shattering my nerves. If I could have walked elsewhere I would have, but the only path to the bottom led along that unscalable hedge. I forgot the cold, the feeling of sprites in my midst, my husband, whenever I had to walk past that gauntlet of horns on a Sunday morning.

And it was a gauntlet, well deserved. A letter had come the day before, forwarded from Oxford. Letters between my mother and me had become increasingly rare. Arthur kept her busy, she said, and I wasn't too eager to tell her what had happened on my side of the Atlantic. I wasn't proud that Michael and I were separated. Nor was I sure of the permanence of any of the arrangements, and rather than tell her where I was, effectively committing myself to unpleasant explanations, I hedged, and told her nothing.

But it hadn't worked. Maybe Arthur did keep her busy cooking and washing, but she still had time to notice a certain lack of the word "we" in my letters. "You haven't mentioned Michael since last spring. I hope everything is all right?" I was ashamed. Tell my mother I was living like some hairy, unkempt, ranting anchoress in an earthen-floored hut? After four years of college, to be a waitress and a potato peeler? Married barely a year, and already separated? And why? For my own childish dreams. *Challenges.* Selfishness, and insecurity. He had not been unfaithful. He had never raised a hand against me. I was never ignored or taken for granted. His only fault was that I could not cope with his goodness. I wanted it all back again, like it was. I decided that seven weeks alone was quite enough.

The novelty of working there, the variety of things I had to do, still appealed to me. I was almost ashamed of the way I enjoyed menial work. Given the choice of typing an essay for Barnes or cleaning out Angel and Andrew's chicken coop, I would still take the coop hands down. In the seven weeks I had been at Bryngessy, the earth had made a massive shift. It was no longer summer, and even autumn seemed to be slipping away from me. My pile of coal on the mountainside was seriously diminished already, but I was reluctant to ask for more, lest Angel and Andrew think I was a wastrel and a sissy. And besides, I wasn't sure how the coal would get up the mountain to me. If I had to carry it, sack by sack, that might be good cause to quit. And go where? Home. If he would have me.

I was purged. Those cold, wet afternoons, between lunch and

supper, I had sat thinking about him, becoming surer than ever that, although the life—apart from the cold—appealed to me, the unabated loneliness did not. It was good to be busy, useful. Three-foot-high stacks of dishes did not daunt me. I rose to the occasion, and when the dishes were done I felt good. I had killed and gutted chickens. I could do anything. I thought about how he had accused me of seeking a challenge. He had been right, but it was not such a negative thing, and he had had no right to mock me for that. He had been wrong to sneer at that. He simply had not realized that it would be harder for a woman to find that challenge than a man. It was a cultural and a sexual problem, I supposed. But it hardly mattered. I knew what I wanted now.

It bothered me that he had had to forward my mother's letter. I had told him not to visit weeks ago, and it was good that he hadn't. But now I wanted him again. The forwarding address written on the envelope was a horrible statement: that he had accepted this situation, acquiesced to my whims, had become accustomed to living alone. Without me. I thought of his father's mistress in South Africa. I was sure the thought had occurred to him, too. Keep the wife at bay thousands of miles away, have fun in absentia. I didn't want him to be suspicious of my fidelity, but that might have been how the forced separation was affecting him. I had been selfish. It was horribly obvious now. I had been unfair to him. For all he knew, I did have a lover in the hills. I worried about his reaction. I didn't want him to react at all. Suddenly all I wanted was what I had had before I ever left Warborough. The cold, being alone, working seven days a week—it was too harsh. I missed his soft edges, the smell of him.

Angel and Andrew were already there. I felt like complaining about the temperature, but I couldn't to them. They must have been just as uncomfortable but they said nothing about it. They always started work earlier than I did, too. It was humbling. Andrew carried a tray full of clean half-pints into the bar as I walked in the front door. "Your husband called," he said to the shelf. Angel was running broth through the blender for lunchtime minestrone. My husband called. How utterly English of him to say it so. An American would have said, "Mike called." Andrew's tone made me feel shameful, yet he would never venture such an honest opinion.

"Did he leave a message?"

"No."

I felt suddenly queasy. "Is it okay if I use the phone?"

"Yes, all right. Angel needs help with the vegetables when you're through."

I went into the dining room where the hotel phone was kept concealed behind a large reed bread basket. The two grandfather clocks, on opposite ends of the room, were not in unison, one low, lonely *tump* just an apprehensive step behind the other. It was amusing to watch them up close, the hands quite clearly pitching ahead with each swag of the pendulum. I had not called him once in the seven weeks I had been gone. He had called me quite a few times. It was catching up to me. The fact that he had called but had not left any message bothered me. I felt terrible. I did not want him to abandon me now. I just hoped it wouldn't be too late.

I dialed the Oxford code and suddenly forgot the rest of the number. I pressed the buttons down in the receiver cradle and thought hard. 0865. Then what? If I could remember the first number I knew I'd have it. The six-toed cat walked in from the passage that Angel said was haunted by a person with big clumpy feet. The cat arched his back up in an impossible stretch, pure contentment from ear to ear, then made a few deprecating sniffs around the cold fireplace. 511. That was it. I dialed again. The English ring was a lesson in tension control on both ends of the line: two sharp honks, a pause, two more, one more.

"Hello, Jones."

"Hello Jones."

"Gay." I had hoped for more enthusiasm. My stomach felt weightless, my knees wavered.

"Why didn't you wait and call when I was here? You know I come down at ten on Sundays."

"I just had a fancy to talk to you. I hoped you'd be in early."

It had been more than a week since I'd last heard his voice, and it was a pleasing surprise. He sounded young, educated, familiar; not at all like the roughened old farmers from the valley who came into the pub with the same expression cemented onto their faces, their voices, all the time. Their manner had settled on them on the back of a tractor over the years. "Give me a pint of bitter, there's a nice lass" sounded the same as "You're a pretty thing a long way from home" which sounded the same as "The horse has spavine and the milch cow's got mastitis." I started to recall what my husband looked like. My husband. My husband and I. How regal it sounded. How sweet and foreign.

"I do have some vegetables to chop . . ."

"Can't we talk first? I miss you."

"What did you want to talk about?"

"Don't be cruel. We haven't talked in ages."

"I had a letter from you a few days ago."

"You haven't written me."

"I haven't got anything to write about. I make soup, I draw beer, I wait tables, I wash sheets, I freeze alone at night. I think I miss you, too."

"It's good to hear you say that. You sure there's no one else to keep you warm there? Come on now, 'fess up."

"Nobody living."

"I get cold, too. Why don't you just come back here and keep me warm?"

I thought of the dark bedroom, the smell of mildew that permeated everything, the wet woodbox, the cramped kitchen. I didn't think of him. I couldn't bear to. "Michael, we've discussed that before."

"Let's discuss it again then. When are you coming back?"

"I don't know yet. Just trying to stay warm takes up most of my free time these days. I haven't had much opportunity to think about it." I wondered why I was being so contrary. Probably wanted, deep down, to make sure of his affection before I committed myself.

"Can I come and see you?"

"See me?" For weeks that possibility had seemed too large a hurdle for me to leap. Now it suddenly seemed attractive as he said it. It was conceivable now. But I wasn't certain yet. Not entirely. I didn't want him feeling sorry for me, or condescending to enter my hovel. I couldn't bear him trying to stuff his good sense down my silly little girl's throat. Seven weeks alone in a shack did wonders for a person's sense. "Are you sure you want to see me again?"

"I want to see you. Is that so very difficult to understand? Don't you want to see me?"

"I think I do, actually."

"Jesus, this hasn't made any sense to me. It's been almost two months. *Two months!* I don't understand what you're trying to prove to yourself. Goodness knows you don't have to prove anything to me—or if you've got a lover up there . . . I mean, you're so wishy-washy. You don't go around demanding a divorce, yet you haven't told me that you love me in months. What the hell am I supposed to think? What's going on with you? Are you all right?"

"Of course I'm all right. I've explained it to you several times already. I just need to be alone for a while, to think things over."

"Then tell me when it's going to be over! Why can't we just talk, kiss, make up and live together like decent married people again? I *want* you here with me; I don't want you working like some country wench in a place like that."

I didn't appreciate the criticism, but I liked the way he was getting riled. He cared. Still, I didn't want him to make me feel stupid again. That was part of the reason why I had left him. I had some self-respect now. He would not be able to snatch it away, because I would not let him. "I can't talk about this now, Michael. I have work to do."

"Gay, you're avoiding the issue again. You're hiding from the truth and refusing to face something that shouldn't be difficult to face. I just can't believe that I'm the cause of all this. I think we have to talk, in person."

He had said it. I wanted to see him, but I would not give in that easily. It demanded a token resistance. "Are you sure you're ready for that, Michael?"

"I'm coming out there tonight."

"You have to go to work tomorrow."

"No, I don't. I'll take the day off. This is more important. We've got to talk."

I heard Angel calling for Andrew to help her with the potatoes and I was stricken with guilt, torn between the spuds and Michael's insistence on coming. I was not at all sure that I could face him without crying and breaking down all of the cold, hard barriers I had managed to construct since late August. As much as I wanted to see him I didn't want to see him; because self-confidence is so tenuous when it is new. I did not want him to unwittingly obliterate what had happened to me by moving in too fast with his logic and good sense. As much as I missed him, I was still not totally convinced that living alone was not the only, the best way to live. No meals to cater, no beds to make, no bathroom doors to shut, no conversational efforts to make, no yardstick of the world visible to which you had to measure up. There was only my own laundry and the hotel's anonymous sheets to account for: less guilt, fewer complications, and tripe only if I wanted it.

But roses? No roses. And no deep, warm, brown eyes to explore, no large hands running sympathetically over my neck, my shoulders, my breasts, my belly. I wasn't in any mood now to weigh that against my dubious freedom. I could hear the potatoes dropping into the stainless steel sink with thick, reprehensible thuds—my jailers.

"I really have to go."

"Say you love me."

"No."

"Say you don't love me."

"No."

"If you don't say it, it won't be real."

"I don't want anything to be real. Real hurts."

"Real feels good. You can't fuck dreams."

"You want to make a bet? Dreams can fuck you."

"I'll see you later, Gay. Don't go running off with any ghosts before I get there." And then he hung up.

The cat was in the kitchen waiting for his breakfast and Andrew was, ineffectively, peeling potatoes over the compost sack. I snatched the peeler from him and apologized. "Quite all right," he said, and he opened a tin of Go-Cat for the tortoiseshell tom.

We expected a healthy bunch to arrive outside before opening time at noon because it was a bone-dry, clear day—odd enough for late October. We usually had plenty of Sunday-goers, an equal number of hikers and farmers on bad days. There was usually a sizable cluster of five or ten dripping green macs waiting in the cloister for noon. On good days we could count on twice that many if not more, but for some reason there were only two when Andrew unlocked: two old men basking like arthritic, ancient cats on the pillar bottoms lining the nave. They crept in and sat on opposite settles along the walls directly beside the bar; close enough so that one good reach would suffice to refill a glass.

One I recognized: Mr. Modgett's father-in-law, who had taught him all the local legends, and would love to tell them again if you could keep him on one track. He was retired now to his son-in-law's back bedroom, listening to the Honddu Brook trickling over the small dam in their garden, awaiting the death-cart. The other man I did not recognize. A man so gnarled that he looked more like a contorted hazel bush than a human, with knuckles like boulders balanced on pencil-thin fingers and so lined in the face that it was hard to tell if he had eyes or not.

"What will you have, sir?" I called to him, but he appeared not to hear me. Mr. Modgett's father-in-law, thinking my offer was directed at him, asked for some bitter. I went into the back room of the cellar to draw it, and when I came back out the other old man was standing up at the bar, the top of his head no less than two inches from my chin. I looked down into the rumpled, sacklike face trying to detect some sign of life.

Mr. Modgett's father-in-law paid for his bitter with a pound note, which meant he would have at least two more. I asked the other man, again, what he wanted. A glimmer of eyeball appeared from beneath one massive wrinkle, and I thought I saw a smile, or at least a tremulous quiver of one facial crease between nose and mouth. There was something dear, familiar about the old man. It bothered me, even though I did harbor a soft spot for all old men: the older and more helpless the better, like nicely weathered antiques, a pleasure to sit beside. They inspired warmth, affection, and respect in me. I always regretted having been born after both my grandfathers died.

"What would you like, sir?" I repeated for the third time. He nodded in the direction of Mr. Modgett's father-in-law, which I presumed meant bitter. I drew a pint for him in the back room and set it down at a table; he looked too fragile to carry it. I saw him trying to muster some expression again as he hobbled the ten steps back to the settle beside the table.

"Lovely day," said Mr. Modgett's father-in-law to everyone. I knew that he wouldn't hear me anyway, so I didn't answer; I just nodded hugely and smiled. The other old man still did not make a sound, but he clasped his pint in both hands and drank. I had the feeling that he was watching me, but I couldn't tell for sure, because I could not see his eyes. Andrew popped in from the kitchen and spoke in his usual distracted fragments.

"Not too busy?"

"No. I'm surprised. It looks like the St. David's Parish Convalescent Home here today."

"The other one?"

"I've never seen him before. Quiet."

"Um." He threw up one hand in some incomprehensible gesture of acknowledgment, or maybe it was resignation. He withdrew into the kitchen, leaving behind a draft of baking bread. Mr. Modgett's father-in-law was smiling, entertaining himself with memories, slowly tapping one foot to inaudible music played decades ago by now-deceased musicians. I dried some glasses and hoped for more business to distract me from thinking about that telephone call and the inevitable visit. The wrinkled one still had his face pointed disconcertingly in my direction. He took his bitter very seriously. When it was gone he set a silver coin on the table; I couldn't tell if it was a ten or a fifty, and he stood up and came to the bar again.

"Another one?" I asked, but he just stared. He was awfully familiar just then, but I could not place him. An old shepherd I had seen in the market in Abergavenny? Maybe at the cattle show in Hereford? Flustered, I turned to go to his table for the empty glass, but he said something. He said, "Gay," and that was all.

I watched him turn and walk out, bent over like a steam-treated cruck, practically leaving a trail of ashes and dust. He wore a long, dirty, black coat with a hood, tied with a rough woven belt, with worn reddish leather boots. He scuffed slowly, painfully, up the steps. He turned to the right toward the parish church, and was gone. Mr. Modgett's father-in-law was singing to himself. Andrew poked his head through the door again. "Any lunches?"

"He could probably use one."

"Right."

I served him a plowman's lunch: a lump of cheese, a crust of granary bread, a pickle, an onion, a sweet crabapple. He seemed to chew forever. I noticed that the sky had suddenly gone dark. Any potential hikers had probably heard the forecast and shied away. Two farmers came in, and one intrepid couple hardly visible inside their heavy hiking gear. We closed early and Andrew told me to enjoy the rest of the day off. I wondered how that would be possible, as I put on my coat, not looking forward to going back to my gelid cottage. I peered out the door at the dark, low, cold clouds. Andrew called over from the bar. "Gay," he said, "just a minute."

He had been wiping the tables clean; the ashtrays and coasters were piled up on top of the bar. "Look what I found." He had something in the palm of his hand. It was still very dark outside and the pub was only faintly lit by the glow of six small gas hurricane lamps on the walls. "It was on that table," he motioned toward the one by the settle, beside the bar.

I looked down into his hand but I saw only a small glint from some round object. "I can't see. Put it in the light." I turned up the gas on the closest lamp and the small round thing winked back in the light. It was a coin: thin, silver, with a well-rubbed effigy in the center. "What's that?"

"Some sort of a coin."

"I can see that. I wasn't aware that we had any foreigners in here today."

"No." Andrew picked the tiny coin up and rotated it in the light. "It's very old, I think."

"Let me see it." He handed it to me and I looked closely at the face. It was almost worn smooth, but on the reverse side some print was still visible. It had a good shine to it, but one side was clipped and the ends were worn to a sharp, narrow edge. "I can just barely make it out. Something like *G . . . Rex.* I don't know. Maybe it says *Dux.* I've never seen such a coin."

"Perhaps someone found it in the ruins. I'll save it for the people at the university," Andrew said. I gave the coin back to him, and took to the hills.

The weather had turned sharply colder since that morning, if that was possible, and the clouds, coming and going, had spread the hills with snow. I decided to walk myself warm before going back to the cottage to wait for Michael. Scaling the gentler slopes to gaze down over the ruins of the priory, I thought it looked like dominoes nestled in a giant's palm. The mountains were brilliant with the sun and the snow, the forever green grass still peeking through wherever it could. But there was nothing else to see. Nothing but rabbits, pheasants, sheep, cows, horses. Nothing until I had been going for over an hour, lost in trying to reconcile myself to Michael's visit. The sky suddenly began to tinker with the earth, heavy, sodden clouds parting to give glimpses of pure blue sky. The sleet fell in quick spurts and I had not had the foresight to carry an umbrella up into the hills with me. It would ruin my boots probably, soak my coat, but I didn't care. Between storms the clouds would separate like dancers. The sun broke through in strips creating crazy rainbows everywhere that appeared and disappeared almost as fast as I could count them. Some of them persisted for several minutes, some jumped up almost directly beside me, following me as I walked, the two ends perfectly, brilliantly visible until the next cloud passed over.

The rainbows were everywhere, mincing along my line of vision, creeping up into nothingness as a cloud passed over, softly reappearing color by color when the sun shot through once again. They were like living prisms, breathing wheels of color, waltzing through the skies in that valley like angels gone berserk. It was a sight like I had never seen before: like a once-in-a-lifetime comet, or a total eclipse of the sun. I guessed that the valley must be prone to rainbows because I had seen one there once before—but it was so much more romantic to suppose that God was showing off just for me that day.

Unlike the parish churches of England which were now locked against vandals, most of the little churches of Monmouthshire were usually kept open. There was generally not much worth plundering in them. I walked back in the direction of St. David's, beside the ruins of the priory. There wasn't a soul inside—odd, sad for a Sunday. I learned later from Andrew that Sunday mass was postponed that day until after dark. Apparently the dogs at the stud farm down the road raised a fury when the bells rang in the daylight, but they stayed quiet when the bells rang at night. The windows of the little church were small and set high in the thick walls, probably because it had served as a place of refuge in those turbulent times when the Welsh Marches were a bitterly contested region. There was a worn Norman font just inside the south door, and a red velveteen curtain separating the sacristy from the nave. I sat down in one of the rear pews.

Perhaps I was sequestering myself at Bryngessy because I did not want Michael to see me for what I really suspected I was. I didn't believe him when he said he loved me; it did not make sense, after sixteen months of knowing him, that he could still love me. I had been unfaithful. I had made him look foolish in front of his friends. I had an American accent and I wore trousers to work. How could I ever hope to be more than a fading novelty? A ghost? But what was love anyway but ephemera? How could one grasp and hold a feeling? It is no more than a shiver in the dark. Something glimpsed out of the corner of your eye, like a white sheet moving like a satin octopus through the ruins at dusk. Love was something totally beyond the rational control of your will, your consciousness.

I thought of Bryngessy, William, Gaie de Mauro. All settled back into the earth forever, waiting perhaps for another misguided young knight to come along and try, in vain, to resurrect dreams, old barns, ruined hermitages. I was not prepared to be another pioneer like that, having one vision after another vanish until the end, when I myself would be the vision that vanished, a victim of my own dreams.

The Bible was open on the pulpit up front. I got up, and out of some quasi-religious impulse, climbed into the pulpit to read it. "For love is as strong as death," I read. And I wondered, out over my congregation of ghosts: Is death a necessary ingredient of love? Would we love a thing as much if we knew that it would last eternally? Love may be as strong as death, but it is not stronger; and, of the two, death will always win out. Whereas love can waver, glimmer, be snuffed out, death will persist and override. But if true love is as strong as death, then it exists beyond the grave. Lovers will never find their peace, then, until they are both dead.

Like William and Gaie? I was always hearing ghost stories, and I believed them, after a fashion. But when faced with one that was so real, so familiar, so warmly human, how could I ever really believe that he had been a ghost? A ghost was dead: bones and hair and a newborn skeleton; something in a shroud; a mere puff of fog on a dark night; an imagination come to life; a dream. Either ghosts are as real as we are, or this whole world is just a fantasy in God's mind. If I could really believe that what I made love to that night was just a shadow, then the burden of it might not have driven me into the wilderness alone like this. If I thought the whole incident was the product of a lustful and adulterous brain, then I would not be there lamenting, repenting, doing penance, away from the one I loved. And I did love Michael. I was sure of that now.

It is all so futile, so vain. These stone walls crumbling, rain coming in through the gaps in the roof. Not even Gaie's grave had been eternal. The flesh will fall away, but the soul will stay behind, and suffer. Why do we live at all, except for love? Why do we die, except for love?

That is what I had wrought upon my marriage, I thought. We kill the things we love best, like William killed Gaie, and then erected a monument—a church—over her remains. But it did not bring her back. He had to wear his armor the rest of his life, to protect his heart. The only good thing to come of his love was death, because in physical death he could forget her. Love was painful, for two loves seldom die together. Only after death can they be truly together without fear, without regret, without jealousy and sin. We never lie perfectly still until death, and even then, who knows? The grave may not be a soft enough bed for some, like William. Death was not enough to keep him from roaming abroad, from searching for the half that was missing.

It was too cold to stand still in there for long. At the evening

[256]

service there would be people crowded in to emanate warmth. They would probably turn on the electric fires that hung from the ceiling above the pews, oddly anachronistic beside the oil lamps on the walls. I pulled on my mittens, and saw something flit behind the back row of pews. I walked back to see.

It was a butterfly. A common little cabbage white, it looked like, twirling madly in a dusty stream of sunlight coming through the west windows. It must have just hatched in a warm, protected nook somewhere in the chapel; but in that bitter weather it would soon freeze. I turned to watch it, looping in the rays of light, moving its small wings so fast that it seemed not to move at all. The butterfly made a few daringly wide arcs, then settled onto the font where a beam of setting sunlight was shining.

I had once joked with Michael, after squashing cabbage worms —the cabbage white's embryonic form—that God would get even with him for that some day. He would be reincarnated as the butterfly. The Etruscans had a quaint superstition that the souls of the dead were reincarnated as butterflies. The little white flexed its wings slowly, luxuriously, enjoying the sun before it disappeared, enjoying its last hours of life. I couldn't think of a lovelier place to die.

It occurred to me, with stunning clarity, that there really *are* ghosts in this world, in one form or another, only I was incapable of understanding them. Something extraordinary had happened at Bryngessy, but I was only human. I could not see beyond my own dimension, over the walls of my limited comprehension. The musicians of Cadfor, the knights in armor, would have to play their same scenarios over and over again, pitifully, for the rest of eternity perhaps. Maybe someday someone would come along who could understand and bridge the centuries and the dimensions that separated us from the answers. There is only one reality distinguishable to us, I thought, and that exists in the present. I had been walking those hills for weeks hoping for, expecting, a miracle, or at least another dream come true. I did not realize until then that ghosts cannot answer your prayers, but only men.

Andrew was just parking his van in the drive between the church and the farmhouse when I walked out. He made a big, imprecise gesture with one arm out the window, beckoning me over. "I found out about that other old man," he said.

"Who was he?"

"Lewis down the road sold his house to a maiden aunt called Williams, and it was her old father. They just moved in last week. She tries to keep him pretty much tied down because he's a crazy old loon, deaf as a board, but he broke loose this morning and wandered all the way down here. She caught up with him just after he left, told me to watch out for him in future because now he knows where the pub is, he's sure to come back."

"What about the coin?"

"Oh, I don't know about that. It's probably Roman. I left it with Angel, to show to a professor at Cardiff University who plans to come up next spring to see about some digs again. Miss Williams paid for her father's drink, though. He never carries any money, she said. The coin must have come from someone else, maybe dropped by accident by one of the hikers."

I was glad that Andrew had caught me, told me. I didn't want things to get out of hand again, especially with Michael coming. He made an oversized, meaningless guffaw, signaling the end of the conversation. I walked back up the hill to my cottage.

He came after dark, when the blackness had settled so firmly over the cottage that even with the light from two lamps, there were thick shadows around the room. He knocked on the window first, then clumped around to the door, coming right on in, huffing like a train. "How can you do this every day? It's bloody awful out there! I kept running into boulders, and it goes almost straight up! Did you inherit goat's hooves from your Norwegian ancestors?"

"It helps to know the way, and to have a flashlight," I said, from behind the stove. I goaded the coals into producing a great flash of flame, just as soon extinguished when I shut the heavy iron door.

"Here, let me," he said, taking the iron poker from my hand. He adjusted the damper beneath the firebox and one on the pipe. The fire seemed to leap up with pleasure. He tossed in a few more coals, and shut the door. I could see the fire dancing through the cracks around the top burners.

"It's warmer already. I suppose someone should have shown me how to use it weeks ago, but as you might have gathered I don't get many visitors up here."

He hung his coat on the wall peg, not saying anything, and I saw him, for the first time in almost two months. It was almost like seeing him for the first time. I had not imagined that he would seem so foreign after that short time apart; he had not seemed that way to me since our first week together. I heard his accent all over again, noticed the cut of his dark hair, the way he was shaped inside of the Shetland sweater and blue jeans and Wellington boots. "Come and sit down. I can make us a pot of tea."

"I've brought some wine. Wouldn't that be nicer?"

"I haven't had any dinner. If I drank wine I don't know how much talking we'd accomplish, and besides, the only loo is out the back, inside a three-sided wood shack."

"I've brought some Chinese take-away. Do you have a pot where we can heat it up?" He handed me a plastic shopping bag and our fingers touched. I was almost embarrassed, with a hot, white, childish jolt of recognition. He bent over my chair and kissed me on the forehead, cheek, lips. "You're changed," he said. "You're much quieter, calmer. Have I interrupted something?"

There were no eyes in the dark that night, nor were the spirits blowing over the top of the mountain with their usual ferocity. The black night was still, without distraction. Nothing would interrupt us. "I haven't gotten used to you yet. Give me a few minutes. It's been a while." I got up, took the various cartons out of the bag, set them on the table, and went to find the cookpot.

"Sweet and sour chicken, beef chow mein, fried rice, egg rolls, and vegetable chop suey. I was hungry. That ought to be enough, oughtn't it?"

"I only have one pot."

"Then mix them all up. They all taste the same anyway."

We ate off one plate, with one fork and one spoon, drinking the wine out of one teacup. He didn't say much until after we had finished. Somehow it didn't seem right yet to launch into conversation of a personal nature with one who still seemed so strange. I noticed his smell when he came close; the bedsheets in Warborough had always smelled like that. He pumped water into the empty pot and set it on the stove to heat. He seemed totally comfortable with the primitive surroundings. "Got any washing-up liquid?"

"In the cupboard."

He squeezed some Fairy Soap into the pot and came back to the table. "We'll just let that cook for a while and it'll wipe out clean later." He poured some more wine into the cup—the bottle was half-empty. "Reminds me of that night at your college, only we drank it out of a paper bag then."

"Long time ago."

"Only a little over a year. But you're right. It does seem like a long time. Sip?"

I took a drink and passed the cup back to him. Wine usually makes me terminally sleepy, but it must have been the combination of the cold, the food, and Michael that made me more alert than usual. I hadn't worked much that day either, and I had a lot of energy left. "Why did you come?"

He looked at his knuckles; he always did that when he was unsure of what to say next. He flexed his hand, open, closed, open. Nervous. "It's been a long time. I thought that it was time we talked."

His expression was equivocal. I wasn't sure if I should be glad or apprehensive. The worst things occurred to me. Had my mother died? Had his? Was he going to ask for a divorce? Was there another woman? Was he mortally ill? "If you say so."

"I still can't understand why you did this." He gestured with an open hand at the dirt floor.

"It's a dirt floor. It's free."

"No, no, I don't mean that. I mean all of this: the running away, the weird job, your silence all these weeks. What went wrong? I think I was aware of it, but I couldn't really put a finger on when or what it was. You just sort of drifted away. You weren't able to tell me things anymore. I never felt that you were really being honest with me."

I thought about that, and he was right, after a fashion; the difference was that I was simply frightened of telling him things, because he would think I was silly, or immature, or spoiled. I hadn't wanted that job at the History Department with Barnes; I would rather have been a homemaker until I could bribe myself into the university as a student. But I had had to take it or else he would have thought I was a bum, an idler. I didn't feel quite that way anymore, though. Two months of separation were still there, between us. I felt I had nothing, or very little to lose by talking now. I felt that I had successfully proven something by forging out on my own. And that proof somehow made me more credible. "I probably wasn't being honest with you. You were intimidating."

"Why on earth? I loved you, Gay. Why was that so intimidating?"

"It wasn't. It's just that you did everything better. I was afraid to have an opinion around you because yours was always more sensible. Remember the noises I heard in the loo at Cadfor? You and Richard both agreed it was just the wind. You fobbed it off in a matter of one sentence. I really *believe* that what I heard there that night was more than the sound of wind." It wasn't completely true; I doubt I really believed anything, but it sounded good.

"You're entitled to your beliefs. I'm sorry you took it so badly. We didn't mean to make you feel foolish."

"And the night I abandoned the castle? I had good reason. I heard more than just slates falling, but I would never tell you that. Do you really believe that what we heard that night last February was traffic noise? Surely you don't have such a tin ear that you can't tell the difference between music and the sound of squealing tires?"

"Possibly. But Richard's explanation was logical enough."

"Don't you believe that some things defy explanation?"

"I don't deny that." He got up then and paced across to an inky dark corner. Once you left the immediate sphere of light cast by one of the lamps, you might as well have been on the moon. I could just see him—back or front, I wasn't sure—a shape like a man but still conceivably nonhuman, like a ghost. His faint motions were like those of a night bird, black against black. There was a hint of humanness, but for all the world he was phantasmal. "Can't even take my boots off here."

"Didn't you bring shoes or slippers?"

"Left them in the car. It was so wet I thought I'd better wear these." As if someone had been listening, there was a roll of raindrops over the roof and against the north window. An unhappy sound, a draft of chilled wetness blowing in under the door. "Can we sit on the bed together?"

"You can. I'll stay here for now. It's closer to the fire."

He sat and pulled the boots off. There was a hole in one of his socks, and I felt a deep gush of affection. "I've got some news. Good and bad."

I had almost forgotten the apprehension. The way he said it, I felt a little sick. "Bad news first, please. I can't stand the suspense."

"No. Good news first. I've bought a house."

"You mean you've saved that much already?"

"Not much more than I had two months ago, but my father loaned me some, and I got the rest from the building society. It was only £8,000."

"Tell me all about it."

"Well, it's in Charlbury, which has the railway line right into Oxford. It's just a terraced cottage, but has quite a nice garden. It was in decent condition, the owner wanted to sell in a hurry, so I moved as quickly as I could and I got it. Due to move in next week."

"Is it big? Does it have lights? And heat? And indoor plumbing?"

"Yes. It's really quite nice. You must see it. It has three fireplaces: one up, one down, one big one in the kitchen with an Aga stove, and certainly more electric outlets than we've got now. It's probably more than two hundred years old, possibly three; not too mucked up, so it's even got some character. Beamed ceilings, lovely stone mantels, flagstone floors, tiny windows."

"But no central heating."

"No, but we can put that in later."

I had to ask. "Now the bad news, please."

"I don't want to hurt your feelings, but I'm sure it will. You're so abnormally sensitive sometimes."

I braced myself for the worst. My breathing was shallow. I took a gulp of the wine. It somehow softened the blow, plugged my ears slightly so that I didn't hear it as harshly as I might have. "Go on."

"There's been another woman."

I felt the breath leave me and hang in the frozen air before my face, reluctant to return. It was a relief. After the long agony of illness, death was even a welcome relief. Once you are caught in the whirlpool, going down for the third time, it isn't so terrifying; in fact, it is soothing, and death lulls you willingly into the most comfortable, painless sleep. Do not bring me back, please. Do me a favor and let me die now. "But it's over now. It meant nothing."

I inhaled. It hurt, like shards of glass tearing up through my nose, into my brains, down into my lungs. It hurt so much that I couldn't even cry. "Nothing?" I said, sounding, I knew, like a mouse.

"It was just after you left. I thought you were living with some bloke up here, even though you told me differently. After that I even came up once or twice to check, but I never saw anyone lurking around here. You were always alone. I only did it because I thought you were being unfaithful, and lying to me. It was purely revenge, and that's why I'm telling you. It was nothing. I'm sorry. It lasted only a few weeks, and that was all."

"Anyone I know?" I managed to croak.

"No."

"Will you tell me who it was anyway?"

"My lady accountant. She was as dreary as ever. I believe I've laid the ghost now."

"Did she know you were married?"

"Yes."

"Does she have no morals? No shame?"

"I told her we were separated."

"Oh." So it had been my fault. We kill the things we love most. Nothing else mattered. Not my insecurity, the two months of solitude, not the sack of potatoes that had to be peeled by lunchtime tomorrow. "And now?"

"I've bought us a cottage. I want you to come and live in it with me. I need you to live in it with me."

"You really do, Michael?"

"As much as you need me."

I could just dimly see the moon through the south-facing window, high and opalescent, with rounded black clouds charging along, covering its edges. It was late October, nearly Halloween. We would be moved in by Christmas. We could have a tree, pudding, presents. This was real. It was whatever one made of it. Our life together could remain indecisive; me in the hills, the cold and emptiness gnawing away at my conscience and my free will, him alone in the nice new house. Or I could decide now to try to forget what had happened to both of us. We could start over, not in someone else's house, but in our very own.

"I meant to tell you there are climbing roses in the back garden," he said.

"What color?" I said.

"We'll see, shall we?"

12

This is Julius, a canon of the House of Bryngessy Prima, writing in the Chronicle of Ranulph on the death of the founder of our Priory, William the Hermit, former Knight of Hugo de Lacy, the benefactor of our House and late of Ewyas.

William died in his sleep in the night. Brother Aneirin found him in the morning. His wish was to be buried in the meadow to the west of the church, on the mountainside called Chwarel-y Fan, but as that ground is not consecrated and as our water supply flows down from those hills we thought it best, the eleven canons who survive him in this place, to bury William the Hermit with the other founders in the graveyard beyond the Slype. We have buried his iron breastplate in the meadow to partly accede to his last wishes. We would have buried him under the altar of the chapel he built beside the priory if he had not specifically advised us against this.

I am new to the Order and I did not know the Hermit as well as some of the others, but his courage, endurance, strength, and quiet religious devotion were obvious to all. It was known to several who had it from his own mouth that when he was old and full of years and loaded with great age and was to say Mass on some solemn occasion the devil would often on such occasions disturb him in the night with lascivious apparitions.

He was a quiet man who ate and drank sparingly and kept to himself. May God give peace to his soul. Deus ait mercit de nos anemes.

—From the *Chronicle of Ranulph*, Bryngessy Priory, c. 1150